"I want you to make a kill," the old man said. His voice was quavery and high, peevish. "I understand that is what you do."

"Who do you want hit?"

"Your victim is right behind you," the old man said softly.

Halston moved quickly. His reflexes were his life and they were always set on a filed pin. He was off the couch, falling to one knee, turning, hand inside his specially tailored sport coat, gripping the handle of the short-barreled .45. An instant later it was out and pointed at . . .

A cat.

Special Collections from Ace Science Fiction and Fantasy

MAGICATS!

EDITED BY
JACK DANN AND GARDNER DOZOIS

ACE FANTASY BOOKS
NEW YORK

MAGICATS!

An Ace Fantasy Book / published by arrangement with
the editors

PRINTING HISTORY
Ace Original / June 1984
Second printing / September 1984

ISBN: 0-441-51531-2

Ace Fantasy Books are published by The Berkley Publishing Group,
200 Madison Avenue, New York, New York 10016.
PRINTED IN THE UNITED STATES OF AMERICA

Acknowledgment is made for permission to print the following material:

"Space-Time for Springers" by Fritz Leiber. Copyright © 1958 by Ballantine Books, Inc. First published in *Star Science Fiction Stories* No. 4 (Ballantine). Reprinted by permission of the author and the author's agent, Robert P. Mills.

"The Game of Rat and Dragon" by Cordwainer Smith. Copyright © 1955 by Galaxy Publishing Co. for *Galaxy Science Fiction.* Copyright © 1963 by Cordwainer Smith. First published in *Galaxy,* October 1955. Reprinted by permission of the author and the author's agents, Scott Meredith Literary Agency, Inc., 845 Third Avenue, New York, New York 10022.

"The Cat From Hell" by Stephen King. Copyright © 1977 by Dugent Publishing Corp. From *Cavalier,* June 1977. Reprinted by permission of the author and the author's agents, Kirby McCauley, Ltd.

"Out of Place" by Pamela Sargent. Copyright © 1981 by TZ Publications. First published in *The Twilight Zone Magazine,* October 1981. Reprinted by permission of the author and her agent, the Joseph Elder Agency.

"Schrödinger's Cat" by Ursula K. Le Guin. Copyright © 1974, 1982 by Ursula K. Le Guin. From *Universe 5* (Random House). Reprinted by permission of the author and the author's agent, Virginia Kidd.

"Groucho" by Ron Goulart. Copyright © 1981 by TZ Publications, Inc. First published in *The Twilight Zone Magazine,* April 1981. Reprinted by permission of the author.

"My Father, the Cat" by Henry Slesar. Copyright © 1957 by King-Size Publications, Inc. First published in *Fantastic Universe,* December 1957. Reprinted by permission of the author.

"The Cat Man" by Byron Liggett. Copyright © 1960 by Hallie Burnett. From the Spring 1960 *Story*. Reprinted by permission of Hallie Burnett, Inc.

"Some Are Born Cats" by Terry and Carol Carr. Copyright © 1973 by Rand McNally and Co. From *Science Fiction Tales.* Reprinted by permission of the authors.

For Susan Allison

The editors would like to thank the following people for their help and support:

Virginia Kidd, Jane Butler, Perry Knowlton, Adam Deixel, Stuart Schiff, Trina King, Susan Casper, Jeanne Van Buren Dann, Janet Kagen, Michael Swanwick, Bob Walters, Pat LoBrutto, Al Sarrantonio, Tom Whitehead of the Special Collections Department of the Paley Library at Temple University (and his staff, particularly Connie King and John Betancourt), Edward and Audrey Ferman, Kirby McCauley, Brian Perry of *Fat Cat Books* (263 Main Street, Johnson City, New York 13790), Edward Bryant, Manly Wade Wellman, Francis Garfield, the convention staff of ConStellation, Hallie Burnett, Jan Kardys from Scholastic Magazines, Inc., Gene Wolfe, George Scithers, Pamela Sargent, Beth Meacham, and special thanks to our own editor, Susan Allison.

Contents

Preface

By Gardner Dozois
and Jack Dann

Cats may not rank among the very earliest of domesticated animals—that honor is usually reserved for dogs, oxen, horses, and sheep—but even a conservative estimate has them throwing their lot in with the human race no later than about 1500 B.C. This means that people have had cats around the house for at least four thousand years—perhaps even going back as far as the time when the "house" was a skin tent, or a mud-and-wattle hut—and yet in all that time they have *still* not made up their minds just how they feel about them.

Humanity's relationship with the cat is much more complex and contradictory than the simple master-slave (or consumer-consumed) relationship that obtains with most domestic animals. At one time or another throughout history, cats have been worshipped as gods, and been hunted down and slaughtered as emissaries of the Devil. To many Amerindian tribes, they were the only animals without souls, avatars of evil, while to some French peasants they were the earthly embodiment of the Corn Spirit, venerated as the luck of the harvest. Herodotus reports the case of a Greek soldier who was torn apart by an angry Egyptian mob for injuring a cat, while in medieval Europe (no one believes *this* one, but see Barbara Tuchman's *A Distant Mirror* for confirmation) it was a popular pastime to nail cats to a post and then attempt to batter them to death with your head without being blinded in the process (see, there *are* worse forms of popular entertainment than television;

even an evening spent watching old *Gilligan's Island* reruns is classier that *that*). Cats have earned their own sparse livings as catchers of rats and mice, grudgingly tolerated by the farm families they serve, and they have been spoiled and pampered as pets, often with a lavishness and luxury far beyond what many human beings can afford for themselves. Sometimes they are eaten (we're willing to bet that there are still poor people in this country who eat "roof rabbit" every now and then), more often we kill *other* animals to feed to *them* (where *did* you think cat food comes from?). One person will casually drown a sackful of kittens, with no sense of repugnance or remorse, while another will take a sick cat to a veterinarian and spend hundreds of dollars in the attempt to nurse it back to health. Cats probably inspire greater extremes of hate and love than any other animal (with the possible exception of snakes)—we have all known people who clearly love their cats far more than they ever did their children, and who fill their houses with outrageous numbers of them; and we have also all seen grown men and women reduced to cold sweats and trembling terror by the presence of a small, relatively harmless animal dozens of times weaker, smaller, lighter, and less formidable than themselves (not even *poisonous,* for goodness sake!). Folklore portrays cats equally as cold, aloof, and cruel, and as affectionate, playful and loving, and we hold both images in our minds at once with seemingly no feeling of paradox or contradiction. It is perhaps not surprising that cats are one of the few animals that are almost universally believed to have supernatural powers, nor is it really odd that both pro-*and* anti-cat books should find themselves sharing the best-seller lists.

It's probably a reflection of humanity's multifaceted, sophisticated, and passionately contradictory relationship with cats that so much more fiction has been written about them than about any other kind of domestic animal (one is almost tempted to say: than about *any* animal). It would perhaps be possible to find a few good fantasy or SF stories about, say, dogs or horses (let us, mercifully, not even consider the idea of a *Great Science Fiction Stories About Sheep* anthology), but there might be one such story for every ten stories about cats (and we're willing to bet that most of the horse and dog stories would be juvenile fiction, while most cat stories are decidedly *not* aimed at children). There have been a lot of cat stories written over the years. Even eliminating all the cat stories that are not clearly identifiable as fantasy or science fiction (the first and most obvious winnowing screen we employed when putting this book together), we were still left with a huge amount of material to read. For instance, most of the major nineteenth-century writers—Twain, Le Fanu, Saki, Poe, Kipling, Doyle, Stoker, Bierce—wrote fantasy stories about cats, as did early twentieth-century writers such as Lovecraft, Benét, Wodehouse, Blackwood, de la Mare, Sayers, and many others. To say nothing of more contemporary stories.

All told, we must have read close to two hundred stories in the course of researching this book; we had room to use fewer than twenty of them. Further winnowing was obviously in order, and we were forced to make several hard decisions:

The first was that the stories should actually be about *cats*: *Felis catus,* the ordinary, garden-variety house cat (or, at most, his genetically engineered descendants of the far future), and *not* about lions, tigers, leopards, cheetahs, pumas, lynx, jaguars, or black panthers. We lost several good stories at this point—including Kit Reed's "Automatic Tiger," Ward Moore's "The Boy Who Spoke Cat," and Stephen King's "Night of the Tiger"—but then things began to become a bit more manageable. Next, we decided that the story must center around the *cat* itself, that the cat must be an integral part of the plot. This eliminated stories that just happen to have a cat in them somewhere (the protagonist's pet, maybe), but where the cat doesn't really figure in the significant movement of the plot; it eliminated a large number of science fiction stories where the hero has a superpowered cat or catlike creature of some sort as a sidekick (but where the cat's role *remains* that of a sidekick, peripheral to the real action), and an equally large number of fantasy stories where a witch's familiar (usually the traditional black cat) is mentioned in passing but isn't really at the center of the story; it also eliminated the staggeringly large number of SF stories where the protagonists encounter "catlike" aliens—usually either giant talking (or telepathic) cats, four-footed variety (as in Phyllis Gotlieb's "Son of the Morning"), or two-legged catlike humanoids, usually complete with fur, whiskers, tails, and claws (the sensuous Tigerishka, from Fritz Leiber's *The Wanderer*, is probably the classic—and classiest—example).

Next, since most of the nineteenth-century and early twentieth-century material (stories by Poe, Benét, Lovecraft, Stoker, Le Fanu, and so on) was already heavily anthologized and likely to be already familiar to our audience, we decided to concentrate primarily on contemporary stories, stories published during the last thirty years (although we couldn't resist adding one little-known classic by Manly Wade Wellman from a 1939 *Weird Tales*).

Our last—and, we believe, most important—decision was to go for as much variety and diversity in story type as possible.

In most of the classic cat stories from the nineteenth and early twentieth centuries, for instance, the cat is almost invariably evil, a sinister, stalking emissary of Satan, either ghost, demon, killer werebeast, or witch's evil familiar. And while that certainly is a valid expression of one side, the dark side, of humanity's contradictory relationship with cats (represented here in chillers by King, Crowley, Burger, and Liggett), we felt that some of the previous anthologies of cat stories suffered from this unrelieved uniformity of mood, presenting story after story in which the cats are monstrous and evil. We wanted also to examine the more *positive* side of humanity's long association with cats, the light side, the side in which cats are perceived as companions and friends and even benefactors (it is interesting, for example, that while many fantasy writers still tend to portray cats as evil creatures—Wellman and Slesar are exceptions here—science fiction writers almost without exception portray them as helpmates, and often even as guardians).

So, variety is the watchword here. Here you will find both fantasy and science fiction, tragedy and comedy, gentle nostalgia and bone-chilling horror. Cats as victims, cats as killers. Cats who build their own feline societies, cats who accompany humankind to the stars. Cats who can talk. Cats who can fly. Cats who have been reshaped into strange forms by the sophisticated genetic science of the future. Cats who are magicians. Cats who write television scripts. Ghost cats. Noncausal cats. Feral cats. Cats who love and nurture, cats implacably bent on revenge. Cats who save people, cats who are saved by people. Cats who are servants, cats who are masters.

Witches' cats. Cats who guard your dreams, cats who'll haunt your nightmares.

Funny cats. Deadly cats.

Magic cats.

Space-Time
for Springers

By Fritz Leiber

This story has been reprinted before, but it was impossible to even consider not including it in an anthology of science fiction and fantasy stories about cats, as it is quite possibly the single best story of that sort ever to be written.

Fritz Leiber is one of the truly seminal figures in the development of modern fantasy and SF, with a forty-year career that stretches from the "Golden Age" *Astounding* of the 1940's to the present day, with no sign of slackening of vigor or faltering of imagination and invention. Probably no other figure of his generation (with the possible exception of L. Sprague de Camp) has written in as many different genres as Leiber, or been as important as he has been to the development of each. Leiber can be considered one of the fathers of modern "heroic fantasy," and his long sequence of stories about Fafhrd and the Gray Mouser remains one of the most complex and intelligent bodies of work in the entire subgenre of "Sword & Sorcery" (which term Leiber himself is usually credited with coining). He is also widely considered to be one of the best—if not *the* best—writers of the supernatural horror tale since Lovecraft and Poe, and was writing updated "modern" or "urban" horror stories like "Smoke Ghost" and the classic *Conjure Wife* long before the Big Horror Boom of the middle 1970's brought that form to popular attention. In science fiction, stories like "Coming Attraction" and the brilliant *The Big Time,* among many others, were among the best things ever to grace the pages of the H. L.

1

Gold-edited *Galaxy* of the 1950's. *The Big Time* won a well-deserved Hugo Award in 1959, and since then Leiber has gone on to win a slew of other awards—all told, six Hugos and four Nebulas, plus two World Fantasy Awards—one of them the Life Achievement Award—and a Grandmaster of Fantasy Award. Leiber's books include *The Wanderer, Our Lady of Darkness, The Green Millennium, Gather, Darkness,* the collections *The Best of Fritz Leiber, The Book of Fritz Leiber,* and *The Mind Spider,* and the long sequence of Fafhrd/Gray Mouser books, the best of which are probably *The Swords of Lankhmar* and *Swords in the Mist.*

Cats have long been a recurrent motif in Leiber's work—along with chess, the theatre, and slightly kinky sex. Here he tells the story of Gummitch the superkitten—I.Q. 160, potential future author of *Invisible Signs and Secret Wonders* and *Slit Eyes Look at Life*—and his funny and poignant journey toward an odd kind of apotheosis. . . .

Gummitch was a superkitten, as he knew very well, with an I.Q. of about 160. Of course, he didn't talk. But everybody knows that I.Q. tests based on language ability are very one-sided. Besides, he would talk as soon as they started setting a place for him at table and pouring him coffee. Ashurbanipal and Cleopatra ate horsemeat from pans on the floor and they didn't talk. Baby dined in his crib on milk from a bottle and he didn't talk. Sissy sat at table but they didn't pour her coffee and she didn't talk—not one word. Father and Mother (whom Gummitch had nicknamed Old Horsemeat and Kitty-Come-Here) sat at table and poured each other coffee and they *did* talk. Q. E. D.

Meanwhile, he would get by very well on thought projection and intuitive understanding of all human speech—not even to mention cat patois, which almost any civilized animal could play by ear. The dramatic monologues and Socratic dialogues, the quiz and panel show appearances, the felidological expedition to darkest Africa (where he would uncover the real truth behind lions and tigers), the exploration of the outer planets— all these could wait. The same went for the books for which he was ceaselessly accumulating material: *The Encyclopedia of Odors, Anthropofeline Psychology, Invisible Signs and Secret Wonders, Space-Time for Springers, Slit Eyes Look at Life,* et cetera. For the present it was enough to live existence to the hilt and soak up knowledge, missing no experience proper to his age level—to rush about with tail aflame.

So to all outward appearances Gummitch was just a vividly normal kitten, as shown by the succession of nicknames he bore along the magic path that led from blue-eyed infancy toward puberty: Little One, Squawker, Portly, Bumble (for purring not clumsiness), Old Starved-to-Death, Fierso, Lover-boy (affection not sex), Spook and Catnik. Of these only the last perhaps requires further explanation: the Russians had just sent Muttnik up after Sputnik, so that when one evening Gummitch streaked three times across the firmament of the living room floor in the same direction, past the fixed stars of the humans and the comparatively slow-moving heavenly bodies of the two older cats, and Kitty-Come-Here quoted the line from Keats:

> *Then felt I like some watcher of the skies*
> *When a new planet swims into his ken;*

it was inevitable that Old Horsemeat would say, "Ah—Cat-nik!"

The new name lasted all of three days, to be replaced by Gummitch, which showed signs of becoming permanent.

The little cat was on the verge of truly growing up, at least so Gummitch overheard Old Horsemeat comment to Kitty-Come-Here. A few short weeks, Old Horsemeat said, and Gummitch's fiery flesh would harden, his slim neck thicken, the electricity vanish from everything but his fur, and all his delightful kittenish qualities rapidly give way to the earth-bound singlemindedness of a tom. They'd be lucky, Old Horsemeat concluded, if he didn't turn completely surly like Ashurbanipal.

Gummitch listened to these predictions with gay unconcern and with secret amusement from his vantage point of superior knowledge, in the same spirit that he accepted so many phases of his outwardly conventional existence: the murderous side-long looks he got from Ashurbanipal and Cleopatra as he de-voured his own horsemeat from his own little tin pan, because they sometimes were given canned catfood but he never; the stark idiocy of Baby, who didn't know the difference between a live cat and a stuffed teddy bear and who tried to cover up his ignorance by making goo-goo noises and poking indiscrim-inately at all eyes; the far more serious—because cleverly hidden—maliciousness of Sissy, who had to be watched out for warily—especially when you were alone—and whose retarded—even warped—development, Gummitch knew, was Old Horsemeat and Kitty-Come-Here's deepest, most secret, worry (more of Sissy and her evil ways soon); the limited intellect of Kitty-Come-Here, who despite the amounts of coffee she drank was quite as featherbrained as kittens are supposed to be and who firmly believed, for example, that kittens operated in the same space-time as other beings—that to get from *here* to *there* they had to cross the space *between*—and similar fallacies; the mental stodginess of even Old Horsemeat, who although he understood quite a bit of the secret doctrine and talked intelligently to Gummitch when they were alone, nevertheless suffered from the limitations of his status —a rather nice old god but a maddeningly slow-witted one.

But Gummitch could easily forgive all this massed inadequacy and downright brutishness in his felino-human household, because he was aware that he alone knew the real truth about himself and about other kittens and babies as well, the truth which was hidden from weaker minds, the truth that was as intrinsically incredible as the germ theory of disease or the origin of the whole great universe in the explosion of a single atom.

As a baby kitten Gummitch had believed that Old Horsemeat's two hands were hairless kittens permanently attached to the ends of Old Horsemeat's arms but having an independent life of their own. How he had hated and loved those two five-legged sallow monsters, his first playmates, comforters and battle-opponents!

Well, even that fantastic discarded notion was but a trifling fancy compared to the real truth about himself!

The forehead of Zeus split open to give birth to Minerva. Gummitch had been born from the waist-fold of a dirty old terrycloth bathrobe, Old Horsemeat's basic garment. The kitten was intuitively certain of it and had proved it to himself as well as any Descartes or Aristotle. In a kitten-size tuck of that ancient bathrobe the atoms of his body had gathered and quickened into life. His earliest memories were of snoozing wrapped in terrycloth, warmed by Old Horsemeat's heat. Old Horsemeat and Kitty-Come-Here were his true parents. The other theory of his origin, the one he heard Old Horsemeat and Kitty-Come-Here recount from time to time—that he had been the only surviving kitten of a litter abandoned next door, that he had had the shakes from vitamin deficiency and lost the tip of his tail and the hair on his paws and had to be nursed back to life and health with warm yellowish milk-and-vitamins fed from an eyedropper—that other theory was just one of those rationalizations with which mysterious nature cloaks the birth of heroes, perhaps wisely veiling the truth from minds unable to bear it, a rationalization as false as Kitty-Come-Here and Old Horsemeat's touching belief that Sissy and Baby were their children rather than the cubs of Ashurbanipal and Cleopatra.

The day that Gummitch had discovered by pure intuition the secret of his birth he had been filled with a wild instant excitement. He had only kept it from tearing him to pieces by rushing out to the kitchen and striking and devouring a fried scallop, torturing it fiendishly first for twenty minutes.

And the secret of his birth was only the beginning. His intellectual faculties aroused, Gummitch had two days later intuited a further and greater secret: since he was the child of humans he would, upon reaching this maturation date of which Old Horsemeat had spoken, turn not into a sullen tom but into a godlike human youth with reddish golden hair the color of his present fur. He would be poured coffee; and he would instantly be able to talk, probably in all languages. While Sissy (how clear it was now!) would at approximately the same time shrink and fur out into a sharp-clawed and vicious she-cat dark as her hair, sex and self-love her only concerns, fit harem-mate for Cleopatra, concubine to Ashurbanipal.

Exactly the same was true, Gummitch realized at once, for all kittens and babies, all humans and cats, wherever they might dwell. Metamorphosis was as much a part of the fabric of their lives as it was of the insects'. It was also the basic fact underlying all legends of werewolves, vampires and witches' familiars.

If you just rid your mind of preconceived notions, Gummitch told himself, it was all very logical. Babies were stupid, fumbling, vindictive creatures without reason or speech. What could be more natural than that they should grow up into mute sullen selfish beasts bent only on rapine and reproduction? While kittens were quick, sensitive, subtle, supremely alive. What other destiny were they possibly fitted for except to become the deft, word-speaking, book-writing, music-making, meat-getting-and-dispensing masters of the world? To dwell on the physical differences, to point out that kittens and men, babies and cats, are rather unlike in appearance and size, would be to miss the forest for the trees—very much as if an entomologist should proclaim metamorphosis a myth because his microscope failed to discover the wings of a butterfly in a caterpillar's slime or a golden beetle in a grub.

Nevertheless it was such a mind-staggering truth, Gummitch realized at the same time, that it was easy to understand why humans, cats, babies and perhaps most kittens were quite unaware of it. How to safely explain to a butterfly that he was once a hairy crawler, or to a dull larva that he will one day be a walking jewel? No, in such situations the delicate minds of man- and feline-kind are guarded by a merciful mass amnesia, such as Velikovsky has explained prevents us from recalling that in historical times the Earth was catastrophically bumped by the planet Venus operating in the manner of a comet before settling down (with a cosmic sigh of relief, surely!) into its present orbit.

This conclusion was confirmed when Gummitch in the first fever of illumination tried to communicate his great insight to others. He told it in cat patois, as well as that limited jargon permitted, to Ashurbanipal and Cleopatra and even, on the off chance, to Sissy and Baby. They showed no interest whatever, except that Sissy took advantage of his unguarded preoccupation to stab him with a fork.

Later, alone with Old Horsemeat, he projected the great new thoughts, staring with solemn yellow eyes at the old god, but the later grew markedly nervous and even showed signs of real fear, so Gummitch desisted. ("You'd have sworn he was trying to put across something as deep as the Einstein theory or the doctrine of original sin," Old Horsemeat later told Kitty-Come-Here.)

But Gummitch was a man now in all but form, the kitten reminded himself after these failures, and it was part of his destiny to shoulder secrets alone when necessary. He wondered if the general amnesia would affect him when he metamorphosed. There was no sure answer to this question, but he hoped not—and sometimes felt that there was reason for his hopes. Perhaps he would be the first true kitten-man, speaking from a wisdom that had no locked doors in it.

Once he was tempted to speed up the process by the use of drugs. Left alone in the kitchen, he sprang onto the table and started to lap up the black puddle in the bottom of Old Horsemeat's coffee cup. It tasted foul and poisonous and he withdrew with a little snarl, frightened as well as revolted. The dark beverage would not work its tongue-loosening magic, he realized, except at the proper time and with the proper ceremonies. Incantations might be necessary as well. Certainly unlawful tasting was highly dangerous.

The futility of expecting coffee to work any wonders by itself was further demonstrated to Gummitch when Kitty-Come-Here, wordlessly badgered by Sissy, gave a few spoonfuls to the little girl, liberally lacing it first with milk and sugar. Of course Gummitch knew by now that Sissy was destined shortly to turn into a cat and that no amount of coffee would ever make her talk, but it was nevertheless instructive to see how she spat out the first mouthful, drooling a lot of saliva after it, and dashed the cup and its contents at the chest of Kitty-Come-Here.

Gummitch continued to feel a great deal of sympathy for his parents in their worries about Sissy and he longed for the day when he would metamorphose and be able as an acknowledged man-child truly to console them. It was heartbreaking to see how they each tried to coax the little girl to talk, always attempting it while the other was absent, how they seized on each accidentally wordlike note in the few sounds she uttered and repeated it back to her hopefully, how they were more and more possessed by fears not so much of her retarded (they thought) development as of her increasingly obvious maliciousness, which was directed chiefly at Baby . . . though the two cats and Gummitch bore their share. Once she had caught Baby alone in his crib and used the sharp corner of a block to dot Baby's large-domed lightly downed head with triangular red marks. Kitty-Come-Here had discovered her doing it, but the woman's first action had been to rub Baby's head to obliterate the marks so that Old Horsemeat wouldn't see them. That was the night Kitty-Come-Here hid the abnormal psychology books.

Grummitch understood very well that Kitty-Come-Here and Old Horsemeat, honestly believing themselves to be Sissy's parents, felt just as deeply about her as if they actually were and he did what little he could under the present circumstances to help them. He had recently come to feel a quite independent affection for Baby—the miserable little proto-cat was so completely stupid and defenseless—and so he unofficially constituted himself the creature's guardian, taking his naps behind the door of the nursery and dashing about noisily whenever Sissy showed up. In any case he realized that as a potentially adult member of a felino-human household he had his natural responsibilities.

Accepting responsibilities was as much a part of a kitten's life, Gummitch told himself, as shouldering unsharable intuitions and secrets, the number of which continued to grow from day to day.

There was, for instance, the Affair of the Squirrel Mirror.

Gummitch had early solved the mystery of ordinary mirrors and of the creatures that appeared in them. A little observation and sniffing and one attempt to get behind the heavy wall-job in the living room had convinced him that mirror beings were insubstantial or at least hermetically sealed into their other world, probably creatures of pure spirit, harmless imitative ghosts—including the silent Gummitch Double who touched paws with him so softly yet so coldly.

Just the same, Gummitch had let his imagination play with what would happen if one day, while looking into the mirror world, he should let loose his grip on his spirit and let it slip into the Gummitch Double while the other's spirit slipped into his body—if, in short, he should change places with the scentless ghost kitten. Being doomed to a life consisting wholly of imitation and completely lacking in opportunities to show initiative—except for behind-the-scenes judgment and speed needed in rushing from one mirror to another to keep up with the real Gummitch—would be sickeningly dull, Gummitch decided, and he resolved to keep a tight hold on his spirit at all times in the vicinity of mirrors.

But that isn't telling about the Squirrel Mirror. One morning Gummitch was peering out the front bedroom window that overlooked the roof of the porch. Gummitch had already classified windows as semi-mirrors having two kinds of space on the other side: the mirror world and that harsh region filled with mysterious and dangerously organized-sounding noises called the outer world, into which grownup humans reluc-

tantly ventured at intervals, donning special garments for the
purpose and shouting loud farewells that were meant to be reassuring but achieved just the opposite effect. The coexistence
of two kinds of space presented no paradox to the kitten who
carried in his mind the 27-chapter outline of *Space-Time for
Springers*—indeed, it constituted one of the minor themes of
the book.

This morning the bedroom was dark and the outer world
was dull and sunless, so the mirror world was unusually difficult to see. Gummitch was just lifting his face toward it, nose
twitching, his front paws on the sill, when what should rear
up on the other side, exactly in the space that the Gummitch
Double normally occupied, but a dirty brown, narrow-visaged
image with savagely low forehead, dark evil walleyes, and a
huge jaw filled with shovel-like teeth.

Gummitch was enormously startled and hideously frightened. He felt his grip on his spirit go limp, and without voli-
tion he teleported himself three yards to the rear, making use
of that faculty for cutting corners in space-time, traveling by
space-warp in fact, which was one of his powers that Kitty-
Come-Here refused to believe in and that even Old Horsemeat
accepted only on faith.

Then, not losing a moment, he picked himself up by his
furry seat, swung himself around, dashed downstairs at top
speed, sprang to the top of the sofa, and stared for several
seconds at the Gummitch Double in the wall-mirror—not relaxing a muscle strand until he was completely convinced that
he was still himself and had not been transformed into the
nasty brown apparition that had confronted him in the bedroom window.

"Now what do you suppose brought that on?" Old Horsemeat asked Kitty-Come-Here.

Later Gummitch learned that what he had seen had been a
squirrel, a savage, nut-hunting being belonging wholly to the
outer world (except for forays into attics) and not at all to the
mirror one. Nevertheless he kept a vivid memory of his profound momentary conviction that the squirrel had taken the
Gummitch Double's place and been about to take his own. He
shuddered to think what would have happened if the squirrel
had been actively interested in trading spirits with him. Apparently mirrors and mirror-situations, just as he had always
feared, were highly conducive to spirit transfers. He filed the

information away in the memory cabinet reserved for dangerous, exciting and possibly useful information, such as plans
for climbing straight up glass (diamond-tipped claws!) and flying higher than the trees.

These days his thought cabinets were beginning to feel filled to
bursting and he could hardly wait for the moment when the
true rich taste of coffee, lawfully drunk, would permit him to
speak.

He pictured the scene in detail: the family gathered in con-
clave at the kitchen table, Ashurbanipal and Cleopatra
respectfully watching from floor level, himself sitting erect on
chair with paws (or would they be hands?) lightly touching his
cup of thin china, while Old Horsemeat poured the thin black
steaming stream. He knew the Great Transformation must be
close at hand.

At the same time he knew that the other critical situation in
the household was worsening swiftly. Sissy, he realized now,
was far older than Baby and should long ago have undergone
her own somewhat less glamorous though equally necessary
transformation (the first tin of raw horsemeat could hardly be
as exciting as the first cup of coffee). Her time was long over-
due. Gummitch found increasing horror in this mute vam-
pirish being inhabiting the body of a rapidly growing girl,
though inwardly equipped to be nothing but a most blood-
thirsty she-cat. How dreadful to think of Old Horsemeat and
Kitty-Come-Here having to care all their lives for such a
monster! Gummitch told himself that if any opportunity for
alleviating his parents' misery should ever present itself to
him, he would not hesitate for an instant.

Then one night, when the sense of Change was so burstingly
strong in him that he knew tomorrow must be the Day, but
when the house was also exceptionally unquiet with boards
creaking and snapping, taps adrip, and curtains mysteriously
rustling at closed windows (so that it was clear that the many
spirit worlds including the mirror one must be pressing very
close), the opportunity came to Gummitch.

Kitty-Come-Here and Old Horsemeat had fallen into especially sound, drugged sleeps, the former with a bad cold, the
latter with one unhappy highball too many (Gummitch knew
he had been brooding about Sissy). Baby slept too, though
with uneasy whimperings and joggings—moonlight shone full

on his crib past a window shade which had whirringly rolled
itself up without human or feline agency. Gummitch kept vigil
under the crib, with eyes closed but with wildly excited mind
pressing outward to every boundary of the house and even
stretching here and there into the outer world. On this night of
all nights sleep was unthinkable.

Then suddenly he became aware of footsteps, footsteps so
soft they must, he thought, be Cleopatra's.

No, softer than that, so soft they might be those of the
Gummitch Double escaped from the mirror world at last and
padding up toward him through the darkened halls. A ribbon
of fur rose along his spine.

Then into the nursery Sissy came prowling. She looked slim
as an Egyptian princess in her long thin yellow nightgown and
as sure of herself, but the cat was very strong in her tonight,
from the flat intent eyes to the dainty canine teeth slightly
bared—one look at her now would have sent Kitty-Come-Here
running for the telephone number she kept hidden, the telephone number of the special doctor—and Gummitch realized
he was witnessing a monstrous suspension of natural law in
that this being should be able to exist for a moment without
growing fur and changing round pupils for slit eyes.

He retreated to the darkest corner of the room, suppressing
a snarl.

Sissy approached the crib and leaned over Baby in the
moonlight, keeping her shadow off him. For a while she
gloated. Then she began softly to scratch his cheek with a long
hatpin she carried, keeping away from his eye, but just barely.
Baby awoke and saw her and Baby didn't cry. Sissy continued
to scratch, always a little more deeply. The moonlight glittered
on the jeweled end of the pin.

Gummitch knew he faced a horror that could not be
countered by running about or even spitting and screeching.
Only magic could fight so obviously supernatural a manifestation. And this was also no time to think of consequences, no
matter how clearly and bitterly etched they might appear to a
mind intensely awake.

He sprang up onto the other side of the crib, not uttering a
sound, and fixed his golden eyes on Sissy's in the moonlight.
Then he moved forward straight at her evil face, stepping
slowly, not swiftly, using his extraordinary knowledge of the
properties of space *to walk straight through her hand and arm*

as they flailed the hatpin at him. When his nose-tip finally paused a fraction of an inch from hers his eyes had not blinked once, and she could not look away. Then he unhesitatingly flung his spirit into her like a fistful of flaming arrows and he worked the Mirror Magic.

Sissy's moonlit face, feline and terrified, was in a sense the last thing that Gummitch, the real Gummitch-kitten, ever saw in this world. For the next instant he felt himself enfolded by the foul black blinding cloud of Sissy's spirit, which his own had displaced. At the same time he heard the little girl scream, very loudly but even more distinctly, *"Mommy!"*

That cry might have brought Kitty-Come-Here out of her grave, let alone from sleep merely deep or drugged. Within seconds she was in the nursery, closely followed by Old Horsemeat, and she had caught up Sissy in her arms and the little girl was articulating the wonderful word again and again, and miraculously following it with the command—there could be no doubt, Old Horsemeat heard it too—"Hold me tight!"

Then Baby finally dared to cry. The scratches on his cheek came to attention and Gummitch, as he had known must happen, was banished to the basement amid cries of horror and loathing chiefly from Kitty-Come-Here.

The little cat did not mind. No basement would be one-tenth as dark as Sissy's spirit that now enshrouded him for always, hiding all the file drawers and the labels on all the folders, blotting out forever even the imagining of the scene of first coffee-drinking and first speech.

In a last intuition, before the animal blackness closed in utterly, Gummitch realized that the spirit, alas, is not the same thing as the consciousness and that one may lose—sacrifice—the first and still be burdened with the second.

Old Horsemeat had seen the hatpin (and hid it quickly from Kitty-Come-Here) and so he knew that the situation was not what it seemed and that Gummitch was at the very least being made into a sort of scapegoat. He was quite apologetic when he brought the tin pans of food to the basement during the period of the little cat's exile. It was a comfort to Gummitch, albeit a small one. Gummitch told himself, in his new black halting manner of thinking, that after all a cat's best friend is his man.

From that night Sissy never turned back in her development. Within two months she had made three years' progress in speaking. She became an outstandingly bright, light-footed, high-spirited little girl. Although she never told anyone this, the moonlit nursery and Gummitch's magnified face were her first memories. Everything before that was inky blackness. She was always very nice to Gummitch in a careful sort of way. She could never stand to play the game "Owl Eyes."

After a few weeks Kitty-Come-Here forgot her fears and Gummitch once again had the run of the house. But by then the transformation Old Horsemeat had always warned about had fully taken place. Gummitch was a kitten no longer but an almost burly tom. In him it took the psychological form not of sullenness or surliness but an extreme dignity. He seemed at times rather like an old pirate brooding on treasures he would never live to dig up, shores of adventure he would never reach. And sometimes when you looked into his yellow eyes you felt that he had in him all the materials for the book *Slit Eyes Look at Life*—three or four volumes at least—although he would never write it. And that was natural when you come to think of it, for as Gummitch knew very well, bitterly well indeed, his fate was to be the only kitten in the world that did not grow up to be a man.

The Game of
Rat and Dragon

By Cordwainer Smith

The late Cordwainer Smith—in "real" life Dr. Paul M. A. Linebarger, scholar and statesman—created a science fiction cosmology unique in its scope and complexity: a millennia-spanning Future History, logically outlandish and elegantly strange, set against a vivid, richly colored, mythically intense universe where animals assume the shape of men, vast plano-form ships whisper through multidimensional space, immortality can be bought, and the mysterious Lords of the Instrumentality rule a haunted Earth too old for history. Smith's books include the long novel *Norstrilia,* and the collections *Space Lords, The Best of Cordwainer Smith, You Will Never Be the Same, Stardreamer, Quest of the Three Worlds,* and *The Instrumentality of Mankind.*

Here, in what may well be the most imaginative of the science fiction extrapolations in this anthology, he shows us a future in which travelers can flit between the stars in the blinking of an eye . . . *if* they are willing to dare the dark and twisted dimensions of "space three," the "up-and-out," and face the "dragons" that dwell there, malevolent and implacably deadly creatures who strike without warning out of the black hollow nothingness of multidimensional space, and who can only be defeated by—a cat.

1. The Table

Pinlighting is a hell of a way to earn a living. Underhill was furious as he closed the door behind himself. It didn't make much sense to wear a uniform and look like a soldier if people didn't appreciate what you did.

He sat down in his chair, laid his head back in the headrest, and pulled the helmet down over his forehead.

As he waited for the pin-set to warm up, he remembered the girl in the outer corridor. She had looked at it, then looked at him scornfully.

"Meow." That was all she had said. Yet it had cut him like a knife.

What did she think he was—a fool, a loafer, a uniformed nonentity? Didn't she know that for every half-hour of pinlighting, he got a minimum of two months' recuperation in the hospital?

By now the set was warm. He felt the squares of space around him, sensed himself at the middle of an immense grid, a cubic grid, full of nothing. Out in that nothingness, he could sense the hollow aching horror of space itself and could feel the terrible anxiety which his mind encountered whenever it met the faintest trace of inert dust.

As he relaxed, the comforting solidity of the Sun, the clockwork of the familiar planets and the moon rang in on him.

Our own solar system was as charming and as simple as an ancient cuckoo clock filled with familiar ticking and with reassuring noises. The odd little moons of Mars swung around their planet like frantic mice, yet their regularity was itself an assurance that all was well. Far above the plane of the ecliptic, he could feel half a ton of dust more or less drifting outside the lanes of human travel.

Here there was nothing to fight, nothing to challenge the mind, to tear the living soul out of a body with its roots dripping in effluvium as tangible as blood.

Nothing ever moved in on the solar system. He could wear the pin-set forever and be nothing more than a sort of telepathic astronomer, a man who could feel the hot, warm protection of the sun throbbing and burning against his living mind.

Woodley came in.

"Same old ticking world," said Underhill. "Nothing to report. No wonder they didn't develop the pin-set until they began to planoform. Down here with the hot sun around us, it feels so good and so quiet. You can feel everything spinning and turning. It's nice and sharp and compact. It's sort of like sitting around home."

Woodley grunted. He was not much given to flights of fantasy.

Undeterred, Underhill went on, "It must have been pretty good to have been an ancient man. I wonder why they burned up their world with war. They didn't have to planoform. They didn't have to go out to earn their livings among the stars. They didn't have to dodge the rats or play the game. They couldn't have invented pinlighting because they didn't have any need of it, did they, Woodley?"

Woodley grunted, "Uh-huh." Woodley was twenty-six years old and due to retire in one more year. He already had a farm picked out. He had gotten through ten years of hard work pinlighting with the best of them. He had kept his sanity by not thinking very much about his job, meeting the strains of the task whenever he had to meet them and thinking nothing more about his duties until the next emergency arose.

Woodley never made a point of getting popular among the partners. None of the partners liked him very much. Some of them even resented him. He was suspected of thinking ugly thoughts of the partners on occasion, but since none of the partners ever thought a complaint in articulate form, the other pinlighters and the chiefs of the Instrumentality left him alone.

Underhill was still full of the wonder of their job. Happily he babbled on, "What does happen to us when we planoform? Do you think it's sort of like dying? Did you ever see anybody who had his soul pulled out?"

"Pulling souls is just a way of talking about it," said Woodley. "After all these years, nobody knows whether we have souls or not."

"But I saw one once. I saw what Dogwood looked like when he came apart. There was something funny. It looked wet and sort of sticky as if it were bleeding and it went out of him—and you know what they did to Dogwood? They took him away, up in that part of the hospital where you and I never go—way up at the top part where the others are, where the others always have to go if they are alive after the rats of the up-and-out have gotten them."

Woodley sat down and lit an ancient pipe. He was burning something called tobacco in it. It was a dirty sort of habit, but it made him look very dashing and adventurous.

"Look here, youngster. You don't have to worry about that stuff. Pinlighting is getting better all the time. The partners are getting better. I've seen them pinlight two rats forty-six million miles apart in one and a half milliseconds. As long as people had to try to work the pin-sets themselves, there was always the chance that with a minimum of four-hundred milliseconds for the human mind to set a pinlight, we wouldn't light the rats up fast enough to protect our planoforming ships. The partners have changed all that. Once they get going, they're faster than rats. And they always will be. I know it's not easy, letting a partner share your mind—"

"It's not easy for them, either," said Underhill.

"Don't worry about them. They're not human. Let them take care of themselves. I've seen more pinlighters go crazy from monkeying around with partners than I have ever seen caught by the rats. How many of them do you actually know of that got grabbed by rats?"

Underhill looked down at his fingers, which shone green and purple in the vivid light thrown by the tuned-in pin-set, and counted ships. The thumb for the *Andromeda*, lost with crew and passengers, the index finger and the middle finger for *Release Ships 43* and *56*, found with their pin-sets burned out and every man, woman, and child on board dead or insane. The ring finger, the little finger, and the thumb of the other hand were the first three battleships to be lost to the rats—lost as people realized that there was something out there *underneath space itself* which was alive, capricious, and malevolent.

Planoforming was sort of funny. It felt like—

Like nothing much.

Like the twinge of a mild electric shock.

Like the ache of a sore tooth bitten on for the first time.

Like a slightly painful flash of light against the eyes.

Yet in that time, a forty-thousand-ton ship lifting free above Earth disappeared somehow or other into two dimensions and appeared half a light-year or fifty light-years off.

At one moment, he would be sitting in the Fighting Room, the pin-set ready and the familiar solar system ticking around inside his head. For a second or a year (he could never tell how long it really was, subjectively), the funny little flash went through him and then he was loose in the up-and-out, the terrible open spaces between the stars, where the stars themselves felt like pimples on his telepathic mind and the planets were too far away to be sensed or read.

Somewhere in this outer space, a gruesome death awaited, death and horror of a kind which man had never encountered until he reached out for interstellar space itself. Apparently the light of the suns kept the Dragons away.

Dragons. That was what people called them. To ordinary people, there was nothing, nothing except the shiver of planoforming and the hammer blow of sudden death or the dark spastic note of lunacy descending into their minds.

But to the telepaths, they were dragons.

In the fraction of a second between the telepaths' awareness of a hostile something out in the black, hollow nothingness of space and the impact of a ferocious, ruinous psychic blow against all living things within the ship, the telepaths had sensed something like the dragons of ancient human lore, beasts more clever than beasts, demons more tangible than demons, hungry vortices of aliveness and hate compounded by unknown means out of the thin, tenuous matter between the stars.

It took a surviving ship to bring back the news—a ship in

which, by sheer chance, a telepath had a light-beam ready, turning it out at the innocent dust so that, within the panorama of his mind, the dragon dissolved into nothing at all and the other passengers, themselves non-telepathic, went about their way not realizing that their own immediate deaths had been averted.

From then on, it was easy—almost.

Planoforming ships always carried telepaths. Telepaths had their sensitiveness enlarged to an immense range by the pin-sets, which were telepathic amplifiers adapted to the mammal mind. The pin-sets in turn were electronically geared into small dirigible light bombs. Light did it.

Light broke up the dragons, allowed the ships to reform three-dimensionally, skip, skip, skip, as they moved from star to star.

The odds suddenly moved down from a hundred to one against mankind to sixty to forty in mankind's favor.

This was not enough. The telepaths were trained to become ultrasensitive, trained to become aware of the dragons in less than a millisecond.

But it was found that the dragons could move a million miles in just under two milliseconds and that this was not enough for the human mind to activate the light beams.

Attempts had been made to sheath the ships in light at all times.

This defense wore out.

As mankind learned about the dragons, so too, apparently, the dragons learned about mankind. Somehow they flattened their own bulk and came in on extremely flat trajectories very quickly.

Intense light was needed, light of sunlike intensity. This could be provided only by the light bombs. Pinlighting came into existence.

Pinlighting consisted of the detonation of ultra-vivid miniature photonuclear bombs, which converted a few ounces of a magnesium isotope into pure visible radiance.

The odds kept coming down in mankind's favor, yet ships were being lost.

It became so bad that people didn't even want to find the ships because the rescuers knew what they would see. It was sad to bring back to Earth three hundred bodies ready for burial and two hundred or three hundred lunatics, damaged beyond repair, to be wakened, and fed, and cleaned, and put to sleep, wakened and fed again until their lives were ended.

Telepaths tried to reach into the minds of the psychotics who had been damaged by the dragons, but they found nothing there beyond vivid spouting columns of fiery terror bursting from the primordial id itself, the volcanic source of life.

Then came the partners.

Man and partner could do together what man could not do alone. Men had the intellect. Partners had the speed.

The partners rode their tiny craft, no larger than footballs, outside the spaceships. They planoformed with the ships. They rode beside them in their six-pound craft ready to attack.

The tiny ships of the partners were swift. Each carried a dozen pinlights, bombs no bigger than thimbles.

The pinlighters threw the partners—quite literally threw—by means of mind-to-firing relays directly at the dragons.

What seemed to be dragons to the human mind appeared in the form of gigantic rats in the minds of the partners.

Out in the pitiless nothingness of space, the partners' minds responded to an instinct as old as life. The partners attacked, striking with a speed faster than man's, going from attack to attack until the rats or themselves were destroyed. Almost all the time it was the partners who won.

With the safety of the interstellar skip, skip, skip of the ships, commerce increased immensely, the population of all the colonies went up, and the demand for trained partners increased.

Underhill and Woodley were a part of the third generation of pinlighters and yet, to them, it seemed as though their craft had endured forever.

Gearing space into minds by means of the pin-set, adding the partners to those minds, keying up the minds for the tension of a fight on which all depended—this was more than human synapses could stand for long. Underhill needed his two months' rest after half an hour of fighting. Woodley needed his retirement after ten years of service. They were young. They were good. But they had limitations.

So much depended on the choice of partners, so much on the sheer luck of who drew whom.

2. The Shuffle

Father Moontree and the little girl named West entered the
room. They were the other two pinlighters. The human com-
plement of the Fighting Room was now complete.

Father Moontree was a red-faced man of forty-five who had
lived the peaceful life of a farmer until he reached his fortieth
year. Only then, belatedly, did the authorities find he was
telepathic and agree to let him late in life enter upon the career
of pinlighter. He did well at it, but he was fantastically old for
this kind of business.

Father Moontree looked at the glum Woodley and the musing Underhill. "How're the youngsters today? Ready for a
good fight?"

"Father always wants a fight," giggled the little girl named
West. She was such a little little girl. Her giggle was high and
childish. She looked like the last person in the world one
would expect to find in the rough, sharp dueling of pinlighting.

Underhill had been amused one time when he found one of
the most sluggish of the partners coming away happy from
contact with the mind of the girl named West.

Usually the partners didn't care much about the human
minds with which they were paired for the journey. The partners seemed to take the attitude that human minds were complex and fouled up beyond belief, anyhow. No partner ever
questioned the superiority of the human mind, though very
few of the partners were much impressed by that superiority.

The partners liked people. They were willing to fight with
them. They were even willing to die for them. But when a partner liked an individual the way, for example, that Captain
Wow or the Lady May liked Underhill, the liking had nothing
to do with intellect. It was a matter of temperament, of feel.

Underhill knew perfectly well that Captain Wow regarded
his, Underhill's, brains as silly. What Captain Wow liked was
Underhill's friendly emotional structure, the cheerfulness and
glint of wicked amusement that shot through Underhill's un-
conscious thought patterns, and the gaiety with which Underhill faced danger. The words, the history books, the ideas, the
science—Underhill could sense all that in his own mind—reflected back from Captain Wow's mind, as so much rubbish.

Miss West looked at Underhill. "I bet you've put stickum on the stones."

"I did not!"

Underhill felt his ears grow red with embarrassment. During his novitiate, he had tried to cheat in the lottery because he got particularly fond of a special partner, a lovely young mother named Murr. It was so much easier to operate with Murr and she was so affectionate toward him that he forgot pinlighting was hard work and that he was not instructed to have a good time with his partner. They were both designed and prepared to go into deadly battle together.

One cheating had been enough. They had found him out and he had been laughed at for years.

Father Moontree picked up the imitation-leather cup and shook the stone dice which assigned them their partners for the trip. By senior rights he took first draw.

He grimaced. He had drawn a greedy old character, a tough old male whose mind was full of slobbering thoughts of food, veritable oceans full of half-spoiled fish. Father Moontree had once said that he burped cod liver oil for weeks after drawing that particular glutton, so strongly had the telepathic image of fish impressed itself upon his mind. Yet the glutton was a glutton for danger as well as for fish. He had killed sixty-three dragons, more than any other partner in the service, and was quite literally worth his weight in gold.

The little girl West came next. She drew Captain Wow. When she saw who it was, she smiled.

"I *like* him," she said. "He's such fun to fight with. He feels so nice and cuddly in my mind."

"Cuddly, hell," said Woodley. "I've been in his mind, too. It's the most leering mind in this ship, bar none."

"Nasty man," said the little girl. She said it declaratively, without reproach.

Underhill, looking at her, shivered.

He didn't see how she could take Captain Wow so calmly. Captain Wow's mind *did* leer. When Captain Wow got excited in the middle of a battle, confused images of dragons, deadly rats, luscious beds, the smell of fish, and the shock of space all scrambled together in his mind as he and Captain Wow, their consciousnesses linked together through the pinset, became a fantastic composite of human being and Persian cat.

That's the trouble with working with cats, thought Underhill. It's a pity that nothing else anywhere will serve as partner. Cats were all right once you got in touch with them telepathically. They were smart enough to meet the needs of the flight, but their motives and desires were certainly different from those of humans.

They were companionable enough as long as you thought tangible images at them, but their minds just closed up and went to sleep when you recited Shakespeare or Colegrove, or if you tried to tell them what space was.

It was sort of funny realizing that the partners who were so grim and mature out here in space were the same cute little animals that people had used as pets for thousands of years back on Earth. He had embarrassed himself more than once while on the ground saluting perfectly ordinary non-telepathic cats because he had forgotten for the moment that they were not partners.

He picked up the cup and shook out his stone dice.

He was lucky—he drew the Lady May.

The Lady May was the most thoughtful partner he had ever met. In her, the finely bred pedigree mind of a Persian cat had reached one of its highest peaks of development. She was more complex than any human woman, but the complexity was all one of emotions, memory, hope, and discriminated experience—experience sorted through without benefit of words.

When he had first come into contact with her mind, he was astonished at its clarity. With her he remembered her kittenhood. He remembered every mating experience she had ever had. He saw in a half-recognizable gallery all the other pinlighters with whom she had been paired for the fight. And he saw himself radiant, cheerful, and desirable.

He even thought he caught the edge of a longing—

A very flattering and yearning thought: *What a pity he is not a cat.*

Woodley picked up the last stone. He drew what he deserved—a sullen, scarred old tomcat with none of the verve of Captain Wow. Woodley's partner was the most animal of all the cats on the ship, a low, brutish type with a dull mind. Even telepathy had not refined his character. His ears were half chewed off from the first fights in which he had engaged. He was a serviceable fighter, nothing more.

Woodley grunted.

Underhill glanced at him oddly. Didn't Woodley ever do anything but grunt?

Father Moontree looked at the other three. "You might as well get your partners now. I'll let the Go-captain know we're ready to go into the up-and-out."

3. The Deal

Underhill spun the combination lock on the Lady May's cage. He woke her gently and took her into his arms. She humped her back luxuriously, stretched her claws, started to purr, thought better of it, and licked him on the wrist instead. He did not have the pin-set on, so their minds were closed to each other, but in the angle of her mustache and in the movement of her ears, he caught some sense of the gratification she experienced in finding him as her partner.

He talked to her in human speech, even though speech meant nothing to a cat when the pin-set was not on.

"It's a damn shame, sending a sweet little thing like you whirling around in the coldness of nothing to hunt for rats that are bigger and deadlier than all of us put together. You didn't ask for this kind of fight, did you?"

For answer, she licked his hand, purred, tickled his cheek with her long fluffy tail, turned around and faced him, golden eyes shining.

For a moment, they stared at each other, man squatting, cat standing erect on her hind legs, front claws digging into his knee. Human eyes and cat eyes looked across an immensity which no words could meet, but which affection spanned in a single glance.

"Time to get in," he said.

She walked docilely to her spheroid carrier. She climbed in. He saw to it that her miniature pin-set rested firmly and comfortably against the base of her brain. He made sure that her claws were padded so that she could not tear herself in the excitement of battle.

Softly he said to her, "Ready?"

For answer, she preened her back as much as her harness would permit and purred softly within the confines of the frame that held her.

He slapped down the lid and watched the sealant ooze around the seam. For a few hours, she was welded into her projectile until a workman with a short cutting arc would remove her after she had done her duty.

He picked up the entire projectile and slipped it into the ejection tube. He closed the door of the tube, spun the lock, seated himself in his chair, and put his own pin-set on.

Once again he flung the switch.

He sat in a small room, *small, small, warm, warm,* the bodies of the other three people moving close around him, the tangible light in the ceiling bright and heavy against his closed eyelids.

As the pin-set warmed, the room fell away. The other people ceased to be people and became small glowing heaps of fire, embers, dark red fire, with the consciousness of life burning like old red coals in a country fireplace.

As the pin-set warmed a little more, he felt Earth just below him, felt the ship slipping away, felt the turning Moon as it swung on the far side of the world, felt the planets and the hot, clear goodness of the sun which kept the dragons so far from mankind's native ground.

Finally, he reached complete awareness.

He was telepathically alive to a range of millions of miles. He felt the dust which he had noticed earlier high above the ecliptic. With a thrill of warmth and tenderness, he felt the consciousness of the Lady May pouring over into his own. Her consciousness was as gentle and clear and yet sharp to the taste of his mind as if it were scented oil. It felt relaxing and reassuring. He could sense her welcome of him. It was scarcely a thought, just a raw emotion of greeting.

At last they were one again.

In a tiny remote corner of his mind, as tiny as the smallest toy he had ever seen in his childhood, he was still aware of the room and the ship, and of Father Moontree picking up a telephone and speaking to a Go-captain in charge of the ship.

His telepathic mind caught the idea long before his ears could frame the words. the actual sound followed the idea the way that thunder on an ocean beach follows the lightning inward from far out over the seas.

"The Fighting Room is ready. Clear to planoform, sir."

4. The Play

Underhill was always a little exasperated the way that Lady May experienced things before he did.

He was braced for the quick vinegar thrill of planoforming, but he caught her report of it before his own nerves could register what happened.

Earth had fallen so far away that he groped for several milliseconds before he found the Sun in the upper rear right-hand corner of his telepathic mind.

That was a good jump, he thought. *This way we'll get there in four or five skips.*

A few hundred miles outside the ship, the Lady May thought back at him. "O warm, O generous, O gigantic man! O brave, O friendly, O tender and huge partner! O wonderful with you, with you so good, good, good, warm, warm, now to fight, now to go, good with you . . ."

He knew that she was not thinking words, that his mind took the clear amiable babble of her cat intellect and translated it into images which his own thinking could record and understand.

Neither one of them was absorbed in the game of mutual greeting. He reached out far beyond her range of perception to see if there was anything near the ship. It was funny how it was possible to do two things at once. He could scan space with his pin-set mind and yet at the same time catch a vagrant thought of hers, a lovely, affectionate thought about a son who had had a golden face and a chest covered with soft, incredibly downy white fur.

While he was still searching, he caught the warning from her.

We jump again!

And so they had. The ship had moved to a second planoform. The stars were different. The sun was immeasurably far behind. Even the nearest stars were barely in contact. This was good dragon country, this open, nasty, hollow kind of space. He reached farther, faster, sensing and looking for danger, ready to fling the Lady May at danger wherever he found it.

Terror blazed up in his mind, so sharp, so clear, that it came through as a physical wrench.

The little girl named West had found something—something immense, long, black, sharp, greedy, horrific. She flung Captain Wow at it.

Underhill tried to keep his own mind clear. "Watch out!" he shouted telepathically at the others, trying to move the Lady May around.

At one corner of the battle, he felt the lustful rage of Captain Wow as the big Persian tomcat detonated light while he approached the streak of dust which threatened the ship and the people within.

The light scored near misses.

The dust flattened itself, changing from the shape of a sting ray into the shape of a spear.

Not three milliseconds had elapsed.

Father Moontree was talking human words and was saying in a voice that moved like cold molasses out of a heavy jar. "C-a-p-t-a-i-n." Underhill knew that the sentence was going to be "Captain, move fast!"

The battle would be fought and finished before Father Moontree got through talking.

Now, fractions of a millisecond later, the Lady May was directly in line.

Here was where the skill and speed of the partners came in. She could react faster than he. She could see the threat as an immense rat coming directly at her.

She could fire the light-bombs with a discrimination which he might miss.

He was connected with her mind, but he could not follow it.

His consciousness absorbed the tearing wound inflicted by the alien enemy. It was like no wound on Earth—raw, crazy pain which started like a burn at his navel. He began to writhe in his chair.

Actually he had not yet had time to move a muscle when the Lady May struck back at their enemy.

Five evenly spaced photonuclear bombs blazed out across a hundred-thousand miles.

The pain in his mind and body vanished.

He felt a moment of fierce, terrible, feral elation running through the mind of the Lady May as she finished her kill. It was always disappointing to the cats to find out that their enemies disappeared at the moment of destruction.

Then he felt her hurt, the pain and the fear that swept over both of them as the battle, quicker than the movement of an eyelid, had come and gone. In the same instant there came the sharp and acid twinge of planoform.

Once more the ship went skip.

He could hear Woodley thinking at him. "You don't have to bother much. This old son-of-a-gun and I will take over for a while."

Twice again the twinge, the skip.

He had no idea where he was until the lights of the Caledonia space port shone below.

With a weariness that lay almost beyond the limits of thought, he threw his mind back into rapport with the pin-set, fixing the Lady May's projectile gently and neatly in its launching tube.

She was half dead with fatigue, but he could feel the beat of her heart, could listen to her panting, and he grasped the grateful edge of a "Thanks" reaching from her mind to his.

5. The Score

They put him in the hospital at Caledonia.

The doctor was friendly but firm. "You actually got touched by that dragon. That's as close a shave as I've ever seen. It's all so quick that it'll be a long time before we know what happened scientifically, but I suppose you'd be ready for the insane asylum now if the contact had lasted several tenths of a millisecond longer. What kind of cat did you have out in front of you?"

Underhill felt the words coming out of him slowly. Words were such a lot of trouble compared with the speed and the joy of thinking, fast and sharp and clear, mind to mind! But words were all that could reach ordinary people like this doctor.

His mouth moved heavily as he articulated words. "Don't call our partners cats. The right thing to call them is partners. They fight for us in a team. You ought to know we call them partners, not cats. How is mine?"

"I don't know," said the doctor contritely. "We'll find out for you. Meanwhile, old man, you take it easy. There's nothing but rest that can help you. Can you make yourself sleep, or would you like us to give you some kind of sedative?"

"I can sleep," said Underhill. "I just want to know about the Lady May."

The nurse joined in. She was a little antagonistic. "Don't you want to know about the other people?"

"They're okay," said Underhill. "I knew that before I came in here."

He stretched his arms and sighed and grinned at them. He could see they were relaxing and were beginning to treat him as a person instead of a patient.

"I'm all right," he said. "Just let me know when I can go see my partner."

A new thought struck him. He looked wildly at the doctor. "They didn't send her off with the ship, did they?"

"I'll find out right away," said the doctor. He gave Underhill a reassuring squeeze of the shoulder and left the room.

The nurse took a napkin off a goblet of chilled fruit juice.

Underhill tried to smile at her. There seemed to be something wrong with the girl. He wished she would go away. First she had started to be friendly and now she was distant again. *It's a nuisance being telepathic,* he thought. *You keep trying to reach even when you are not making contact.*

Suddenly she swung around on him.

"You pinlighters! You and your damn cats!"

Just as she stamped out, he burst into her mind. He saw himself a radiant hero, clad in his smooth suede uniform, the pin-set crown shining like ancient royal jewels around his head. He saw his own face, handsome and masculine, shining out of her mind. He saw himself very far away and he saw himself as she hated him.

She hated him in the secrecy of her own mind. She hated

him because he was—she thought—proud and strange and rich, better and more beautiful than people like her.

He cut off the sight of her mind and, as he buried his face in the pillow, he caught an image of the Lady May.

She is *a cat*, he thought. *That's all she is—a* cat!

But that was not how his mind saw her—quick beyond all dreams of speed, sharp, clever, unbelievably graceful, beautiful, wordless and undemanding.

Where would he ever find a woman who could compare with her?

The Cat
From Hell

By Stephen King

Stephen King is without doubt the foremost contemporary practitioner of the modern horror story (a subgenre that he is almost single-handedly responsible for bringing to a widespread public in the 1970's), and one of the most successful writers in the country by any standard. In the last few years, King has gone from triumph to triumph with books such as *Salem's Lot, The Shining, The Stand, Firestarter,* and *Cujo,* all of which have been made—or are currently in the process of being made—into films or television movies. His short fiction has been collected in *Night Shift.* His most recent books are the novels *The Dark Tower: The Gunslinger, Christine* and *The Pet Sematary.*

King has an uncanny talent for discovering what really scares us, what dark dreams and monsters actually drive the machinery of contemporary society, existing unexamined behind the bland facade of our humdrum everyday lives.

Here he gives us a chilling little story about a professional killer and a black-and-white cat. After reading this story, you may never feel completely easy again around your *own* cat— that sleek four-footed killing machine who may even now be purring beside you as you read. . . .

Halston thought the old man in the wheelchair looked sick, terrified, and ready to die. He had experience in seeing such things. Death was Halston's business; he had brought it to eighteen men and six women in his career as an independent hitter. He knew the death look.

The house—mansion, actually—was cold and quiet. The only sounds were the low snap of the fire on the big stone hearth and the low whine of the November wind outside.

"I want you to make a kill," the old man said. His voice was quavery and high, peevish. "I understand that is what you do."

"Who did you talk to?" Halston asked.

"With a man named Saul Loggia. He says you know him."

Halston nodded. If Loggia was the go-between, it was all right. And if there was a bug in the room, anything the old man—Drogan—said was entrapment.

"Who do you want hit?"

Drogan pressed a button on the console built into the arm of his wheelchair and it buzzed forward. Close-up, Halston could smell the yellow odors of fear, age, and urine all mixed. They disgusted him, but he made no sign. His face was still and smooth.

"Your victim is right behind you," Drogan said softly.

Halston moved quickly. His reflexes were his life and they were always set on a filed pin. He was off the couch, falling to one knee, turning, hand inside his specially tailored sport coat,

35

gripping the handle of the short-barrelled .45 hybrid that hung
below his armpit in a spring-loaded holster that laid it in his
palm at a touch. A moment later it was out and pointed at . . .
a cat.

For a moment Halston and the cat stared at each other. It
was a strange moment for Halston, who was an unimaginative
man with no superstitions. For that one moment as he knelt on
the floor with the gun pointed, he felt that he knew this cat,
although if he had ever seen one with such unusual markings
he surely would have remembered.

Its face was an even split: half black, half white. The divid-
ing line ran from the top of its flat skull and down its nose to
its mouth, straight-arrow. Its eyes were huge in the gloom, and
caught in each nearly circular black pupil was a prism of fire-
light, like a sullen coal of hate.

And the thought echoed back to Halston: *We know each
other, you and I.*

Then it passed. He put the gun away and stood up. "I ought
to kill you for that, old man. I don't take a joke."

"And I don't make them," Drogan said. "Sit down. Look
in here." He had taken a fat envelope out from beneath the
blanket that covered his legs.

Halston sat. The cat, which had been crouched on the back
of the sofa, jumped lightly down into his lap. It looked up at
Halston for a moment with those huge dark eyes, the pupils
surrounded by thin green-gold rings, and then it settled down
and began to purr.

Halston looked at Drogan questioningly.

"He's very friendly," Drogan said. "At first. Nice friendly
pussy has killed three people in this household. That leaves
only me. I am old, I am sick . . . but I prefer to die in my own
time."

"I can't believe this," Halston said. "You hired me to hit a
cat?"

"Look in the envelope, please."

Halston did. It was filled with hundreds and fifties, all of
them old. "How much is it?"

"Six thousand dollars. There will be another six when you
bring me proof that the cat is dead. Mr. Loggia said twelve
thousand was your usual fee?"

Halston nodded, his hand automatically stroking the cat in
his lap. It was asleep, still purring. Halston liked cats. They

were the only animals he did like, as a matter of fact. They got along on their own. God—if there was one—had made them into perfect, aloof killing machines. Cats were the hitters of the animal world, and Halston gave them his respect.

"I need not explain anything, but I will," Drogan said. "Forewarned is forearmed, they say, and I would not want you to go into this lightly. And I seem to need to justify myself. So you'll not think I'm insane."

Halston nodded again. He had already decided to make this peculiar hit, and no further talk was needed. But if Drogan wanted to talk, he would listen.

"First of all, you know who I am? Where the money comes from?"

"Drogan Pharmaceuticals."

"Yes. One of the biggest drug companies in the world. And the cornerstone of our financial success has been this." From the pocket of his robe he handed Halston a small, unmarked vial of pills. "Tri-Dormal-phenobarbin, compound G. Prescribed almost exclusively for the terminally ill. It's extremely habit-forming, you see. It's a combination pain-killer, tranquilizer, and mild hallucinogen. It is remarkably helpful in helping the terminally ill face their conditions and adjust to them."

"Do you take it?" Halston asked.

Drogan ignored the question. "It is widely prescribed throughout the world. It's a synthetic, was developed in the fifties at our New Jersey labs. Our testing was confined almost solely to cats, because of the unique quality of the feline nervous system."

"How many did you wipe out?"

Drogan stiffened. "That is an unfair and prejudicial way to put it."

Halston shrugged.

"In the four-year testing period which led to FDA approval of Tri-dormal-G, about fifteen thousand cats . . . uh, expired."

Halston whistled. About four thousand cats a year. "And now you think this one's back to get you, huh?"

"I don't feel guilty in the slightest," Drogan said, but that quavering, petulant note was back in his voice. "Fifteen thousand test animals died so that hundreds of thousands of human beings—"

"Never mind that," Halston said. Justifications bored him.

"That cat came here seven months ago. I've never liked cats. Nasty, disease-bearing animals . . . always out in the fields . . . crawling around in barns . . . picking up god knows what germs in their fur . . . always trying to bring something with its insides falling out into the house for you to look at . . . it was my sister who wanted to take it in. She found out. She paid." He looked at the cat sleeping on Halston's lap with dead hate.

"You said the cat killed three people."

Drogan began to speak. The cat dozed and purred on Halston's lap under the soft, scratching strokes of Halston's strong and expert killer's fingers. Occasionally a pine knot would explode on the hearth, making it tense like a series of steel springs covered with hide and muscle. Outside the wind whined around the big stone house far out in the Connecticut countryside. There was winter in that wind's throat. The old man's voice droned on and on.

Seven months ago there had been four of them here— Drogan, his sister Amanda, who at seventy-four was two years Drogan's elder, her lifelong friend Carolyn Broadmoor ("of the Westchester Broadmoors," Drogan said), who was badly afflicted with emphysema, and Dick Gage, a hired man who had been with the Drogan family for twenty years. Gage, who was past sixty himself, drove the big Lincoln Mark IV, cooked, served the evening sherry. A day-maid came in. The four of them had lived this way for nearly two years, a dull collection of old people and their family retainer. Their only pleasures were *The Hollywood Squares* and waiting to see who would outlive whom.

Then the cat had come.

"It was Gage who saw it first, whining and skulking around the house. He tried to drive it away. He threw sticks and small rocks at it, and hit it several times. But it wouldn't go. It smelled the food, of course. It was little more than a bag of bones. People put them out beside the road to die at the end of the summer season, you know. A terrible, inhumane thing."

"Better to fry their nerves?" Halston asked.

Drogan ignored that and went on. He hated cats. He always had. When the cat refused to be driven away, he had instructed Gage to put out poisoned food. Large, tempting dishes of Calo cat food spiked with Tri-Dormal-G, as a matter

of fact. The cat ignored the food. At that point Amanda
Drogan had noticed the cat and had insisted they take it in.
Drogan had protested vehemently, but Amanda had gotten
her way. She always did, apparently.

"But she found out," Drogan said. "She brought it inside
herself, in her arms. It was purring, just as it is now. But it
wouldn't come near me. It never has . . . yet. She poured it a
saucer of milk. 'Oh, look at the poor thing, it's starving,' she
cooed. She and Carolyn both cooed over it. Disgusting. It was
their way of getting back at me, of course. They knew the way
I've felt about felines ever since the Tri-Dormal-G testing program twenty years ago. They enjoyed teasing me, baiting me
with it." He looked at Halston grimly. "But they paid."

In mid-May, Gage had gotten up to set breakfast and had
found Amanda Drogan lying at the foot of the main stairs in a
litter of broken crockery and Little Friskies. Her eyes bulged
sightlessly up at the ceiling. She had bled a great deal from the
mouth and nose. Her back was broken, both legs were broken,
and her neck had been literally shattered like glass.

"It slept in her room," Drogan said. "She treated it like a
baby . . . 'Is oo hungwy, darwing? Does oo need to go out and
do poopoos?' Obscene, coming from an old battle-axe like my
sister. I think it woke her up, meowing. She got his dish. She
used to say that Sam didn't really like his Friskies unless they
were wetted down with a little milk. So she was planning to go
downstairs. The cat was rubbing against her legs. She was old,
not too steady on her feet. Half-asleep. They got to the head
of the stairs and the cat got in front of her . . . tripped
her . . ."

Yes, it could have happened that way, Halston thought. In
his mind's eye he saw the old woman falling forward and outward, too shocked to scream. The Friskies spraying out as she
tumbled head over heels to the bottom, the bowl smashing. At
last she comes to rest at the bottom, the old bones shattered,
the eyes glaring, the nose and ears trickling blood. And the
purring cat begins to work its way down the stairs, contentedly
munching Little Friskies . . .

"What did the coroner say?" he asked Drogan.

"Death by accident, of course. But I knew."

"Why didn't you get rid of the cat then? With Amanda
gone?"

Because Carolyn Broadmoor had threatened to leave if he

did, apparently. She was hysterical, obsessed with the subject.
She was a sick woman, and she was nutty on the subject of
spiritualism. A Hartford medium had told her (for a mere
twenty dollars) that Amanda's soul had entered Sam's feline
body. Sam had been Amanda's, she told Drogan, and if Sam
went, *she* went.

Halston, who had become something of an expert at reading
between the lines of human lives, suspected that Drogan and
the old Broadmoor bird had been lovers long ago, and the old
dude was reluctant to let her go over a cat.

"It would have been the same as suicide," Drogan said. "In
her mind she was still a wealthy woman, perfectly capable of
packing up that cat and going to New York or London or even
Monte Carlo with it. In fact she was the last of a great family,
living on a pittance as a result of a number of bad investments
in the sixties. She lived on the second floor here in a specially-
controlled, super-humidified room. The woman was seventy,
Mr. Halston. She was a heavy smoker until the last two years
of her life, and the emphysema was very bad. I wanted her
here, and if the cat had to stay . . ."

Halston nodded and then glanced meaningfully at his
watch.

"Near the end of June, she died in the night. The doctor
seemed to take it as a matter of course . . . just came and wrote
out the death certificate and that was the end of it. But the cat
was in the room. Gage told me."

"We all have to go sometime, man," Halston said.

"Of course. That's what the doctor said. But I knew. I
remembered. Cats like to get babies and old people when
they're asleep. And steal their breath."

"An old wives' tale."

"Based on fact, like most so-called old wives' tales,"
Drogan replied. "Cats like to knead soft things with their
paws, you see. A pillow, a thick shag rug . . . or a blanket. A
crib blanket or an old person's blanket. The extra weight on a
person who's weak to start with . . ."

Drogan trailed off, and Halston thought about it. Carolyn
Broadmoor asleep in her bedroom, the breath rasping in and
out of her damaged lungs, the sound nearly lost in the whisper
of special humidifiers and air-conditioners. The cat with the
queer black-and-white markings leaps silently onto her
spinster's bed and stares at her old and wrinkle-grooved face

with those lambent, black-and-green eyes. It creeps onto her thin chest and settles its weight there, purring . . . and the breathing slows . . . slows . . . and the cat purrs as the old woman slowly smothers beneath its weight on her chest.

He was not an imaginative man, but Halston shivered a little.

"Drogan," he said, continuing to stroke the purring cat. "Why don't you just have it put away? A vet would give it the gas for twenty dollars."

Drogan said, "The funeral was on the first of July. I had Carolyn buried in our cemetery plot next to my sister. The way she would have wanted it. Only July third I called Gage to this room and handed him a wicker basket . . . a picnic hamper sort of thing. Do you know what I mean?"

Halston nodded.

"I told him to put the cat in it and take it to a vet in Milford and have it put to sleep. He said, 'Yes, sir,' took the basket, and went out. Very like him. I never saw him alive again. There was an accident on the turnpike. The Lincoln was driven into a bridge abutment at better than sixty miles an hour. Dick Gage was killed instantly. When they found him there were scratches on his face."

Halston was silent as the picture of how it might have been formed in his brain again. No sound in the room but the peaceful crackle of the fire and the peaceful purr of the cat in his lap. He and the cat together before the fire would make a good illustration for that Edgar Guest poem, the one that goes: "The cat on my lap, the hearth's good fire/ . . . A happy man, should you enquire."

Dick Gage moving the Lincoln down the turnpike toward Milford, beating the speed limit by maybe five miles an hour. The wicker basket beside him—a picnic hamper sort of thing. The chauffeur is watching traffic, maybe he's passing a big cab-over Jimmy and he doesn't notice the peculiar black-on-one-side, white-on-the-other face that pokes out of one side of the basket. Out of the driver's side. He doesn't notice because he's passing the big trailer truck and that's when the cat jumps onto his face, spitting and clawing, its talons raking into one eye, puncturing it, deflating it, blinding it. Sixty and the hum of the Lincoln's big motor and the other paw is hooked over the bridge of the nose, digging in with exquisite, damning pain—maybe the Lincoln starts to veer right, into the path of the Jimmy, and its airhorn blares ear-shatteringly, but Gage can't hear it because the cat is yowling, the cat is spread-eagled over his face like some huge furry black spider, ears laid back, green eyes glaring like spotlights from hell, back legs jittering and digging into the soft flesh of the old man's neck. The car veers wildly back the other way. The bridge abutment looms. The cat jumps down and the Lincoln, a shiny black torpedo, hits the cement and goes up like a bomb.

Halston swallowed hard and heard a dry click in his throat. "And the cat came back?"

Drogan nodded. "A week later. On the day Dick Gage was buried, as a matter of fact. Just like the old song says. The cat came back."

"It survived a car crash at sixty? Hard to believe."

"They say each one has nine lives. When it comes back . . . that's when I started to wonder if it might not be a . . . a . . ."

"Hellcat?" Halston suggested softly.

"For want of a better word, yes. A sort of demon sent . . ."

"To punish you."

"I don't know. But I'm afraid of it. I feed it, or rather, the woman who comes in to do for me feeds it. She doesn't like it either. She says that face is a curse of God. Of course, she's local." The old man tried to smile and failed. "I want you to kill it. I've lived with it for the last four months. It skulks around in the shadows. It looks at me. It seems to be . . . waiting. I lock myself in my room every night and still I wonder if I'm going to wake up one early morning and find it . . . curled up on my chest . . . and purring."

The wind whined lonesomely outside and made a strange hooting noise in the stone chimney.

"At last I got in touch with Saul Loggia. He recommended you. He called you a stick, I believe."

"A one-stick. That means I work on my own."

"Yes. He said you'd never been busted, or even suspected. He said you always seem to land on your feet . . . like a cat."

Halston looked at the old man in the wheelchair. And suddenly his long-fingered, muscular hands were lingering just above the cat's neck.

"I'll do it now, if you want me to," he said softly. "I'll snap its neck. It won't even know—"

"No!" Drogan cried. He drew in a long, shuddering breath.

Color had come up in his sallow cheeks. "Not . . . not here. Take it away."

Halston smiled humorlessly. He began to stroke the sleeping cat's head and shoulders and back very gently again. "All right," he said. "I accept the contract. Do you want the body?"

"No. Kill it. Bury it." He paused. He hunched forward in the wheelchair like some ancient buzzard. "Bring me the tail," he said. "So I can throw it in the fire and watch it burn."

Halston drove a 1973 Plymouth with a custom Cyclone Spoiler engine. The car was jacked and blocked, and rode with the hood pointing down at the road at a twenty-degree angle. He had rebuilt the differential and the rear end himself. The shift was a Pensy, the linkage was Hearst. It sat on huge Bobby Unser Wide Ovals and had a top end of a little past one-sixty.

He left the Drogan house at a little past 9:30. A cold rind of crescent moon rode overhead through the tattering November clouds. He rode with all the windows open, because that yellow stench of age and terror seemed to have settled into his clothes and he didn't like it. The cold was hard and sharp, eventually numbing, but it was good. It was blowing that yellow stench away.

He got off the turnpike at Placer's Glen and drove through the silent town, which was guarded by a single yellow blinker at the intersection, at a thoroughly respectable thirty-five. Out of town, moving up S.R. 35, he opened the Plymouth up a little, letting her walk. The tuned Spoiler engine purred like the cat had purred on his lap earlier this evening. Halston grinned at the simile. They moved between frost-white November fields full of skeleton cornstalks at a little over seventy.

The cat was in a double-thickness shopping bag, tied at the top with heavy twine. The bag was in the passenger bucket seat. The cat had been sleepy and purring when Halston put it in, and it had purred through the entire ride. It sensed, perhaps, that Halston liked it and felt at home with it. Like himself, the cat was a one-stick.

Strange hit, Halston thought, and was surprised to find that he was taking it seriously *as* a hit. Maybe the strangest thing about it was that he actually liked the cat, felt a kinship with

it. If it had managed to get rid of those three old crocks, more
power to it . . . especially Gage, who had been taking it to
Milford for a terminal date with a crewcut veterinarian who
would have been more than happy to bundle it into a ceramic-
lined gas chamber the size of a microwave oven. He felt a kinship, but no urge to renege on the hit. He would do it the
courtesy of killing it quickly and well. He would park off the
road beside one of these November-barren fields and take it
out of the bag and stroke it and then snap its neck and sever its
tail with his pocket knife. And, he thought, the body I'll bury
honorably, saving it from the scavengers. I can't save it from
the worms, but I can save it from the maggots.

He was thinking these things as the car moved through the
night like a dark blue ghost and that was when the cat walked
in front of his eyes, up on the dashboard, tail raised arro-
gantly, its black-and-white face turned toward him, its mouth
seeming to grin at him.

"Ssssshhhh—" Halston hissed. He glanced to his right and
caught a glimpse of the double-thickness shopping bag, a hole
chewed—or clawed—in its side. Looked ahead again . . . and
the cat lifted a paw and batted playfully at him. The paw
skidded across Halston's forehead. He jerked away from it
and the Plymouth's big tires wailed on the road as it swung er-
ratically from one side of the narrow blacktop to the other.

Halston batted at the cat on the dashboard with his fist. It
was blocking his field of vision. It spat at him, arching its
back, but it didn't move. Halston swung again, and instead of
shrinking away, it leaped at him.

Gage, he thought. *Just like Gage—*

He stamped the brake. The cat was on his head, blocking his
vision with its furry belly, clawing at him, gouging at him.
Halston held the wheel grimly. He struck the cat once, twice, a
third time. And suddenly the road was gone, the Plymouth
was running down into the ditch, thudding up and down on its
shocks. Then, impact, throwing him forward against his seatbelt, and the last sound he heard was the cat yowling inhu-
manly, the voice of a woman in pain or in the throes of sexual
climax.

He struck it with his closed fists and felt only the springy,
yielding flex of its muscles.

Then, second impact. And darkness.

•   •   •

The moon was down. It was an hour before dawn.

The Plymouth lay in a ravine curdled with groundmist. Tangled in its grille was a snarled length of barbed wire. The hood had come unlatched, and tendrils of steam from the breached radiator drifted out of the opening to mingle with the mist.

No feeling in his legs.

He looked down and saw that the Plymouth's firewall had caved in with the impact. The back of that big Cyclone Spoiler engine block had smashed into his legs, pinning them.

Outside, in the distance, the predatory squawk of an owl dropping onto some small, scurrying animal.

Inside, close, the steady purr of the cat.

It seemed to be grinning, like Alice's Cheshire had in Wonderland.

As Halston watched it stood up, arched its back, and stretched. In a sudden limber movement like rippled silk, it leaped to his shoulder. Halston tried to lift his hands to push it off.

His arms wouldn't move.

Spinal shock, he thought. *Paralyzed. Maybe temporary. More likely permanent.*

The cat purred in his ear like thunder.

"Get off me," Halston said. His voice was hoarse and dry. The cat tensed for a moment and then settled back. Suddenly its paw batted Halston's cheek, and the claws were out this time. Hot lines of pain down to his throat. And the warm trickle of blood.

Pain.

Feeling.

He ordered his head to move to the right, and it complied. For a moment his face was buried in smooth, dry fur. Halston snapped at the cat. It made a startled, disgruntled sound in its throat—*yowk!*—and leaped onto the seat. It stared up at him angrily, ears laid back.

"Wasn't supposed to do that, was I?" Halston croaked.

The cat opened its mouth and hissed at him. Looking at that strange, schizophrenic face, Halston could understand how Drogan might have thought it was a hellcat. It—

His thoughts broke off as he became aware of a dull, tingling feeling in both hands and forearms.

Feeling. Coming back. Pins and needles.

The cat leaped at his face, claws out, spitting.

Halston shut his eyes and opened his mouth. He bit at the cat's belly and got nothing but fur. The cat's front claws were clasped on his ears, digging in. The pain was enormous, brightly excruciating. Halston tried to raise his hands. They twitched but would not quite come out of his lap.

He bent his head forward and began to shake it back and forth, like a man shaking soap out of his eyes. Hissing and squalling, the cat held on. Halston could feel blood trickling down his cheeks. It was hard to get his breath. The cat's chest was pressed over his nose. It was possible to get some air in by mouth, but not much. What he did get came through fur. His ears felt as if they had been doused with lighter fluid and then set on fire.

He snapped his head back, and cried out in agony—he must have sustained a whiplash when the Plymouth hit. But the cat hadn't been expecting the reverse and it flew off. Halston heard it thud down in the back seat.

A trickle of blood ran in his eye. He tried again to move his hands, to raise one of them and wipe the blood away.

They trembled in his lap, but he was still unable to actually move them. He thought of the .45 special in its holster under his left arm.

If I can get to my piece, kitty, the rest of your nine lives are going in a lump sum.

More tingles now. Dull throbs of pain from his feet, buried and surely shattered under the engine block, zips and tingles from his legs—it felt exactly the way a limb that you've slept on does when it's starting to wake up. At that moment Halston didn't care about his feet. It was enough to know that his spine wasn't severed, that he wasn't going to finish out his life as a dead lump of body attached to a talking head.

Maybe I had a few lives left myself.

Take care of the cat. That was the first thing. *Then get out of the wreck*—maybe someone would come along, that would solve both problems at once. Not likely at 4:30 in the morning on a back road like this one, but barely possible. And—

And what was the cat doing back there?

He didn't like having it on his face, but he didn't like having it behind him and out of sight, either. He tried the rear-view mirror, but that was useless. The crash had knocked it awry and all it reflected was the grassy ravine he had finished up in.

A sound from behind him, like low, ripping cloth.

Purring.

Hellcat my ass. It's gone to sleep back there.

And even if it hadn't, even if it was somehow planning murder, what could it do? It was a skinny little thing, probably weighed all of four pounds soaking wet. And soon . . . soon he would be able to move his hands enough to get his gun. He was sure of it.

Halston sat and waited. Feeling continued to flood back into his body in a series of pins-and-needles incursions. Absurdly (or maybe in instinctive reaction to his close brush with death) he got an erection for a minute or so. *Be kind of hard to beat off under present circumstances,* he thought.

A dawn-line was appearing in the eastern sky. Somewhere a bird sang.

Halston tried his hands again and got them to move an eighth of an inch before they fell back.

Not yet. But soon.

A soft thud on the seatback beside him. Halston turned his head and looked into the black-white face, the glowing eyes with their huge dark pupils.

Halston spoke to it.

"I have never blown a hit once I took it on, kitty. This could be a first. I'm getting my hands back. Five minutes, ten at most. You want my advice? Go out the window. They're all open. Go out and take your tail with you."

The cat stared at him.

Halston tried his hands again. They came up, trembling wildly. Half an inch. An inch. He let them fall back limply. They slipped off his lap and thudded to the Plymouth's seat. They glimmered there palely, like large tropical spiders.

The cat was grinning at him.

Did I make a mistake? he wondered confusedly. He was a creature of hunch, and the feeling that he had made one was suddenly overwhelming. Then the cat's body tensed, and even as it leaped, Halston knew what it was going to do and he opened his mouth to scream.

The cat landed on Halston's crotch, claws out, digging.

At that moment, Halston wished he *had* been paralyzed. The pain was gigantic, terrible. He had never suspected that there could be such pain in the world. The cat was a spitting coiled spring of fury, clawing at his balls.

Halston *did* scream, his mouth yawning open, and that was when the cat changed direction and leaped at his face, leaped at his mouth. And at that moment Halston knew that it was something more than a cat. It was something possessed of a malign, murderous intent.

He caught one last glimpse of that black-and-white face below the flattened ears, its eyes enormous and filled with lunatic hate. It had gotten rid of the three old people and now it was going to get rid of John Halston.

It rammed into his mouth, a furry projectile. He gagged on it. Its front claws pinwheeled, tattering his tongue like a piece of liver. His stomach recoiled and he vomited. The vomit ran down into his windpipe, clogging it, and he began to choke.

In this extremity, his will to survive overcame the last of the impact paralysis. He brought his hands up slowly to grasp the cat. *Oh my God,* he thought.

The cat was forcing its way into his mouth, flattening its body, squirming, working itself further and further in. He could feel his jaws creaking wider and wider to admit it.

He reached to grab it, yank it out, destroy it . . . and his hands clasped only the cat's tail.

Somehow it had gotten its entire body into his mouth. Its strange, black-and-white face must be crammed into his very throat.

A terrible thick gagging sound came from Halston's throat, which was swelling like a flexible length of garden hose.

His body twitched. His hands fell back into his lap and the fingers drummed senselessly on his thighs. His eyes sheened over, then glazed. They stared out through the Plymouth's windshield blankly at the coming dawn.

Protruding from his open mouth was two inches of bushy tail . . . half-black, half-white. It switched lazily back and forth.

It disappeared.

A bird cried somewhere again. Dawn came in breathless silence then, over the frost-rimmed fields of rural Connecticut.

The farmer's name was Will Reuss.

He was on his way to Placer's Glen to get the inspection sticker renewed on his farm truck when he saw the late morning sun twinkle on something in the ravine beside the road. He pulled over and saw the Plymouth lying at a drunken, canted angle in the ditch, barbed wire tangled in its grille like a snarl of steel knitting.

He worked his way down, and then sucked in his breath sharply. "Holy moley," he muttered to the bright November day. There was a guy sitting bolt upright behind the wheel, eyes open and glaring emptily into eternity. The Roper organization was never going to include him in its presidential poll again. His face was smeared with blood. He was still wearing his seatbelt.

The driver's door had been crimped shut, but Reuss managed to get it open by yanking with both hands. He leaned in and unstrapped the seatbelt, planning to check for ID. He was reaching for the coat when he noticed that the dead guy's shirt was rippling, just above the belt-buckle. Rippling . . . and bulging. Splotches of blood began to bloom there like sinister roses.

"What the Christ?" He reached out, grasped the dead man's shirt, and pulled it up.

Will Reuss looked—and screamed.

Above Halston's navel, a ragged hole had been clawed in his flesh. Looking out was the gore-streaked black-and-white face of a cat, its eyes huge and glaring.

Reuss staggered back, shrieking, hands clapped to his face. A score of crows took cawing wing from a nearby field.

The cat forced its body out and stretched in obscene languor.

Then it leaped out the open window. Reuss caught sight of it moving through the high dead grass and then it was gone.

It seemed to be in a hurry, he later told a reporter from the local paper.

As if it had unfinished business.

Out of Place

By Pamela Sargent

To understand the language of beasts! This is a dream that has persisted throughout the ages, from Aesop to Doctor Doolittle. If we *could* understand the speech of animals, though, would we necessarily like what they had to say?

Perhaps. Or perhaps *not*. . . .

Pamela Sargent has emerged as one of the foremost writer-editors of her generation. Her novels include the recent (and highly acclaimed) *The Golden Space,* as well as *Cloned Lives, The Sudden Star,* and *Watchstar.* Her anthologies include the acclaimed *Women of Wonder, More Women of Wonder, The New Women of Wonder,* and *Bio-Futures.* Her short fiction has been collected in *Starshadows.* Her most recent books are *Earthseed* and *The Alien Upstairs,* both novels.

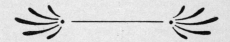

*"For something is amiss or out of place
When mice with wings can wear a human face."*

—THEODORE ROETHKE,
"The Bat"

Marcia was washing the breakfast dishes when she first heard her cat thinking. "I'm thirsty, why doesn't she give me more water, there's dried food on the sides of my bowl." There was a pause. "I wonder how she catches the food. She can't stalk anything, she always scares the birds away. She never catches any when I'm nearby. Why does she put it into those squares and round things when she just has to take it out again? What is food, anyway? What is water?"

Very slowly, Marcia put down the cup she was washing, turned off the water, and faced the cat. Pearl, a slim Siamese, was sitting by her plastic bowls. She swatted the newspaper under them with one paw, then stretched out on her side. "I want to be combed, I want my stomach scratched. Why isn't he here? He always goes away. They should both be here, they're supposed to serve me." Pearl's mouth did not move, but Marcia knew the words were hers. For one thing, there was no one else in the house. For another, the disembodied voice had a feline whine to it, as if the words were almost, but not quite, meows.

Oh, God, Marcia thought, I'm going crazy. Still eyeing the

cat, she crept to the back door and opened it. She inhaled some fresh air and felt better. A robin was pecking at the grass. "Earth, yield your treasures to me. I hunger, my young cry out for food." This voice had a musical lilt. Marcia leaned against the door frame.

"I create space." The next voice was deep and sluggish. "The universe parts before me. It is solid and dark and damp, it covers all, but I create space. I approach the infinite. Who has created it? A giant of massive dimensions must have moved through the world, leaving the infinite. It is before me now. The warmth—ah!"

The voice broke off. The robin had caught a worm.

Marcia slammed the door shut. Help, she thought, and then: I wonder what Dr. Leroy would say. A year of transactional analysis and weekly group-therapy sessions had assured her that she was only a mildly depressed neurotic; though she had never been able to scream and pound her pillow in front of others in her group and could not bring herself to call Dr. Leroy Bill, as his other clients did, the therapy had at least diminished the frequency of her migraines, and the psychiatrist had been pleased with her progress. Now she was sure that she was becoming psychotic; only psychotics heard voices. There was some satisfaction in knowing Dr. Leroy had been wrong.

Pearl had wandered away. Marcia struggled to stay calm. If I can hear her thoughts, she reasoned, can she hear mine? She shivered. "Pearl," she called out in a wavering voice. "Here, kitty. Nice Pearl." She walked into the hall and toward the stairs.

The cat was on the top step, crouching. Her tail twitched. Marcia concentrated, trying to transmit a message to Pearl. If you come to the kitchen right now, she thought, I'll give you a whole can of Super Supper.

The cat did not move.

If you don't come down immediately, Marcia went on, I won't feed you at all.

Pearl was still.

She doesn't hear me, Marcia thought, relieved. She was now beginning to feel a bit silly. She had imagined it all; she would have to ask Dr. Leroy what it meant.

"I could leap from here," Pearl thought, "and land on my feet. I could leap and sink my claws in flesh, but then I'd be punished." Marcia backed away.

The telephone rang. Marcia hurried to the kitchen to answer it, huddling against the wall as she clung to the receiver. "Hello."

"Marcia?"

"Hi, Paula."

"Marcia, I don't know what to do, you're going to think I'm crazy."

"Are you at work?"

"I called in sick. I think I'm having a nervous breakdown. I heard the Baron this morning, I mean I heard what he was thinking, 'They're stealing everything again, they're stealing it,' and then he said, 'But the other man will catch them and bring some of it back, and I'll bark at him and he'll be afraid even though I'm only being friendly.' I finally figured it out. He thinks the garbage men are thieves and the mailman catches them later."

"Does he think in German?"

"What?"

"German shepherds should know German, shouldn't they?" Marcia laughed nervously. "I'm sorry, Paula. I heard Pearl, too. I also overheard a bird and a worm."

"I was afraid the Baron could hear my thoughts, too. But he doesn't seem to." Paula paused. "Jesus. The Baron just came in. He thinks my perfume ruins my smell. His idea of a good time is sniffing around to see which dogs pissed on his favorite telephone poles. What are we going to do?"

"I don't know." Marcia looked down. Pearl was rubbing against her legs. "Why doesn't she comb me," the cat thought. "Why doesn't she pay attention to me? She's always talking to that thing. I'm much prettier."

Marcia said, "I'll call you back later."

Doug was sitting at the kitchen table when Marcia came up from the laundry room.

"You're home early."

Doug looked up, frowning under his beard. "Jimmy Barzini brought his hamster to Show and Tell, and the damn thing started to talk. We all heard it. That was the end of any order in the classroom. The kids started crowding around and asking it questions, but it just kept babbling, as if it couldn't understand them. Its mouth wasn't moving, though. I thought at first that Jimmy was throwing his voice, but he wasn't. Then I figured out that we must be hearing the hamster's thoughts somehow, and then Mrs. Price came in and told me the white rats in her class's science project were talking, too, and after that Tallman got on the P.A. system and said school would close early.''

"Then I'm not crazy," Marcia said. "Or else we all are. I heard Pearl. Then Paula called up and said Baron von Ribbentrop was doing it.''

They were both silent for a few moments. Then Marcia asked, ''What did it say? The hamster, I mean.''

''It said, 'I want to get out of this cage.' ''

Did cats owned by Russians speak Russian? Marcia had wondered. Did dogs in France transmit in French? Either animals were multilingual or one heard their thoughts in one's native tongue; she had gathered this much from the news.

Press coverage and television news programs were now given over almost entirely to this phenomenon. Did it mean that animals had in fact become intelligent, or were people simply hearing, for the first time, the thoughts that had always been there? Or was the world in the midst of a mass psychosis?

It was now almost impossible to take a walk without hearing birds and other people's pets expressing themselves at length. Marcia had discovered that the cocker spaniel down the street thought she had a nice body odor, while Mr. Sampson's poodle next door longed to take a nip out of her leg. Cries of "Invader approaching!" had kept her from stepping on an anthill. She was afraid to spend time in her yard since listening to a small snake: "I slither. The sun is warm. I coil. I strike. Strike or be struck. That is the way of it. My fangs are ready.''

Marcia found herself hiding from this cacophony by staying indoors, listening instead to the babble on the radio and television as animal behaviorists, zoo officials, dog breeders, farmers, psychiatrists, and a few cranks offered their views. A Presidential commission was to study the matter, an advisor to the President had spoken of training migratory birds as observers to assure arms control. Marcia had heard many theories. People were picking up the thoughts of animals and somehow translating them into terms they could understand. They were picking up their own thoughts and projecting them onto the nearest creatures. The animals' thoughts were a manifestation of humankind's guilt over having treated other living, sentient beings as slaves and objects. They were all racists—or "speciesists," as one philosopher had put it on "Good Morning, America"; the word had gained wide currency.

Marcia had begun to follow Pearl around the house, hoping for some insight into the cat's character; it had occurred to her that understanding a cat's point of view might yield some wisdom. Pearl, however, had disappointed her. The cat's mind was almost purely associative; she thought of food, of being scratched behind the ears, of sex, of sharpening her claws on the furniture. "I want to stalk those birds in the yard," she would think. "I like to feel the grass on my paws but it tickles my nose, when I scratched that dog next door on the nose, he yipped, I hate him, why did my people scream at me when I caught a mouse and put it on their pillow for them, I'm thirsty, why don't they ever give me any tuna fish instead of keeping it all to themselves?" Pearl reminded Marcia, more than anything, of her mother-in-law, whose conversations were a weakly linked chain.

Yet she supposed she still loved the cat, in spite of it. In the evening, Pearl would hop on her lap as she watched television with Doug, and Marcia would stroke her fur, and Pearl would say, "That feels good," and begin to purr. At night, before going to bed, Marcia had always closed the bedroom door, feeling that sex should be private, even from cats. Now she was glad she had done so. She was not sure she wanted to know what Pearl would have had to say about that subject.

The President had gone on television to urge the nation to return to its daily tasks, and Doug's school had reopened. Marcia, alone again for the day, vacuumed the living room while thinking guiltily that she had to start looking for another job. The months at home had made her lazy; she had too easily settled into a homemaker's routine and wondered if this meant she was unintelligent. Persisting in her dull-wittedness, she decided to do some grocery shopping instead of making a trip to the employment agency.

Doug had taken the bus to work, leaving her the car. She felt foolish as she drove down the street. Anton's Market was only a block away and she could have taken her shopping cart, but she could not face the neighborhood's animals. It was all too evident that Mr. Sampson's poodle and a mixed-breed down the road bore her ill will because she was Pearl's owner. She had heard a report from India on the morning news. Few people there were disturbed by recent events, since audible animal contemplation had only confirmed what many had already believed; that animals had souls. Several people there had in fact identified certain creatures as dead relatives or ancestors.

As she parked behind Anton's Market and got out of the car, she noticed a collie pawing at Mr. Anton's garbage cans. "Bones," the dog was thinking. "I know there are bones in there. I want to gnaw on one. What a wonderful day! I smell a bitch close by." The collie barked. "Why do they make it so hard for me to get the bones?" The dog's mood was growing darker. It turned toward Marcia's car. "I hate them, I hate those shiny rolling carapaces, I saw it, one rolled and growled as it went down the street and it didn't even see her, she barked and whined and then she died, and the thing's side opened and a man got out, and the thing just sat there on its wheels and purred. I hate them." The dog barked again.

When Marcia entered the store, she saw Mr. Anton behind the cash register. "Where's Jeannie?" she asked.

Mr. Anton usually seemed cheerful, as if three decades of waiting on his customers had set his round face in a perpetual smile. But today his brown eyes stared at her morosely. "I had to let her go, Mrs. Bochner," he replied. "I had to let the other butchers go, too. Thirty years, and I don't know how long I can keep going. My supplier won't be able to get me any more meat. There's a run on it now in the big cities, but after that—" He shrugged. "May I help you?" he went on, and smiled, as if old habits were reasserting themselves.

Marcia, peering down the aisle of canned goods, noticed that the meat counter was almost empty. Another customer, a big-shouldered, gray-haired man, wandered over with a six-pack of beer. "I don't know what things are coming to," the man said as he fumbled for his wallet. "I was out in the country with my buddy last weekend. You can't hardly sleep with all the noise. I heard one of them coyotes out there. You know what it said? It said, 'I must beware the two-legged stalker.' And you know who it meant. Then it howled."

"You should have seen '60 Minutes,'" Mr. Anton said. "They did a story about the tuna fishermen, and how they're going out of business. They showed one of the last runs. They shouldn't have stuff like that on when kids are watching. My grandson was crying all night." He draped an arm over the register. "A guy has a farm," he said. "How does he know it's actually a concentration camp? All the cows are bitching, that's what they say. You can't go into a barn now without hearing their complaints." He sighed. "At least we can still get milk—the cows can't wander around with swollen udders. But what the hell happens later? They want bigger stalls, they want better feed, they want more pasture. What if they want to keep all the milk for their calves?"

"I don't know," Marcia said, at a loss.

"The government should do something," the gray-haired man uttered.

"The chickens. They're all crazy from being crowded. It's like a nuthouse, a chicken farm. The pigs—they're the worst, because they're the smartest. You know what I feel like? I feel like a murderer—I've got blood on my hands. I feel like a cannibal."

Marcia had left the house with thoughts of hamburgers and slices of baked Virginia ham. Now she had lost her appetite. "What are you going to do?"

"I don't know," Mr. Anton replied. "I'm trying to get into legumes, vegetables, fresh produce, but that puts me in competition with John Ramey's fruit and vegetable market. I'm going to have to get a vegetarian advisor, so I'll know what to stock. There's this vegetarian college kid down the street from me. She's thinking of setting up a consulting firm."

"Well," Marcia said, looking down at the floor.

"I can give you some potato salad, my wife made it up fresh. At least potatoes don't talk. Not yet."

Doug nibbled at his dinner of bean curd and vegetables. "Have you noticed? People are getting thinner."

"Not everybody. Some people are eating more starch."

"I guess so," Doug said. "Still, it's probably better for us in the long run. We'll live longer. I know I feel better."

"I suppose. I don't know what we're going to do when Pearl's cat food runs out." Marcia lowered her voice when she spoke of Pearl.

After supper, they watched the evening news. Normality, of a sort, had returned to the network broadcast; the first part of the program consisted of the usual assortment of international crises, Congressional hearings, and press conferences. Halfway through the broadcast, it was announced that the President's Labrador retriever had died; the *Washington Post* was claiming that the Secret Service had disposed of the dog as a security risk.

"My God," Marcia said.

There was more animal news toward the end of the program. Family therapists in California were asking their clients to bring their pets to sessions. Animal shelters all over the country were crowded with dogs and cats that workers refused to put to sleep. Medical researchers were abandoning animal studies and turning to computer models. Race tracks were closing because too many horseplayers were getting inside information from the horses. There were rumors in Moscow that the Kremlin had been secretly and extensively fumigated, and that there were thousands of dead mice in the city's sewers. There was a story about a man named MacDonald, whose column, "MacDonald's Farm," was made up of sayings and aphorisms he picked up from his barnyard animals. His column had been syndicated and was being published in several major newspapers, putting him in direct competition with Farmer Bob, a "Today" show commentator who also had a column. Marcia suspected editorial tampering on the part of both men, since MacDonald's animals sounded like Will Rogers, while Farmer Bob's reminded her of Oscar Wilde.

Pearl entered the room as the news was ending and began to claw at the rug. "I saw an interesting cat on Phil Donahue this morning," Marcia said. "A Persian. Kind of a philosopher. His owner said that he has a theory of life after death and thinks cats live on in a parallel world. The cat thinks that all those strange sounds you sometimes hear in the night are actually the spirits of cats. What's interesting is that he doesn't think birds or mice have souls."

"Why don't you look for a job instead of watching the tube all day?"

"I don't watch it all day. I have to spend a lot of time on meals, you know. Vegetarian cooking is very time-consuming when you're not used to it."

"That's no excuse. You know I'll do my share when you're working."

"I'm afraid to leave Pearl alone all day."

"That never bothered you before."

"I never heard what she was thinking before."

Pearl was stretching, front legs straight out, back arched. "I want to sleep on the bed tonight," the cat was thinking. "Why can't I sleep on it at night, I sleep there during the day. They keep it all to themselves. They let that woman with the red fur on her head sleep there at night, but not me."

Doug sucked in his breath. Marcia sat up. "He pushed her on it," the cat went on, "and they shed their outer skins, and he rolled around and rubbed her, but when I jumped up on the bed, he shooed me away."

Marcia said, "You bastard." Doug was pulling at his beard. "When did this happen?" He did not answer. "It must have been when I was visiting my sister, wasn't it? You son of a bitch." She got to her feet, feeling as though someone had punched her in the stomach. "Red fur on her head. It must have been Emma. I always thought she was after you. Jesus Christ, you couldn't even go to a motel."

"I went out with some friends for a few beers," Doug said in a low voice. "She drove me home. I didn't expect anything to happen. It didn't mean anything. I would have told you if I thought it was important, but it wasn't, so why bother you with it? I don't even like Emma that much." He was silent for a moment. "You haven't exactly been showing a lot of interest in sex, you know. And ever since you stopped working, you don't seem to care about anything. At least Emma talks about something besides housework and gossip and Phil Donahue."

"You didn't even close the door," Marcia said, making fists of her hands. "You didn't even think of Pearl."

"For God's sake, Marcia, do you think normal people care if a cat sees them?"

"They do now."

"I'm thirsty," Pearl said. "I want some food. Why doesn't anybody clean my box? It stinks all the time. I wish I could piss where I like."

Doug said, "I'm going to kill that cat." He started to lunge across the room.

"No, you're not." Marcia stepped in front of him, blocking his way. Pearl scurried off.

"Let me by."

"No."

She struggled with him. He knocked her aside and she screamed, swung at him, and began to cry. They both sat down on the floor. Marcia cursed at him between sobs while he kept saying he was sorry. The television set blared at them until Doug turned it off and got out some wine. They drank for a while and Marcia thought of throwing him out, then remembered that she didn't have a job and would be alone with Pearl.

Doug went to bed early, exhausted by his apologizing. Marcia glared at the sofa resentfully; it was Doug who should sleep there, not she.

Before she went to sleep, she called Pearl. The cat crept up from the cellar while Marcia took out some cat food. "Your favorite," she whispered to the cat. "Chicken livers. Your reward. Good kitty."

Marcia had heard a sharp crack early that morning. The poodle next door was dead, lying in the road. When Mr. Sampson found out, he strode across the street and started shouting at Mr. Hornig's door.

"Come out, you murderer," he hollered. "You come out here and tell me why you shot my dog. You bastard, get out here!"

Marcia stood in her front yard, watching; Doug was staring out the bay window at the scene. The Novaks' cocker spaniel sat on the edge of Marcia's lawn. "I smell death," the spaniel thought. "I smell rage. What is the matter? We are the friends of man, but must we die to prove our loyalty? We are not friends, we are slaves. We die licking our masters' hands."

Mr. Hornig opened his door; he was holding a rifle. "Get the hell off my lawn, Sampson."

"You shot my dog." Mr. Sampson was still wearing his pajamas; his bald pate gleamed in the sun. "I want to know why. I want an answer right now before I call the cops."

Mr. Hornig walked out on his porch and down the steps; Mrs. Hornig came to the door, gasped, and went after her husband, wresting the weapon from him. He pulled away from her and moved toward Mr. Sampson.

"Why?" Mr. Sampson cried. "Why did you do it?"

"I'll tell you why. I can live with your damn dog yapping all the time, even though I hate yappy dogs. I don't even care about him leaving turds all over my yard and running around loose. But I won't put up with his spying and his goddamn insults. That dog of yours has a dirty mind."

"Had," Mr. Sampson shouted. "He's dead now. You killed him and left him in the street."

"He insulted my wife. He was laughing at her tits. He was right outside our bedroom window, and he was making fun of her tits." Mrs. Hornig retreated with the rifle. "He says we stink. That's what he said. He said we smell like something that's been lying outside too long. I take a shower every day, and he says I stink. And he said some other things I won't repeat."

Mr. Sampson leaned forward. "You fool. He didn't understand. How the hell could he help what he thought? You didn't have to listen."

"I'll bet I know where he got his ideas. He wouldn't have thought them up all by himself. I shot him and I'm glad. What do you think of that, Sampson?"

Mr. Sampson answered with his fist. Soon the two pudgy men were rolling in the grass, trading punches. A few neighborhood children gathered to watch the display. A police car appeared; Marcia looked on as the officers pulled the two men away from each other.

"My God," Marcia said as she went inside. "The police came," she said to Doug, who was now stretched out on the sofa with the Sunday *New York Times*. She heard Pearl in the next room, scratching at the dining room table. "Good and sharp," Pearl was saying. "I have them good and sharp. My claws are so pretty. I'm shedding. Why doesn't somebody comb me?"

"I've let you down," Doug said suddenly. Marcia tensed. "I don't mean just with Emma, I mean generally." They had not spoken of that incident since the night of Pearl's revelation.

"No, you haven't," Marcia said.

"I have. Maybe we should have had a kid. I don't know."

"You know I don't want kids now. Anyway, we can't afford it yet."

"That isn't the only reason," Doug said, staring at the dining room entrance, where Pearl now sat, licking a paw, silent for once. "You know how possessive Siamese cats are. If we had a kid, Pearl would hate it. The kid would have to listen to mean remarks all day. He'd probably be neurotic."

Pearl gazed at them calmly. Her eyes seemed to glow.

"Maybe we should get rid of her," Doug went on.

"Oh, no. You're just mad at her still. Anyway, she loves you."

"No, she doesn't. She doesn't love anyone."

"Pet me," Pearl said. "Somebody better scratch me behind the ears, and do it nicely."

"We have chickens today," Mr. Anton said as Marcia entered the store. "I'll be getting beef in next week." He leaned against the counter, glancing at the clock on the wall; it was almost closing time. "Jeannie's coming back on Tuesday. Things'll be normal again."

"I suppose," Marcia said. "You'll probably be seeing me on Saturdays from now on. I finally found a job. Nothing special, just office work." She paused. "Doesn't it make you feel funny?" She waved a hand at the chickens.

"It did at first. But you have to look at it this way. First of all, chickens are stupid. I guess nobody really knew how stupid until they could hear them thinking. And cows—well, it's like my supplier said. No one's going to hurt some nice animal, but a lot of them don't have nice things to say about people, and some of them sound like real troublemakers. You know who's going to get the axe, so to speak. It's a good thing they don't know we can hear them." Mr. Anton lowered his voice. "And the pigs. Think they're better than we are, that's what they say. Sitting around in a pen all day, and thinking they're better. They'll be sorry."

As Marcia walked home with her chicken and eggs, the street seemed quieter that evening. The birds still babbled: "My eggs are warm." "The wind lifts me, and carries me to my love." "The wires hum under my feet." "I am strong, my nest is sound, I want a mate." A squirrel darted up a tree. "Tuck them away, tuck them away. I have many acorns in my secret place. Save, save, save. I am prepared."

She did not hear the neighborhood pets. Some were inside; others were all too evident. She passed the bodies of two gray cats, then detoured around a dead mutt. Her eyes stung. We've always killed animals, she thought. Why should this be different?

Louise Novak was standing by her dead cocker spaniel,

crying. "Louise?" Marcia said as she approached the child. Louise looked up, sniffing. Marcia gazed at the spaniel, remembering that the dog had liked her.

"Dad killed her," the girl said. "Mrs. Jones overheard her and told everybody Dad hits Mom. Dad said she liked Mom and me best, he heard her think it. He said she hated him and chewed his slippers on purpose and she wanted to tear out his throat because he's mean. I wish she had. I hate him. I hope he dies."

When Marcia reached her own house, she saw the car in the driveway; Doug was home. She heard him moving around upstairs as she unpacked her groceries and put them away. Pearl came into the kitchen and meowed, then scampered to the door, still meowing. "I want to go outside. Why doesn't she let me out? I want to stalk birds, I want to play."

Pearl was so unaware, so insistent, so perfect in her otherness. You'd better be careful, Marcia thought violently. You'd better keep your mind quiet when our friends are here if you know what's good for you, or you'll stay in the cellar. And you'd better watch what you think about me. Appalled, she suddenly realized that under the right circumstances, she could dash the cat's brains out against the wall.

"I want to go outside."

"Pearl," Marcia said, leaning over the cat. "Pearl, listen to me. Try to understand. I know you can't, but try anyway. You can't go outside, it's dangerous. You have to stay here. You have to stay inside for your own good. I know what's best. You have to stay inside from now on."

Schrödinger's Cat

By Ursula K. Le Guin

At first glance, the story that follows—by Ursula K. Le Guin, winner of the National Book Award in children's literature and multiple Nebula and Hugo awards, author of such landmark books as *The Left Hand of Darkness, The Dispossessed, The Wizard of Earthsea,* and the recent *Eye of the Heron*—might seem like some surrealistic fantasy dreamed up by the likes of Salvador Dali or Max Ernst. Here is a world where dogs can talk and everything is burning hot: your children's hair, a lover's kiss, a knife or fork or carpenter's tool. In this place the burners on your stove get hot by themselves and can't be turned off because they were never turned *on* in the first place. Here everything moves at lightning speed: children grow up before your eyes, and worms shoot through your garden like subway trains.

Only a yellow cat can move slowly, fluidly, through this burning world . . . and only the cat is cool to the touch.

He is the most famous cat known to science, the fabled Schrödinger's Cat, who is paradoxically both dead and alive at the same time. . . .

This is a wry and fascinating story about quantum mechanics and reality, one that will leave you wondering if the world of everyday reality outside your window is quite so real after all.

As things appear to be coming to some sort of climax, I have withdrawn to this place. It is cooler here, and nothing moves fast.

On the way here I met a married couple who were coming apart. She had pretty well gone to pieces, but he seemed, at first glance, quite hearty. While he was telling me that he had no hormones of any kind, she pulled herself together, and by supporting her head in the crook of her right knee and hopping on the toes of the right foot, approached us shouting, "Well, what's *wrong* with a person trying to express themselves?" The left leg, the arms and the trunk, which had remained lying in the heap, twitched and jerked in sympathy.

"Great legs," the husband pointed out, looking at the slim ankle. "My wife has great legs."

A cat has arrived, interrupting my narrative. It is a striped yellow tom with white chest and paws. He has long whiskers and yellow eyes. I never noticed before that cats had whiskers above their eyes; is that normal? There is no way to tell. As he has gone to sleep on my knee, I shall proceed.

Where?

Nowhere, evidently. Yet the impulse to narrate remains. Many things are not worth doing, but almost anything is worth telling. In any case, I have a severe congenital case of Ethica laboris puritanica, or Adam's Disease. It is incurable except by total decephalization. I even like to dream when asleep, and to try and recall my dreams: it assures me that I haven't wasted seven or eight hours just lying there. Now here I am, lying, here. Hard at it.

Well, the couple I was telling you about finally broke up. The pieces of him trotted around bouncing and cheeping, like little chicks, but she was finally reduced to nothing but a mass of nerves: rather like fine chicken-wire, in fact, but hopelessly tangled.

So I came on, placing one foot carefully in front of the other, and grieving. This grief is with me still. I fear it is part of me, like foot or loin or eye, or may even be myself: for I seem to have no other self, nothing further, nothing that lies outside the borders of grief.

Yet I don't know what I grieve for: my wife? my husband? my children, or myself? I can't remember. Most dreams are forgotten, try as one will to remember. Yet later music strikes the note and the harmonic rings along the mandolin-strings of the mind, and we find tears in our eyes. Some note keeps playing that makes me want to cry; but what for? I am not certain.

The yellow cat, who may have belonged to the couple that broke up, is dreaming. His paws twitch now and then, and once he makes a small, suppressed remark with his mouth shut. I wonder what a cat dreams of, and to whom he was speaking just then. Cats seldom waste words. They are quiet beasts. They keep their counsel, they reflect. They reflect all day, and at night their eyes reflect. Overbred Siamese cats may be as noisy as little dogs, and then people say, "They're talking," but the noise is further from speech than is the deep silence of the hound or the tabby. All this cat can say is meow, but maybe in his silences he will suggest to me what it is that I have lost, what I am grieving for. I have a feeling that he knows. That's why he came here. Cats look out for Number One.

It was getting awfully hot. I mean, you could touch less and less. The stove-burners, for instance; now, I know that stove-burners always used to get hot, that was their final cause, they existed in order to get hot. But they began to get hot without having been turned on. Electric units or gas rings, there they'd be when you came into the kitchen for breakfast, all four of them glaring away, the air above them shaking like clear jelly with the heat waves. It did no good to turn them off, because they weren't on in the first place. Besides, the knobs and dials were also hot, uncomfortable to the touch.

Some people tried hard to cool them off. The favorite technique was to turn them on. It worked sometimes, but you could not count on it. Others investigated the phenomenon, tried to get at the root of it, the cause. They were probably the most frightened ones, but man is most human at his most frightened. In the face of the hot stove-burners they acted with exemplary coolness. They studied, they observed. They were like the fellow in Michelangelo's "Last Judgment" who has clapped his hands over his face in horror as the devils drag him down to Hell—but only over one eye. The other eye is busy looking. It's all he can do, but he does it. He observes. Indeed, one wonders if Hell would exist if he did not look at it. However, neither he nor the people I am talking about had enough time left to do much about it. And then finally of course there were the people who did not try to do or think anything about it at all.

When hot water came out of the cold-water taps one morning, however, even people who had blamed it all on the Democrats began to feel a more profound unease. Before long, forks and pencils and wrenches were too hot to handle without gloves; and cars were really terrible. It was like opening the door of an oven going full blast, to open the door of your car. And by then, other people almost scorched your fingers off. A kiss was like a branding iron. Your child's hair flowed along your hand like fire.

Here, as I said, it is cooler; and, as a matter of fact, this animal is cool. A real cool cat. No wonder it's pleasant to pet his fur. Also he moves slowly, at least for the most part, which is all the slowness one can reasonably expect of a cat. He hasn't that frenetic quality most creatures acquired—all they did was ZAP and gone. They lacked presence. I suppose birds always tended to be that way, but even the hummingbird used to halt for a second in the very center of his metabolic frenzy, and hang, still as a hub, present, above the fuchsias—then gone again, but you knew something was there besides the blurring brightness. But it got so that even robins and pigeons, the heavy impudent birds, were a blur; and as for swallows, they cracked the sound barrier. You knew of swallows only by the small, curved sonic booms that looped about the eaves of old houses in the evening.

Worms shot like subway trains through the dirt of gardens, among the writhing roots of roses.

You could scarcely lay a hand on children, by then: too fast to catch, too hot to hold. They grew up before your eyes.

But then, maybe that's always been true.

I was interrupted by the cat, who woke and said meow once, then jumped down from my lap and leaned against my legs diligently. This is a cat who knows how to get fed. He also knows how to jump. There was a lazy fluidity to his leap, as if gravity affected him less than it does other creatures. As a matter of fact there were some localized cases, just before I left, of the failure of gravity; but this quality in the cat's leap was something quite else. I am not yet in such a state of confusion that I can be alarmed by grace. Indeed, I found it reassuring. While I was opening a can of sardines, a person arrived.

Hearing the knock, I thought it might be the mailman. I miss mail very much, so I hurried to the door and said, "Is it the mail?" A voice replied, "Yah!" I opened the door. He came in, almost pushing me aside in his haste. He dumped down an enormous knapsack he had been carrying, straightened up, massaged his shoulders, and said, "Wow!"

"How did you get here?"

He stared at me and repeated, "How?"

At this, my thoughts concerning human and animal speech recurred to me, and I decided that this was probably not a man, but a small dog. (Large dogs seldom go yah, wow, how, unless it is appropriate to do so.)

"Come on, fella," I coaxed him. "Come, come on, that's a boy, good doggie!" I opened a can of pork and beans for him at once, for he looked half-starved. He ate voraciously, gulping and lapping. When it was gone he said "Wow!" several times. I was just about to scratch him behind the ears when he stiffened, his hackles bristling, and growled deep in his throat. He had noticed the cat.

The cat had noticed him some time before, without interest, and was now sitting on a copy of *The Well-Tempered Clavichord* washing sardine oil off its whiskers.

"Wow!" the dog, whom I had thought of calling Rover, barked. "Wow! Do you know what that is? *That's Schrödinger's cat!*"

"No, it's not; not any more; it's my cat," I said, unreasonably offended.

"Oh, well, Schrödinger's dead, of course, but it's his cat. I've seen hundreds of pictures of it. Erwin Schrödinger, the great physicist, you know. Oh, wow! To think of finding it here!"

The cat looked coldly at him for a moment, and began to wash its left shoulder with negligent energy. An almost religious expression had come into Rover's face. "It was meant," he said in a low, impressive tone. "Yah. It was *meant*. It can't be a mere coincidence. It's too improbable. Me, with the box; you, with the cat; to meet—here—now." He looked up at me, his eyes shining with happy fervor. "Isn't it wonderful?" he said. "I'll get the box set up right away." And he started to tear open his huge knapsack.

While the cat washed its front paws, Rover unpacked. While the cat washed its tail and belly, regions hard to reach gracefully, Rover put together what he had unpacked, a complex task. When he and the cat finished their operations simultaneously and looked at me, I was impressed. They had come out even, to the very second. Indeed it seemed that something more than chance was involved. I hoped it was not myself.

"What's that?" I asked, pointing to a protuberance on the outside of the box. I did not ask what the box was, as it was quite clearly a box.

"The gun," Rover said with excited pride.

"The gun?"

"To shoot the cat."

"To shoot the cat?"

"Or to *not shoot* the cat. Depending on the photon."

"The photon?"

"Yah! It's Schrödinger's great *Gedankenexperiment*. You see, there's a little emitter here. At Zero Time, five seconds after the lid of the box is closed, it will emit one photon. The photon will strike a half-silvered mirror. The quantum mechanical probability of the photon passing through the mirror is exactly one-half, isn't it? So! If the photon passes through, the trigger will be activated and the gun will fire. If the photon is deflected, the trigger will not be activated and the gun will not fire. Now, you put the cat in. The cat is in the box. You close the lid. You go away! You stay away! What happens?" Rover's eyes were bright.

"The cat gets hungry?"

"The cat gets shot—or not shot," he said, seizing my arm, though not, fortunately, in his teeth. "But the gun is silent, perfectly silent. The box is soundproof. There is no way to know whether or not the cat has been shot until you lift the lid of the box. There is NO way! Do you see how central this is to the whole of quantum theory? Before Zero Time the whole system, on the quantum level or on our level, is nice and simple. But after Zero Time the whole system can be represented only by a linear combination of two waves. We cannot predict the behavior of the photon, and thus, once it has behaved, we cannot predict the state of the system it has determined. We cannot predict it! God plays dice with the world! So it is beautifully demonstrated that if you desire certainty, any certainty, you must create it yourself!"

"How?"

"By lifting the lid of the box, of course," Rover said, looking at me with sudden disappointment, perhaps a touch of suspicion, like a Baptist who finds he has been talking church matters not to another Baptist as he thought, but to a Methodist, or even, God forbid, an Episcopalian. "To find out whether the cat is dead or not."

"Do you mean," I said carefully, "that until you lift the lid of the box, the cat has neither been shot nor not been shot?"

"Yah!" Rover said, radiant with relief, welcoming me back to the fold. "Or maybe, you know, both."

"But why does opening the box and looking reduce the system back to one probability, either live cat or dead cat? Why don't we get included in the system when we lift the lid of the box?"

There was a pause. "How?" Rover barked distrustfully.

"Well, we would involve ourselves in the system, you see, the superposition of two waves. There's no reason why it should only exist *inside* an open box, is there? So when we came to look, there we would be, you and I, both looking at a live cat, and both looking at a dead cat. You see?"

A dark cloud lowered on Rover's eyes and brow. He barked twice in a subdued, harsh voice, and walked away. With his back turned to me he said in a firm, sad tone, "You must not complicate the issue. It is complicated enough."

"Are you sure?"

He nodded. Turning, he spoke pleadingly. "Listen. It's all we have—the box. Truly it is. The box. And the cat. And they're here. The box, the cat, at last. Put the cat in the box. Will you? Will you let me put the cat in the box?"

"No," I said, shocked.

"Please. Please. Just for a minute. Just for half a minute! Please let me put the cat in the box!"

"Why?"

"I can't stand this terrible uncertainty," he said, and burst into tears.

I stood some while indecisive. Though I felt sorry for the poor son of a bitch, I was about to tell him, gently, No, when a curious thing happened. The cat walked over to the box, sniffed around it, lifted his tail and sprayed a corner to mark his territory, and then lightly, with that marvelous fluid ease, leapt into it. His yellow tail just flicked the edge of the lid as he jumped, and it closed, falling into place with a soft, decisive click.

"The cat is in the box," I said.

"The cat is in the box," Rover repeated in a whisper, falling to his knees. "Oh, wow. Oh, wow. Oh, wow."

There was silence then: deep silence. We both gazed, I afoot, Rover kneeling, at the box. No sound. Nothing happened. Nothing would happen. Nothing would ever happen, until we lifted the lid of the box.

"Like Pandora," I said in a weak whisper. I could not quite recall Pandora's legend. She had let all the plagues and evils out of the box, of course, but there had been something else, too. After all the devils were let loose, something quite different, quite unexpected, had been left. What had it been? Hope? A dead cat? I could not remember.

Impatience welled up in me. I turned on Rover, glaring. He returned the look with expressive brown eyes. You can't tell me dogs haven't got souls.

"Just exactly what are you trying to prove?" I demanded.

"That the cat will be dead, or not dead," he murmured submissively. "Certainty. All I want is certainty. To know for *sure* that God *does* play dice with the world."

I looked at him for a while with fascinated incredulity. "Whether he does, or doesn't," I said, "do you think he's going to leave you a note about it in the box?" I went to the box, and with a rather dramatic gesture, flung the lid back. Rover staggered up from his knees, gasping, to look. The cat was, of course, not there.

Rover neither barked, nor fainted, nor cursed, nor wept. He really took it very well.

"Where is the cat?" he asked at last.

"Where is the box?"

"Here."

"Where's here?"

"Here is now."

"We used to think so," I said, "but really we should use larger boxes."

He gazed about him in mute bewilderment, and did not flinch even when the roof of the house was lifted off just like the lid of a box, letting in the unconscionable, inordinate light of the stars. He had just time to breathe, "Oh, wow!"

I have identified the note that keeps sounding. I checked it on the mandolin before the glue melted. It is the note A, the one that drove Robert Schumann mad. It is a beautiful, clear tone, much clearer now that the stars are visible. I shall miss the cat. I wonder if he found what it was we lost?

Groucho

Ron Goulart has long been one of the funniest writers in SF,
with an unerring instinct for all that is bizarre, zany, cock-
eyed, gonzo, and just plain downright *weird* in contemporary
society. His books include the novels *The Sword Swallowers,
After Things Fell Apart, When the Waker Sleeps,* and *A
Talent for the Invisible,* among more than fifty others. His
short fiction has been collected in *Broke Down Engine and
Other Troubles With Machines, What's Become of Screw-
loose? and Other Inquiries, The Chameleon Corps and Other
Shape Changers,* and *Nuzenbolts and More Troubles With
Machines.* His most recent books include the novels *Cowboy
Heaven, Hail Hibbler,* and *Skyrocket Steele.*

Here he proposes a theory about the inner workings of
Hollywood and the television industry that *may* be dubious—
or it may not. Come to think of it, have you *seen* some of the
television shows they've had on lately? These days, they may
all be being written by cats. . . .

It wasn't a wolf that killed him, but it wasn't exactly a dog either. The police, never able to reach a satisfactory conclusion as to what ripped Buzz Stover to pieces, finally wrote his death off as due to an attack by some sort of wild animal that had somehow strayed into his Hollywood Hills neighborhood. They had to fudge a little to do that and ignore items such as a sworn statement by Buzz's nearest neighbor, a respected rock composer, that he had seen a large gray dog leaving Buzz's house on the night of his death. The hound left by way of the front door, whistling an old Broadway show tune. The police, even in Southern California, aren't especially anxious to follow up leads like that and so the exact cause of Buzz's death remains a mystery to just about everyone. I'm probably the only person, with the possible exception of Panda Cruz, who knows who actually destroyed Buzz and why. But, as I long ago resolved, it's best never to talk about the murder cases you happen to get tangled in. Especially the supernatural ones.

When I had lunch with Buzz on that gray rainy day this past spring I tried to warn him about his own delving into the supernatural.

"Delving? What kind of candy-apple word is that?" He bounced, a feisty sneer on his plump little face, on the leatherette banquette. "Is that the kind of verbiage you put into the ads you grind out at that advertising sweatshop where—"

"Hush!" suggested a gaunt old gentleman at a nearby table

in the dim, exclusive Beverly Hills restaurant.

"Up yours, grandpappy!" Buzz flashed him a finger, returned his attention to me. "I didn't come to this vastly over-priced bistro to—"

"Do you know who you just gave the finger to? That's Jean Alch, the most respected French film director of the 1950s. He won—"

"He's got gravy on his rugby shirt. And the '50s are dead and gone." He picked up his Otranto's menu, put it back down near his water goblet. "I shouldn't even be eating. I'm still in mourning."

"Yes, I was sorry to hear about Warren getting killed in that car accident. You guys had been partners for—"

"Six glorious years." Buzz was a small chunky man of thirty-six, who persisted in wearing silken warm-up suits to lunch. "It's lousy enough losing a writing partner when your shows are doing so-so, but *Goon Squad* is number two on the tube all across this great land of ours right now. Honesty compels me to admit that Warren Gish, rest his soul, was equally responsible for the brilliant *Goon Squad* scripts that pushed the show to its present pinnacle."

"I thought Warren did the plots and all the dialogue and you just did the polish."

"It is truly incredible that someone in the ad game, a Hollywood hanger-on for all these many years, can be so dumb," said Buzz, hunching. "My polishing is what made those scripts work, what made Curly Hudnut and Dip Gomez into our nation's leading macho TV stars."

"How are you going to continue the scripting?"

"Scripting? Where do you get your vocabulary, from back issues of *Writer's Digest* lying around your barber shop?"

"I heard you've been having trouble finding a new associate anywhere near as good as Warren was," I said. "The producers of *Goon Squad* supposedly weren't satisfied with your first solo script."

Buzz winced. "Naw, they loved it . . . but I would feel better with a new assistant," he said. "In fact, I . . . well, call me sentimental, but I wish there were some way I could get Warren back. See, that night when the poor bastard had his fatal crash, we'd had a little squabble at a party out in Malibu just a little while before. I feel bad."

"You punched him in the snoot."

"Only once." Buzz held up a single finger.

"Ah, he does it yet again," muttered Jean Alch.

"This one isn't for you, Uncle Wiggly," said Buzz. He gave a forlorn shake of his head. "I can't believe Warren's been gone a month. God."

"You really did have a fight that night?"

"All great teams fight—Martin and Lewis, Hecht and MacArthur, Rodgers and Hammerstein," Buzz told me. "You don't know what it means to be overflowing with talent. Putting two highly gifted people like Warren and me together, it's going to cause a few sparks."

"I hear he kicked you in the groin," I said, "that night."

"Naw, only the knee." Buzz, wincing again, leaned back to gaze up at the crystal chandelier directly above us. "Did you have any trouble getting shown to this table today?"

"Nope."

He nodded, pensive. "He made me spell my name twice, Otranto himself who's known me since he was salad chef at Udolpho's seven years ago," he said. "I'm getting a little invisible, I fear. It usually starts at posh places like this, they stop seeing you. It spreads to parking lot attendants, then receptionists, producers, the works. In six months you can cease to exist altogether."

"Maybe, considering what's been happening, you ought to take a vacation or—"

"Who told you to suggest that to me?"

"Nobody, Buzz. You seem sort of—"

"Listen, I know you're one of the few guys I can trust in this goofy town." He was leaning toward me, elbows on the table. "That script I did on my own was a complete turkey. Couple more like that and . . . brrr. I fade out completely."

"C'mon, a new collaborator and—"

"Nope, I need Warren's help to save me."

"How can you expect to—"

"Do you ever watch *Strange, Isn't It?*" His voice had dropped to a whisper.

"Once. I don't go in for that *Real People* sort of—"

"You know Panda Cruz, don't you, the love of my life?"

"The slim redhead?"

"No, you're thinking of . . . oh, right. Last time we met, at the screening of *Six Demented Coeds*, Panda was a redhead," he answered, remembering. "She's a blonde now, working as a secretary for Gossamer-Stein, the halfwits who produce *Strange, Isn't It?*" He rubbed his plump little hands together. "There was this old bimbo on the show last week, a Mrs. Brill from Oxnard. She can contact the *dead*."

"Nobody can do that, Buzz."

"Mrs. Brill can," he assured me. "Panda and I drove out to her dump day before yesterday. She's going to get me through to Warren."

"You actually believe you can—"

"It works. Really. She had me talking to my dead mother. I swear."

"Doing anyone's mother is easy. That can be faked by any fortune-teller."

"You can't fake my mom. I tell you this old bimbo is legit. She's got occult powers."

"Okay, so she puts you in touch with the spirit of Warren Gish. Then what? You plan to sit around the seance while he dictates a *Goon Squad* story through this woman?"

After glancing carefully around Otranto's, Buzz replied, "She may, if all the signs are right . . . and certain essential rituals are performed . . . she may get Warren to come back."

"Come back? How?"

"You know, reincarnate."

"As who?"

"There's the tricky part. She doesn't know exactly where he'll pop up. But she guarantees he will come back in some form and save my apples." He straightened up, smiling tentatively. "Going to be terrific, together again, turning out top-notch scripts, winning Emmy awards."

"You mentioned certain rituals. What exactly do you have to do?"

Buzz studied his stubby fingernails. "Black magic stuff," he said finally. "We have to take off our clothes and . . . um . . . sacrifice a goat. Things like that."

"Things like that can get you in considerable trouble."

"Maybe, but it's worth it," Buzz said. "They're not going to bench me just yet. Nope."

My advertising agency responsibilities took me out of town the day after that lunch with Buzz. One of our clients, the Arends Labs, was test-marketing a new liquid headache remedy in Phoenix, Arizona. The stuff was called Brainwash and, although it apparently relieved the stubbornest headache in under ninety seconds, it was causing approximately one customer in three to experience violent and fantastic hallucinations. I flew in to help the Arends publicity man come up with a plausible story to soothe everybody. Usually these sorts of troubleshooting jobs take no more than two or three days, but in this instance Junior Arends also came out from the main office in Orlando, Florida. I was in Phoenix nearly two days before I realized Junior had appropriated two cases of the suspect headache cure and was consuming several bottles of Brainwash a night. The resulting hallucinations prompted him, eventually, to join a marimba band that was playing backup at a male strippers club in a sleazy sector of town. By the time I located him, got him detoxified and coauthored some copy that pacified the mayor, the governor and various health officers, a week and half of my life had passed into oblivion.

Buzz never spoke much about the session with Mrs. Brill, the psychic, whereat he and Panda performed certain occult rites and got a message across to his recently deceased partner. "It was degrading, but damn effective," was all Buzz would say when I asked him about it over the phone on my return. He was more talkative about the reincarnation of Warren Gish.

It had been a rainy evening, about a week after the seance, and Buzz was sitting alone in the spacious living room of his hillside house. The night was chill and misty as well. Panda, who now and then lived with him, was over in Burbank at the taping of the *Strange, Isn't It?* show.

"Rape, incest, torture, terminal cancer," Buzz was mumbling, striving to come up with a topic he hadn't used on *Goon Squad*. "Child molesting, sodomy, bubonic plague . . . Geeze, I ought to be able to switch something. Is there a twist on abortion nobody's come up with? Could we get by with bestiality again?"

A faint scratching sounded.

Buzz leaped up out of his leather lounge chair, dropping his pencils and his legal tablet. He'd been rather tense since the occult encounter.

The scratching was repeated, louder. The kitchen door rattled as though something were being tossed against it.

"Do I owe anybody money? Is there anyone who wants to break my arms and legs?"

Deciding it was okay to pad through his big shadowy house, he went to investigate, turning on lights as he did.

"What?" he asked from the middle of the kitchen.

More scratching, more rattling of the outer screen door. The yellow back door kept him from seeing what was out there.

"Who is it?"

"Meow, meow."

After flipping the back area floodlights on, Buzz carefully opened the door.

There was a cat out there, a fat furry one the color of butterscotch pudding.

"Hello, pussy."

"Hello yourself, asshole," said the cat.

Buzz jumped backward, hitting his hip a good one on his butcher block table. "A joke, right? Some crazed ventriloquist is lurking out there." He walked again toward the open doorway. "We don't audition for *Strange, Isn't It?* here. Take your cat over to Burbank for—"

"Let me in, old boy. I'm getting soaked," called the cat. "Having fur is a crock, but since—"

"Warren? Warren Gish?"

"They call me Groucho now. Open up already, huh?"

Hand shaking some, Buzz flung open the screen door, nearly swatting the talking cat off the damp redwood porch. "Groucho? What kind of halfwit name is that for a—"

"I didn't pick it, obviously, old boy," said Groucho, coming into the kitchen. "The cat I got stuck in was already named Groucho. See, I even have a tag under my flea collar with the name on it."

"This is a . . . a miracle."

Groucho shook himself, began rubbing at an ear with his paw. "Get me a towel or something, schmuck."

Buzz grabbed the whole roll out of the rack over the yellow tile sink. "I was anticipating you'd . . . I figured you were going to come back . . . you know, as a person."

"Lot you know about reincarnation," the cat said. "Rush in and summon me back from the other side, use that old skwack in Oxnard of all places to get a lock on my spirit. Typical Buzz Stover move."

"Isn't this better than being dead?"

"The people who own Groucho fed me nothing but Yowl!"

"What is it?"

"Yowl! is the new meaty-like food for contented cats," explained Groucho. "Use some of those towels, I'm soggy."

"Oh, sure. Sorry." He crouched down beside his reincarnated partner. "What's it like on the other side?"

"Can't tell you."

"Rules?"

"Don't remember. When I came jolting back here, the details got lost. Rub vigorously, can you?"

Buzz struggled to massage the dampness out of the wet cat. "How come you can talk? Most cats don't have the power to—"

"It's all part of the mumbo jumbo you worked on me," explained Groucho. "All I know is that right after you dragged my spirit back for that conference in Oxnard I blacked out. I awakened in Pasadena eating Yowl! out of a recycled TV dinner tray. Everybody was calling me Groucho."

"You came all the way here from Pasadena on foot?"

"It's a regular *Lassie, Come Home*, huh?"

Crumbling up the tattered, wet paper towels, Buzz stood up and away from the butterscotch cat. "I did miss you, Warren."

"Can't you smack Panda instead? I didn't realize, by the way, she was so skinny. When you two stripped down for that mystical ritual, I saw more ribs than tits on her."

"Listen, Warren, I hope you didn't come back just to bicker and squabble."

"You have to address me as Groucho."

"A dumb name."

"Even so, that's the way reincarnation seems to work."

"Would you like something to drink, Groucho?"

"Milk." The cat strolled in the direction of the blue refrigerator. "Can't handle booze anymore, found that out in Pasadena. Something to do with the feline metabolism I'm stuck with."

"I only have skim, because Panda mostly drinks the milk and she's—"

"On a diet. So she can grow even skinnier."

"Everybody doesn't have to be zoftig, War—Groucho. Even one of your wives, remember, was sort of slender."

The cat shuddered. "We don't talk about Estrellita."

"You know, if I can pay you a compliment, that's a cute voice you have now. Has a trace of your old one, but with a sort of—"

"Looney Tunes quality added?"

"I was being sincere," Buzz told him. "You're a very hard guy to flatter."

"Cat. I'm a very hard *cat* to flatter."

"I didn't order a cat. We just asked, you know, for reincarnation. In fact, I've been eyeing strangers all week, hoping one of them might be you. Nearly got punched by a stunt man in a bar over—"

"Spare me the tacky details, old boy." He went four-footing into the hall, heading for the vast living room.

"I honestly did miss you," said Buzz, following. "Despite our ups and downs, you were the best writing partner I—"

"Okay, short change, what's the problem?" Groucho hopped up into the big leather chair Buzz had vacated.

"I'm having trouble with the *Goon Squad* scripts."

"I imagined you would," said Groucho. "The instant I smacked into that stone wall and realized I'd bought the farm, the last thought that flashed through my brain was, 'That little asshole is going to bomb out without my help.' "

"That's touching, that you thought of me at the last moment."

"Okay, old boy, grab a pencil." Groucho licked at the fur on his side. "I've been kicking around a neat switch on the basic incest plot."

"One more switch on incest?"

"Just listen, old boy, and trust me," said Groucho.

Buzz laughed. "Boy, it's great to have you back."

Although I didn't get to meet Groucho in those early weeks of Buzz's collaboration with him, I had no doubt the cat housed the spirit of Warren Gish. There was simply no other way to account for the fantastic improvement in Buzz's allegedly solo scripts. He simply couldn't have written anywhere near that well on his own and unaided. I began to hear talk that his new *Goon Squad* script dealing with rape, incest and leprosy was a solid contender for an Emmy. It certainly looked as though Buzz was going to maintain his position as one of the town's top television writers.

Right about then I had to leave town again unexpectedly.

There was new trouble with Brainwash, this time in the East Moline, Illinois, test market. The Arends Lab chemists had ironed out the hallucination kinks, but now something like seventy-two percent of the people who tried the new headache liquid woke up the next morning to find the palms of their hands covered with hair. The agency sent me to help the client's people whip up radio spots downplaying the social stigma of hairy palms. Unfortunately Junior Arends showed up in East Moline and, perhaps hoping for more hallucinations, guzzled down eleven bottles of Brainwash. I found him asleep in my room the next afternoon and covered from head to toe with short curly fur. What with one thing and another I didn't return to LA until nearly three weeks had passed.

When I went into the agency the next day, my lovely secretary grabbed at my sleeve as I was heading for my private office. "He's in there," she whispered, uneasy. "With a cage."

"Who?"

"That bouncy little man."

"Oh, Buzz Stover."

She nodded her extremely pretty head. "Yes, with a cage on his lap. He insisted on waiting to see you."

"He probably brought over Groucho, his new . . . his new cat."

"The cage," she informed me, "is empty."

Buzz was crouched in one of my imitation leather sofas with a cat carrying case on his knees. "They've betrayed me," he announced as soon as I shut the door.

I bent, staring in through the wire crosshatch of the small cage. It was empty. "You don't, do you, think you have a cat in there, Buzz?"

"Am I stark raving goofy?" He stood, bouncing on the balls of his feet, waving the cage the way an altar boy waves an incense holder at religious ceremonies. "Did I claw my way to the halfwit pinnacle of Hollywood success by imagining I'm lugging invisible pussycats around?" He sank back on the sofa, making it sigh. "My alleged love and my traitorous partner have knifed me in the back."

I eased behind my large metal desk, tapped at the immense pile of stuff that had accumulated in my in-box. "How exactly?"

"She wooed him away."

"This is still Panda we're talking about?"

"How many loves of my life do you think I have? When I fall, it's for keeps."

"Panda did something to Groucho?"

"Kidnapped him," he said. "Except it's all kosher."

'Where's the cat . . . Warren?"

"He's living with her in her mansion in Bel Air."

"Since when does a secretary on a TV show like—"

"She bought the damn house, made the halfwit down payment with some of the money they gave her," he said. "Do you know who used to live there? Orlando Busino, the great silent screen lover. It's a veritable mansion, a palace of luxury."

I rocked once in my swivel chair. "I don't think I understand what Panda's done," I told him, "Did she make some kind of scriptwriting deal and go into partnership with your cat?"

"No, no, don't be a halfwit. She's Groucho's agent." He whapped his fist on the empty cage. "She sold his services to Yowl! They've been beating the bushes for months hunting for a perfect cat to star in their TV commercials. I have to admit Groucho does look terrific on camera. Takes direction like a vet, has a sneer on his kisser that is perfect when they mention the rival products."

"Does he . . . he doesn't talk on these commercials?"

"Of course not, he only talks to me and Panda," said Buzz. "Even in Hollywood you couldn't get by with letting a cat talk all over the place. But because Warren's spirit is inside that cat, he's better at commercials than any other cat known to man."

"How'd Panda manage to—"

"She was insidiously clever." His fingers drummed on the top of the carrying case. "Naturally, since she was with me a good part of the time, I confided all in her. Groucho, having known her in his previous incarnation, was cordial, too. At first it was a dream of bliss. The scripts were nifty. I had them about ready to give me a pay hike. Yet all the while I was nursing a viper, in the person of that raven-tressed—"

"I thought she was a redhead."

"No, she was a blonde, but she switched again," he explained. "Listen, the point is, Yowl! is one of the sponsors of that idiotic piece of crap, *Strange, Isn't It?* She heard about their quest for a cat, smuggled Groucho out to an audition while I was on location in Apple Valley with *Goon Squad*."

"He's your cat, isn't he? Legally you—"

"Ah, but there again she was diabolically smart." He dealt the cage a heavy whack. "Panda went to the people who used to own Groucho and she bought him. She owns that damned Judas."

"How does he feel about this?"

"It's gone to his head. Starring in commercials, being fawned over," said Buzz. "Warren was a great writer, but he originally came out here to try to get into the movies. As an actor. This is one of his boyhood dreams coming true and he's ditched me for it."

"Is the money better?"

"Sure, they're pulling in a bloody fortune from Yowl!" he said forlornly. "When this thing really gets rolling, there'll be a multimedia blitz. Panda and Groucho will net a million bucks easy."

"What do you plan to do?"

"Panda's still allowing him to collaborate with me . . . some."

"How much?"

"Well, Groucho is busy most of the time with the TV spots, the magazine ads and all. I'm darn lucky if I get at him for an hour a week. Barely enough time for a plot session."

"Might be wise to look for a new partner."

"Nope, there is only one Warren Gish."

"You could give writing alone another try."

He stood up, the cat cage swinging in his hand. "Perfect dreams don't come along very often. If I can't work with him, I don't think I can work at all."

"You're romanticizing, Buzz. When Warren was alive and in his original body, you fought all the time."

"We fought, sure, punched each other out, but we wrote some dynamite scripts." He pointed a warning finger at me. "I got him back and we are going to keep on working together."

"That could," I warned, "mean trouble."

"For Panda, not for me." With the empty cat case dangling in his grip, he went stalking out of my office.

• • •

Since I never saw him again, alive or dead, most of the rest
of this account is based only on what I am fairly certain is
what happened.

You probably know what a substantial hit Groucho was.
The first cycle of Yowl! commercials doubled sales in less than
a month. The cat caught the public fancy, you saw him on the
covers of *Time, Life, Us, People, Mammon* and even *Vogue*.
There were, soon, Groucho posters, Groucho toys, Groucho
lunch boxes, Groucho calendars, a Groucho biography turned
out by the same man who'd done bios of Lola Turbinado, Dip
Gomez and Leroy Blurr. The money was such that within four
months Panda, now a platinum blonde, was able to buy the
Bel Air mansion outright. Because of Groucho's burgeoning
fame, the cat's schedule became increasingly crowded. He appeared on talk shows, never talking of course but letting
Panda hold him on her lap and act as spokesperson. He did
supermarket openings, hospital tours, movie premieres. It
became impossible for Buzz to work with Groucho more than
once every three or four weeks.

When Buzz was able to reach his reincarnated partner on
the phone, Groucho was aloof and indifferent.

"Listen," Buzz would begin, "about this expanded two-
hour *Goon Squad* they want. Do you really think our switch
on the rape and brain tumor plot will stretch for two frapping
hours?"

"Trust me, old boy."

"They have their doubts at the network."

"That's what they get paid for. Those of us . . . oops, here's
the photog from *Movieland* magazine. Bye."

The network didn't accept the two-hour script, even when
Buzz changed the brain tumor to lung cancer. They ordered a
major rewrite. When Buzz went rushing over to the Bel Air
mansion, the rejected script tucked up tight under his arm,
they wouldn't even let him on the grounds. Panda had hired a
couple of hefty fellows, both weightlifting trophy winners, to
guard the wrought iron gates and keep out fans and tourists.
There was a small dinner party for the top Yowl! executives
that night and Panda didn't want Buzz barging in.

Stubborn, he pretended to drive away. Instead he parked his
Mercedes a few blocks off, sat in it muttering to himself. The

night grew darker, clouds hid the moon. Finally, at midnight, Buzz went skulking back toward the mansion. He skirted the high stone wall and found a spot where a fallen tree trunk allowed him to boost himself over. Panda hadn't as yet gotten around to having an electric alarm system installed. Buzz's advent went unnoticed.

Hunched low, still hugging the failed script to him, he got to the shrubs near the open garages and hid. By a few minutes after midnight the last of the visitors had driven off.

A pleased smile touched his face when he saw Panda, in an absolutely stunning satin evening gown, standing at the top of the marble front stairway with Groucho himself cradled in her arms.

She placed the butterscotch cat on the marble, patted his furry backside. "Do your business, Groucho, and hurry back," she told him. "It's late and you need plenty of sleep. We start taping your special tomorrow."

"I may chase a bird or two, but I'll be back soon," the cat promised, padding down the smooth steps.

Buzz waited until Panda closed the door and then whispered, "Hey, Groucho."

The cat halted, tail switching. He glanced toward the pile of shadows where Buzz was ducked. "That you, old boy?"

"Over here, in front of the garages."

"They had orders to give you the old heave-ho tonight." Groucho came, backside swaying, over to him. "How'd you—"

"They shot us down." He held out the script. "We've got to fix this. Quick or we could lose the damn show."

"Why do you keep saying we?"

"Because we're still a team and—"

"You're getting solo credits on the scripts now," the cat reminded. "Warren Gish is dead. Groucho the cat is a national, indeed an international, favorite. Do you know how much we'll take in over the next—"

"Okay, you can make more dough doing commercials and gobbling swill. But you are a *writer* at heart."

"Nope, I'm an actor," corrected the cat. "You know, old boy, I always wanted this. To be a star. Not a walk-on or a bit. But a real damn star."

"You have to drop this, Groucho, and get back to helping me out." He shook the script near the cat's nose. "I need you.

If you don't help me, I'll go to Yowl! and—"

"Easy there, old boy," warned the cat. "I'm really enjoying this present incarnation. Woe to him who mucks it up."

"You've got to help me out."

Grouncho shook his furry head. "Nope, I'm through saving your bacon."

· Buzz let the script drop, made a grab for the cat.

Groucho's fur stood up like thousands of exclamation points. Making a hissing sound, he backed toward one of the open garages, clawing at Buzz. "Watch it."

Buzz, angry, made another grab and got hold of the cat around the middle. "I'm going to take you away from Panda. You're going to help me save . . . ow!"

The cat had raked him, hard, across the face. Blood came running down Buzz's cheek. "You son of a bitch!" He kept his hold on the struggling animal.

Groucho dug into Buzz's midsection with his back claws. "Jerk," he said.

The front claws ripped into his face again.

Buzz cried out in pain and then, catching the snarling cat by the tail, he sent it whizzing across the shadowy garage.

There was an enormous thud when Groucho's skull connected with the wall.

Charging into the garage, Buzz caught up a tire iron from the concrete flooring. He ran to the place where the dazed cat, wobbling, was trying to stand.

"Why won't you help me? Why?" Buzz chanted that, smashing at Groucho's small skull with the iron.

The cat made a harsh keening noise and died.

"Oh, Jesus." Buzz rose. "I've killed my partner."

"Groucho, are you fighting again?" came Panda's voice from the doorway of the mansion.

Buzz ducked low beside the dead animal, breath held.

"You act so much like a cat sometimes, it's spooky." She went back inside and closed the door.

Buzz crept out and retrieved the script, came back and scooped up the cat on it.

There was a back door and, trying not to look down at the grimacing cat, he made his way out into the night.

Behind a row of thorny shrubs near the back wall of the estate he dug a hole with his hands. In it he buried both Groucho and the script.

• • •

Five days later the producers of *Goon Squad* gave Buzz an ultimatum. Come up with an acceptable revise right away or step down off the show. That night he took his spare carbon copy of the two-hour scripts and spread the pages out on the living room rug.

There was a hot desert wind blowing, brushing at the windows, rattling shutters.

"No reason I can't do this myself." He wandered among the sprawl of pages.

Something scratched at the kitchen door.

The noise persisted, the screen door clattered.

Buzz crossed the kitchen threshold. "Somebody out there?"

There was a clawing on the door.

"Okay, we'll see what the hell is going on." He went striding across the floor and yanked the wooden door open.

Standing half inside the screen door was a large gray police dog. The hair on its back was bristling, its teeth showed.

"I'm back again, old boy," the dog said and came leaping for his throat.

My Father, the Cat

By Henry Slesar

Henry Slesar has worked extensively in the mystery-suspense field and for television—winning both the Edgar Award and the Emmy—as well as producing well over a hundred SF and fantasy stories, many of which originally appeared in slick prestige markets like *Playboy*. Here he relates a wise and gentle fable about the sacrifices that people—and cats!— must sometimes be willing to make for those they love. . . .

My mother was a lovely, delicate woman from the coast of Brittany, who was miserable sleeping on less than three mattresses, and who, it is said, was once injured by a falling leaf in her garden. My grandfather, a descendant of the French nobility whose family had ridden the tumbrils of the Revolution, tended her fragile body and spirit with the same loving care given rare, brief-blooming flowers. You may imagine from this his attitude concerning marriage. He lived in terror of the vulgar, heavy-handed man who would one day win my mother's heart, and at last, this persistent dread killed him. His concern was unnecessary, however, for my mother chose a suitor who was as free of mundane brutality as a husband could be. Her choice was Dauphin, a remarkable white cat which strayed onto the estate shortly after his death.

Dauphin was an unusually large Angora, and his ability to speak in cultured French, English, and Italian was sufficient to cause my mother to adopt him as a household pet. It did not take long for her to realize that Dauphin deserved a higher status, and he became her friend, protector, and confidante. He never spoke of his origin, nor where he had acquired the classical education which made him such an entertaining companion. After two years, it was easy for my mother, an unworldly woman at best, to forget the dissimilarity in their species. In fact, she was convinced that Dauphin was an enchanted prince, and Dauphin, in consideration of her illusions, never dissuaded her. At last, they were married by an understanding clergyman of the locale, who solemnly filled in the marriage application with the name of M. Edwarde Dauphin.

I, Etienne Dauphin, am their son.

To be candid, I am a handsome youth, not unlike my mother in the delicacy of my features. My father's heritage is evident in my large, feline eyes, and in my slight body and quick movements. My mother's death, when I was four, left me in the charge of my father and his coterie of loyal servants, and I could not have wished for a finer upbringing. It is to my father's patient tutoring that I owe whatever graces I now possess. It was my father, the cat, whose gentle paws guided me to the treasure houses of literature, art, and music, whose whiskers bristled with pleasure at a goose well cooked, at a meal well served, at a wine well chosen. How many happy hours we shared! He knew more of life and the humanities, my father, the cat, than any human I have met in all my twenty-three years.

Until the age of eighteen, my education was his personal challenge. Then, it was his desire to send me into the world outside the gates. He chose for me a university in America, for he was deeply fond of what he called "that great raw country," where he believed my feline qualities might be tempered by the aggressiveness of the rough-coated barking dogs I would be sure to meet.

I must confess to a certain amount of unhappiness in my early American years, torn as I was from the comforts of the estate and the wisdom of my father, the cat. But I became adapted, and even upon my graduation from the university, sought and held employment in a metropolitan art museum. It was there I met Joanna, the young woman I intended to make my bride.

Joanna was a product of the great American southwest, the daughter of a cattle-raiser. There was a blooming vitality in her face and her body, a lustiness born of open skies and desert. Her hair was not the gold of antiquity; it was new gold, freshly mined from the black rock. Her eyes were not like old-world diamonds; their sparkle was that of sunlight on a cascading river. Her figure was bold, an open declaration of her sex.

She was, perhaps, an unusual choice for the son of a fairylike mother and an Angora cat. But from the first meeting of our eyes, I knew that I would someday bring Joanna to my father's estate to present her as my fiancee.

I approached that occasion with understandable trepidation. My father had been explicit in his advice before I departed for America, but on no point had he been more emphatic than secrecy concerning himself. He assured me that revelation of my paternity would bring ridicule and unhappiness upon me. The advice was sound, of course, and not even Joanna knew that our journey's end would bring us to the estate of a large, cultured, and conversing cat. I had deliberately fostered the impression that I was orphaned, believing that the proper place for revealing the truth was the atmosphere of my father's home in France. I was certain that Joanna would accept her father-in-law without distress. Indeed, hadn't nearly a score of human servants remained devoted to their feline master for almost a generation?

We had agreed to be wed on the first of June, and on May the fourth, emplaned in New York for Paris. We were met at Orly Field by Francois, my father's solemn manservant, who had been delegated not so much as escort as he was chaperone, my father having retained much of the old world proprieties. It was a long trip by automobile to our estate in Brittany, and I must admit to a brooding silence throughout the drive which frankly puzzled Joanna.

However, when the great stone fortress that was our home came within view, my fears and doubts were quickly dispelled. Joanna, like so many Americans, was thrilled at the aura of venerability and royal custom surrounding the estate. Francois placed her in the charge of Madame Jolinet, who clapped her plump old hands with delight at the sight of her fresh blonde beauty, and chattered and clucked like a mother hen as she led Joanna to her room on the second floor. As for myself, I had one immediate wish: to see my father, the cat.

He greeted me in the library, where he had been anxiously awaiting our arrival, curled up in his favorite chair by the fireside, a wide-mouthed goblet of cognac by his side. As I entered the room, he lifted a paw formally, but then his reserve was dissolved by the emotion of our reunion, and he licked my face in unashamed joy.

Francois refreshed his glass, and poured another for me,

and we toasted each other's well-being.

"To you, *mon purr,*" I said, using the affectionate name of my childhood memory.

"To Joanna," my father said. He smacked his lips over the cognac, and wiped his whiskers gravely. "And where is this paragon?"

"With Madame Jolinet. She will be down shortly."

"And you have told her everything?"

I blushed. "No, *mon purr,* I have not. I thought it best to wait until we were home. She is a wonderful woman," I added impulsively. "She will not be—"

"Horrified?" my father said. "What makes you so certain, my son?"

"Because she is a woman of great heart," I said stoutly. "She was educated at a fine college for women in Eastern America. Her ancestors were rugged people, given to legend and folklore. She is a warm, human person—"

"Human," my father sighed, and his tail swished. "You are expecting too much of your beloved, Etienne. Even a woman of the finest character may be dismayed in this situation."

"But my mother—"

"Your mother was an exception, a changeling of the Fairies. You must not look for your mother's soul in Joanna's eyes." He jumped from his chair, and came towards me, resting his paw upon my knee. "I am glad you have not spoken of me, Etienne. Now you must keep your silence forever."

I was shocked. I reached down and touched my father's silky fur, saddened by the look of his age in his gray, gold-flecked eyes, and by the tinge of yellow in his white coat.

"No, *mon purr,*" I said. "Joanna must know the truth. Joanna must know how proud I am to be the son of Edwarde Dauphin."

"Then you will lose her."

"Never! That cannot happen!"

My father walked stiffly to the fireplace, staring into the gray ashes. "Ring for Francois," he said. "Let him build the fire. I am cold, Etienne."

I walked to the cord and pulled it. My father turned to me and said: "You must wait, my son. At dinner this evening, perhaps. Do not speak of me until then."

"Very well, father."

When I left the library, I encountered Joanna at the head of the stairway, and she spoke to me excitedly.

"Oh, Etienne! What a *beautiful* old house. I know I will love it! May we see the rest?"

"Of course," I said.

"You look troubled. Is something wrong?"

"No, no. I was thinking how lovely you are."

We embraced, and her warm full body against mine confirmed my conviction that we should never be parted. She put her arm in mine, and we strolled through the great rooms of the house. She was ecstatic at their size and elegance, exclaiming over the carpeting, the gnarled furniture, the ancient silver and pewter, the gallery of family paintings. When she came upon an early portrait of my mother, her eyes misted.

"She was lovely," Joanna said. "Like a princess! And what of your father? Is there no portrait of him?"

"No," I said hurriedly. "No portrait." I had spoken my first lie to Joanna, for there was a painting, half-completed, which my mother had begun in the last year of her life. It was a whispering little watercolor, and Joanna discovered it to my consternation.

"What a magnificent cat!" she said. "Was it a pet?"

"It is Dauphin," I said nervously.

She laughed. "He has your eyes, Etienne."

"Joanne, I must tell you something—"

"And this ferocious gentleman with the moustaches? Who is he?"

"My grandfather. Joanna, you must listen—"

Francois, who had been following our inspection tour at shadow's-length, interrupted. I suspected that his timing was no mere coincidence.

"We will be serving dinner at seven-thirty," he said. "If the lady would care to dress—"

"Of course," Joanna said. "Will you excuse me, Etienne?"

I bowed to her, and she was gone.

At fifteen minutes to the appointed dining time, I was ready, and hastened below to talk once more with my father. He was in the dining room, instructing the servants as to the placement of the silver and accessories. My father was proud of the excellence of his table, and took all his meals in the splendid manner. His appreciation of food and wine was unsurpassed in my experience, and it had always been the greatest of pleasures for me to watch him at table, stalking across the damask and dipping delicately into the silver dishes prepared for him. He pretended to be too busy with his dinner preparations to engage me in conversation, but I insisted.

"I must talk to you," I said. "We must decide together how to do this."

"It will not be easy," he answered with a twinkle. "Consider Joanna's view. A cat as large and as old as myself is cause enough for comment. A cat that speaks is alarming. A cat that dines at table with the household is shocking. And a cat whom you must introduce as your—"

"Stop it!" I cried. "Joanna must know the truth. You must help me reveal it to her."

"Then you will not heed my advice?"

"In all things but this. Our marriage can never be happy unless she accepts you for what you are."

"And if there is no marriage?"

I would not admit to this possibility. Joanna was mine; nothing could alter that. The look of pain and bewilderment in my eyes must have been evident to my father, for he touched my arm gently with his paw and said:

"I will help you, Etienne. You must give me your trust."

"Always!"

"Then come to dinner with Joanna and explain nothing. Wait for me to appear."

I grasped his paw and raised it to my lips. "Thank you, father!"

He turned to Francois, and snapped: "You have my instructions?"

"Yes, sir," the servant replied.

"Then all is ready. I shall return to my room now, Etienne. You may bring your fiancee to dine."

I hastened up the stairway, and found Joanna ready, strikingly beautiful in shimmering white satin. Together, we descended the grand staircase and entered the room.

Her eyes shone at the magnificence of the service set upon the table, at the soldiery array of fine wines, some of them already poured into their proper glasses for my father's enjoyment: *Haut Medoc*, from *St. Estephe*, authentic *Chablis*, *Epernay Champagne*, and an American import from the Napa

Valley of which he was fond. I waited expectantly for his appearance as we sipped our aperitif, while Joanna chatted about innocuous matters, with no idea of the tormented state I was in.

At eight o'clock, my father had not yet made his appearance, and I grew ever more distraught as Francois signalled for the serving of the *bouillon au madere*. Had he changed his mind? Would I be left to explain my status without his help? I hadn't realized until this moment how difficult a task I had allotted for myself, and the fear of losing Joanna was terrible within me. The soup was flat and tasteless on my tongue, and the misery in my manner was too apparent for Joanna to miss.

"What is it, Etienne?" she said. "You've been so morose all day. Can't you tell me what's wrong?"

"No, it's nothing. It's just—" I let the impulse take possession of my speech. "Joanna, there's something I should tell you. About my mother, and my father—"

"Ahem," Francois said.

He turned to the doorway, and our glances followed his.

"Oh, Etienne!" Joanna cried, in a voice ringing with delight.

It was my father, the cat, watching us with his gray, gold-flecked eyes. He approached the dining table, regarding Joanna with timidity and caution.

"It's the cat in the painting!" Joanna said. "You didn't tell me he was here, Etienne. He's beautiful!"

"Joanna, this is—"

"Dauphin! I would have known him anywhere. Here, Dauphin! Here, kitty, kitty, kitty!"

Slowly, my father approached her outstretched hand, and allowed her to scratch the thick fur on the back of his neck.

"Aren't you the pretty little pussy! Aren't you the sweetest little thing!"

"Joanna!"

She lifted my father by the haunches, and held him in her lap, stroking his fur and cooing the silly little words that women address to their pets. The sight pained and confused me, and I sought to find an opening word that would allow me to explain, yet hoping all the time that my father would himself provide the answer.

Then my father spoke.

"Meow," he said.

"Are you hungry?" Joanna asked solicitously. "Is the little pussy hungry?"

"Meow," my father said, and I believed my heart broke then and there. He leaped from her lap and padded across the room. I watched him through blurred eyes as he followed Francois to the corner, where the servant had placed a shallow bowl of milk. He lapped at it eagerly, until the last white drop was gone. Then he yawned and stretched, and trotted back to the doorway, with one fleeting glance in my direction that spoke articulately of what I must do next.

"What a wonderful animal," Joanna said.

"Yes," I answered. "He was my mother's favorite."

The Cat Man

By Byron Liggett

You may occasionally have met one of those people—usually old, usually living alone—who keep *lots* of cats. And we mean *lots*—six, seven, eight, nine, maybe even *dozens* of cats. And if you talk to such a person, especially if you dare to hint (oh, so gently!) that perhaps this is just too much of a good thing, then he or she is quite likely to smile at you and say something like: "Oh, there's no such thing as too *many* cats!"

Obviously, they have never read the chilling and absolutely riveting story that follows. . . .

Its real name is Tao Atoll, and it still carries that name on some maps. But after the Cat Man came to the Tuamotus, people started calling it "Cat Island," and it has been known by that name ever since.

Cat Island is a crescent-shaped little atoll that lies about seventy miles north-west of Puka-Puka. As far back as anyone can remember, it has been taboo to the native Polynesians. They wouldn't go near it for all the money in the world. I don't know what native superstition put the original hex on it, but everyone knows why it is taboo today. No one—white or Polynesian—visits it now; they wouldn't dare.

I'll never forget the first day I met the Cat Man. Between the World Wars, I was making an easy living running a mail boat among the islands. The mail contract didn't pay much, but I gathered in a nice percentage hauling supplies and picking up a charter job now and then. I was sitting in the Chinaman's at Papeete having my usual, when a native cabbie brought this little gent in to see me.

I liked him the first time I saw him. He was a small, dried-up little fellow, past fifty, I'd say. He had pale blue eyes and a magnificent head of white hair. He was dressed in a grey linen suit and carried a cane which drew attention to his slight rheumatic limp. He had a kind, intelligent face.

The cabbie pointed me out to him and he shuffled over to my table. He seemed relieved to have found me.

"I understand you are Captain Rogers?" he asked.

"That's right," I said and stood up. "What can I do for you?"

The little guy took the empty chair I waved him to. He folded both hands over his cane and looked at me with an intense, serious expression.

"I'm told you have a boat I might charter."

His manner and the cut of his clothes made me smell money. Instinctively, I began juggling for a bargaining position.

"I have a sloop, sir," I admitted, "but I also have other obligations at present. Just what did you have in mind?"

He must have recognized my pitch, because he didn't seem the least disappointed.

"My name is Foster, Captain," he said, "Gerald W. Foster." He paused, as though waiting for me to recognize the name. When I didn't, he continued, "I'm a writer. I want to charter your boat to take me to Tao Atoll."

"Tao Atoll?" I blurted out. "What in the world do you want to go there for? There's nothing there but palm trees and rats!"

The man was undeterred. "Well, you see, Captain, I've just bought the island and—"

"Bought it?" I said, incredulously.

The little fellow began to get irritated, and I suddenly realized I was stepping on his dream.

"Captain, I didn't seek you out to ask your advice on the matter. I've purchased a twenty-five year lease on the island from the local government, and I intend to live there the rest of my life. I assure you, I've investigated the project thoroughly."

With that I had him pegged. I'd seen others like him come to French Oceania with that same gleam in their eyes. Some of them came to write, some to paint, and some just came in an effort to escape from themselves. *Soif des îles*—thirst for the islands—is the phrase the French have for it.

The little gent went on to explain that he wanted my sloop to haul him to the island and set him up. He wanted me to carry all his supplies, some building materials, and a couple of local carpenters to build him a cabin. He unfolded his plans with the confidence of a man who had planned his project well and who knew exactly what he wanted.

He didn't seem the slightest concerned about expenses. So,

when we got down to the financial end of the deal, I quoted him a haggling price one-third over the one I had hoped to get. He staggered me again when he whipped out his chequebook and made out the full amount in advance payment. Like I said, I knew I would like the Cat Man the first time I laid eyes on him!

I had five days in port before I had to start my next mail run to the islands. The natives Mr. Foster had hired began loading my boat the next day. He must have spent a fortune for the materials and supplies they were loading on my sloop.

I lined up a couple of Chinese carpenters for the trip, and they beat a stiff price out of me. I could've got native help for a quarter of the price but none of the natives would tackle the tabooed atoll. The Chinks knew that, too, and were out to make a killing. What did I care? After all, it was his money I was spending. This was a cost-plus deal, so far as I was concerned.

I was supervising the stowing of his gear when Foster himself brought the cats aboard. They were just ordinary-looking cats, and he carried them in two net bags slung over his arms.

"What are those things for, Mr. Foster?" I asked.

He smiled. "They are my pets, Captain. They'll keep me company in my exile. They could prove useful, too. You said yourself there were lots of rats on Tao."

I shrugged. His answers made a lot of sense, if you happened to like cats, but I don't care for the damned beasts. I looked them over when he dropped them to the deck.

"Some of them look like females," I remarked.

The Cat Man nodded and smiled. "Yes, Captain," he said. "I'm taking four females and two toms. I expect I'll have a nice crop of kittens before long. Don't you think kittens are cute?"

"Guess they are, if you like 'em. You're liable to get more kittens than you bargained for," I added more prophetically than I realized.

The weather was nice and our trip through the islands was a smooth one. The two Chinese carpenters slept on the deck. The old man spent most of his time feeding and playing with his cats, which were given the run of the ship after we left port.

We set our course for Tao Atoll after I made my mail delivery to Puka-Puka. In all my years in the islands, I had only stopped at Tao twice—once just to take a look at a hexed island, and once to repair a damaged rudder. I don't think anyone else had visited it for years. It was the most useless piece of Pacific real estate I'd ever seen.

It was late evening when we tacked into the sheltered lagoon of the atoll and dropped anchor. I don't think the Cat Man slept a wink that night. He just sat on the cabin roof and gazed towards the beach. He certainly had a bad case of island fever. I couldn't help wondering if the old boy would find what it was he seemed to be looking for.

His damned cats were fascinated by the island, too. They squatted along the gunwales and fixed their shiny little eyes on the shore, their tails twitching expectantly. I would be glad to get rid of them. Cats always gave me the creeps.

I stayed anchored at Tao while Mr. Foster got himself established. His carpenters built him a cosy little place with large screen windows. They made him bookcases for the hundreds of books he'd brought. They constructed a cistern to catch and store his water supply. They even built him a small boat dock with the scraps of lumber left over.

While we worked, the six cats investigated their new home. In no time at all, each of them had caught and killed one of the scrawny, emaciated rats that infested the island. I hated rats even more than I did cats, so my attitude softened a little. Perhaps the old man was right; the cats might prove useful, after all.

The construction jobs completed, I prepared to leave the atoll. I made a deal with Mr. Foster to stop at the island every three months on my mail run around the islands. I promised to keep him supplied with anything he needed. We both realized that I was going to be his only contact with the rest of the world.

We shook hands on the miniature dock when I was ready to shove off. Suddenly he snapped his fingers to indicate a sudden recollection.

"By the way, Captain, you'd better add a case of beef and a case of salmon to that order I gave you. It might come in handy for cat food."

This was too much! After years of living and dealing with people who considered any canned food an expensive luxury, I was understandably shocked.

"Cat food?"

The old man seemed amused at my lack of imagination. "Certainly," he said. "You don't expect the rats on this island to last forever, do you? I wouldn't want to see my little pets go hungry."

As usual, the little gent made sense. I had to admit there probably wouldn't be much left of the rodent population by the time I returned.

"O.K., Mister Foster," I agreed. "I'll bring your cat food. A pretty damned penny you're going to pay to feed these animals, but I guess you can spend your own money the way you want."

We parted amicably, and I maneuvered the sloop out of the lagoon with the tide. I set course for the Marquesas Islands and took one last look at the Cat Man's low atoll before it sank below the horizon.

I worked the islands in a counter-clockwise direction, and averaged four complete trips a year. My home port was Papeete, the capital of the Societies. I covered my route around Tahiti first, then south along the Tubuais. I had four stops in the Tuamotus before I sailed north for the Marquesas and then completed my circular route back to Papeete. The whole trip usually consumed a day or two over two months, which left me plenty of time for a charter job between runs. The new stop at Tao would add three days to my regular journey, but I didn't mind. The Cat Man appeared to be loaded with money, and I could see he was going to be a darned good customer.

On my next stop at Tao, three months later, I saw the happiest man I'd ever remembered seeing. He was brown as a nut, and his face radiated health and good humour. If it weren't for his pile of white hair, he would have looked twenty years younger. Once again I had to admire him. He had come to the islands to find his private little Utopia, and he had found it!

The little fellow bubbled over with excitement as he went through the books and mail I delivered to him. He extracted a cheque from one envelope and endorsed it to me in payment for the supplies I had brought, and asked me to bring the balance of the money to him on my next trip. I was impressed at the amount of the cheque. I had never heard of him before, but apparently he made a good living with his typewriter.

I picked up his pile of finished manuscripts and promised to see that they were airmailed to New York. He ordered the usual supplies and doubled his previous order for cat food. Two of his females had litters of kittens. He showed them to me proudly, and I could see he got a lot of pleasure from their company. He'd been right about the rats, too. Hardly any were left on the once-infested island.

On my next stop, he had another stack of manuscripts for me, and more new kittens. They were certainly thriving on the atoll. The old man was thriving, too. I couldn't get over the fact that he was enjoying his self-imposed exile on that dreary little palm-tree prison, and my esteem for him continued to grow. I delivered a load of cash from his previous cheque, and he endorsed new ones to me. He put the money in a strong box he kept in his cabin. Again he doubled his order for cat food.

By the time three years had passed, that damned atoll was crawling with cats. I could hear them yowling at the sight of my sloop when I entered the lagoon: they knew I was carrying the commissary. Mr. Foster met my dory while standing on his dock in a mob of cats. For the first time, I noticed a tight look about his features and a slight nervousness in his manner. I had an uneasy feeling that my miracle man was beginning to wear at the seams.

But his greeting was warmer than usual. "Good day, Captain Rogers. I certainly am glad to see you."

We had to practically kick our way through the cats to get to his cabin. The old man yelled at them and waved his cane threateningly. My curiosity got the better of me.

"Mister Foster," I asked, "how many cats do you think you have now?"

He answered with a noticeable lack of enthusiasm.

"Oh, I don't know—over a hundred, I guess."

"Well, at least you don't have to worry about the rats any more," I chuckled.

He turned to me with an amused smile. "Rats?" he asked. "I don't have to worry about anything any more. They've climbed the palms and cleaned out all the bird nests on the island. The birds won't come near the place now. They've caught and eaten just about every insect on the atoll. I ran out of food for them a week ago, and the little devils haven't given me a moment's peace. I finally had to stop writing and spend all my time fishing for them."

I could see the animals could be quite a problem if they were

hungry. I was making a good profit on the cat food I was hauling him, but the situation appeared to be getting out of hand.

"Looks like you brought too many females in your original
batch," I said. "Want me to take half of them with me when I
leave, and drop them over the side?"

The Cat Man drew back in horror.

"Oh, heavens no!" he gasped. "I couldn't consider such a
thing." Then his face brightened and his usual kind expression
returned. He stooped and picked up a purring, half-grown kitten.

"My pets are really quite interesting, Captain Rogers. Of
course, there are so many now, they've lost their individuality
to me to some extent, but the feline society they have organ-
ized is fascinating."

He turned and pointed to the window. "See that ragged-
eared big tom rubbing against the screen?"

I could see the mangy-looking beast. He looked as if he'd
been in a thousand fights and lost every one of them.

"That one is the king of my tribe, and he has a goon squad
of young toms who back him up. They have their pick of the
females. And the care the mother cats give to their young ones
is something wonderful to witness. I admit they're getting to
be a problem, but life here would be pretty dull without
them."

He didn't quite convince me this time.

I tried another angle. "At least let me try to round up a
couple of natives who aren't too superstitious to come here
and do your fishing for you. There's enough fish in that
lagoon to feed a million cats."

The old man shook his white head vigorously.

"No, no, Captain. I came here to get away from people so I
could write. I'll put up with a thousand cats before I'll share
my solitude with anyone."

I didn't push the issue. It was his life, his world; he had
made it for himself. I left him the supplies he'd ordered, and
tossed in an extra case of beef from my own stores. It would
take a lot of rations to feed a hundred cats for three months. I
noted that the finished manuscripts he handed me were about
half their usual bulk.

The story of the Cat Man and his pets had spread throughout
French Oceania. By now, the rations I was hauling for his

beasts were making up a large part of my load, and Tao Atoll was a subject of much amusement in Papeete. Several people with apparently nothing else to do were always waiting for me to return from my trip with news of the old man and his cats. He didn't realize it, but he was a famous man in the South Pacific, and not because of his writing, either.

On my next trip I found him beginning to crack. He'd run short of food again, and the cats were really starting to wear him down. I saw something else in his face that I'd never seen before. It was fear.

As usual, he met me standing on his dock, completely surrounded with a yowling pack of hungry cats.

"Did you bring the cat food, Captain Rogers?" he yelled over the din.

"Everything you ordered, sir," I answered, as I tossed him the rope from my dory.

Again, we had to kick our way through the cats to reach his cabin. The old man surely was mistaken in his last estimate of their population. It appeared to me there were closer to two hundred cats. On an island a mile long and a hundred yards wide, that's a lot of cats.

He started complaining about his pets as soon as we got into the cabin, ready to admit they were now a serious problem.

"These last two weeks have been a nightmare, Captain," he whined. "I started fishing a month ago, when it became obvious that their rations wouldn't last. I've never seen such voracious beasts."

His face was lined with worry. He had lost his neat, tidy appearance, and his face looked haunted. His island Utopia was rapidly turning into a hell. His dream was threatening to disintegrate before his eyes.

"I'm afraid we'll have to do something about the cats after all," he complained. "I have no manuscripts for you this time. These animals haven't given me any peace. Their mating screams and their begging voices! The toms have taken to eating the new-born kittens and the fights are practically continuous. I must do something!"

I wasn't surprised to hear him talk this way. I'd seen the initial signs of a crack-up on my last trip. The old man was beginning to recognize realities.

"Shall I bring you some poison for them on my next trip, Mister Foster?" I offered.

"Poison?" He flinched, as I knew he would. He closed his eyes and squeezed his forehead with nervous fingers. Then he opened his eyes and looked at me.

"No, definitely not," he said. "I could never be that cruel. Their being here is my own doing, and no fault of the cats. There must be some other solution."

I smiled and patted the old man on the shoulder. "I hope you'll forgive me, Mister Foster, but I anticipated your getting fed up with the cats. I brought along a couple of dogs for you this trip."

Now it was the Cat Man's turn to be surprised. "Dogs?" he exclaimed. Then a gleam of hope came into his eyes.

"That's right, Mister Foster. I thought maybe you could tie them up around your cabin. They'd keep the cats from bothering you."

He was pleased. His eyes grew brighter and the old smile returned to his face. He snatched my hand and wrung it gratefully. I was glad I'd brought them. If he hadn't consented to my leaving them, I planned to kick them overboard before I sailed anyhow, and let them swim to shore. I liked the little guy too much to see a mess of cats ruin his paradise.

"They're both males, too," I added as I turned to go after the dogs. "You won't have to worry about their breeding you out of your island."

The folks back in Papeete got a kick when I told them about the dogs. I had rounded up the meanest canines I could find in the Tuamotus. They didn't even like themselves, and they would both go wild at the sight of a cat. However, the way things turned out, I guess I wasn't as smart as I thought I was. Two dogs were a pretty poor match for two hundred hungry cats.

The cats had about taken over completely by the time I reached Tao on my next tip. I could hear them yowling as I entered the lagoon. I was listening for the barking of the dogs, but I never heard a yip.

I saw the old man's face peering at me from his screened window as I rowed the dory towards his dock. Just before I reached the dock, I heard his door slam. I looked up to see him scurrying towards me, and thrashing with his cane. The leaping, screaming cats made way for him, but they were bold as hell. They'd just jump out of range of the cane and stand there spitting at him with their backs arched.

Foster had to knock about a dozen of them into the water before he could grab my rope. We fought our way to his cabin. I noticed the dog chains and empty collars as I dashed through the doors. The screams of the hungry cats were deafening.

When I finally got my breath and faced the old man, I was shocked. I hope I never see a look like that on a human face again. His eyes were sunken, his skin stretched over his sharp cheek bones, and his lips drawn in a thin line against his yellowed teeth. He was filthy, and he obviously hadn't shaved for days.

He didn't have to tell me what he'd been through. The din of the cats tearing at the screens told the story. I would have dreaded the prospect of staying there a day, let alone weeks. The poor man had lived through a hell of his own making. I knew he wasn't completely mad yet, or he wouldn't have had the courage to meet me at the dock.

"The dogs!" I shouted. "Where are the dogs?"

The Cat Man was glaring at me like an idiot.

"They ate them," he said, in a strange metallic voice. "Two weeks ago. They killed and ate them—down to the last hair and toenail. The dogs killed a few of the cats and the cats ate their own corpses. They've been after me ever since."

In spite of his appearance, I could see the old man still had a good grip on himself. Best thing I could do was to get those cats fed before they ripped us both to pieces. I snatched up his cane and went for the door.

A couple of the beasts leaped on my back from the roof as I dashed for the dock. They gave me some nasty bites and scratches before I shook them off. I killed five with the cane before they learned my reach was longer than old Foster's. Each stricken cat was immediately eaten by his famished brothers and sisters.

I loaded the dory with cases of cat food from the sloop, and rowed to within twenty feet of the beach. For two hours I sat and tossed them open tins until my fingers were covered with blisters made by the can opener.

When the last cat had slunk away, gorged, I beached the dory and made my way back to the old man's cabin. He was sitting with his head on the table—asleep!

A couple of hours' rest, a bath, a shave, and some of the

fear gone out of his face, and the little gent looked something like his old self. We had coffee and got down to cases. I put it to him squarely.

"I don't suppose I can make you leave this place?"

He wagged his head, "Never, Captain."

I figured as much. Characters like Mr. Foster have that dogged determination that moves mountains. Guess that's why I liked him.

"Well, then," I continued, "we're going to have to do something about the cats. I'm going to bring a load of poison next trip."

In spite of the horrifying experience he'd been through, the word "poison" still made him grimace. "Must it be poison, Captain?" he asked hopefully.

"Now don't try to talk me out of it," I warned. "I'm going to get rid of these cats if I have to tie you up to do it."

He agreed, reluctantly. "I suppose you're right. It seems impossible to control them, and I must get back to my writing."

I hated to leave him with the cats again, but I had no choice. I had brought even more cat food than he'd ordered, but it still wasn't enough. I raided my own stores and gave him all I could part with. I handed him my carbine on my last trip in the dory.

"Better take this, just in case," I urged him. He accepted it with the air of a person indulging another's whim. I fished a box of cartridges out of my pocket and tossed it to him.

"Careful with these and don't waste them," I warned. "There are only fifty rounds in that box, and that's all I have."

He accepted the box with a sad but grateful smile. As I pulled away from the dock, I yelled my last bit of advice.

"Aim at the toms!"

I should have shot fifty of the cats myself before I left. That way the rations would have gone a lot further. However, I had already decided to make a quick trip and return with the poison as soon as I could. Besides, I couldn't bear the thought of shooting them while the Cat Man was watching. He feared them, but he still couldn't stand to see them hurt.

I hurried through my business in Papeete, and was back at sea in three days. The hurricane caught me in the Tubuais. It wasn't the worst blow that ever hit the islands, but it was the worst that I'd been through. I weathered the storm on one of the atolls with the natives. My sloop snapped her moorings and was driven among the palms. It was almost a total wreck.

When the sea calmed down, I hired a native out-rigger to take me back to Papeete. It was a long, miserable trip, but we made it. I guess I had a foolish notion I could hire or buy another boat and go about my business, or at least get the old man's stuff to him at Tao. I hadn't realized how bad the hurricane had been until I saw Papeete.

The Society Islands had taken the full force of the storm, and the results were appalling. Ninety per cent of the boats and ships tied up were wrecked or damaged. You couldn't hire, buy, or steal a deep water boat. I forgot about my own misfortunes when I got a glimpse at the destruction in the harbour at Papeete. All I could think of was that poor old guy on that island with all those cats!

Not being able to get a boat, I had to do the next best thing. I bought bolts, caulking, sail cloth, and everything else that I thought the natives and I could carry on the out-rigger, and headed back to the Tubuais. I figured we could put my own sloop together again, at least good enough to get back to Cat Island.

Natives hate work and I just about killed those boys of mine with it. We took that pile of scrap lumber and began re-assembling it. I drove them from dawn to dusk, relentlessly, and worked after dark by lantern light. What we needed and didn't have, we made. In six weeks we had the sloop in shape. I'll admit she wasn't very sound, but I knew she'd stand quite a bit of sailing if I kept her out of rough weather.

All the time we laboured I was spurred on by thoughts of the old man on Tao. He had rations for those hungry cats for only three months, and the morning we refloated the sloop made three months to the day since I had left him. Counting time I would lose going back to Papeete to replenish my supplies, it would take another month to get there.

Like the other white men in the islands, I never gave much thought to native taboos. They are based on cultural habits and legends rather than on factual data. However, a nervous uneasiness came over me twenty-six days later, when I was one day out of Tao. The sea was calm. The wind was light and steady and the sky was a clean, pale blue. Everything was normal for that time of the year, but I had a feeling I was leaving the world of the living and sailing towards the gates of hell.

I slipped into the lagoon just after midnight, and dropped anchor. Immediately a moan of sound rose from the black outline of the atoll and came across the moonlight-drenched mirror of water. My scalp rippled and I felt the skin tighten on the back of my neck. The starving beasts had heard me, and they were yowling for their rations.

I searched in vain for a light in the old man's shack. I gave him about a dozen yells across the lagoon, but was answered only by rising peaks in the continuous moaning of the cats. I searched for a sign of life from shore, and then I saw them. Cat eyes! Hundreds of them reflecting the light from the full moon, and glittering like silver sequins scattered on the black velvet shore of the atoll. They were still there, hungry and waiting. A wave of nausea swept over me as I realized I was too late. I wondered how many the old man had killed before they got him.

I waited for the sky to turn grey in the east before I unlimbered the dory. I didn't want to tackle that island until daylight. When the sun came up, I armed myself with two billy clubs, and started rowing towards the shore. When I approached the beach I saw a sight I'll remember the rest of my life. Several of the cats were splashing and diving in the shallow waters close to the shore, and swimming around like seals. They were fishing!

Two of the big toms swam out to meet my dory and tried to climb over the side. I brained them with the billy. I didn't try to make the dock. It was completely covered with the damned beasts and I was afraid they'd leap into the dory and swamp me when I tried to tie up. The beach was literally carpeted with cats. They were screaming at me in a maddening crescendo as though I were personally responsible for their plight. As I rowed down to the far end of the beach they followed me on the shore, an evil, mottled wave of spitting fur.

Again I opened tins of food to throw to them until my fingers were raw. When I emptied the dory I rowed back to the dock. About half of the cats follwed me back and were waiting there to meet me. I vetoed the dock and shot the dory towards the beach with swift strokes. Just before she touched bottom, I shipped the oars, grabbed up my billy clubs, and got ready to jump.

I landed running, swinging my clubs like a windmill. I was killing cats with practically every swing, but they still tried to swarm over me. I yelled when I felt their teeth. The damned animals were insane. They were so crazy from hunger they would attack anything.

I literally beat my way to the old man's cabin, and very nearly didn't make it. The screens were torn as I knew they'd be. I didn't stop to open the door. I hit it with my shoulder and my momentum carried me through it with splinters flying. In a haze of pain and anger I saw the cats fighting over something in the center of the floor. I knew that something had to be Mr. Foster.

I went as crazy as the cats then. Ignoring the beasts that were clinging to my body, I began to beat a hole through that writhing pile of fur before me. The clubs rose and fell as I methodically smashed their bodies, until I could see what they were fighting over. It was a pile of snow-white hair attached to a bit of scalp.

I think I went completely out of my head. I don't know how I got out of that cabin, but I do know I must have been crazy to drop one of my clubs and grab up the old man's hair. I remember running for the beach with cats clinging all over me. I dived over the prow of the beached dory and smashed into it in a headlong swan dive.

That dive saved my life. The force of my body striking the stern unbeached the dory and sent it shooting out into the lagoon. I ripped the cats off me and knocked them silly with the remaining club.

I threw my shredded clothes away and doctored my hundreds of scratches and bites on the way back to Papeete. I made a full report to the French Governor, but I could tell he didn't believe me. Nevertheless, he sent a launch full of local police to investigate Tao a week later. When that launch got back, my stories about Cat Island sounded like Sunday School tales.

The police long boat didn't even make the beach at Tao. The swimming cats met them in the lagoon. They climbed the oars and tried to eat the investigators on the spot. The police got out of there fast. They reported the cats had completely covered the atoll, and were fishing the lagoon like penguins. That's how its name "Cat Island" became official.

Everyone gives that atoll a wide berth now. No one has gone near it for years. I sail by it on my regular runs but I never stop. Sometimes I get to thinking about all that money the old man had in that strong box, and play with the idea of going back after it. When such a silly notion comes over me I just count my scars and dig out a little souvenir from my sea chest. Every time I look at old man Foster's hair I change my mind.

Some Are
Born Cats

By Terry and Carol Carr

Have you ever considered that the tabby sitting contentedly on your lap, or bumping gently up against your leg, or nagging you for some chicken or tuna fish or liver, just *might* be an incognito shape-shifting alien spy from Arcturus?

No? Well, maybe you ought to *start* thinking about such things, then.

It may already be . . . too late.

Terry Carr is one of the most prominent and respected editors in science fiction. In addition to editing the prestigious original anthology series *Universe* and the long-running *Best Science Fiction of the Year* series, Carr was the editor of the famous "Ace Specials" SF book line, perhaps the most critically acclaimed publishing venture of the late 1960's, and a showcase for (then) new writers such as Joanna Russ, R. A. Lafferty, D. G. Compton, and many others. Carr is currently engaged in recreating an "Ace Specials" line (the first of the new Specials will be released in 1984), and the line promises once again to be a showcase for a lot of hot new talent. As a writer, Terry Carr has produced a handful of wry, elegantly crafted stories such as "The Dance of the Changer and the Three," "Hop-Friend," and "Virra," as well as the novel *Cirque*. His short fiction is collected in *The Light at the End of the Universe*.

Carol Carr is best known for her marvelously funny story "Look, You Think You've Got Troubles?" about a Nice Jewish Girl who marries a Martian. (Oy!) She has sold to *Orbit*, and has a new story coming up in *Omni*.

"Maybe he's an alien shape-changing spy from Arcturus," Freddie said.

"What does that mean?" asked the girl.

Freddie shrugged. "Maybe he's not a cat at all. He could be some kind of alien creature that came to Earth to spy on us. He could be hiding in the shape of a cat while he studies us and sends back reports to Arcturus or someplace."

She looked at the cat, whose black body lay draped across the top of the television set, white muzzle on white paws, wide green eyes open and staring at them. The boy and the girl lay on her bed, surrounded by schoolbooks.

"You're probably right," she said. "He gives me the creeps."

The girl's name was Alyson, and it was her room. She and Freddie spent a lot of their time together, though it wasn't a real Thing between them. Nothing official, nor even unofficial. They'd started the evening doing homework together, but now they were watching "Creature Features," with the sound turned down.

"He always does that," Alyson said. "He gets up on the television set whenever there's a scary movie on, and he drapes his tail down the side like that and just *stares* at me. I'm watching a vampire movie, and I happen to glance up and there he is, looking at me. He never blinks, even. It really freaks me out sometimes."

The cat sat up suddenly, blinking. It yawned and began an elaborate washing of its face. White paws, white chest, white face, and the rest of him was raven black. With only the television screen illuminating the room, he seemed to float in the darkness. On the screen now was a commercial for campers; a man who looked Oriental was telling them that campers were the best way to see America.

"What kind of a name is Gilgamesh?" Freddie asked. "That's his name, isn't it?"

"It's ancient Babylonian or something like that," Alyson told him. "He was kind of a god; there's a whole long story about him. I just liked the name, and he looked so scraggly and helpless when he adopted us, I thought maybe he could use a fancy name. But most of the time I just call him Gil anyway."

"Is George short for anything?" the boy asked. George was her other cat, a placid Siamese. George was in some other part of the house.

"No, he's just George. He looks so elegant, I didn't think he needed a very special name."

"Gilgamesh, you ought to pay more attention to George," the boy said. "He's a *real* cat; he acts like a cat would really act. You don't see *him* sitting on top of horror shows and acting weird."

"George gets up on the television set too, but he just goes to sleep," Alyson said.

The cat, Gilgamesh, blinked at them and slowly lay down again, spreading himself carefully across the top of the TV set. He didn't look at them.

"Do you mean Gil could be just hypnotizing us to think he's a cat?" Alyson asked. "Or do you suppose he took over the body of a real cat when he arrived here on Earth?"

"Either way," Freddie said. "It's how he acts that's the tip-off. He doesn't act like a cat would. Hey, Gil, you really ought to study George—he knows what it's all about."

Gilgamesh lay still, eyes closed. They watched the movie, and after it, the late news. An announcer jokingly reported that strange lights had been seen in the skies over Watsonville, and he asked the TV weatherman if he could explain them. The weatherman said, "We may have a new wave of flying saucers moving in from the Pacific." Everybody in the studio laughed.

Gilgamesh jumped off the television set and left the room.

Freddie's Saturday morning began at eight o'clock with the

"World News Roundup of the Week." He opened one eye cautiously and saw an on-the-spot reporter interviewing the families of three sky divers whose parachutes had failed to open.

Freddie was about to go downstairs for breakfast when the one woman reporter in the group smilingly announced that Friday night, at 11:45 P.M., forty-two people had called the studio to report a flying-saucer sighting. One man, the owner of a fish store, referred to "a school of saucers." The news team laughed, but Freddie's heartbeat quickened.

It took him twenty minutes to get through to Alyson, and when she picked up the phone, he was caught unprepared, with a mouthful of English muffin.

"Hello? Hello?"

"Mmgfghmf."

"Hello? Who *is* this?"

"Chrglfmhph."

"Oh, my goodness! Mom! I think it's one of those obscene calls!" She sounded deliriously happy. But she hung up.

Freddie swallowed and dialed again.

"Boy, am I glad it's you," Alyson said. "Listen, you've got to come right over—it's been one incredible thing after another ever since you left last night. First, the saucers—did you hear about them?—and then Gil freaking out, then a real creepy obscene telephone call."

"Hold it, hold it," Freddie said. "I'll meet you back of the house in five minutes."

When he got there, Alyson was lying stomach down on the lawn, chewing a blade of grass. She looked only slightly more calm than she sounded.

"Freddie," she said almost tragically. "How much do you know?"

"About as much as the next guy."

"No, seriously—I mean about the saucers last night. Did you see them?"

"I was asleep. Did you?"

"*See* them! I practically *touched* them." She looked deep into his eyes. "But Freddie, that's not the important part."

"What is? What?"

"Gilgamesh. I seriously believe he's having a nervous breakdown. I hate to think of what else it could be." She got up. "Wait right here. I want you to see this."

Freddie waited, a collage of living-color images dancing in

his head: enemy sky divers, a massacred school of flying saucers, shape-changing spies from Arcturus. . . .

Alyson came back holding a limp Gilgamesh over her arm.

"He was in the litter pan," she said significantly. "He was covering it up."

"Covering what up?"

"His doo-doo, silly."

Freddie winced. There were moments when he wished Alyson were a bit more liberated.

Gilgamesh settled down to Alyson's lap and purred frantically.

"He has *never*, not once before, covered it up," she insisted. "He always gets out of the box when he's finished and scratches on the floor near it. George comes along eventually and does it for him."

Gilgamesh licked one paw and applied it to his right ear. It was a highly adorable action, one that never failed to please. He did it twice more—lick, tilt head, rub; lick, tilt head, rub—then stopped and looked at Freddie out of the corner of his eye.

"You see what I mean?" Alyson said. "Do you know what that look means?"

"He's asking for approval," said Freddie. "No doubt about it. He wants to know if he did it right."

"Exactly!"

Gilgamesh tucked his head between his white paws and closed his eyes.

"He feels that he's a failure," Alyson interpreted.

"Right."

Gilgamesh turned over on his back, let his legs flop, and began to purr. His body trembled like a lawn mower standing still.

Freddie nodded. "Overdone. Everything he does is self-conscious."

"And you know when he's not self-conscious? When he's staring. But he doesn't look like a cat then, either."

"What did he do last night, when the saucers were here?"

Alyston sat up straight; Gilgamesh looked at her suspiciously.

"He positively freaked," she said. "He took one look and his tail bushed out and he arched his back. . . ."

"That's not so freaky. And kind of cat would do that."

"I know . . . it's what comes next." She paused dramatically. "In the middle of this bushy-tailed fit, he stopped dead in his tracks, shook his head, and trotted into the house to find George. Gil woke him up and chased him onto the porch. Then you know what he did? He put a paw on George's shoulder, like they were old buddies. And you know how George is—he just went along with it; he'll groove on anything. But it was so weird. George wanted to leave, but Gil keep him there by washing him. George can't resist a wash—he's too busy grooving to do it himself—so he stayed till the saucers took off."

Freddie picked up Alyson's half-chewed blade of grass and put it in his mouth. "You think that Gil, for reasons of his own, manipulated George into watching saucers with him?"

Gilgamesh stopped being a lawn mower long enough to bat listlessly at a bumblebee. Then he looked at Alyson slyly and resumed his purring.

"That's exactly what I think. What do you think?"

Freddie thought about it for a while, gazing idly at Gilgamesh. The cat avoided his eyes.

"Why would he want George to watch flying saucers with him?" Freddie asked.

Alyson shrugged elaborately, tossing her hair and looking at the clear blue of the sky. *"I* don't know. Flying saucers are spaceships, aren't they? Maybe Gilgamesh came here in one of them."

"But why would he want *George* to look at one?"

"I'll tell you what," said Alyson. "Why don't you ask Gilgamesh about that?"

Freddie glanced again at the cat; Gilgamesh was lying preternaturally still, as though asleep, yet too rigid to be truly asleep. Playing 'possum, Freddie thought. Listening.

"Hey, Gil," he said softly. "Why did you want George to see the flying saucers?"

Gilgamesh made no acknowledgment that he had heard. But Freddie noticed that his tail twitched.

"Come on, Gil, you can tell *me,"* he coaxed. "I'm from Procyon, myself."

Gilgamesh sat bolt upright, eyes wide and shocked. Then he seemed to recollect himself, and he swatted at a nonexistent bee, chased his tail in a circle, and ran off around the corner of the house.

"You nearly got him that time," Alyson said. "That line about being from Procyon blew his mind."

"Next time we tie him to a chair and hang a naked light bulb over his head," Freddie said.

After school Monday, Freddie stopped off at the public library and did a little research. They kept files of the daily newspapers there, and Freddie spent several hours checking through the papers for the last several months for mentions of flying saucers or anything else unusual.

That evening, in Alyson's room, Freddie said, "Let's skip the French vocabulary for a while. When did you get Gilgamesh?"

Alyson had George on her lap; the placid Siamese lay like a dead weight except for his low-grade purr. Alyson said, "Three weeks ago. Gil just wandered into the kitchen, and we thought he was a stray—I mean, he couldn't have belonged to anybody, because he was so dirty and thin, and anyway, he didn't have a collar."

"Three weeks ago," Freddie said. "What day, exactly?"

She frowned, thinking back. "Mmm . . . it was a Tuesday. Three weeks ago tomorrow, then."

"That figures," Freddie said. "Alyson, do you know what happened the day before Gilgamesh just walked into your life?"

She stared wonderingly at him for a moment, then something lit in her eyes. "That was the night the sky was so loud!"

"Yes," said Freddie.

Alyson sat up on the bed, shedding both George and the books from her lap in her excitement. "And then that Tuesday we asked Mr. Newcomb in science class what had caused it, and he just said a lot of weird stuff that didn't mean anything, remember? Like he really didn't know, but he was a teacher, and he thought he had to be able to explain everything."

"Right," said Freddie. "An unexplainable scientific phenomenon in the skies, and the next day Gilgamesh just happened to show up on your doorstep. I'll bet there were flying saucers that night, too, only nobody saw them."

George sleepily climbed back onto the bed and settled down in Alyson's lap again. She idly scratched his ear, and he licked her hand, then closed his eyes and went to sleep again.

"You think it was flying saucers that made all those weird noises in the sky?" Alyson asked.

"Sure," he said. "Probably. Especially if that was the night before Gilgamesh got here. I wonder what his mission is?"

"What?" said Alyson.

"I wonder why he's here, on Earth. Do you think they're really planning to invade us?"

"Who?" she asked. "You mean people from flying saucers? Oh, Freddie, cool it. I mean a joke's a joke, and Gilgamesh *is* pretty creepy, but he's only a little black-and-white cat. He's not some invader from Mars!"

"Arcturus," Freddie said. "Or maybe it's really Procyon; maybe that's why he was so startled when I said that yesterday."

"Freddie! He's a *cat!*"

"You think so?" Freddie asked. "Let me show you something about your innocent little stray cat."

He got off the bed and silently went to the door of the bedroom. Grasping the knob gently, he suddenly threw the door open wide.

Standing right outside the door was Gilgamesh. The black-and-white cat leaped backward, then quickly recovered himself and walked calmly into the room, as though he had just been on his way in when the door opened. But Freddie saw that his tail was fully bushed out.

"You still think he's a cat?" Freddie asked.

"Freddie, he's just a little weird, that's all—"

"Weird? This cat's so weird he's probably got seven hearts and an extra brain in his back! Alyson, this is no ordinary cat!"

Gilgamesh jumped up on the bed, studied how George was lying, and arranged himself in a comparable position next to Alyson. She petted him for a moment, and he began to purr his odd high-pitched purr.

"You think he's just a cat?" Freddie asked. "He sounds like a cricket."

"Freddie, are you serious?" Alyson said. Freddie nodded. He'd done his research at the library, and he was sure something strange was going on.

"Well, then," said Alyson. "I know what we can do. We'll take him to my brother and see if he's really a cat or not."

"Your brother? But he's a chiropractor."

Alyson smiled. "But he has an X-ray machine. We'll *see* if Gilgamesh really has those extra hearts and all."

On her lap, George continued to purr. Next to her, Gilgamesh seemed to have developed a tic in the side of his face, but he continued to lie still.

• • •

Alyson's brother, the chiropractor, had his office in the Watsonville Shopping Center, next door to the Watsonville Bowling Alley. His receptionist told them to wait in the anteroom, the doctor would be with them in a moment.

Alyson and Freddie sat down on a black sofa, with the carrying case between them. From inside the case came pitiful mews and occasional thrashings about. From inside the office came sounds of pitiful cries and the high notes of Beethoven's Fifth. Somebody made a strike next door; the carrying case flew a foot into the air. Freddie transferred it to his lap and held it steady.

A young man with longish brown hair and a white jacket opened the door.

"Hey sister, hi Freddie. What's happening?"

Alyson pointed to the carrying case. "This is the patient I told you about, Bob."

"Okay. Let's go in and take a look."

He opened the case. Gilgamesh had curled himself into a tight ball of fur, his face pressed against the corner. When the doctor lifted him out, Freddie saw that the cat's eyes were clenched shut.

"I've never seen him so terrified," Alyson said. "Weird, freaky, yes, but never this scared."

"I still don't understand why you didn't take him to a vet if you think he's sick," her brother said.

Alyson grinned ingratiatingly. "You're cheaper."

"Hmpf."

All this time the doctor had been holding the rigid Gilgamesh in the air. As soon as he put him down on the examining table, the cat opened his eyes to twice their normal size, shot a bushy tail straight up, and dashed under the table. He cowered there, face between paws. Alyson's brother crawled under the table, but the cat scrambled to the opposite side of the room and hid behind a rubber plant. Two green eyes peeked through the leaves.

"I think stronger measures are indicated," the doctor said. He opened a drawer and removed a hypodermic needle and a small glass bottle.

Freddie and Alyson approached the rubber plant from each end, then grabbed.

Freddie lifted the cat onto the examining table. Gilgamesh froze, every muscle rigid—but his eyes darted dramatically around the room, looking for escape.

The doctor gave him the shot, and within seconds he was a boneless pussycat who submitted docilely to the indignities of being X-rayed in eight different positions.

Ten minutes later Alyson's brother announced the results—no abnormalities; Gilgamesh was a perfectly healthy cat.

"Does he have any extra hearts?" Alyson said. "Anything funny about his back?"

"He's completely normal," said her brother. "Doesn't even have any extra toes." He saw the worried expression on her face. "Wasn't that what you wanted to find out?"

"Sure," said Alyson. "Thanks a lot. I'm really relieved."

"Me, too," said Freddie. "Very."

Neither of them looked it.

"Lousy job," said Gilgamesh.

They turned to look at him, mouths open. The cat's mouth was closed. He was vibrating like a lawn mower again, purring softly.

Freddie looked at the doctor. "Did someone just say something?"

"Somebody just said, 'Lousy job,' " said the doctor. "I thought it was your cat. I must be losing my mind. Alyson?" She looked to be in shock. "Did you hear anything?"

"No. I didn't hear him say 'Lousy job' or anything like that." Still in a daze, she went over to the cat and stroked him on the head. Then she bent down and whispered something in his ear.

"Just haven't got the knack," said Gilgamesh. "Crash course." He smiled, closed his eyes, and fell asleep. But there was no doubt that it was he who had spoken.

Freddie, who had just got over the first wave of disbelief, said, "What was in that injection, anyway?"

"Sodium pentothal. Very small dose. I think I'd better sit down." The doctor staggered to the nearest chair, almost missing it.

"Hey, Alyson?" the doctor said.

"Huh?"

"Maybe you'd better tell me why you really brought your cat in here."

"Well," said Alyson.

"Come on, little sister, give," he said.

Alyson looked at the floor and mumbled, "Freddie thinks he's a spy from outer space."

"From Arcturus," said Freddie.

"Procyon," said Gilgamesh. He yawned and rolled onto his side.

"Wait a minute," said the doctor. "Wait a minute, I want to get something straight." But he just stared at the cat, at Freddie, at Alyson.

Freddie took advantage of the silence. "Gilgamesh, you were just talking, weren't you?"

"Lemme sleep," Gilgamesh mumbled.

"What's your game, Gil?" Freddie asked him. "Are you spying on us? You're really some shapeless amoeba-like being that can rearrange its protoplasm at will, aren't you? Are your people planning to invade Earth? When will the first strike hit? Come on, *talk!*"

"Lemme sleep," Gilgamesh said.

Freddie picked up the cat and held him directly under the fluorescent light of the examining table. Gilgamesh winced and squirmed, feebly.

"Talk!" Freddie commanded. "Tell us the invasion plans."

"No invasion," Gilgamesh whined. "Lemme down. No fair drugging me."

"Are you from Procyon?" Freddie asked him.

"Are you from Killarney?" the cat sang, rather drunkenly. "Studied old radio broadcasts, sorry. Sure, from Procyon. Tried to act like a cat but couldn't get the hang of it. Never can remember what to do with my tail."

"What are you doing on Earth?" Freddie demanded.

"Chasing a runaway," the cat mumbled. "Antisocial renegade, classified for work camps. Jumped bail and ran. Tracked him to Earth, but he's been passing as a native."

"As a *human being?*" Alyson cried.

"As a cat. It's George. Cute li'l George, soft and lazy, lies in the sun all day. Irresponsible behavior. Antisocial. Never gets anything done. Got to bring him back, put him in a work camp."

"Wait a minute," Freddie broke in. "You mean you came to Earth to find an escaped prisoner? And George is it? You mean you're a *cop?*"

"Peace officer," Gilgamesh protested, trying to sit up straight. "Law and order. Loyalty to the egg and arisian pie. Only George *did* escape, so I had to track him down. I always get my amoeba."

Alyson's brother dazedly punched his intercom button.

"Miss Blanchard, you'd better cancel the rest of my appointments," he said dully.

"But you *can't* take George away from me!" Alyson cried. "He's my *cat!*"

"Just a third-class amoeba," Gilgamesh sniffed. "Hard to control, though. More trouble than he's worth."

"Then leave him here!" Alyson said. "If he's a fugitive, he's safe with me! I'll give him sanctuary. I'll sign parole papers for him. I'll be responsible—"

Gilgamesh eyed her blearily. "Do you know what you're saying, lady?"

"Of course I know what I'm saying! George is my cat, and I love him—I guess you wouldn't know what that means. George stays with me, no matter what. You go away. Go back to your star."

"Listen, Alyson, maybe you should think about this . . ." Freddie began.

"Shaddup, kid," said Gilgamesh. "I'll tell you, George was never anything to us but a headache. Won't work, just wants to lie around looking decorative. If you want him, lady, you got him."

There was a silence. Freddie noticed that Alyson's brother seemed to be giggling softly to himself.

After long moments, Alyson asked, "Don't I have to sign something?"

"Nah, lady," said Gilgamesh. "We're not barbarians. I've got your voice recorded in my head. George is all yours, and good riddance. He was a blot on the proud record of the Procyon Co-Prosperity Sphere." Gilgamesh got to his feet and marched rigidly to the window of the office. He turned and eyed them greenly.

"Listen, you tell George one thing for me. Tell him he's dumb lucky he happened to hide out as a cat. He can be lazy and decorative here, but I just want you to know one thing: there's no such thing as a decorative amoeba. An amoeba works, or out he goes!"

Gilgamesh disappeared out the window.

On the way back to Alyson's house, Freddie did his best to contain himself, but as they approached her door, he broke their silence. "I told you so, Alyson."

"Told me what?" Alyson opened the door and led him up the stairs to her room.

"That the cat was an alien. A shape-changer, a spy hiding out here on Earth."

"Pooh," she said. "You thought he was from Arcturus. Do you know how far Arcturus is from Procyon?"

They went into her room. "Very far?" Freddie asked.

"Oh, *boy!*" Alyson said. "Very *far!*" She shook her head disgustedly.

George was lying in the middle of the bed, surrounded by schoolbooks. He opened one eye as the two of them tramped into the room, then closed it again and contented himself with a soft purr.

Alyson sat on the side of the bed and rubbed George's belly. "Sweet George," she said. "Beautiful little pussycat."

"Listen, Alyson," said Freddie, "maybe you ought to think about George a little bit. I mean, you're responsible for him now—"

"He's my cat," Alyson said firmly.

"Yeah, well, sort of," Freddie said. "Not really, of course, because really he's an alien shape-changing amoeba from Procyon. And worse than that, remember what Gilgamesh said, he's a runaway. He's a dropout from interstellar society. Who knows, maybe he even uses drugs!"

Alyson rested a level gaze on Freddie, a patient, forgiving look. "Freddie," she said softly, "some of us are born cats, and some of us achieve catness."

"What?"

"Well, look, if *you* were an amoeba from Procyon and you were sent off to the work camps, wouldn't you rather come to Earth and be a cat and lie around all day sunning yourself and getting scratched behind the ears? I mean, it just makes *sense*. It proves George is *sane!*"

"It proves he's lazy," Freddie muttered.

George opened his eyes just a slit and looked at Freddie—a look of contented wonder. Then he closed his eyes again and began to purr.

The Cat Lover

By Knox Burger

In the beginning of the grisly (but ultimately rather touching) story that follows by Knox Burger, the narrator warns us: "The story is about a cat, and if you are a wildly dedicated cat lover, I suggest you do not read it."

Maybe you should *not,* particularly if you are easily upset.

But we suspect that you'll go ahead anyway. . . .

As the fiction editor of *Collier's* in the 1950's, Knox Burger published early stories by Ray Bradbury and the very first fiction of Jack Finney and Kurt Vonnegut. He was a correspondent in the Pacific during World War II, a book editor in the 1960's, and has operated his own literary agency in New York since 1970.

I met Harrington only once, and somehow I don't expect our paths to cross again.

For a year or so before our encounter, I'd heard his name in conversations with our mutual friend George Levy. In addition to George, Harrington and I had in common a cleaning lady named Lavinia, a tough, stringy old woman who was ruthlessly honest in her opinions as well as her personal habits. I have known George and Lavinia for many years, and have never had occasion to doubt anything either of them has ever told me. From them, I have pieced out the story about to be related—or that part of it I didn't witness myself. The story is about a cat, and if you are a wildly dedicated cat lover, I suggest you do not read it.

A bachelor, Harrington lived alone in a small ground-floor apartment in Greenwich Village. Everything I'd heard about him led me to believe he was a pretty cold fish whose only indulgence was cats.

And he was ostentatiously unsentimental about those. He didn't talk baby talk to them, or permit them to sleep on his bed. In the years he'd lived in the city he'd run through three cats, Inagain, Carrie Chapman and, finally, Finnigan. Lavinia had endured them all. Long before I met him, she used to talk to me about Harrington's cats, lamenting the furniture they'd scratched. She couldn't understand how a man otherwise so fastidious could be so unconcerned about his cat's shedding on his chairs and scratching the woodwork.

"Mistuh Harrington's slipcover's ruined," Lavinia would announce mournfully to me.

"Hardly noticeable," Harrington would insist to George Levy.

Carrie Chapman was a rather stupid, if pedigreed Persian. Harrington didn't look forward to her coming into heat, and his apprehension turned out to be justified. One night she escaped from his apartment, apparently through a window open no more than an inch and a half, and the next morning Harrington heard her keening apprehensively out in his rubbly little back yard. He peered out and saw her crouched beside the fence, surrounded by four neighborhood toms. He opened the kitchen window, and in she sprang.

But the worst had happened.

Finnigan was one of five. Harrington managed to give away the others, and Finnigan would have gone too, except that while he was still a kitten, Carrie Chapman came into heat again and left on another streetwalking expedition—this time never to return.

Finnigan's father failed to leave a mark on his appearance. The kitten had Carrie's luxuriant pinkish-orange fur, yellow eyes, and great thick bottlebrush of a tail. But where Carrie had been selfish and placid, Finnigan was lively and intelligent and crawling with charm.

He was knockkneed, and this gave him a funny chorusboy's walk. He loved to lie in a big wing chair facing the hearth of Harrington's little fireplace, blinking his eyes in a straight-faced parody of understanding as Harrington talked to him, raking the upholstery with the long claws of his forefeet. According to Lavinia, Finnigan had managed to run through two tough twill slipcovers before he was a year old.

Finnigan would submit to caresses from other people, with a taut, exaggerated air of patience; and he never purred, except when Harrington or Lavinia stroked him. Finnigan's favorite foods were cantaloupe melon and a cat food we shall call Brand X.

It was at the end of their second year together that Harrington noticed that Finnigan seemed uncomfortable. His ears would flatten back against his head, and he would move in a spavined, halting gait, as if his hips were broken and had been badly wired. Something inside was hurting, and his anger, his frustration, were evidenced in the querulous sound of his mewing. He stalked the little apartment in some anxious private search. His body would contract with shudders. One day Harrington saw blood on the newspapers in his box.

The veterinary kept nodding maddeningly as Harrington explained the cat's symptoms. Yes, he'd seen a good deal of the same trouble lately. "It's probably a condition called cystitis, caused by a deposit of stones in the bladder. Do you feed him a canned food called Brand X? . . . That's probably it. Too many bones. Calcium builds up and can't be absorbed. I'll catheterize the animal, but it's not a guarantee that the condition won't return. And sometimes it just goes away. But no more Brand X. Liver!"

Harrington lifted Finnigan out of his box.

"Organ meats! Kidney! No fish! No milk!"

Harrigan stroked Finnigan reassuringly as the cat gazed around the office with narrowed eyes.

"If the trouble recurs," the vet was saying, "the cat should be destroyed."

Harrington returned three days later to pick up Finnigan, who seemed quite chipper, and was obviously glad to see him.

Lavinia, who shopped for Harrington, bought fresh organ meats three or four times a week and received strict instructions not to feed Finnigan the prohibited foods.

But the symptoms returned in two weeks' time. Finnigan bled, and his eyes blinked in pain. He chased himself, with frantic, convulsive movements as he tried to bite at the hurt. He ate almost nothing, and all his charm and independence seemed to collapse inward. His strength failed. When he sat in his favorite chair by the fireplace and tried to sharpen his claws, his efforts were a travesty of his former prowess. The nap of the slipcover was hardly roughened.

Finnigan's eyes grew cloudy and hostile. He tried to hide himself in dark places. Another catheterization produced only temporary relief. Harrington took the cat to another vet, who gave it injections and received a bad scratch under his left eye.

The injections had no effect. Finnigan continued to decline. Harrington disliked having to leave him alone in the apartment during the days, and disliked having to return at night to find the cat hiding in a closet or under the bed, panting and miserable. Lavinia nearly refused to work in the apartment any longer, so dominated was it by the sick animal.

Harrington debated having the cat "put away," but the impersonality of that act made him recoil, and there were still occasions when Finnigan would make some shadow of an overture to him, and act as if he might get better. But he didn't, and as he declined, Harrington's nerves went to pieces.

He took Finnigan to the original vet one Saturday, but the cat was so violent and anguished on being left that Harrington put him back in the box and returned home.

That night, Finnigan's howling and panting seemed to be more desperate than ever, and Harrington realized that he was going to have to do something about it, all by himself, and right now.

He thought of chloroform, but he didn't know where he could get it at this hour, or how he'd go about administering it, or how long it took to have its effect. It occurred to him that New York was a hard place to kill an animal.

As he was running tapwater into his fifth tumbler of whiskey, the idea came to him, the simple, classical, obvious idea: How did you kill a cat? You drowned it. It would be over in seconds, and the emotional strain involved in doing it himself seemed somehow appropriate. Finnigan had been brave for weeks; certainly he himself could be brave for a minute or two. At a delicatessen around the corner he obtained a burlap sack. Returning with it to the apartment, he lifted Finnigan gently from the kitchen floor and carried him down to the basement. He set the cat down on the drainboard and ran a washtub full of cold water, high, up to the taps.

He held the sack open on the drainboard. Perhaps Finnigan thought it was a game, perhaps he was too sick to care, or perhaps he really knew, and wanted it to happen. At any rate, tail erect, eyes preternaturally bright, Finnigan walked into the mouth of the sack, as if to see whether that dark interior was where his pain and trouble lay.

Harrington closed the neck of the sack. Squeezing it as hard as he could, he plunged it into the tub. There was a terrible thrashing in the water. Harrington realized his eyes were closed, his teeth clenched, and that he was standing as far away from the tub as he was able to and still hold the dreadful burden under the water. He had no idea how long it was before the struggles subsided and he turned and looked down at the sack eddying limply in the tub. The water sloshed gently back and forth.

His right hand was stiff with the effort of his grip as he let slip the neck of the sack. The thought occurred to him then that he had made no plans to handle the remains. Perhaps he could get the body cremated. But right now he knew that he could not bear to touch or even look at what he had done. He started up the stairs two at a time, but halfway up the thought of that poor bagged body floating somewhere between the bottom of the tub and the water's surface drove him to turn and go down again.

Without looking, Harrington reached into the hateful water and pulled the plug. Then he went upstairs to his apartment.

It happened that I was sailing for Europe on business the next afternoon, and that night I was being dined and bon voyaged by the Levys. About one o'clock in the morning, as I was preparing to leave, their telephone rang, and after a quick, puzzled frown toward his wife, George answered it. It was Harrington, drunk as a lord, and filled with guilt and an overpowering need to tell someone what he'd done. This he did, at some length, to the accompaniment of a sympathetic obligato of reassuring sounds from George, who finally persuaded him to go to bed.

Shortly after my return from Europe, George called on me and asked if I'd like to accompany him on a visit to Harrington's apartment. I said I would.

Harrington turned out to be a rather shy, contained man of perhaps forty-five. His apartment was neat and pleasant, and I could detect the dedicated hand of Lavinia on the gleaming brass andirons of the fireplace and the rich lustre of the wide pine plank floors. I recognized the two comfortable-looking wing chairs on either side of the fireplace from the descriptions I'd gleaned from George and Lavinia. As I made a move toward the one on the left, Harrington raised a hand.

"Not that one, please. It's—Finnigan's."

I nodded in embarrassed sympathy, and sat down on the edge of a couch. My feeling was one of deference to an understandable idiosyncrasy: if a man wants to maintain a particular piece of furniture as a memorial to a dead pet, I feel its his own business.

"I just had it re-covered a month ago." Harrington seemed to speak with a kind of admiration as he rubbed a fussy hand over the slipcovered arm of the chair. "And it's fraying already. That animal's strength is amazing." He shook his head and disappeared into the kitchen to make drinks.

As Harrington left the room, George and I looked at each other rather oddly. Then he rose to examine the cat's chair. His eyebrows went up as he bent over the arm, and he turned to beckon me. I went over and looked at the chair arm. It was scratched and worn, a sharp contrast to the crisp newness of the rest of the slipcover, which was marred only by the presence of a thin matting of fine reddish cat hairs on the seat.

"What the hell?" I said. "I thought he'd drowned it." And Lavinia wouldn't allow all this hair, I thought.

"Maybe he's got another one," George said. "But he mentioned Finnigan by *name* just then. Shh, here he comes."

"I gather you've heard about my cat," Harrington said to me as he entered the room and set the drinks down on a coffee table.

I told him I had, and that I sympathized.

"I thought I'd lost him there for a while," he said.

It was not an easy remark to respond to. I looked at George.

"Nick's been away in Europe," George explained. "As a matter of fact, the night before he sailed he was at my house. It was the night you phoned, after you'd—done it."

Harrington shook his head reminiscently.

"You did drown him, didn't you?" I'm sure I sounded rather dubious.

A small, mirthless grin showed itself on Harrington's face. "I did and I didn't. You see, it didn't work."

I looked at George; his face was curiously watchful.

"You mean he recovered?"

"Oh yes. Hasn't our Lavinia told you? Physically he's in fine health."

I shook my head and explained I'd only just returned and hadn't gotten around to calling Lavinia yet.

"Oh, well, then you don't know the most dramatic part of the story. After I'd let the water out of the tub and telephoned the Levys, I went to bed. The next morning was Saturday. Usually I sleep late on Saturday, but I realized one of the other tenants might go down to the basement ahead of me, so I set my alarm for seven and drank myself to sleep. My God, the dreams! Guilt, pursuit, fear—a psychoanalyst's field day. Well, I got some sleep, and was up half an hour before the alarm rang. Still drunk and depressed, I went directly down to the basement.

"The sack lay, wet and flat, on the bottom of the tub. Shapeless. Empty . . ." (As he warmed to his story, I realized it had the practiced, professional tone of being an oft-told tale.) "I stood very still," he went on. "My first impulse was that I must have blacked out somehow, that I had already disposed of the body. But while I stood there, the whole scene of the night before came sharply to my mind.

"And right then I heard a sound, a thin, hideous sound that

made me think of a snake. I looked down. There was a damp spot at my feet. I stepped back. Finnigan was there, underneath the tubs, his pink hair gnarled and tufted where it had dried unlicked.'' Harrington passed a hand over his eyes. "It was terrible, dreadful. He lay without moving, his eyes slitted, his head raised a fraction of an inch from the cold concrete floor. As I looked at him, he made that awful sound again, a sort of hiss. I was horrified. The end of that ratty tail flicked infinitesimally against the floor, and his haunches tightened almost imperceptibly. I didn't know if he was gathering for a spring, or what.

"I turned and simply ran up the stairs. Lavinia was due that afternoon, and by the time she arrived I was so potted I could scarcely babble out what had, uh, happened.''

Harrington shook his head. "It took three days to coax Finnigan out of the basement. Lavinia finally did it. That was three months ago. I called on the vet, and told him what had happened, and a little while later I called him to report that the symptoms of the cystitis had cleared up entirely. The vet can't account for it. Sometimes the deposits in the bladder simply break up and dissolve away. It's possible, I suppose, that Finnigan's—uh, immersion was a factor in clearing up the condition, and that's some comfort for me, I suppose. But I haven't actually managed to *touch* the poor beast since that night. And I've never seen him really sound asleep, either. He just sits and stares at me . . .'' Harrington trailed off miserably.

"Where's the cat now?'' George asked him gently.

"Oh, probably out in the back yard. He shows no inclination to run away, and I feel it's hardly right to try to find another home for him. He's really quite alienated from the *pet* status by now. It's as if he were on earth for the sole purpose of hating me. We sit by the fire, and he's very decorative still, with his great tail swishing back and forth. And I can be *positive* he's dozing, but when I look directly at him, those big yellow eyes are staring right into mine. And if I make an overture toward him, Finnigan hisses or backs away . . .'' Harrington sighed and rose. He signalled us to follow him out to the kitchen.

"He has access to the back yard,'' he said, indicating a hinged wooden panel in place of one of the panes in the window over the sink. Pushing the panel out, he leaned toward the opening. *"Puss, Puss, Puss?''* he called. In a moment he let the panel fall back into place. "No use. Of course, I'll never have another cat in here. He's a complete loner by now."

We returned to the living room. "I'm sorry you couldn't see him. Lovely animal, even if he is poor company. And he's still young. There's no reason to think he won't live a long, long time." Harrington dug the heels of his hands into his eyes, as if to rub out the cat's existence.

And it was on that note that George and I said our good-byes.

A few days later, in my apartment, I was watching Lavinia dust books. I told her I'd met Mr. Harrington, and that he'd told me what happened after he'd tried to drown his cat.

"What was that?" Lavinia asked me.

"Why, that the cat recovered, and that he's pretty difficult to live with, pretty bitter."

"You see that cat?" Lavinia asked me, doggedly polishing backstraps.

I said I hadn't.

"Mister B., that cat ain't bitter about *nobody* no more. That cat ain't *there*. I found that cat in the tub, and I th'ew the carcass right out into the garbage. If Mr. Harrin'ton want to go aroun' croonin' to that poor dead thing, and puttin' out livers and lights into little dishes . . ."

"But Lavinia," I interrupted. "I was there. I saw the big wing chair. The slipcover looked new—and Mr. Harrington *said* it was—"(Lavinia nodded.) "—and yet the arm was almost in tatters. And the seat was covered with—"

"I don't bother that chair, and it don't bother me." Lavinia seemed quite agitated. "That's the deadest, drownedest cat I ever see. Ain't *no* cat in that house. You say they's cat hairs, scratch marks, on the new cover for Finnigan's chair. I say my church don' teach nothin' about ghost cats—an' I'm much too old to be fixin' to find out now."

I myself am not nearly so definite about which reality I believe in; as Harrington said, however, Finnigan does seem destined—one way or another—to live a long, long time.

Jade Blue

By Edward Bryant

Multiple Nebula-winner Edward Bryant became a full-time writer in 1969, and over the past fourteen years has established himself as one of the most popular and respected writers of his generation. Bryant's stories have appeared everywhere from *Orbit* to *National Lampoon* to *Penthouse,* including almost all of the SF magazines and anthologies. His books include the well-known *Cinnabar* (either a collection of short stories or a "mosaic novel," depending on your own definition), *Phoenix Without Ashes,* a novelization of a television script by Harlan Ellison, three acclaimed short-story collections, *Among the Dead, Wyoming Sun*, and *Particle Theory*, and, as editor, the anthology *2076: The American Tricentennial*.

The story that follows takes place in Cinnabar, Bryant's fabulous Victorian city of the far future, a glittering *fin de siècle* world peopled by immortals and simulacra and rococo statues that nod as you pass, a paradoxical, perfumed world of manners and refinement and sudden brutality, a place where machines bend time, and dreams—and nightmares—can come true.

There, in Cinnabar, you will meet one of Bryant's most engaging and memorable characters, the catmother Jade Blue, the only one who might be able to save a small boy from the vampiric shadow-creatures of his dreams. . . .

What? You don't *know* what a catmother is?

Read on. . . .

"And this," said Timnath Obregon, "is the device I have invented to edit time."

The quartet of blurred and faded ladies from the Craterside Park Circle of Aesthetes made appreciative sounds; the whisper of a dry wind riffling the plates of a long-out-of-print art folio.

"Time itself."

"Fascinating, yes."

"Quite."

The fourth lady said nothing, but pursed wrinkled lips. She fixed the inventor in a coquettish gaze. Obregon averted his eyes. How, he wondered, did he deserve to be appreciated in this fashion? He had begun to wish the ladies would leave him to his laboratory.

"Dear Mr. Obregon," said the hitherto silent one. "You have no idea how much we appeciate the opportunity to visit your laboratory. This district of Cinnabar was growing tedious. It is so refreshing to encounter an eminent personality such as yourself."

Obregon's smile was strained. "I thank you, but my fame may be highly transitory."

Four faces were enraptured.

"My APE—" The inventor took a cue from the concert of rising eyebrows. "Ah, that's my none-too-clever acronym for the artificial probability enhancer. My device seems on the brink of being invented simultaneously—or worse, first—by a competitor at the Tancarae Institute. One Dr. Sebastian Le Goff."

"Then this machine is not yet, um, fully invented?"

"Not fully developed. No, I'm afraid not." Obregon thought he heard one of the ladies *tsking*, an action he had previously believed only a literary invention. "But it's very, very close to completion," he hastened to say. "Here, let me show you. I can't offer a full demonstration, of course, but—" He smiled winningly.

Obregon seated himself before the floor-to-ceiling crystal pillar which was the APE. He placed his hands on a brushed-metal console. "These are the controls. The keyboard is for the programming of probability changes." He stabbed the panel with an index finger; the crystal pillar glowed fluorescent orange. "The device is powered inductively by the vortical time streams which converge in the center of Cinnabar." His finger darted again and the pillar resumed its transparency. "For now I'm afraid that's all I can show you."

"Very pretty, though."

"I think blue would be so much more attractive."

"I found the most cunning sapphire curtain material yesterday."

"Tea would be marvelous, Mr. Obregon."

"Please, ladies. Call me Timnath." The inventor walked to a tangle of plastic tubing on an antiseptic counter. "I'm an habitual tea drinker, so I installed this instant brewing apparatus." He slid a white panel aside and removed five delicate double-handled cups. "The blend for today is black dragon pekoe. Satisfactory with everyone?"

Nodding of heads; brittle rustle of dying leaves.

"Cream and sugar?"

The tall one: "Goat cream, please."

The short one: "Two sugars, please."

The most indistinct one: "Nothing, thank you."

The flirtatious one: "Mother's milk, if you would."

Obregon punched out the correct combinations on the tea-maker's panel and rotated the cups under the spigot.

From behind him one of the ladies said, "Timnath, what will you do with your machine?"

Obregon hesitated. "I'm not sure, really. I've always rather liked the way things are. But I've invented a way of changing them. Maybe it's a matter of curiosity."

Then he turned and distributed the tea. They sat and sipped and talked of science and the arts.

"I firmly believe," said the inventor, "that science *is* an art."

"Yes," said the flirtatious lady. "I gather that you pay little attention to either the practical or commercial applications of technology." She smiled at him from behind steepled fingers.

"Quite so. Many at the Institute call me a dilettante."

The tall lady said, "I believe it's time to go. Timnath, we thank you for allowing us to impose. It has been a pleasure." She dashed her teacup to the tile floor. Her companions followed suit.

Startled by their abruptness, Obregon almost forgot to smash his own nearly empty cup. He stood politely as the ladies filed past him to the door. Their postures were strangely alike; each in her brown dress reminded him of the resurrectronic cassowaries he admired at the Natural History Club.

"A pleasure," repeated the tall lady.

"Quite." (The short one.)

Exit the flirt. "Perhaps I'll be seeing you again soon?" Her gaze lingered and Obregon looked aside, mumbling some pleasantry.

The fourth lady, the one whose features had not seemed to jell, paused in the doorway. She folded her arms so that the hands tucked into her armpits. She jumped up and down, flapping her truncated limbs. "Scraw! Scraw!" The soft door whuffed shut.

Taken aback, Obregon felt the need for another cup of tea and he sat down. On the table a small black cylinder stood on end. It could have been a tube of lip-salve. Apparently it had been forgotten by one of his guests. Curious, he picked it up. It was very light. He unscrewed one end; the cylinder was empty. Obregon raised the object to his nose. There was the distinct acrid tang of silver iodide emulsion.

"It appears," said Obregon softly, "to be an empty film cannister."

A child's scream in a child's night. A purring, enfolding comfort. A loneliness of nightmares and the waking world and the indistinct borderland. A feline reassurance.

"Don't cry, baby. I'll hold you close and rock you."

George buried his face in the soft blue fur which blotted his tears. "Jade Blue, I love you."

"I know," said the catmother softly. "I love you too. Now sleep."

"I can't," George said. "They'll find me again." His voice rose in pitch and his body moved restlessly; he clutched at Jade Blue's warm flank. "They'll get me in the shadows, and some will hold me down, and the one will reach for—"

"Dreams," said Jade Blue. "They can't hurt you." Feeling inside her the lie. Her fingerpads caressed the boy's head and drew it close again.

"I'm afraid." George's voice was distantly hysterical.

The governess guided the boy's head. "Drink now." His lips found the rough nipple and sucked instinctively. Her milk soothed, gently narcotic, and he swallowed slowly. "Jade Blue," the whisper was nearly inaudible. "I love you." The boy's body began to relax.

Jade Blue rocked him slowly, carefully wiping away the thin trickle of milk from one corner of his mouth, then lay down and cuddled the boy against her. After a time she also slept.

And awoke, night-wary. She was alone. With an angry snarl, quickly clipped off, she struggled from the bed. Jade Blue extended all her senses and caught a subtle scent of fear, a soft rub of something limp on flagstones, the quick flash of shadow on shadow.

A black, vaguely anthropomorphic shape moved in the darkness of the doorway. There were words, but they were so soft as to seem exhaled rather than spoken: "Forget it, pussy." A mouth gaped and grinned. "He's ours, cat."

Jade Blue screamed and leaped with claws outthrust. The shadow figure did not move; it squeaked and giggled as the catmother tore it apart. Great portions of shadowstuff, light as ash, flew about the room. The mocking laughter faded.

She paused in the doorway, flanks heaving, sucking in breath. Her wide, pupilless eyes strained to intercept the available light. Sharp-pointed ears tilted forward. The enormous house, very quiet; except—

Jade Blue padded swiftly down the hall, easily threading the irregular masses of inert sculpture. She ran silently, but in her mind:

Stupid cat! That shadow was a decoy, a diversion.
Foolish woman! The boy is my trust.
Find him. If anything has happened to him, I will be
punished.
If anything has happened to him, I shall kill myself.
A sound. The game room.
They couldn't have taken him far.
That bitch Merreile! I could tear out her throat.
How could she do it to him?
Close now. Quietly.

The double doors of the game room stood ajar. Jade Blue
slipped between their baroquely carved edges. The room was
large and echoing with the paraphernalia of childhood: glaze-
eyed hobbyhorses, infinite shelves of half-assembled model
kits, ranks of books and tapes and dot-cases, balls, mallets,
frayed creatures spilling stuffing, instruments of torture, gam-
ing boards, and an infrared spectrometer. The catmother
moved carefully through George's labyrinth of memories.

In a cleared space in the far end she found him. George lay
on his back, spread-eagled, straining weakly against intangible
fetters. Around him flocked the moving shadows, dark suc-
cubus-shapes. One of them crouched low over the boy and
brushed shadow lips around flesh.

George's mouth moved and he mewed weakly, like a kitten.
He raised his head and stared past the shadows at Jade Blue.

The catmother resisted her first berserker reaction. Instead
she stepped quickly to the near wall and found the lighting
panel. She pressed a square, and dim illumination glowed
from the walls; pressed harder and the light brightened, then
seared. Proper shadows vanished. The moving shadow creatures raveled like poorly woven fabric and were gone. Jade
Blue felt an ache beginning in her retinas and dimmed the light
to a bearable level.

On the floor George was semiconscious. Jade Blue picked
him up easily. His eyes were open, their movements rapid and
random, but he was seeing nothing. Jade Blue cradled the boy
close and walked down the long hallways to their bedroom.

George was dreamless the remainder of the long night.
Once, closer to wakening, he stirred and lightly touched
Jade Blue's breasts. "Kitty, kitty," he said. "Nice kitty."
Friendlier shadows closed about them both until morning.

• • •

When George awoke he felt a coarse grade of sand abrade the inside of his eyelids. He rubbed with his fists, but the sensation lingered. His mouth was dry. George experimentally licked the roof of his mouth; it felt like textured plastic. There was no taste. He stretched, winced, joints aching. The syndrome was familiar; it was the residue of bad dreams.

"I'm hungry." He reclined against crumpled blue stain. A seed of querulousness, "I'm hungry." Still no response. "Jade Blue?" He was hungry, and a bit lonely. The two conditions were complementary in George, and both omnipresent.

George swung his legs off the bed. "Cold!" He drew on the pair of plush slippers; then, otherwise naked, he walked into the hall.

Sculptures in various stages of awakening nodded at George as he passed. The stylization of David yawned and scratched its crotch. " 'Morning, George."

"Good morning, David."

The replica of a Third Cycle odalisque ignored him as usual.

"Bitch," George mumbled.

"Mommy's boy," mocked the statue of Victory Rampant.

George ignored her and hurried past.

The abstract Pranksters Group tried to cheer him up, but failed miserably.

"Just shut up," said George. "All of you."

Eventually the sculptures were left behind and George walked down a paneled hallway.

The hall finally described a klein turn, twisted in upon itself, and exited into the laboratory of Timnath Obregon.

Luminous pearl walls funneled him toward the half-open door. George saw a quick swirl of lab smock. He was suddenly conscious of the silence of his steps. He knew he should announce himself. But then he overheard the dialogue:

"If his parents would come home, that might help." The voice was husky, the vowels drawn out. Jade Blue.

"Not a chance," said Obregon's tenor. "They're too close to City Center by now. I couldn't even begin to count the subjective years before they'll be back."

George waited outside the doorway and listened.

Jade Blue's voice complained. "Well, couldn't they have

found a better time for a second honeymoon? Or third, or fourth, or whatever.''

A verbal shrug. ''They are, after all, researchers with a curious bent. And the wonders which lie closer to the center of Cinnabar are legendary. I can't blame them for their excursion. They *had* lived in this family group a rather long time.''

''Oh shit, you idiot human! You're rationalizing.''

''Not entirely. George's mother and father are sentients. They have a right to their own life.''

''They also have responsibilities.'' Pause. ''Merreile. That fathersucking little—''

''They couldn't have known when they hired her, Jade Blue. Her, um, peculiarities didn't become apparent until she had been George's governess for several months. Even then, no one knew the ultimate results.''

''No one knew! No one cared, you mean.''

''That's a bit harsh, Jade—''

''Listen, you pale imitation of an open mind. Can't you see? They're the most selfish people alive. They want to take nothing from themselves, give nothing to their son.''

Silence for a few seconds.

Jade Blue again: ''You're a kind man, but so damned obtuse!''

''I'm quite fond of George,'' said the inventor.

''And I also. I love him as one of my own. It's too bad his own parents don't.''

In the hallway George was caught in an ambivalence of emotion. He missed his parents horribly. But he also loved Jade Blue. So he began to cry.

Obregon tinkered with a worms' warren of platinum filaments.

Jade Blue paced the interior of the laboratory and wished she could switch her vestigial tail.

George finished his milk and licked the last cookie crumb from his palm.

A large raven flapped lazily through a window in the far end of the lab. ''Scraw! Scraw!''

''Ha!'' The inventor snapped his fingers and glistening panes slid into place; the doors shut; the room was sealed. Apparently confused, the raven fluttered in a tight circle, screaming in hoarse echoes.

"Jade, get the boy down!" Obregon reached under the APE's console and came up with a cocked and loaded crossbow. The bird saw the weapon, snap-rolled into a turn and dive, darted for the closest window. It struck the pane and rebounded.

George let Jade Blue pull him down under one of the lab tables.

Wings beat furiously as the raven caromed off a wall, attempting evasive action. Obregon coolly aimed the crossbow and squeezed the trigger. The short square-headed quarrel passed completely through the raven and embedded itself in the ceiling. The bird, wings frozen in mid-flap, cartwheeled through the air and struck the floor at Obregon's feet. Stray black feathers autumnleafed to the floor.

The inventor gingerly toed the body; no movement. "Fool. Such underestimation." He turned to Jade Blue and his nephew, who were extracting themselves from beneath the table. "Perhaps I'm less distracted than you charge."

The catmother licked delicately at her rumpled blue fur. "Care to explain all this?"

Obregon picked up the body of the raven with the air of a man lifting a package of particularly fulsome garbage. "Simulacrum," he said. "A construct. If I dissected it properly I'd discover a quite sophisticated surveillance and recording system." He caught Jade Blue's unblinking green eyes. "It's a spy, you see." He dropped the carcass into the disposer, where it vanished in a golden flare and the transitory odor of well-done meat.

"It was big," said George.

"Good observation. Wingspread of at least two meters. That's larger than any natural raven."

"Who," asked Jade Blue, "is spying?"

"A competitor, fellow named Le Goff, a man of no certain ethics and fewer scruples. A day ago he brought his spies here to check the progress of my new invention. It was all done very clumsily so that I'd notice. Le Goff is worse than a mere thief. He mocks me." Obregon gestured toward the artificial probability enhancer.

"It's *that* he wishes to complete before I do."

"A crystal pillar?" said Jade Blue. "How marvelous."

"Quiet, cat. My machine can edit time. I will be able to alter the present by modifying the past."

"Is that all it does?"

Obregon seemed disgusted. "In my own home I don't need mockery."

"Sorry. You sounded pompous."

The inventor forced a laugh. "I suppose so. It's Le Goff who has driven me to that. All I've ever wanted was to be left in peace to work my theories. Now I feel I'm being forced into some sort of confrontation."

"And competition?"

Obregon nodded. "Just why, I don't know. I worked with Le Goff for years at the Institute. He was always a man of obscure motives."

"You're a good shot," said George.

Obregon self-consciously set the crossbow on the console. "It's a hobby. I'd only practiced with stationary targets before."

"Can I try it?"

"I think you're probably too small. It takes a great deal of strength to cock the bow."

"I'm not too small to pull the trigger."

"No," said Obregon. "You're not." He smiled. "After lunch we'll go out to the range. I'll let you shoot."

"Can I shoot a bird?"

"No, not a live one. I'll have some simulacrae made up."

"Timnath," said Jade Blue. "I don't suppose— No, probably not."

"What."

"Your machine. It can't change dreams."

Mother, Father, help me I don't want the dreams any more. Just the warm black that's all. Mother? Father? Why did you go when will you come back? You leave me left me make me hurt.

Uncle Timnath, get them bring them back. Tell them I hurt I need. Make them love me.

Jade Blue, rock me hold me love me bring them back now. No no don't touch me there you're like Merreile I don't want more bad dreams don't hurt don't—

And Merreile would come into his bedroom each evening to take him from his toys and prepare him for bed. She would undress him slowly and slip the nightshirt over his head, then sit cross-legged at the foot of the bed while he lay back against the pillow.

"A story before sleeping? Of course, my love. Shall I tell again of the vampires?

"Do you remember my last telling, love? No? Perhaps I caused you to forget." And she would smile, showing the bands of scarlet cartilage where most people had teeth.

"Once upon a time, there was a little boy, much like you, who lived in an enormous old house. He was alone there, except for his parents and his loving governess.

"Oh, quite true that there were vampires hiding in the attic, but they weren't much like living creatures at all. They seldom ventured from the attic and the boy was never allowed to go there. His parents had forbidden him, despite the fact that the attic was filled with all manner of interesting and enjoyable things.

"The boy's curiosity grew and grew until one night he slipped out of his room and quietly climbed the stairs to the attic. At the top of the flight he paused, remembering his parents' warning. Then he recalled what he had heard about the strange treasures that lay within. He knew that warnings come from dull people and should be ignored. That barriers are made to be crossed. And then he opened the attic door.

"Inside were rows of tables stacked high with every sort of game and toy imaginable. Between were smaller tables laden with candy and cakes and pitchers of delicious drink. The boy was never happier.

"At that moment the vampires came out to play. They looked much like you and me, except that they were black and very quiet and just as thin as shadows.

"They crowded around the boy and whispered to him to come join their games. They loved the boy very much, because people came so seldom to the attic to visit. They were very honest (for folk so thin cannot hold lies) and the boy knew how silly his parents' warnings had been. Then they went off to the magic lands in the far end of the attic and played for hours and hours.

"What games, darling? I will show you."

And then Merreile would switch off the light and reach for him.

No, it can't change dreams, Timnath had said, musing. Then, looking through the catmother's eyes as though jade were glass, he said, *Give me time; I must think on it.*

They sat and talked in the blue bedroom.

"Did you ever have children like me?" George hugged his drawn-up knees.

"Not like you."

"I mean, were they kittens, or more like babies?"

"Both if you like. Neither." Her voice was neutral.

"You're not playing fair. Answer me." The child's voice was ancient, petulant from long practice.

"What do you want to know?"

George's fists beat a rapid tattoo on his knees. "Your children, what were they like? I want to know what happened to them."

Silence for a while. Small wrinkles under Jade Blue's lip, as though she held something bitter in her mouth. "They were never like anything."

"I don't understand."

"Because they *weren't*. They came from Terminex the computer. They lived in him and died in him; he placed the bright images in my brain."

George sat straighter; this was better than a bedtime story. "But why?"

"I'm the perfect governess. My maternal instincts are augmented. I've hostages in my mind." Each word was perfectly cut with gemstone edges.

Petulance softened to a child's compassion. "It makes you very sad."

"Sometimes."

"When I'm sad I cry."

"I don't," said Jade Blue. "I can't cry."

"I'll be your son," said George.

The hall of diurnal statues was still. Jade Blue prowled the shadows, seeking the slight sounds and odors and temperature differentials. The encroaching minutes frustrated and made her frantic. The many nights of sleepless watch—and the eventual betrayal by her body. Again she looked for a lost child.

Not in the game room this time; the hobbyhorses grinned vacantly.

Nor in the twenty gray parlors where George's ancestors

kept an embalmed and silent vigil from their wall niches.

Nor in the attic, dusty and spiderwebbed.

Not in the dining hall, arboretum, kitchens, aquatorium, library, observatory, family rooms, or linen closets.

Not—Jade Blue ran down the oak hallway and the minute signs vindicated her caprice. She ran faster and when she hurled herself into the corner which kleined into the approach to Timnath Obregon's laboratory, her stomach turned queasily.

The door slid open at a touch. The lab was dimly illuminated by the distorted yellow lights of Cinnabar. Several things occurred at once:

—In front of her, a startled figure looked up from the console of Obregon's APE. A reeled measuring tape dropped and clattered on tile.

—Across the lab a group of capering shadow figures stopped the act they were committing on George's prone body and looked toward the door.

—A screeching bird-shape flapped down from the dark ceiling and struck at Jade Blue's eyes.

The catmother ducked and felt claws cut harmless runnels through fur. She rolled onto her back and lashed out, her own claws extended. She snagged something heavy that screamed and buffeted her face with feathered wings. She knew she could kill it.

Until the booted foot came down on her throat and Jade Blue looked up past the still-struggling bird-thing at whoever had been examining Obregon's invention. "Sorry," said the man, and pressed harder.

"George!" Her voice was shrill, strangled. "Help." And then the boot was too heavy to let by any words at all. The darkness thickened intolerably.

The pressure stopped. Jade Blue could not see, but—painfully—she could again breathe. She could hear, but she didn't know what the noises were. There were bright lights and Timnath's concerned face, and arms lifting her from the floor. There was warm tea and honey poured into a saucer. George was hugging her and his tears put salt in the tea.

Jade Blue rubbed her throat gingerly and sat up; she realized she was on a white lab table. On the floor a little way from the table was an ugly mixture of feathers and wet red flesh. Something almost unrecognizable as a man took a ragged breath.

"Sebastian," said Timnath, kneeling beside the body. "My dear friend." He was crying.

"Scraw!" said the dying man; and died.

"Did you kill him?" said Jade Blue, her voice hoarse.

"No, the shadows did."

"How?"

"Unpleasantly." Timnath snapped his fingers twice and the glittering labrats scuttled out from the walls to clean up the mess.

"Are you all right?" George stood very close to his governess. He was shivering. "I tried to help you."

"I think you did help me. We're all alive."

"He did, and we are," said Timnath. "For once, George's creations were an aid rather than a hindrance."

"I still want you to do something with your machine," said Jade Blue.

Timnath looked sadly down at the body of Sebastian Le Goff. "We have time."

Time progressed helically, and one day Timnath pronounced his invention ready. He called George and Jade Blue to the laboratory. "Ready?" he said, pressing the button which would turn on the machine.

"I don't know," said George, half hiding behind Jade Blue. "I'm not sure what's happening."

"It will help him," said Jade Blue. "Do it."

"He may be lost to you," said Timnath.

George whimpered. "No."

"I love him enough," said the governess. "Do it."

The crystal pillar glowed bright orange. A fine hum cycled up beyond the auditory range. Timnath tapped on the keyboard: GEORGE'S DREAMS OF THE SHADOW VAMPIRES ARE AS NEVER WERE. MERREILE NEVER EXISTED. GEORGE IS OPTIMALLY HAPPY.

The inventor paused, then stabbed a special button: REVISE.

The crystal pillar glowed bright orange. A fine hum cycled up beyond the auditory range. Timnath taped on the keyboard: GEORGE'S DREAMS OF THE SHADOW VAM-

PIRES ARE AS NEVER WERE. MERREILE NEVER
EXISTED. GEORGE IS REASONABLY HAPPY.

Timnath   considered,   then   pushed   another   button:
ACTIVATE. "That's it," he said.

"Something's leaving us," Jade Blue whispered.

They heard a scuff of footsteps in the outer hall. Two
people walking. There was the clearing of a throat, a parental
cough.

"Who's there?" said Jade Blue, knowing.

Tom Cat

By Gary Jennings

What is this story about? Well . . . there are some stories that are difficult to synopsize. Take this one by Gary Jennings—a frequent contributor to *The Magazine of Fantasy & Science Fiction* and author of the recent best-seller *Aztecs*—about a cat named Puffpuss who some believe might become the President of the United States in a future incarnation. . . . Well, no, that's not quite right. Maybe it's about Swami Sri Ghosh and his crusade to secure a large donation for the Ghosh Almighty Pagoda . . . or about a girl named Alice Aforethought and the swinging life of the International Jet Set. . . . No, it's *really* about a young man named Tom whose rich aunt, who supports him, suddenly decides to leave all her money to her cat, see, and so he glues fur all over himself, and practices purring and playing with balls of string. . . .

Tom soon discovers that it takes a lot of practice to be a cat, and that there are some strange surprises in store for those who ply the feline trade. . . .

Well, anyway, read on . . . you'll see what we mean.

It isn't that Tom Welch has anything against work. One of his mottoes is "don't knock it till you try it," and work simply happens to be one of the things he's never tried. His rich Aunt Emma put him through the best schools and afterward settled on him an allowance that now enables him just *barely* to drone along with the Beautiful People of the Jet Set.

"But only in jet economy class, Aunt Emma," he complains, fidgeting about the drawing room of her Boston town house. "Just look at that dingy old Aston Martin of mine. Every other boy my age is driving a brand new Smetana-Moldau."

"Humph. How old are you now, young Thomas?"

"Forty-two, auntie."

"Shame on you. When your dear uncle was your age, he was forty-three."

"That's the dotty sort of answer I'm always getting," Tom laments to his friend Shelby Melancolli II, as they loll on the beach at Deauville.

"What did you say to that?" asks Shelby.

"What *could* I say? That I'll certainly be forty-three next year."

"Then you're plenty old enough," says his aunt, "to have learned to live within your allowance. I'm sure those Jet People of yours would understand."

"Jet *Set*, auntie. Beautiful People."

"Whatever they are. No, not another penny, young Thomas. If you spend it all now, there'll be nothing for you to inherit later."

"That's the dotty sort of answer I'm always getting," Tom grumbles to Shelby at Acapulco.

Shelby nods understandingly. "After all, it's not as if you'll be sponging off the old girl forever."

"Of course not," says Tom. "One of these days she'll die."

"And you'll inherit."

"I'm her nearest and dearest."

"Her only, I thought."

"Her only *and* her nearest and dearest. I do little things like reading aloud to her whenever I stop by. Since she turned ninety, her vision has gone quite dim."

"You're looking frightfully dissipated, young Thomas," says his aunt, peering narrowly.

"That's uncle's old moose head, auntie. I'm over here."

"Fidgeting about, as usual. Sit down and start reading. Jennings, bring us the latest literature."

"Yes, m'lady."

"I'll just settle here with my knitting. Very well, Thomas, you may begin."

"Yowr!"

"Aunt Emma, that's the cat you're knitting at."

"Oh, dear! My poor Puffpuss. Izzums hurt? Izzums angry?"

"Izzums gone, auntie, over the balustrade. That's your knitting you're fondling."

"Stop correcting your elders. Get on with the reading."

"Yes, Aunt Emma. Ahem. 'From what HIDDEN FOUNTAINS, you may ask, came the WISDOM of Amenhotep IV, Leonardo da Vinci, Francis Bacon? These illustrious Wise Men discovered and perfected certain *secret methods* of enhancing their MENTAL POWER. And those selfsame MYSTIC ARTS have been preserved from generation to generation, in the keeping of the Brotherhood of Rosicrucians . . .' " Tom pauses. "Rosicrucians, auntie? Have we finished with Inner Light Unfoldment already? Or was that Scientology last week?"

"Scientology," says Aunt Emma with a sniff, "is old hat. Too modern. The Rosicrucians make it clear that we must *plumb the past* for the source of TRUE KNOWLEDGE. My eyes are opened at last."

"Her eyes get opened about twice a month," says Tom to Shelby on Mykonos. "But still she holds conversations with the newel post."

"Aren't you afraid she'll really fall for one of these isms? Dotty old women often leave their fortunes to some swindling swami."

"Not Aunt Scrooge. She'd no more do that than leave everything to Puffpuss."

"Speaking of pussycats, here comes a girl you ought to meet. Alice, shake hands with Thos. Welch. Thos., let me make you acquainted with Alice Aforethought."

Tom's eyes bulge. "My, you look nice," he breathes huskily.

"I *am* nice," says Alice.

"She *is* nice, Aunt Emma, and I am smitten," says Tom. "But she is upper crust and I am unworthy of her. The only reason she consorts with me is that I'm a curiosity—the first non-millionaire she's ever met. It's so humiliating when I can't even charter a quick flight to Les Halles for onion soup at midnight."

"For the forty-second time, young Thomas, I will not increase your allowance. Not a penny."

"You never take me anywhere," pouts Alice.

"But, Alice, how can I?" says Tom. "I mean to say, you're *there*. What I mean, if any other girl wanted to go someplace, *this* is where she'd want to go. You're at Juan-les-Pins, at the poshest of posh parties. Just look around you. There's Wallie and the Duke. And over there's Liz and Dick, and Grace and Rainier, and Meg and Tony. And yonder is Gore and Myron and Myra, and Brigitte and Whatsisname. And here come our host and hostess. Hello, Jackie. *Kalimera,* Ari."

"Hello, Alice and Tommy."

"*Kalimera,* Alice and Tommy."

"There, Alice. What more could a girl want?"

"You never take me anywhere."

"Have you thought of supplementing your allowance, old boy?" asks Shelby at Bimini.

"How?"

"A spot of work, perhaps. Some gentlemanly occupation. Just as a stopgap until Aunt Emma is one with the ages."

"Work, eh? Well . . ." Tom sighs and squares his shoulders. "Don't knock it till you try it, I've always said."

So Tom sends out a number of seductively worded letters, all beginning, "Dear Sir: I am a graduate of Harverd . . ." but they bring him not so much as an offer of a minor vice-presidency.

"You never take me anywhere," pouts Alice at Marbella.

"Darling, look—out in the bay—J. Paul's yacht. Let's go with him on a cruise around the world."

"I've been there."

"All right," says Tom with sudden resolve. "I'll take you somewhere you've never been. To the altar. Alice, will you be mine?"

"Marry you?" says Alice, perking up. *"Quelle nouvelle.* No boy's ever propositioned me that way before."

"Proposed to you, Alice."

"I meant proposed. It's so quaint it's cute."

"Then you *will* be mine? Forsaking all others, cleaving only to one another, to have and to hold, for better or worse, in sickness and in health, for richer or poorer, that none shall put asunder, till death do us part?"

"I guess so."

"Those three little words!" cries Tom in joy. "They've made me the happiest man alive. Oh, Alice! We'll be married immediately after the funeral."

"Funeral?" squeaks Alice. "You mean we have to wait for your Aunt Enema to die?"

"Aunt Emma, dearest."

"Well, I won't! I'll marry someone else."

"She'll marry someone else!" Tom bleats brokenly. He staggers into Aunt Emma's drawing room, one arm flung across his eyes. "I have come home to Boston to Beacon Hill to die."

"To die is but a small step for a man," says an unfamiliar voice. "Upward or downward on the great stepladder of To Be."

Tom yanks his arm from his eyes and stares at a small, bald, grease-brown man enveloped in a voluminous fur coat that hangs clear to his grease-brown shoes, worn without socks. He looks like a wienie walking around in its bun.

"Ah, Thomas," says Aunt Emma. "This is Sir Sri Jawaharlal Ghosh."

"Pleased to meet you, Sir Sri."

"A pleasure. Yiss."

"Not Sir Sri, Thomas," his aunt corrects him. "The more respectful address is Swami Ghosh."

"A swami? Great Scott!"

"No, dear. Swamis come from India."

"Yiss."

"All very interesting, auntie, indeed it is. But listen, I must tell you this. I love Alice Aforethought and she loves me. We want to get married and settle down."

"Settle down?" his aunt says absently.

"Our own little rose-covered yacht. The patter of little deck shoes and all that. We simply can't do it on my pittance."

"Not another pitty," says Aunt Emma. "I mean penny. Now, swami, you were saying?"

"I was speaking, Mrs. Madam, of your estimable cat, Pisspiss."

"Puffpuss."

"Yiss, yiss. With application of the mystic influences, as was teached to your humble servant by an ancient hermit lama in Tibet, this cat's future is limitless. *Om mani padme hum*."

"Swami Ghosh, you have opened my eyes!" exults Aunt Emma. She turns and speaks to a floor lamp nearby. "Thomas, would you believe it? Puffpuss might someday be President of the United States."

"The cat?" says Shelby at Gstaad.

"Or a worm," says Tom. "If it lives an upstanding worm life it becomes, perhaps, a newt in its next incarnation. Then the newt, living and dying unsmirched, comes back as, oh, a wombat. And so on up the great stepladder of To Be until it culminates gloriously in, say, Spiro Agnew."

"And Puffpuss is destined for similar eminence."

"All that's necessary is for Aunt Emma to endow the Ghosh Almighty Pagoda. The whole congregation will then sit around chanting—*Oh, Manny!* or however it goes—to help Puffpuss lead a more meaningful cat life and forge on to bigger things."

"I warned you. A swindling swami."

"Yiss. I mean yes. He's utterly repulsive."

"Resembles a wienie, I believe you said."

"Walking around in its bun. He wears this nasty, fuzzy coat flayed from some Himalayan creature. An abdominal something."

"Abominable."

"You said it. And if I don't work fast, he'll be fleecing me as well. I must act before auntie is mulcted. But how?"

"Have you thought of giving Aunt Emma a leg up on that great stepladder of To Be?"

"Hm. Well, I've nothing actually *against* murder, of course. Don't knock it, I always say, until you try it. But before I do anything drastic, I'll have one last talk with her."

"Do that. Maybe she'll say something to put you in a killing rage."

"Aunt Emma, why is the music room swarming with stout old ladies in floral hats?"

"The girls from my club, young Thomas. They've come to hear the swami lecture on the Ghosh Almighty philosophy. Ah, so good to see you, Contessa Francesca."

"That's your begonia centerpiece, auntie."

"Hush, Thomas. The swami is about to speak."

"*Om,* dearly beloveds, *mani padme hum.* We shall begin the service with the ritual singing of our hymn, the Monsoon Moon Song . . ."

Moodily, Tom retreats to the drawing room, where he sits watching Puffpuss perform an elaborate toilet, until finally the service is over and Aunt Emma returns on the arm of Swami Ghosh.

"I'm glad you're still here, young Thomas. I have something to say that concerns both you and the swami."

"Yes, Aunt Emma?" says Tom apprehensively.

"Yiss, Mrs. Madam?" says the swami expectantly.

"Swami, the girls have just joined me in subscribing handsomely to the endowment of the Ghosh Almighty Pagoda. Thomas, your already ample allowance will continue as long as you live. The remainder of my estate—all six billion dollars—I have decided to bequeath to Puffpuss."

"*Auntie!*"

"*Madam!*"

"He will need campaign funds. Puffpuss-for-President posters and such. Pins."

"But Mrs. Madam, that may be ages hence!"

"Precisely. Long after you and my nephew have ceased to need or want the money, it will still be intact for Puffpuss."

"But—but—in the meantimes, Mrs. Madam, the Almighty Pagoda would be a fitting repository for it. Yiss, and a fitting home for the future President, too, through all his interim incarnations. I bespeech you, dear Mrs. Madam, not to be hasty!"

"My mind is made up, dear swami. And not another word from you either, Thomas. Thomas? Where is that boy?"

He is in the study across the hall, at the telephone, frantically dictating cablegrams to both Shelby and Alice: COME AT ONCE. When he departs, by way of the foyer, he finds Jennings helping a few remaining clubwomen into their several minks and sables, and Tom's eye falls on one fur as yet unclaimed.

"Jennings," says Aunt Emma some time later, "what is all that hysterical shouting in the foyer?"

"It's Sir Sri, m'lady. It seems one of the guests must have walked off by mistake with his bun. I mean his coat."

In a hotel room not far away, Tom is busy with glue pot, shears and fur, crooning while he works, "Swa-mee . . . *how*-I-love-ya, *how*-I-love-ya . . . my-y-y dear old swami . . ."

Alice, arriving breathless at the hotel, pounds on Tom's door, finds it unlocked and bursts in.

"I came as fast as I—*eek!*"

"Meow."

"Tommy! What on earth has happened?"

"Call me Puffpuss, dear."

"Tommy, was it burglars? You're bound hand and foot."

"Just got tangled in this yarn while I was playing with it. Untie me, sweetest. And do call me Puffpuss."

"Yes, P—uh, dear. What *are* you up to?"

"Practicing. Make a lap, darling." He bounds into it, curls up and says, "Tell me honestly now, how does this sound for purring? *Futterfutterfutterfutter . . .*"

"You sound awful. You look awful! You're shedding all over me!" She leaps distractedly from the chair, spilling Tom off her lap.

"Notice that, Alice? Landed on my four feet."

"Oh, this is terrible. This is tragic."

"Well, it's not easy. Takes a lot of close observation, assiduous practice to be a cat. I think I've got pretty good at it."

"I don't like it when you lick under your leg like that."

"Don't knock it till—ah, hello, Shelby. Meow."

"Shelby! Thank God you've come! Tommy thinks he's a cat!"

"You must be mistaken, old boy."

"I'm a cat okay. Look at me."

"I am. You must be mistaken, old boy."

"And I'm not just any cat. I am a cat named Puffpuss, to

whom my dotty Aunt Emma is about to bequeath six billion dollars.''

"Six bil— Damned if it *isn't* Puffpuss. Remember him well. Seen him many a time at dotty Aunt Emma's. Alice, you've never met Puffpuss. This is Puffpuss.''

"Of *course*. Puffpuss. Pwetty kitty, come to Awice. Awice pet you. Itchy kitchy kitchy.''

"Futterfutterfutterfutter . . .''

"He's pleased," says Shelby. "He's purring. Exactly the way I remember Puffpuss purring. That's Puffpuss, all right.''

"Now," says Tom, "I'm not," as he stands up and shucks off the disguise.

"Right. Now you're Tom. Explain things, Tom.''

"Dotty Aunt Emma's having her lawyer in tomorrow. Before he gets there, I do. I simply drop the real cat out the window—to you, Alice; give him a good home, dear—and I take his place. Auntie will accept me unquestioningly.''

"But there'll be other people," says Alice. "The lawyer and all.''

"Nobody contradicts Aunt Emma. Besides, I'll have substantiation. Shelby, you'll be the vet.''

"Check. I'll go now and start practicing my catside manner.''

"Do. And you, Alice, practice catching cats.''

"Thomas," says Aunt Emma, entering her drawing room just as Tom wheels around from the window. Outside there is a faint noise of "plump" and "oof!" in a girl's voice. "What are you doing up before noon?''

"Couldn't sleep, auntie. I was worried that someone ought to be watching over our future President.''

"How touching. Where is he, then?''

"Saw him in the study a moment ago. I'll send him in.''

Tom steps into the hall, steps into his disguise, calls out, "Here he comes now, auntie," and saunters back into the drawing room on all fours.

"Yes, there's my puzzums.''

Tom fawns against the old lady's legs while she reaches down to scratch his back. Then he stretches out beside her rocking chair, futterfuttering contentedly.

"Jennings, I heard the front bell. Is that Lawyer Kalbfuss?''

"No, m'lady. It's Sir Sri."

"Yiss." The swami oozes in, now wearing only a rather dirty dhoti. "I came to bespeech you again—" His eyes widen. "Dear Mrs. Madam, what is that?"

Tom lays back his ears and whiskers.

"Do you mean Puffpuss?"

"The cat? That is the cat? The same cat you had yesterday?"

"Of course. Do you suppose I change cats at whim?"

Tom bristles his fur and hisses.

"Puffpuss seems to have taken a slight dislike to you, Swami Ghosh," says Aunt Emma. She adds suspiciously, "You're not by any chance a Democrat?"

"Madam," says the swami, standing smally tall in his sockless shoes. "I am of the highest Indian caste. A Brahman."

"In Boston it's Brahmin."

"Something about this cat," says the swami, staring at Tom's fluffed-up fur, "*is* familiar. Yiss."

"If you came here just to addle me," says Aunt Emma, "my mind is made up."

"Surely so," says the swami hastily. "Only, dear Mrs. Madam, have we assured ourselfs that this cat has the *qualities* for the Presidentdom?"

"*You* assured *me*."

"*With* the proper guidings in the Ghosh Almighty principles. However, not yet having had that guidings, the cat appears phlegmatic. Has he ever, for instance, catched a mice? One would expect one's President—"

"Puffpuss is six years old. In human terms, that would be forty-two. You can hardly expect him to gambol like a kitten."

"Perhaps not, Mrs. Madam. But regard him. You have been rocking on his tail for five minutes, and he has not so much as—"

"Er—*yeowr!*" yelps Tom, coming suddenly alert and bounding away from the chair.

"He does sound a bit hoarse," says Aunt Emma worriedly.

Pausing only to glare tigerishly at the swami, Tom begins to gambol like a kitten. He pounces at the fringe of the rug, then bats at the tassels of a drapery.

"And now he seems quite frenetic. I wonder if he could be coming down with something. Thomas!"

Tom gambols out the door, stands up and sticks just his head back in. The swami jumps. "Yes, auntie?"

"Telephone Dr. Udderweiss to come and have a look at Puffpuss."

"Yes, auntie."

In the study, he dials Shelby and says, "Dr. Udderweiss, come at once. Oh, and meantime tell Alice to get me some mice."

"Aren't they feeding you, old boy?"

Tom gambols into the drawing room again, as Jennings and another gentleman arrive.

"Counselor Kalbfuss is here, m'lady."

The lawyer edges into the room, looking apprehensively at Tom gamboling behind him.

"Good morning, Kalbfuss. That's Puffpuss."

"That is the—er—heir? I thought, Emma, you said it was to be a cat."

"What does that look like? A canary?"

"Well, no."

"Meow."

"Bless my soul, it is a cat."

"Kalbfuss, it was you who *gave* me Puffpuss. To console me when my husband passed away."

"It was just a kitten then. I had no idea . . ."

Tom bounds into Aunt Emma's lap and begins playfully to undo her knitting.

"Puffpuss *has* been a great consolation to me. Now, in gratitude, I intend to provide for his future. Prepare the necessary papers, Kalbfuss. Jennings, you will witness my signature. Thomas, see who that is at the door. Get off my lap, Puffpuss, you're shedding. Thomas!"

"Just going, auntie," Tom calls back, as soon as he has gamboled out of the drawing room.

"From Miss Alice Aforethought," says a palsied, ancient messenger boy at the door. He hands Tom a gorgeously gift-wrapped Tiffany box.

"Why is this box squeaking?"

"Tiffany's finest first-water, flawless, blue-white mice, sir."

"Confound it, I wanted plain old gray house mice."

Haughty sniff. "Try Cartier's, sir."

Tom is fussing with various household fluids in the butler's pantry when the doorbell rings again.

"Emil Udderweiss, D.V.M.,'' says Shelby, wearing a monocle, a Van Dyke and a small round mirror perched on his forehead. "Why are you dyeing those mice?"

"Give me a minute to get upstairs, Shelby, and then you come."

Tom is again gamboling about the drawing room when Shelby sweeps grandly in and demands, "Is there a patient in the house?"

"Ah, Udderweiss,'' says Aunt Emma. "I called you to give a checkup—"

"How right you were. My superb medical intuition perceives that instantly. The poor dumb creature. Lost all its pelt, I see.'' Shelby strides to Swami Ghosh and lifts one of his eyelids. "Moribund. Terminal. Tragic.'' He picks up a telephone, dials swiftly and barks, "The wagon!"

"No, no, no,'' says Aunt Emma, as the swami backs terrified into a corner. "It was Puffpuss I wanted you to look at."

"To admire, you mean. Never saw a finer specimen of *Felis felis*. Just see how he gambols. Living all nine lives to the hilt."

"Do you really think so, doctor?"

"All cat, that cat. Observe, he's caught a mouse."

Tom drops it in the middle of the rug and looks proud.

"Odd,'' says the swami, still somewhat shaken but still unbowed. "This mice is wet. Something seems fishy here. Yiss."

"Fishy indeed!'' scoffs Shelby. "*Mus domesticus*. All mouse, that mouse."

"Thank you, Udderweiss,'' says Aunt Emma. "I'm so relieved about Puffpuss. Kalbfuss, let's get on with the paperwork."

"A moment, doctor,'' says the swami spitefully, peering into Shelby's little black bag. "I see no shots record for this cat. Are all his immunities up to date?"

"Hm. You have a point. One can always do with a shot."

"Yiss."

"*Fitzrowr!*"

"Hold his head, please, counselor.'' Shelby strides to the sideboard and dollops brandy into a snifter. "Force his jaws, Jennings."

"*Fitzr*—ulp."

"Not those kind of shot!'' rages the swami.

"Good for man or beast,'' says Shelby, taking one himself.

"Merciful heavens," says Lawyer Kalbfuss.

A siren sounds suddenly outside, and four burly men in white elbow into the room. "Isolation ward," says Shelby with a jerk of his head, and the four men bear the swami away kicking and screaming.

"Merciful heavens," says Aunt Emma.

"A shock, no doubt, madam. But thank Hippocrates you called me in time. A Himalayan form of hydrophobia, the abominable snowmania. You saw how he was foaming at the cat."

"Merciful heavens."

"Futterfutterfutterfutter . . . hic."

"You think it went well, then?" says Shelby some days later, at a secret meeting in the butler's pantry.

"Perfectly," says Tom. "The will is all signed, sealed and I am irrefutably recognized as Puffpuss. Kalbfuss had me put my pawprints on some of the papers."

"That's just what they made Swami Ghosh do."

"Who did?"

"The Bide-a-Wee Home & Clinic. He's up for adoption."

"We can't go on meeting like this, Tommy," says Alice, still later. "This fence hurts my—hurts me."

"I've told you, dear, auntie is a light sleeper. Whenever she wakes up she likes to look out and see me here serenading the moon. There she is at the window now. *Meowrrrooo*, moon."

"It's been months now, and we're no better off than before. It still looks like that old lady will outlive us all. We'll soon be too old to have kittens. I mean kids."

"We'll adopt Sir Sri."

"Be serious, Tommy!"

"Okay, we'll buy us a whole orphanage. We'll be rich, Alice!"

"When? I don't intend to spend the best years of my life straddling a back fence."

"There's auntie again. *Meowrrrooo*, moon."

Another window rattles up somewhere. "Shut up, you infernal feline!"

Whiz.

Thunk.

"Ow!"

"Sorry, Alice, I think that shoe was meant for me."

"This is too much! I can't endure any more!"

"Alice!"

"Farewell forever, you—you—infernal feline!"

"Hell hath no fury," sighs Shelby, still later, at Tom's fence, "like a woman."

"You don't mean—?"

"Yes. Alice has blown your cover. She's in there now, returning Puffpuss to the bosom of your aunt. You can't go home again."

Lights begin going on in every window of the house. "Your Aunt Emma is so indignant that she's even disowning the real Puffpuss. She's leaving everything to Jennings."

"Ya-*hoooo!*" comes an exuberant cry from indoors.

"That was Jennings."

"Oh, well," says Tom. "Can't win 'em all."

"You don't seem adequately dashed. Six billion dollars done and gone. Sweet Alice been and bolted."

"The fact is, there's someone else."

"Come now, old boy. In that getup how could you even have *met* someone else?"

"Here. On this very fence."

"You can't mean—?" Shelby is speechless.

"She's Siamese. They do say that Orientals make the best wives. Her name is Ah Sin."

"I say, old boy, this is letting down the side."

"Here she comes now. Isn't she smashing?"

Shelby goggles, speechless.

"Futterfutterfutterfutter . . ."

"Futterfutterfutterfutter . . ."

"But—but—old boy, how will you live? How will you support a family?"

"I'll become a cat burglar," Tom murmurs carelessly, as he and Ah Sin move off along the fence top, together into the moonset.

"Old boy!" calls Shelby, in one last appeal. "These mixed marriages never work!"

And back come Tom's last words, dim from the dark far distance. "Don't knock it till you try it . . ."

Sonya, Crane Wessleman, and Kittee

By Gene Wolfe

Cats have been providing love and companionship for people for thousands of years now, but in the future, when we have sophisticated genetic-engineering techniques at our disposal, might we not be tempted to . . . improve a bit on the classic formula?

The story that follows is about the desperation and isolation of ordinary people. It's about love, and loneliness . . . and a very special breed of cat.

Gene Wolfe is perceived by many critics to be one of the best—perhaps *the* best—SF and fantasy writers working today. His tetralogy *The Book of the New Sun*—consisting of *The Shadow of the Torturer, The Claw of the Conciliator, The Sword of the Lictor,* and *The Citadel of the Autauch*—has been hailed as a masterpiece, a seminal work, and is quite probably the standard against which subsequent science-fantasy books of the 1980's will be judged. *The Shadow of the Torturer* won the World Fantasy Award. *The Claw of the Conciliator* won the Nebula Award. Wolfe has also won a Nebula Award for his story "The Death of Doctor Island." His other books include *Peace, The Fifth Head of Cerberus,* and *The Devil in a Forest.* His short fiction has been collected in *The Island of Doctor Death and Other Stories and Other Stories* and *Gene Wolfe's Book of Days.*

The relation between Sonya and Crane Wessleman was an odd one, and might perhaps have been best described as a sort of suspended courtship, the courtship of a poor girl by a wealthy boy, if they had not both been quite old. I do not mean to say that they are old *now*. Now Sonya is about your age and Crane Wessleman is only a few years older, but they do not know one another. If they had, or so Sonya often thought, things might have been much different.

At the time I am speaking of every citizen of the United States received a certain guaranteed income, supplemented if there were children, and augmented somewhat if he or she worked in certain underpaid but necessary professions. It was a very large income indeed in the mouths of conservative politicians and insufficient to maintain life according to liberal politicans, but Sonya gave them both the lie. Sonya without children or augmentation lived upon this income, cleanly but not well. She was able to do this because she did not smoke, or attend any public entertainment that was not free, or use drugs, or drink except when Crane Wessleman poured her a small glass of one of his liqueurs. Then she would hold it up to the light to see if it were yellow or red or brown, and sniff it in a delicate and ladylike way, and roll a half teaspoon on her tongue until it was well mixed with her saliva, and then swallow it. She would go on exactly like this, over and over, until she had finished the glass, and when she had swallowed it all it would make her feel somewhat younger; not a great deal

younger, say about two years, but somewhat younger; she enjoyed that. She had been a very attractive girl, and a very
attractive woman. If you can imagine how Debbie Reynolds
will look when she attends the inauguration of John-John
Kennedy, you will about have her. With her income she rented
two rooms in a converted garage and kept them very clean.

Crane Wessleman met Sonya during that time when he still
used, occasionally, to leave his house. His former partner had
asked him to play bridge, and when he accepted had called a
friend, or (to be truthful) had his wife call the friend's wife,
to beg the name of an unattached woman of the correct age
who might make a fourth. A name had been given, a mistake
made, Sonya had been called instead, and by the time the partner's wife realized what had occurred Sonya had been nibbling
her petits fours and asking for sherry instead of tea. The
partner did not learn of his wife's error until both Crane
Wessleman and Sonya were gone, and Crane Wessleman never
learned of it. If he had, he would not have believed it. The
next time the former partner called, Crane Wessleman asked
rather pointedly if Sonya would be present.

She played well with him, perhaps because she was what
Harlan Ellison would call an empath—Harlan meaning she
gut-dug whether or not Crane Wessleman was going to make
the trick—or perhaps only because she had what is known as
card sense and the ability to make entertaining inconsequential
talk. The partner's wife said she was cute, and she was quite
skillful at flattery.

Then the partner's wife died of a brain malignancy; and the
partner, who had only remained where he was because of her,
retired to Bermuda; and Crane Wessleman stopped going out
at all and after a very short time seldom changed from his pajamas and dressing gown. Sonya thought that she had lost him
altogether.

Sonya had never formed the habit of protesting the decisions of fate, although once when she was much, much
younger she had assisted a male friend to distribute mimeo-
graphed handbills complaining of the indignity of death and
the excretory functions—a short girl with blond braids and
chino pants, you saw her—but that had been only a favor.
Whatever the handbills said, she accepted those things. She accepted losing Crane Wessleman too, but at night when she was
trying to go to sleep, she would sometimes think of Crane

Wessleman among The Things That Might Have Been. She
did not know that the partner's wife was dead or that the partner had moved to Bermuda. Nor did she know how they had
first gotten her name. She thought that she was not called
again because of something—a perfectly innocent thing which
everyone had forgotten in five minutes—she had said to the
partner's wife. She regretted it, and tried to devise ways, in the
event that she was ever asked again, of making up for it.

It was not merely that Crane Wessleman was rich and
widowed, although it was a great deal that. She liked him,
knowing happily and secretly as she did that he was hard to
like; and, deeper, there was the thought of something else: of
opening a new chapter, a wedding, flowers, a new last name, a
not dying as she was. And then four months after the last
game Crane Wessleman himself called her.

He asked her to have dinner with him, at his home; but he
asked in a way that made it clear he assumed she possessed
means of transportation of her own. It was to be in a week.

She borrowed, reluctantly and with difficulty, certain small
items of wearing apparel from distant friends, and when the
evening came she took a bus. You and I would have called it a
helicopter, you understand, but Sonya called it a bus, and the
company that operated it called it a bus, and most important,
the driver called it a bus and had the bus driver mentality,
which is not a helicopter pilot mentality at all. It was the
ascendant heir of those cheap wagons Boswell patronized in
Germany. Sonya rode for half because she had a Golden Age
card, and the driver resented that.

When she got off the bus she walked a considerable distance
to get to the house. She had never been there before, having
always met Crane Wessleman at the former partner's, and so
she did not know exactly where it was although she had looked
it up on a map. She checked the map from time to time as she
went along, stopping under the infrequent streetlights and
waving to the television cameras mounted on them so that if
the policeman happened to be looking at the time and saw her
he would know that she was all right.

Crane Wessleman's house was large, on a lot big enough to
be called an estate without anyone's smiling; the house set a
hundred yards back from the street. A Tudor house, as Sonya
remarked with some pleasure—but there was too much shrubbery, and it had been allowed to grow too large. Sonya

thought roses would be nicer, and as she came up the long
front walk she put pillar roses on the gas lantern posts Crane
Wessleman's dead wife had caused to be set along it. A brass
plate on the front door said:

> C. WESSLEMAN
> AND
> KITTEE

and when Sonya saw that she *knew*.

If it had not been for the long walk she would have turned
around right there and gone back down the path past the gas
lamps; but she was tired and her legs hurt, and perhaps she
would not really have gone back anyway. People like Sonya
are often quite tough underneath.

She rang the bell and Kittee opened the door. Sonya knew,
of course, that it was Kittee, but perhaps you or I might not.
We would have said that the door was opened by a tall, naked
girl who looked a good deal like Julie Newmar; a deep-
chested, broad-shouldered girl with high cheekbones and an
unexpressive face. Sonya had forgotten about Julie Newmar;
she knew that this was Kittee, and she disliked the thing, and
the name Crane Wessleman had given it with the whining
double *e* at the end. She said in a level, friendly voice, "Good
evening, Kittee. My name is Sonya. Would you like to smell
my fingers?" After a moment Kittee did smell her fingers, and
when Sonya stepped through the door Kittee moved out of the
way to let her in. Sonya closed the door herself and said,
"Take me to Master, Kittee," loudly enough, she hoped, for
Crane Wessleman to hear. Kittee walked away and Sonya
followed her, noticing that Kittee was not really completely
naked. She wore a garment like a short apron put on backward.

The house was large and dirty, although the air filtration
units would not allow it to be dusty. There was an odor Sonya
attributed to Kittee, and the remains of some of Crane
Wessleman's meals, plates with dried smears still on them, put
aside and forgotten.

Crane Wessleman had not dressed, but he had shaved and
wore a clean new robe and stockings as well as slippers. He
and Sonya chatted, and Sonya helped him unpack the meal he

had ordered for her and put it in the microwave oven. Kittee helped her set the table, and Crane Wessleman said proudly, "She's wonderful, isn't she." And Sonya answered, "Oh yes, and very beautiful. May I stroke her?" and ran her fingers through Kittee's soft yellow hair.

Then Crane Wessleman got out a copy of a monthly magazine called *Friends*, put out for people who owned them or were interested in buying, and sat beside Sonya as they ate and turned the pages for her, pointing out the ads of the best producers and reading some of the poetry put at the ends of the columns. "You don't know, really, what they were anymore," Crane Wessleman said. "Even the originators hardly know." Sonya looked at the naked girl and Crane Wessleman said, "I call her Kittee, but the germ plasm may have come from a gibbon or a dog. Look here."

Sonya looked, and he showed her a picture of what seemed to be a very handsome young man with high cheekbones and an unexpressive face. "Look at that smile," Crane Wessleman said, and Sonya did and noticed that the young man's lips were indeed drawn back slightly. "Kittee does that sometimes too," Crane Wessleman said. Sonya was looking at him instead of at Kittee, noticing how the fine lines had spread across his face and the way his hands shook.

After that Sonya came about once a week for a year. She learned the way perfectly, and the bus driver grew accustomed to her, and she invented a pet of her own, an ordinary imaginary chow dog, so that she could take a certain amount of leftover meat home.

The next to last time, Crane Wessleman pointed out another very handsome young man in *Friends*, a young man who cost a great deal more than Sonya's income for a year, and said, "After I die I am going to see to it that my executor buys one like this for Kittee. I want her to be happy." Then, Sonya felt, he looked at her in a most significant way; but the last time she went he seemed to have forgotten all about it and only showed Sonya a photograph he had taken of himself with Kittee sitting beside him very primly, and the remote control camera he had used, and told her how he had ordered it by mail.

The next week Crane Wessleman did not call at all, and when it was two days past the usual time Sonya tried to call him, but no one answered. Sonya got her purse, and boarded the bus, and searched the area around Crane Wessleman's front door until she found a key hidden under a stone beneath some of the shrubbery.

Crane Wessleman was dead, sitting in his favorite chair. He had been dead, Sonya decided, for several days, and Kittee had eaten a portion of his left leg. Sonya said aloud, "You must have been very hungry, weren't you, Kittee, locked in here with no one to feed you."

In the kitchen she found a package of frozen *mouton Sainte-Menebould*, and when it was warm she unwrapped it and set it on the dining-room table, calling, "Kittee! Kittee! Kittee!" and wondering all the time whether Crane Wessleman might not have left her a small legacy after all.

The Witch's Cat

By Manly Wade Wellman

Here's a lively and little-known story by Manly Wade Wellman about a home-loving cat who finds himself forced to be a
very reluctant familiar. . . .

Manly Wade Wellman sold his first fantasy story to *Weird
Tales* in 1927, and has kept right on selling novels and stories
without noticeable letup for the subsequent fifty-six years.
Although Wellman has published science fiction, he has had
his biggest impact within the fantasy genre, and is perceived by
many critics as one of the finest modern practitioners of the
"dark fantasy" or "weird fantasy" tale. As a fantasist,
Wellman is probably best known for his series of stories detail-
ing the strange adventures of "John the Minstrel" or "Silver
John," scary and vividly evocative tales set against the background of a ghost-and-demon-haunted rural Appalachia that,
in Wellman's hands, is as bizarre and beautiful as many
another writer's entirely imaginary fantasy world. The "Silver
John" stories have been collected in *Who Fears the Devil?*,
generally perceived as Wellman's best book; it is certainly his
most influential. In recent years, there have also been "Silver
John" novels as well: *The Old Gods Waken, After Dark, The
Lost and the Lurking,* and, most recently, *The Hanging
Stones*. Wellman's other short stories have been assembled in
the mammoth collection *Worse Things Waiting*, which won a
World Fantasy Award as the Best Anthology/Collection in
1975. In 1980, Wellman won another World Fantasy Award,
this one the prestigious Life Achievement Award.

Old Jael Bettiss, who lived in the hollow among the cypresses, was not a real witch.

It makes no difference that folk thought she was, and walked fearfully wide of her shadow. Nothing can be proved by the fact that she was as disgustingly ugly without as she was wicked within. It is quite irrelevant that evil was her study and profession and pleasure. She was no witch; she only pretended to be.

Jael Bettiss knew that all laws providing for the punishment of witches had been repealed, or at the least forgotten. As to being feared and hated, that was meat and drink to Jael Bettiss, living secretly alone in the hollow.

The house and the hollow belonged to a kindly old villager, who had been elected marshal and was too busy to look after his property. Because he was easy-going and perhaps a little daunted, he let Jael Bettiss live there rent-free. The house was no longer snug; the back of its roof was broken in, the eaves drooped slackly. At some time or other the place had been painted brown, before that with ivory black. Now both coats of color peeled away in huge flakes, making the clapboards seem scrofulous. The windows had been broken in every small, grubby pane, and mended with coarse brown paper, so that they were like cast and blurred eyes. Behind was the muddy, bramble-choked back yard, and behind that yawned the old quarry, now abandoned and full of black water. As for the inside—but few ever saw it.

Jael Bettiss did not like people to come into her house. She
always met callers on the old cracked doorstep, draped in a
cloak of shadowy black, with gray hair straggling, her nose as
hooked and sharp as the beak of a buzzard, her eyes filmy and
sore-looking, her wrinkle-bordered mouth always grinning
and showing her yellow, chisel-shaped teeth.

The near-by village was an old-fashioned place, with stone
flags instead of concrete for pavements, and the villagers were
the simplest of men and women. From them Jael Bettiss made
a fair living, by selling love philtres, or herbs to cure sickness,
or charms to ward off bad luck. When she wanted extra
money, she would wrap her old black cloak about her and,
tramping along a country road, would stop at a cowpen and
ask the farmer what he would do if his cows went dry. The
farmer, worried, usually came at dawn next day to her hollow
and bought a good-luck charm. Occasionally the cows would
go dry anyway, by accident of nature, and their owner would
pay more and more, until their milk returned to them.

Now and then, when Jael Bettiss came to the door, there
came with her the gaunt black cat, Gib.

Gib was not truly black, any more than Jael Bettiss was
truly a witch. He had been born with white markings at muzzle, chest and forepaws, so that he looked to be in full evening
dress. Left alone, he would have grown fat and fluffy. But
Jael Bettiss, who wanted a fearsome pet, kept all his white
spots smeared with thick soot, and underfed him to make him
look rakish and lean.

On the night of the full moon, she would drive poor Gib
from her door. He would wander to the village in search of
food, and would wail mournfully in the yards. Awakened
householders would angrily throw boots or pans or sticks of
kindling. Often Gib was hit, and his cries were sharpened by
pain. When that happened, Jael Bettiss took care to be seen
next morning with a bandage on head or wrist. Some of the
simplest villagers thought that Gib was really the old woman,
magically transformed. Her reputation grew, as did Gib's un-
popularity. But Gib did not deserve mistrust—like all cats, he
was a practical philosopher, who wanted to be comfortable
and quiet and dignified. At bottom, he was amiable. Like all
cats, too, he loved his home above all else; and the house in
the hollow, be it ever so humble and often cruel, was home. It
was unthinkable to him that he might live elsewhere.

In the village he had two friends—black-eyed John Frey, the storekeeper's son, who brought the mail to and from the county seat, and Ivy Hill, pretty blond daughter of the town marshal, the same town marshal who owned the hollow and let Jael Bettiss live in the old house. John Frey and Ivy Hill were so much in love with each other that they loved everything else, even black-stained, hungry Gib. He was grateful; if he had been able, he would have loved them in return. But his little heart had room for one devotion only, and that was given to the house in the hollow.

One day, Jael Bettiss slouched darkly into old Mr. Frey's store, and up to the counter that served for postoffice. Leering, she gave John Frey a letter. It was directed to a certain little-known publisher, asking for a certain little-known book. Several days later, she appeared again, received a parcel, and bore it to her home.

In her gloomy, secret parlor, she unwrapped her purchase. It was a small, drab volume, with no title on cover or back. Sitting at the rickety table, she began to read. All evening and most of the night she read, forgetting to give Gib his supper, though he sat hungrily at her feet.

At length, an hour before dawn, she finished. Laughing loudly and briefly, she turned her beak-nose toward the kerosene lamp on the table. From the book she read aloud two words. The lamp went out, though she had not blown at it. Jael Bettiss spoke one commanding word more, and the lamp flamed alight again.

"At last!" she cried out in shrill exultation, and grinned down at Gib. Her lips drew back from her yellow chisels of teeth. "At last!" she crowed again. "Why don't you speak to me, you little brute? . . . Why don't you, indeed?"

She asked that final question as though she had been suddenly inspired. Quickly she glanced through the back part of the book, howled with laughter over something she found there, then sprang up and scuttled like a big, filthy crab into the dark, windowless cell that was her kitchen. There she mingled salt and malt in the palm of her skinny right hand. After that, she rummaged out a bundle of dried herbs, chewed them fine and spat them into the mixture. Stirring again with her forefinger, she returned to the parlor. Scanning the book to refresh her memory, she muttered a nasty little rime. Finally she dashed the mess suddenly upon Gib.

He retreated, shaking himself, outraged and startled. In a corner he sat down, and bent his head to lick the smeared fragments of the mixture away. But they revolted his tongue and palate, and he paused in the midst of this chore, so important to cats; and meanwhile Jael Bettiss yelled, "Speak!"

Gib crouched and blinked, feeling sick. His tongue came out and steadied his lips. Finally he said: "I want something to eat."

His voice was small and high, like a little child's, but entirely understandable. Jael Bettiss was so delighted that she laughed and clapped her bony knees with her hands, in self-applause.

"It worked!" she cried. "No more humbug about me, you understand? I'm a real witch at last, and not a fraud!"

Gib found himself able to understand all this, more clearly than he had ever understood human affairs before. "I want something to eat," he said again, more definitely than before. "I didn't have any supper, and it's nearly——"

"Oh, stow your gab!" snapped his mistress. "It's this book, crammed with knowledge and strength, that made me able to do it. I'll never be without it again, and it'll teach me all the things I've only guessed at and mumbled about. I'm a real witch now, I say. And if you don't think I'll make those ignorant sheep of villagers realize it——"

Once more she went off into gales of wild, cracked mirth, and threw a dish at Gib. He darted away into a corner just in time, and the missile crashed into blue-and-white china fragments against the wall. But Jael Bettiss read aloud from her book an impressive gibberish, and the dish reformed itself on the floor; the bits crept together and joined and the cracks disappeared, as trickling drops of water form into a pool. And finally, when the witch's twig-like forefinger beckoned, the dish floated upward like a leaf in a breeze and set itself gently back on the table. Gib watched warily.

"That's small to what I shall do hereafter," swore Jael Bettiss.

When next the mail was distributed at the general store, a dazzling stranger appeared.

She wore a cloak, an old-fashioned black coat, but its

drapery did not conceal the tall perfection of her form. As for her face, it would have stirred interest and admiration in larger and more sophisticated gatherings than the knot of letter-seeking villagers. Its beauty was scornful but inviting, classic but warm, with something in it of Grecian sculpture and Oriental allure. If the nose was cruel, it was straight; if the lips were sullen, they were full; if the forehead was a suspicion low, it was white and smooth. Thick, thunder-black hair swept up from that forehead, and backward to a knot at the neck. The eyes glowed with strange, hot lights, and wherever they turned they pierced and captivated.

People moved away to let her have a clear, sweeping pathway forward to the counter. Until this stranger had entered, Ivy Hill was the loveliest person present; now she looked only modest and fresh and blond in her starched gingham, and worried to boot. As a matter of fact, Ivy Hill's insides felt cold and topsy-turvy, because she saw how fascinated was the sudden attention of John Frey.

"Is there," asked the newcomer in a deep, creamy voice, "any mail for me?"

"Wh-what name, ma'am?" asked John Frey, his brown young cheeks turning full crimson.

"Bettiss. Jael Bettiss."

He began to fumble through the sheaf of envelopes, with hands that shook. "Are you," he asked, "any relation to the old lady of that name, the one who lives in the hollow?"

"Yes, of a sort." She smiled a slow, conquering smile. "She's my—aunt. Yes. Perhaps you see the family resemblance?" Wider and wider grew the smile with which she assaulted John Frey. "If there isn't any mail," she went on, "I would like a stamp. A one-cent stamp."

Turning to his little metal box on the shelf behind, John Frey tore a single green stamp from the sheet. His hand shook still more as he gave it to the customer and received in exchange a copper cent.

There was really nothing exceptional about the appearance of that copper cent. It looked brown and a little worn, with Lincoln's head on it, and a date—1917. But John Frey felt a sudden glow in the hand that took it, a glow that shot along his arm and into his heart. He gazed at the coin as if he had never seen its life before. And he put it slowly into his pocket, a different pocket from the one in which he usually kept change, and placed another coin in the till to pay for the stamp. Poor Ivy Hill's blue eyes grew round and downright miserable. Plainly he meant to keep that copper piece as a souvenir. But John Frey gazed only at the stranger, raptly, as though he were suddenly stunned or hypnotized.

The dark, sullen beauty drew her cloak more tightly around her, and moved regally out of the store and away toward the edge of town.

As she turned up the brush-hidden trail to the hollow, a change came. Not that her step was less young and free, her figure less queenly, her eyes dimmer or her beauty short of perfect. All these were as they had been; but her expression became set and grim, her body tense and her head high and truculent. It was as though, beneath that young loveliness, lurked an old and evil heart—which was precisely what did lurk there, it does not boot to conceal. But none saw except Gib, the black cat with soot-covered white spots, who sat on the doorstep of the ugly cottage. Jael Bettiss thrust him aside with her foot and entered.

In the kitchen she filled a tin basin from a wooden bucket, and threw into the water a pinch of coarse green powder with an unpleasant smell. As she stirred it in with her hands, they seemed to grow skinny and harsh. Then she threw great palmfuls of the liquid into her face and over her head, and other changes came. . . .

The woman who returned to the front door, where Gib watched with a cat's apprehensive interest, was hideous old Jael Bettiss, whom all the village knew and avoided.

"He's trapped," she shrilled triumphantly. "That penny, the one I soaked for three hours in a love-philtre, trapped him the moment he touched it!" She stumped to the table, and patted the book as though it were a living, lovable thing.

"You taught me," she crooned to it. "You're winning me the love of John Frey!" She paused, and her voice grew harsh again. "Why not? I'm old and ugly and queer, but I can love, and John Frey is the handsomest man in the village!"

The next day she went to the store again, in her new and dazzling person as a dark, beautiful girl. Gib, left alone in the hollow, turned over in his mind the things that he had heard.

The new gift of human speech had brought with it, of necessity, a human quality of reasoning; but his viewpoint and his logic were as strongly feline as ever.

Jael Bettiss' dark love that lured John Frey promised no good to Gib. There would be plenty of trouble, he was inclined to think, and trouble was something that all sensible cats avoided. He was wise now, but he was weak. What could he do against danger? And his desires, as they had been since kittenhood, were food and warmth and a cozy sleeping-place, and a little respectful affection. Just now he was getting none of the four.

He thought also of Ivy Hill. She liked Gib, and often had shown it. If she won John Frey despite the witch's plan, the two would build a house all full of creature comforts—cushions, open fires, probably fish and chopped liver. Gib's tongue caressed his soot-stained lips at the savory thought. It would be good to have a home with Ivy Hill and John Frey, if once he was quit of Jael Bettiss. . . .

But he put the thought from him. The witch had never held his love and loyalty. That went to the house in the hollow, his home since the month that he was born. Even magic had not taught him how to be rid of that cat-instinctive obsession for his own proper dwelling-place. The sinister, strife-sodden hovel would always call and claim him, would draw him back from the warmest fire, the softest bed, the most savory food in the world. Only John Howard Payne could have appreciated Gib's yearnings to the full, and he died long ago, in exile from the home he loved.

When Jael Bettiss returned, she was in a fine trembling rage. Her real self shone through the glamor of her disguise, like murky fire through a thin porcelain screen.

Gib was on the doorstep again, and tried to dodge away as she came up, but her enchantments, or something else, had made Jael Bettiss too quick even for a cat. She darted out a hand and caught him by the scruff of the neck.

"Listen to me," she said, in a voice as deadly as the trickle of poisoned water. "You understand human words. You can talk, and you can hear what I say. You can do what I say, too." She shook him, by way of emphasis. "Can't you do what I say?"

"Yes," said Gib weakly, convulsed with fear.

"All right, I have a job for you. And mind you do it well, or else——" She broke off and shook him again, letting him imagine what would happen if he disobeyed.

"Yes," said Gib again, panting for breath in her tight grip. "What's it about?"

"It's about that little fool, Ivy Hill. She's not quite out of his heart. . . . Go to the village tonight," ordered Jael Bettiss, "and to the house of the marshal. Steal something that belongs to Ivy Hill."

"Steal something?"

"Don't echo me, as if you were a silly parrot." She let go of him, and hurried back to the book that was her constant study. "Bring me something that Ivy Hill owns and touches —and be back here with it before dawn."

Gib carried out her orders. Shortly after sundown he crept through the deepened dusk to the home of Marshal Hill. Doubly black with the soot habitually smeared upon him by Jael Bettiss, he would have been almost invisible, even had anyone been on guard against his coming. But nobody watched; the genial old man sat on the front steps, talking to his daughter.

"Say," the father teased, "isn't young Johnny Frey coming over here tonight, as usual?"

"I don't know, daddy," said Ivy Hill wretchedly.

"What's that daughter?" The marshal sounded surprised. "Is there anything gone wrong between you two young 'uns?"

"Perhaps not, but—oh, daddy, there's a new girl come to town——"

And Ivy Hill burst into tears, groping dolefully on the step beside her for her little wadded handkerchief. But she could not find it.

For Gib, stealing near, had caught it up in his mouth and was scampering away toward the edge of town, and beyond to the house in the hollow.

Meanwhile, Jael Bettiss worked hard at a certain project of wax-modeling. Any witch, or student of witchcraft, would have known at once why she did this.

After several tries, she achieved something quite interesting and even clever—a little female figure, that actually resembled Ivy Hill.

Jael Bettiss used the wax of three candles to give it enough substance and proportion. To make it more realistic, she got some fresh, pale-gold hemp, and of this made hair, like the wig of a blond doll, for the wax head. Drops of blue ink served for eyes, and a blob of berry-juice for the red mouth. All the while she worked, Jael Bettiss was muttering and mumbling words and phrases she had gleaned from the rearward pages of her book.

When Gib brought in the handkerchief, Jael Bettiss snatched it from his mouth, with a grunt by way of thanks. With rusty scissors and coarse white thread, she fashioned for the wax figure a little dress. It happened that the handkerchief was of gingham, and so the garment made all the more striking the puppet's resemblance to Ivy Hill.

"You're a fine one!" tittered the witch, propping her finished figure against the lamp. "You'd better be scared!"

For it happened that she had worked into the waxen face an expression of terror. The blue ink of the eyes made wide round blotches, a stare of agonized fear; and the berry-juice mouth seemed to tremble, to plead shakily for mercy.

Again Jael Bettiss refreshed her memory of goetic spells by poring over the back of the book, and after that she dug from the bottom of an old pasteboard box a handful of rusty pins. She chuckled over them, so that one would think triumph already hers. Laying the puppet on its back, so that the lamplight fell full upon it, she began to recite a spell.

"I have made my wish before," she said in measured tones. "I will make it now. And there was never a day that I did not see my wish fulfilled." Simple, vague—but how many have died because those words were spoken in a certain way over images of them?

The witch thrust a pin into the breast of the little wax figure, and drove it all the way in, with a murderous pressure of her thumb. Another pin she pushed into the head, another into an arm, another into a leg; and so on, until the gingham-clad puppet was fairly studded with transfixing pins.

"Now," she said, "we shall see what we shall see."

Morning dawned, as clear and golden as though wickedness had never been born into the world. The mysterious new paragon of beauty—not a young man of the village but mooned over her, even though she was the reputed niece and namesake of that unsavory old vagabond, Jael Bettiss—walked into the general store to make purchases. One delicate pink ear turned to the gossip of the housewives.

Wasn't it awful, they were agreeing, how poor little Ivy Hill was suddenly sick almost to death—she didn't seem to know her father or her friends. Not even Doctor Melcher could find out what was the matter with her. Strange that John Frey was not interested in her troubles; but John Frey sat behind the counter, slumped on his stool like a mud idol, and his eyes lighted up only when they spied lovely young Jael Bettiss with her market basket.

When she had heard enough, the witch left the store and went straight to the town marshal's house. There she spoke gravely and sorrowfully about how she feared for the sick girl, and was allowed to visit Ivy Hill in her bedroom. To the father and the doctor, it seemed that the patient grew stronger and felt less pain while Jael Bettiss remained to wish her a quick recovery; but, not long after this new acquaintance departed, Ivy Hill grew worse. She fainted, and recovered only to vomit.

And she vomited—pins, rusty pins. Something like that happened in old Salem Village, and earlier still in Scotland, before the grisly cult of North Berwick was literally burned out. But Doctor Melcher, a more modern scholar, had never seen or heard of anything remotely resembling Ivy Hill's disorder.

So it went, for three full days. Gib, too, heard the doleful gossip as he slunk around the village to hunt for food and to avoid Jael Bettiss, who did not like him near when she did magic. Ivy Hill was dying, and he mourned her, as for the boons of fish and fire and cushions and petting that might have been his. He knew, too, that he was responsible for her doom and his loss—that handkerchief that he had stolen had helped Jael Bettiss to direct her spells.

But philosophy came again to his aid. If Ivy Hill died, she died. Anyway, he had never been given the chance to live as her pensioner and pet. He was not even sure that he would have taken the chance—thinking of it, he felt strong, accustomed clamps upon his heart. The house in the hollow was his home forever. Elsewhere he'd be an exile.

Nothing would ever root it out of his feline soul.

On the evening of the third day, witch and cat faced each other across the table-top in the old house in the hollow.

"They've talked loud enough to make his dull ears hear," grumbled the fearful old woman—with none but Gib to see her, she had washed away the disguising enchantment that, though so full of lure, seemed to be a burden upon her. "John Frey has agreed to take Ivy Hill out in his automobile. The doctor thinks that the fresh air, and John Frey's company, will make her feel better—but it won't. It's too late. She'll never return from that drive."

She took up the pin-pierced wax image of her rival, rose and started toward the kitchen.

"What are you going to do?" Gib forced himself to ask.

"Do?" repeated Jael Bettiss, smiling murderously. "I'm going to put an end to that baby-faced chit—but why are you so curious? Get out, with your prying!"

And, snarling curses and striking with her claw-like hands, she made him spring down from his chair and run out of the house. The door slammed, and he crouched in some brambles and watched. No sound, and at the half-blinded windows no movement; but, after a time, smoke began to coil upward from the chimney. Its first puffs were dark and greasy-looking. Then it turned dull gray, then white, then blue as indigo. Finally it vanished altogether.

When Jael Bettiss opened the door and came out, she was once more in the semblance of a beautiful dark girl. Yet Gib recognized a greater terror about her than ever before.

"You be gone from here when I get back," she said to him.

"Gone?" stammered Gib, his little heart turning cold. "What do you mean?"

She stooped above him, like a threatening bird of prey.

"You be gone," she repeated. "If I ever see you again, I'll kill you—or I'll make my new husband kill you."

He still could not believe her. He shrank back, and his eyes turned mournfully to the old house that was the only thing he loved.

"You're the only witness to the things I've done," Jael Bettiss continued. "Nobody would believe their ears if a cat started telling tales, but anyway, I don't want any trace of you around. If you leave, they'll forget that I used to be a witch. So run!"

She turned away. Her mutterings were now only her thoughts aloud:

"If my magic works—and it always works—that car will find itself idling around through the hill road to the other side of the quarry. John Frey will stop there. And so will Ivy Hill—forever."

Drawing her cloak around her, she stalked purposefully toward the old quarry behind the house.

Left by himself, Gib lowered his lids and let his yellow eyes grow dim and deep with thought. His shrewd beast's mind pawed and probed at this final wonder and danger that faced him and John Frey and Ivy Hill.

He must run away if he would live. The witch's house in the hollow, that had never welcomed him, now threatened him. No more basking on the doorstep, no more ambushing wood-mice among the brambles, no more dozing by the kitchen fire. Nothing for Gib henceforth but strange, forbidding wilderness, and scavenger's food, and no shelter, not on the coldest night. The village? But his only two friends, John Frey and Ivy Hill, were being taken from him by the magic of Jael Bettiss and her book. . . .

That book had done this. That book must undo it. There was no time to lose.

The door was not quite latched, and he nosed it open, despite the groans of its hinges. Hurrying in, he sprang up on the table.

It was gloomy in that tree-invested house, even for Gib's sharp eyes. Therefore, in a trembling fear almost too big for his little body, he spoke a word that Jael Bettiss had spoken, on her first night of power. As had happened then, so it happened now; the dark lamp glowed alight.

Gib pawed at the closed book, and contrived to lift its cover. Pressing it open with one front foot, with the other he painstakingly turned leaves, more leaves, and more yet. Finally he came to the page he wanted.

Not that he could read; and, in any case, the characters were strange in their shapes and combinations. Yet, if one looked long enough and levelly enough—even though one were a cat, and afraid—they made sense, conveyed intelligence.

And so into the mind of Gib, beating down his fears, there stole a phrase:

Beware of mirrors. . . .

So that was why Jael Bettiss never kept a mirror—not even now, when she could assume such dazzling beauty.

Beware of mirrors, the book said to Gib, *for they declare the truth, and truth is fatal to sorcery. Beware, also, of crosses, which defeat all spells. . . .*

That was definite inspiration. He moved back from the book, and let it snap shut. Then, pushing with head and paws, he coaxed it to the edge of the table and let it fall. Jumping down after it, he caught a corner of the book in his teeth and dragged it to the door, more like a retriever than a cat. When he got it into the yard, into a place where the earth was soft, he dug furiously until he had made a hole big enough to contain the volume. Then, thrusting it in, he covered it up.

Nor was that all his effort, so far as the book was concerned. He trotted a little way off to where lay some dry, tough twigs under the cypress trees. To the little grave he bore first one, then another of these, and laid them across each other, in the form of an X. He pressed them well into the earth, so that they would be hard to disturb. Perhaps he would keep an eye on that spot henceforth, after he had done the rest of the things in his mind, to see that the cross remained. And, though he acted thus only by chance reasoning, all the demonologists, even the Reverend Montague Summers, would have nodded approval. Is this not the way to foil the black wisdom of the *Grand Albert?* Did not Prospero thus inter his grimoires, in the fifth act of *The Tempest?*

Now back to the house once more, and into the kitchen. It was even darker than the parlor, but Gib could make out a basin on a stool by the moldy wall, and smelled an ugly pungency—Jael Bettiss had left her mixture of powdered water after last washing away her burden of false beauty.

Gib's feline nature rebelled at a wetting; his experience of witchcraft bade him be wary, but he rose on his hind legs and with his forepaws dragged at the basin's edge. It tipped and toppled. The noisome fluid drenched him. Wheeling, he ran back into the parlor, but paused on the doorstep. He spoke two more words that he remembered from Jael Bettiss. The lamp went out again.

And now he dashed around the house and through the brambles and to the quarry beyond.

It lay amid uninhabited wooded hills, a wide excavation from which had once been quarried all the stones for the village houses and pavements. Now it was full of water, from many thaws and torrents. Almost at its lip was parked John

Frey's touring-car, with the top down, and beside it he lolled, slack-faced and dreamy. At his side, cloak-draped and enigmatically queenly, was Jael Bettiss, her back to the quarry, never more terrible or handsome. John Frey's eyes were fixed dreamily upon her, and her eyes were fixed commandingly on the figure in the front seat of the car—a slumped, defeated figure, hard to recognize as poor sick Ivy Hill.

"Can you think of no way to end all this pain, Miss Ivy?" the witch was asking. Though she did not stir, nor glance behind her, it was as though she had gestured toward the great quarry-pit, full to unknown depths with black, still water. The sun, at the very point of setting, made angry red lights on the surface of that stagnant pond.

"Go away," sobbed Ivy Hill, afraid without knowing why. "Please, please!"

"I'm only trying to help," said Jael Bettiss. "Isn't that so, John?"

"That's so, Ivy," agreed John, like a little boy who is prompted to an unfamiliar recitation. "She's only trying to help."

Gib, moving silently as fate, crept to the back of the car. None of the three human beings, so intent upon each other, saw him.

"Get out of the car," persisted Jael Bettiss. "Get out, and look into the water. You will forget your pain."

"Yes, yes," chimed in John Frey, mechanically. "You will forget your pain."

Gib scrambled stealthily to the runningboard, then over the side of the car and into the rear seat. He found what he had hoped to find. Ivy Hill's purse—and open.

He pushed his nose into it. Tucked into a little side-pocket was a hard, flat rectangle, about the size and shape of a visiting-card. All normal girls carry mirrors in their purses—all mirrors show the truth. Gib clamped the edge with his mouth, and struggled to drag the thing free.

"Miss Ivy," Jael Bettiss was commanding, "get out of this car, and come and look into the water of the quarry."

No doubt what would happen if once Ivy Hill should gaze into that shiny black abyss; but she bowed her head, in agreement or defeat, and began slowly to push aside the catch of the door.

Now or never, thought Gib. He made a little noise in his

throat, and sprang up on the side of the car next to Jael Bettiss. His black-stained face and yellow eyes were not a foot from her.

She alone saw him; Ivy Hill was too sick, John Frey too dull. "What are you doing here?" she snarled, like a bigger and fiercer cat than he; but he moved closer still, holding up the oblong in his teeth. Its back was uppermost, covered with imitation leather, and hid the real nature of it. Jael Bettiss was mystified, for once in her relationship with Gib. She took the thing from him, turned it over, and saw a reflection.

She screamed.

The other two looked up, horrified through their stupor. The scream that Jael Bettiss uttered was not deep and rich and young; it was the wild, cracked cry of a terrified old woman.

"I don't look like that," she choked out, and drew back from the car. "Not old——ugly——"

Gib sprang at her face. With all four claw-bristling feet he seized and clung to her. Again Jael Bettiss screamed, flung up her hands, and tore him away from his hold; but his soggy fur had smeared the powdered water upon her face and head.

Though he fell to earth, Gib twisted in midair and landed upright. He had one glimpse of his enemy. Jael Bettiss, no mistake—but a Jael Bettiss with hooked beak, rheumy eyes, hideous wry mouth and yellow chisel teeth—Jael Bettiss exposed for what she was, stripped of her lying mask of beauty!

And she drew back a whole staggering step. Rocks were just behind her. Gib saw, and flung himself. Like a flash he clawed his way up her cloak, and with both forepaws ripped at the ugliness he had betrayed. He struck for his home that was forbidden him — Marco Bozzaris never strove harder for Greece, nor Stonewall Jackson for Virginia.

Jael Bettiss screamed yet again, a scream loud and full of horror. Her feet had slipped on the edge of the abyss. She flung out her arms, the cloak flapped from them like frantic wings. She fell, and Gib fell with her, still tearing and fighting.

The waters of the quarry closed over them both.

Gib thought that it was a long way back to the surface, and a longer way to shore. But he got there, and scrambled out with the help of projecting rocks. He shook his drenched body, climbed back into the car and sat upon the rear seat. At least Jael Bettiss would no longer drive him from the home he loved. He'd find food some way, and take it back there each day to eat. . . .

With tongue and paws he began to rearrange his sodden fur.

John Frey, clear-eyed and wide awake, was leaning in and talking to Ivy Hill. As for her, she sat up straight, as though she had never known a moment of sickness.

"But just what did happen?" she was asking.

John Frey shook his head, though all the stupidity was gone from his face and manner. "I don't quite remember. I seem to have wakened from a dream. But are you all right, darling?"

"Yes, I'm all right." She gazed toward the quarry, and the black water that had already subsided above what it had swallowed. Her eyes were puzzled, but not frightened. "I was dreaming, too," she said. "Let's not bother about it."

She lifted her gaze, and cried out with joy. "There's that old house that daddy owns. Isn't it interesting?"

John Frey looked, too. "Yes. The old witch has gone away—I seem to have heard she did."

Ivy Hill was smiling with excitement. "Then I have an inspiration. Let's get daddy to give it to us. And we'll paint it over and fix it up, and then—" she broke off, with a cry of delight. "I declare, there's a cat in the car with me!"

It was the first she had known of Gib's presence.

John Frey stared at Gib. He seemed to have wakened only the moment before. "Yes, and isn't he a thin one? But he'll be pretty when he gets through cleaning himself. I think I see a white shirt-front."

Ivy Hill put out a hand and scratched Gib behind the ear. "He's bringing us good luck, I think. John, let's take him to live with us when we have the house fixed up and move in."

"Why not?" asked her lover. He was gazing at Gib. "He looks as if he was getting ready to speak."

But Gib was not getting ready to speak. The power of speech was gone from him, along with Jael Bettiss and her enchantments. But he understood, in a measure, what was being said about him and the house in the hollow. There would be new life there, joyful and friendly this time. And he would be a part of it, forever, and of his loved home.

He could only purr to show his relief and gratitude.

Antiquities

By John Crowley

The tall tale is one of the oldest forms of expression, and the tall tale told in a bar is a tradition that must go back nearly to the dawn of civilization. After a few thousand years of inebriated conversation, braggadocio, and straight-faced "whoppers," it occurred to somebody to write some of this stuff down, and the literary mode known as the "bar story" was born. In SF and fantasy, the "bar story" or "club story" has a long and venerable tradition, probably originated by Lord Dunsany's long series of stories about the clubman Jorkens, and including subsequent work by L. Sprague de Camp and Fletcher Pratt (*Tales from Gavagan's Bar*), Arthur C. Clarke (*Tales From the White Hart*), Spider Robinson (*Callahan's Crosstime Saloon*), Sterling Lanier (*The Peculiar Exploits of Brigadier Ffellowes*), and others.

Here World Fantasy Award winner John Crowley—author of the highly acclaimed *Little, Big*, as well as *The Deep* and *Beasts*—continues the tradition with the story that follows, told by a member of the Traveller's Club, in the heyday of the British Empire and the Victorian Age.

So, settle back in your overstuffed armchair, light your cigar, sip your brandy or port, and prepare to listen to the eerie tale of the mysterious Inconstancy Plague that haunted Cheshire in the latter 1880's. . . .

"There was, of course," Sir Jeffrey said, "the Inconstancy Plague in Cheshire. Short-lived, but a phenomenon I don't think we can quite discount."

It was quite late at the Travellers' Club, and Sir Jeffrey and I had been discussing (as we seemed often to do in those years of the Empire's greatest, yet somehow most tenuous, extent) some anomalous irruptions of the foreign and the odd into the home island's quiet life—small, unlooked-for effects which those centuries of adventure and acquisition had had on an essentially stay-at-home race. At least that was my thought. I was quite young.

"It's no good your saying 'of course' in that offhand tone," I said, attempting to catch the eye of Barnett, whom I felt as much as saw passing through the crepuscular haze of the smoking room. "I've no idea what the Inconstancy Plague was."

From within his evening dress Sir Jeffrey drew out a cigar case, which faintly resembled a row of cigars, as a mummy case resembles the human form within. He offered me one, and we lit them without haste, Sir Jeffrey started a small vortex in his brandy glass. I understood that these rituals were introductory—that, in other words, I would have my tale.

"It was in the latter eighties," Sir Jeffrey said. "I've no idea now how I first came to hear of it, though I shouldn't be surprised if it was some flippant note in *Punch*. I paid no attention at first; the 'popular delusions and madness of crowds'

207

sort of thing. I'd returned not long before from Ceylon, and was utterly, blankly oppressed by the weather. It was just starting autumn when I came ashore, and I spent the next four months more or less behind closed doors. The rain! The fog! How could I have forgotten? And the oddest thing was that no one else seemed to pay the slightest attention. My man used to draw the drapes every morning and say in the most cheerful voice, 'Another dismal wet one, eh, sir?' and I would positively turn my face to the wall."

He seemed to sense that he had been diverted by personal memories, and drew on his cigar as though it were the font of recall.

"What brought it to notice was a seemingly ordinary murder case. A farmer's wife in Winsford, married some decades, came one night into the Sheaf of Wheat, a public house, where her husband was lingering over a pint. From under her skirts she drew an old fowling-piece. She made a remark which was later reported quite variously by the onlookers, and gave him both barrels. One misfired, but the other was quite sufficient. We learn that the husband, on seeing this about to happen, seemed to show neither surprise nor anguish, merely looking up and—well, awaiting his fate.

"At the inquest, the witnesses reported the murderess to have said, before she fired, 'I'm doing this in the name of all the others.' Or perhaps it was 'I'm doing this, Sam (his name), to save the others.' Or possibly, 'I've got to do this, Sam, to save you from that other.' The woman seemed to have gone quite mad. She gave the investigators an elaborate and scarifying story which they, unfortunately, didn't take down, being able to make no sense of it. The rational gist of it was that she had shot her husband for flagrant infidelities which she could bear no longer. When the magistrate asked witnesses if they knew of such infidelities—these things, in a small community, being notoriously difficult to hide—the men, as a body, claimed that they did not. After the trial, however, the women had dark and unspecific hints to make, how they could say much if they would, and so on. The murderess was adjudged unfit to stand trial, and hanged herself in Bedlam not long after.

"I don't know how familiar you are with that oppressive part of the world. In those years farming was a difficult enterprise at best, isolating, stultifyingly boring, unremunerative.

Hired men were heavy drinkers. Prices were depressed. The
women aged quickly, what with continual childbirth added to
a load of work at least equal to their menfolk's. What I'm getting at is that it is, or was, a society the least of any conducive
to adultery, amours, romance. And yet for some reason it
appeared, after this murder pointed it up, so to speak, dramatically, that there was a veritable plague of inconstant husbands in northern Cheshire."

"It's difficult to imagine," I said, "what evidence there
could be of such a thing."

"I had occasion to go to the county that autumn, just at the
height of it all," Sir Jeffrey went on, caressing an ashtray with
the tip of his cigar. "I'd at last got a grip on myself and begun
to accept invitations again. A fellow I'd known in Alexandria,
a commercial agent who'd done spectacularly well for himself,
asked me up for the shooting."

"Odd place to go shooting."

"Odd fellow. *Arriviste,* to speak frankly. The hospitality
was lavish; the house was a red-brick Cheshire *faux*-Gothic affair, if you know what I mean, and the impression it gave of
desolation and melancholy was remarkable. And there was no
shooting; poured rain all weekend. One sat about leafing
through novels or playing Cairo whist—which is what we
called bridge in those days—and staring out the windows. One
evening, at a loss for entertainment, our host—Watt was his
name, and . . ."

"What was his name?" I asked.

"Exactly. He'd become a student of mesmerism, or hyp-
notism as he preferred to call it, and suggested we might have
a bit of fun probing our dark underminds. We all declined,
but Watt was insistent, and at last suborned a hearty local
type, old squirearchical family, and—this is important—an in-
veterate, dirt-under-the-nails farmer. His conversation re-
volved, chiefly, around turnips."

"Even his dark undermind's?"

"Ah. Here we come to it. This gentleman's wife was present
at the gathering as well, and one couldn't help noticing the
hangdog air he maintained around her, the shifty eyes, the
nervous start he gave when she spoke to him from behind; and
also a certain dreaminess, an abstraction, that would fall on
him at odd moments."

"Worrying about his turnips, perhaps."

Sir Jeffrey quashed his cigar, rather reproachfully, as though it were my own flippancy. "The point is that this ruddy-faced, absolutely ordinary fellow *was cheating on his wife*. One read it as though it were written on his shirt front. His wife seemed quite as aware of it as any; her face was drawn tight as her reticule. She blanched when he agreed to go under, and tried to lead him away, but Watt insisted he be a sport, and at last she retired with a headache. I don't know what the man was thinking of when he agreed; had a bit too much brandy, I expect. At any rate, the lamps were lowered and the usual apparatus got out, the spinning disc and so on. The squire, to Watt's surprise, went under as though slain. We thought at first he had merely succumbed to the grape, but then Watt began to question him, and he to answer, languidly but clearly, name, age, and so on. I've no doubt Watt intended to have the man stand on his head, or turn his waistcoat back-to-front, or that sort of thing, but before any of that could begin, the man began to speak. To address someone. Someone female. Most extraordinary, the way he was transformed."

Sir Jeffrey, in the proper mood, shows a talent for mimicry, and now he seemed to transform himself into the hypnotized squire. His eyes glazed and half-closed, his mouth went slack (though his moustache remained upright) and one hand was raised as though to ward off an importunate spirit.

" 'No,' says he. 'Leave me alone. Close those eyes—those eyes. Why? Why? Dress yourself, oh God . . .' And here he seemed quite in torment. Watt should of course have awakened the poor fellow immediately, but he was fascinated, as I confess we all were.

" 'Who is it you speak to?' Watt asked.

" 'She,' says the squire. 'The foreign woman. The clawed woman. The cat.'

" 'What is her name?'

" 'Bastet.'

" 'How did she come here?'

"At this question the squire seemed to pause. Then he gave three answers: 'Through the earth. By default. On the *John Deering*.' This last answer astonished Watt, since, as he told me later, the *John Deering* was a cargo ship we had often dealt with, which made a regular Alexandria—Liverpool run.

" 'Where do you see her?' Watt asked.

" 'In the sheaves of wheat.' "

"He meant the pub, I suppose," I put in.

"I think not," Sir Jeffrey said darkly. "He went on about the sheaves of wheat. He grew more animated, though it was more difficult to understand his words. He began to make sounds—well, how shall I put it? His breathing became stertorous, his movements . . ."

"I think I see."

"Well, you can't, quite. Because it was one of the more remarkable things I have ever witnessed. The man was making physical love to someone he described as a cat, or a sheaf of wheat."

"The name he spoke," I said, "is an Egyptian one. A goddess associated with the cat."

"Precisely. It was midway through this ritual that Watt at last found himself, and gave an awakening command. The fellow seemed dazed, and was quite drenched with sweat; his hand shook when he took out his pocket-handkerchief to mop his face. He looked at once guilty and pleased, like—like—"

"The cat who ate the canary."

"You have a talent for simile. He looked around at the company, and asked shyly if he had embarrassed himself. I tell you, old boy, we were hard-pressed to reassure him."

Unsummoned, Barnett materialized beside us with the air of one about to speak tragic and ineluctable prophecies. It is his usual face. He said only that it had begun to rain. I asked for a whisky and soda. Sir Jeffrey seemed lost in thought during these transactions, and when he spoke again it was to muse: "Odd, isn't it," he said, "how naturally one thinks of cats as female, though we know quite well that they are distributed between two sexes. As far as I know, it is the same the world over. Whenever, for instance, a cat in a tale is transformed into a human, it is invariably a woman."

"The eyes," I said. "The movements—that certain sinuosity."

"The air of independence," Sir Jeffrey said. "False, of course. One's cat is quite dependent on one, though he seems not to think so."

"The capacity for ease."

"And spite."

"To return to our plague," I said, "I don't see how a single madwoman and a hypnotized squire amount to one.''

"Oh, that was by no means the end of it. Throughout that autumn there was, relatively speaking, a flurry of divorce actions and breach-of-promise suits. A suicide left a note: 'I can't have her, and I can't live without her.' More than one farmer's wife, after years of dedication and many offspring, packed herself off to aged parents in Chester. And so on.

"Monday morning after the squire's humiliation I returned to town. As it happened, Monday was market day in the village and I was able to observe at first hand some effects of the plague. I saw husbands and wives sitting at far ends of wagon seats, unable to meet each other's eyes. Sudden arguments flaring without reason over the vegetables. I saw tears. I saw over and over the same hangdog, evasive, guilty look I described in our squire.''

"Hardly conclusive.''

"There is one further piece of evidence. The Roman Church has never quite eased its grip in that part of the world. It seems that about this time a number of R.C. wives clubbed together and sent a petition to their bishop, saying that the region was in need of an exorcism. Specifically, that their husbands were being tormented by a succubus. Or succubi—whether it was one or many was impossible to tell.''

"I shouldn't wonder.''

"What specially intrigued me," Sir Jeffrey went on, removing his eyeglass from between cheek and brow and polishing it absently, "is that in all this inconstancy only the men seemed to be accused; the women seemed solely aggrieved, rather than guilty, parties. Now if we take the squire's words as evidence, and not merely 'the stuff that dreams are made on,' we have the picture of a foreign, apparently Egyptian, woman—or possibly women—embarking at Liverpool and moving unnoticed amid Cheshire, seeking whom she may devour and seducing yeomen in their barns amid the fruits of the harvest. The notion was so striking that I got in touch with a chap at Lloyd's, and asked him about passenger lists for the *John Deering* over the last few years.''

"And?"

"There were none. The ship had been in dry dock for two or three years previous. It had made one run, that spring, and then been moth-balled. On that one run there were no passengers. The cargo from Alex consisted of the usual oil,

dates, sago, rice, tobacco—and something called 'antiquities.'
Since the nature of these was unspecified, the matter ended
there. The Inconstancy Plague was short-lived; a letter from
Watt the next spring made no mention of it, though he'd been
avid for details—most of what I know comes from him and his
gleanings of the Winsford *Trumpet,* or whatever it calls itself.
I might never have come to any conclusion at all about the
matter had it not been for a chance encounter in Cairo a year
or so later.

"I was *en route* to the Sudan in the wake of the Khartoum
disaster and was bracing myself, so to speak, in the bar of
Shepheard's. I struck up a conversation with an archaeologist
fellow just off a dig around Memphis, and the talk turned,
naturally, to Egyptian mysteries. The thing that continually
astonished him, he said, was the absolute *thoroughness* of the
ancient Egyptian mind. Once having decided a thing was
ritualistically necessary, they admitted of no deviation in
carrying it out.

"He instanced cats. We know in what high esteem the
Egyptians held cats. If held in high esteem, they must be mummified after death; and so they were. All of them, or nearly
all. Carried to their tombs with the bereaved family weeping
behind, put away with favorite toys and food for the afterlife
journey. Not long ago, he said, some *three hundred thousand*
mummified cats were uncovered at Beni Hassan. An entire cat
necropolis, unviolated for centuries.

"And then he told me something which gave me pause.
More than pause. He said that, once uncovered, all those cats
were disinterred and shipped to England. Every last one."

"Good Lord. Why?"

"I have no idea. They were not, after all, the Elgin Marbles.
This seemed to have been the response when they arrived at
Liverpool, because not a single museum or collector of antiquities displayed the slightest interest. The whole lot had to be
sold off to pay a rather large shipping bill."

"Sold off? To whom, in God's name?"

"To a Cheshire agricultural firm. Who proceeded to chop
up the lot and resell it. To the local farmers, my dear boy. To
use as fertilizer."

Sir Jeffrey stared deeply into his nearly untouched brandy,
watching the legs it made on the side of the glass, as though he
read secrets there. "Now the scientific mind may be able to

believe," he said at last, "that three hundred thousand cats, aeons old, wrapped lovingly in winding cloths and put to rest with spices and with spells, may be exhumed from a distant land—and from a distant past as well—and minced into the loam of Cheshire, and it will all have no result but grain. I am not certain. Not certain at all."

The smoking room of the Travellers' Club was deserted now, except for the weary, unlaid ghost of Barnett. Above us on the wall the mounted heads of exotic animals were shadowed and nearly unnamable; one felt that they had just then thrust their coal-smoked and glass-eyed heads through the wall, seeking something, and that just the other side of the wall stood their vast and unimaginable bodies. Seeking what? The members, long dead as well, who had slain them and brought them to this?

"You've been in Egypt," Sir Jeffrey said.

"Briefly."

"I have always thought that Egyptian women were among the world's most beautiful."

"Certainly their eyes are stunning. With the veil, of course, one sees little else."

"I spoke specifically of those circumstances when they are without the veil. In all senses."

"Yes."

"Depilated, many of them." He spoke in a small, dreamy voice, as though he observed long-past scenes. "A thing I have always found—intriguing. To say the least." He sighed deeply; he tugged down his waistcoat, preparatory to rising; he replaced his eyeglass. He was himself again. "Do you suppose," he said, "that such a thing as a cab could be found at this hour? Well, let us see."

"By the way," I asked when we parted, "whatever came of the wives' petition for an exorcism?"

"I believe the bishop sent it on to Rome for consideration. The Vatican, you know, does not move hastily on these things. For all I know, it may still be pending."

A Little Intelligence

By Robert Silverberg
and Randall Garrett

One of the most prolific authors alive, Robert Silverberg can lay claim to more than 450 fiction and nonfiction books and over 3,000 magazine pieces. Within science fiction, Silverberg rose to his greatest prominence during the late '60s and early '70s, winning four Nebula Awards and a Hugo Award, and publishing dozens of major novels and anthologies, including the renowned novel *Dying Inside* and the influential anthology series *New Dimensions*. In 1980, after four years of self-imposed "retirement," Silverberg started writing again, and the first of his new novels, *Lord Valentine's Castle*, became a nationwide bestseller. His most recent books are *Lord of Darkness*, a historical novel, the collection *Majipoor Chronicles*, and *Valentine Pontifex*, the sequel to *Lord Valentine's Castle*.

Randall Garrett is probably best known as the author of the popular "Lord Darcy" stories, about an alternative twentieth century world where magic works and the Plantagenet Emperor John IV rules a widespread and prosperous Anglo-French Empire upon which the sun has never set. The "Lord Darcy" series includes the well-known novel *Too Many Magicians*, and the short-story collections *Murder and Magic* and *Lord Darcy Investigates*.

In the "Lord Darcy" stories, Garrett successfully blended the mystery story with fantasy, creating a detective who uses magic as one of his criminological tools. Here Silverberg and Garrett—in one of their many collaborations as "Robert Randall"—instead blend the traditional tale of detection with science fiction to create a suspenseful sf mystery centered around a cat, a Sister of the Order of the Holy Nativity, and some very cantankerous aliens . . . a mystery you may be able to solve, if—like the story's protagonist—you have "A Little Intelligence" . . .

215

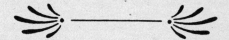

Sister Mary Magdalene felt apprehensive. She glanced worriedly at the priest facing her and said, "But—I don't understand. Why quarter the aliens *here?*"

Her gesture took in her office, the monastery, the convent, the school, the Cathedral of the Blessed Sacrament. "Because," said Father Destry patronizingly, "there is nothing here for them to learn."

The nun eyed Father Destry uneasily. The single votive candle flickering before the statue of the Virgin in the wall niche beside him cast odd shadows over his craggy, unhandsome face. She said, "You mean that the beings of Capella IX are so well versed in the teachings of the Church that they couldn't even learn anything here?" She added with innocent sarcasm, "My, how wonderful for them!"

"Not quite, Sister. The Earth Government isn't worried about the chances of the Pogatha learning anything about the Church. But the Pogatha would be hard put to learn anything about Terrestrial science in a Cathedral."

"The walls are full of gadgets," she said, keeping her voice flat. "Vestment color controls, sound suppressor fields for the confessionals, illumination—"

"I know, I know," the priest interrupted testily. "I'm talking specifically about military information. And I don't expect them to tear down our walls to learn the secrets of the vestment color controls."

Sister Mary Magdalene shrugged. She had been deliberately

baiting Father Destry, and she realized she was taking out on him her resentment against the government for having dumped a delegation of alien beings into her otherwise peaceful life.

"I see," she said. "While the—Pogatha?—Pogatha delegation is here, they're to be kept within the cathedral grounds. The Earth government is assuming they'll be safe here."

"Not only that, but the Pogatha themselves will feel safer here. They know Terrestrial feelings still run high since the war, and they know there could be no violence here. The Government wanted to keep them in a big hotel somewhere—a place that would be as secure as any. But the Pogatha would have none of it."

"And one last question, Father. Why does it fall to the Sisters of the Holy Nativity to put them up? Why can't the Holy Cross Fathers take care of them? I mean—really, I understand that they're alien beings, but they *are* humanoid—"

"Quite so. They are females."

The nun's eyebrows rose. "They are?"

Father Destry blushed faintly. "I won't go into the biology of Capella IX, partly because I don't completely understand it myself. But they do have a matriarchal society. They are oviparous mammals, but the rearing of children is always left to the males, the physically weaker sex. The fighters and diplomats are definitely female."

"In that case"—the nun shrugged in defeat—"if those are the Bishop's wishes, I'll see that they're carried out. I'll make the necessary arrangements." She glanced at her wristwatch and said curtly, "It's almost time for Vespers, Father."

The priest rose. "The Government is preparing a brochure on the—ah—physical needs of the Pogatha. I'll have it sent to you as soon as it arrives."

"*Care and Feeding of Aliens,* eh? Very well, Father. I'll do my best."

"I'm sure you will, Sister." He looked down at his hands as though suddenly unsure of himself. "I know this may be a hard job, Sister, but"—he looked up, smiling suddenly—"you'll make it. The prayers of everyone here will be with you."

"Thank you, Father."

The priest turned and walked out. Sister Mary Magdalene,

unhappily conscious that though she respected Father Destry's learning and piety she could feel no warmth toward him as a person, watched him depart. As he reached the door a lithe coal-black shape padded over to him and rubbed itself lingeringly against the priest's legs.

Father Destry smiled at the cat, but it was a hollow, artificial smile. The priest did not enjoy the affections of Sister Mary Magdalene's pet. He closed the office door.

The cat leaped to the top of the nun's desk.

"Miaou," it said calmly.

"Exactly, Felicity," said Sister Mary Magdalene.

Sister Mary Magdalene spent the next two days reading the digests of the war news. She had not, she was forced to admit, kept up with the war as much as she might have. Granted, a nun was supposed to have renounced the devil, the flesh and the world, but it was sometimes a good idea to check up and see what all three were up to.

When the Government brochure came, she studied it carefully, trying to get a complete picture of the alien race that Earth was fighting. If she was going to have to coddle them, she was going to have to know them.

The beginning of the war was shrouded in mystery. Earth forces had landed on Capella IX 30 years before and had found a civilization two centuries behind that of Earth, technologically speaking. During the next 20 years, the Pogatha had managed to beg, borrow and steal enough technology from the Earth colonies to almost catch up. And then someone had blundered.

There had been an "incident"—and a shooting war had begun. The Pogatha feeling, late in arising, was that Earthmen had no right settling on Capella IX; they were aliens who must be driven off. The colonists refused to abandon 20 years' effort without a fight.

It was a queer war. The colonists, badly outnumbered, had the advantage of technological superiority. On the other hand, they were hindered by the necessity of maintaining a supply line 42 light-years long, which the Pogatha could and did disrupt. The colonists were still dependent on Earth for war material and certain supplies.

The war had waggled back and forth for nearly ten years without any definite advantage to either side. Thermonuclear weapons had not been used, since they would leave only a shattered planet of no use to anyone.

Both sides were weary; both sides wanted to quit, if it could be done without either side losing too much face. Human beings had an advantage in that Earth itself was still whole, but the Pogatha had an almost equal advantage in the length of the colonists' supply lines. Earth would win eventually; that seemed obvious. But at what cost? In the end, Earth would be forced to smash the entire Pogatha civilization. And they did not want to do that.

There was an element of pride in the Pogatha viewpoint. They asked themselves: would not suicide be better than ignominious slaughter at the hands of the alien Earthmen? Unless a peace with honor could be negotiated, the Pogatha would fight to the last Pogath, and would quite likely use thermonuclear bombs in a final blaze of self-destructive glory.

The four Pogatha who were coming to the little convent of the Cathedral Chapter of the Sisters of the Holy Nativity were negotiators that had to be handled with the utmost care. Sister Mary Magdalene was no military expert, and she was not an interstellar diplomat, but she knew that the final disposition of a world might rest with her. It was a heavy cross to bear for a woman who had spent 20 years of her life as a nun.

Sister Mary Magdalene turned her school duties over to Sister Angela. There was mild regret involved in this; one of Sister Mary Magdalene's joys had been teaching the dramatics class in the parochial high school. They had been preparing a performance of *Murder in the Cathedral* for the following month. Well, Sister Angela could handle it well enough.

The supplies necessary for the well-being of the Pogatha were sent by the government, and they consisted mostly of captured goods. A cookbook translated by government experts came with the food, along with a note: *"These foods are not for human consumption. Since they are canned, there is no need to season them. Under no circumstances try to mix them with Terrestrial foods. Where water is called for, use only distilled water, never tap water. For other liquids, use only those provided."*

There was also a book of etiquette and table settings for four. The Pogatha would eat alone. There would be no diplomatic banquets here. Sister Mary Magdalene found ou why when she went, accompanied by Felicity, to talk to the sisters who prepared the meals for the convent.

Sister Elizabeth was a plumpish, smiling woman who loved cooking and good food and who ruled her domain with an almost queenly air. Looking like a contented plump *hausfrau* in her kitchen uniform, she smiled as Sister Mary Magdalene came in.

"Good morning, Sister."

"Have you opened any of the Pogatha food cans yet?" the sister-in-charge wanted to know.

"I didn't know whether I should," Sister Elizabeth said. Seeing Felicity prowling on the worktable in search of scraps of food, she goodnaturedly waved at the cat and said, "Stay away from there, Felicity! That's lunch!"

The cat glowered at her and leaped to the floor.

Sister Mary Magdalene said, "I'd like to have a look at the stuff they're going to eat. Suppose you pick a can at random and we'll open it up."

Sister Elizabeth nodded and went into the storeroom. She returned carrying an ordinary-looking can. Its label was covered with queer script, and it bore a picture of a repulsive-looking little animal. Above the label was pasted a smaller label which real, in Roman characters, VAGHA.

Sister Mary Magdalene flipped open the translated Pogatha cookbook and ran her finger along the "V" section of the index. Finding her reference, she turned the pages and read. After a moment she announced, "It's supposed to be something like rabbit stew. Go ahead and open it."

Sister Elizabeth put it in the opener and pressed the starter. The blade bit in. The top of the can lifted.

"*Whoof!*" said Sister Mary Magdalene.

"*Ugh!*" said Sister Elizabeth.

Even Felicity, who had been so interested that she had jumped up to the table to watch the proceedings, wrinkled her bewhiskered nose in disgust and backed away.

"It's spoiled," Sister Elizabeth said sadly.

But the odor was not quite that of decay. True, there was a background of Limburger cheese overlaid with musk, but this was punctuated pungently with something that smelled like a cross between butyl mercaptan and ammonia.

"No," said Sister Mary Magdalene unhappily. "It says in the book that the foods have distinctive odors."

"With the accent on the *stinc*. Do you mean I have to prepare stuff like that in my kitchen?"

"I'm afraid so," said Sister Mary Magdalene.

"But everything else will smell like that! It'll absolutely ruin everything!"

"You'll just have to keep our own food covered. And remember that ours smells just as bad to them."

Sister Elizabeth nodded, tightlipped, the joviality gone from her face. Now she, too, had her cross to bear.

The appearance of the Pogatha, when they finally arrived, did not shock Sister Mary Magdalene; she had been prepared for the sight of ugly caricatures of human beings by the photographs in the brochure. Nor was she bothered by the faint aroma, not after the much stronger smell of the can of stew. But to have one of them address her in nearly perfect English almost floored her. Somehow she had simply not prepared herself for intelligent speech from alien lips.

Father Destry had brought them in from the spaceport, along with the two Earthmen who were their honor escort. She had been watching the courtyard through the window of her office, and had thought she was quite prepared for them when Father Destry escorted them into the office.

"Sister Mary Magdalene, permit me to introduce our guests. This is Vor Nollig, chief diplomat, and her assistants: Vor Betla, Vor Gontakel and Vor Vun."

And Vor Nollig said, "I am honored, Sister."

The voice was deep, like that of a man's, and there was certainly nothing effeminate about these creatures. The nun, in her surprise, could only choke out a hasty: "Thank you." Then she stood back, trying to keep a pleasant smile on her face while the others spoke their pieces.

They were not tall—no taller than Sister Mary Magdalene's own five five—but they were massively built. Their clothing was full and bright-colored. And, in spite of their alienness, the nun could tell them apart with no difficulty. Vor Nollig and Vor Betla had skins of a vivid cobalt-blue color. Vor Gontakel was green, while Vor Vun was yellow.

The Government brochure, Sister Mary Magdalene recalled, had remarked that the Pogatha had races that differed from each other as did the races of Earth. The blue color was a pigment, while the yellow color was the color of their blood

—thus giving the Pogatha a range of yellow-green-blue shades according to the varying amount of pigment in the skin.

In an odd parallel to Earth history, the Blues had long been the dominant race, holding the others in subjection. It had been less than a century ago that the Yellows had been released from slavery, and the Greens were still poverty-stricken underdogs. Only the coming of the Earthmen had brought the three races together in a common cause.

Father Destry was introducing the two Earthmen.

". . . Secretary Masterson and Secretary Bass. They will be staying at the Holy Cross Monastery during the negotiations."

Sister Mary Magdalene had recovered her composure by now. Looking around with a sweeping gesture that took in Father Destry, the four aliens, the stocky Masterson and the elongated Bass, she said, "Won't you all sit down?"

"You are most gracious," said Vor Nollig brusquely, "but our trip has been a long one, and we are most anxious to—ah —the word—freshen up, is it?"

The nun nodded. "I'll show you to your rooms."

"You are most kind."

"I think you'll find everything prepared. If you don't, just ask for whatever you'll need."

She left the men in her office and escorted the four Pogatha outside, across to the part of the convent where they would be staying. When the aliens were installed in their rooms, Sister Mary Magdalene returned to her office and was surprised to find Father Destry and the two U.N. Secretaries still there. She had supposed that the priest would have taken the U.N. men over to the monastery.

"About the Pogatha," said Secretary Masterson with a nervous quirk of his fleshy lips. "Be rather careful with them, will you, Sister? They're rather—uh—prejudiced, you see."

"So am I. Against them, that is."

"No, no. I don't mean prejudiced against you or any other human. Naturally we don't expect much genuine warmth between peoples who are fighting. But I'm referring to the strong racial antipathy among themselves."

"Between the Blues, Yellows and the Greens," Secretary Bass put in. "They try to be polite to each other, but there's no socializing. It's a different kind of prejudice entirely, Sister."

"Yes," Masterson said. "Any one of them might be willing

to sit down to talk to you, but not while one of another color was around."

"I see," said the sister. "I'll keep that in mind. Is there anything else I should remember?"

Secretary Masterson smiled understandingly. "It's hard to say. Handling an alien race isn't easy—but remember, they don't expect us to do everything right. They just want us to show that we're not purposely trying to offend them."

"I'll do my best," said Sister Mary Magdalene.

An hour later, Sister Mary Magdalene decided that she, in her capacity as a hostess here at the convent, had best go around to see how her guests were doing. Her robes swished softly as she went down the hallway. Behind her, Felicity padded silently along.

Sister Mary Magdalene paused outside Vor Nollig's door and rapped. After a moment it opened a little. The alien was dimly visible just inside the doorway.

"Yes, Sister?" said Vor Nollig.

Sister Mary Magdalene forced herself to smile ingratiatingly. "I hope everything's satisfactory."

"Oh, yes. Yes indeed." The door opened another few inches, far enough to let the nun see that Vor Betla stood behind Vor Nollig.

"Please you yes come in?" asked Vor Betla diffidently. There was something in the alien's tone that indicated that the invitation had been offered in an attempt at politeness, and that the Pogatha woman was not anxious to have it actually accepted.

Sister Mary Magdalene was still trying to decide what she should say when suddenly Vor Betla looked down and in a startled voice said, "What is?"

The nun's glance went to the floor. Felicity was standing there, her gleaming green eyes observing the Pogath woman intently. Sister Mary Magdalene scooped the cat up affectionately and held it against her. "This is Felicity. My cat."

"Gat?" said Vor Betla, puzzled.

"Cat," Vor Nollig corrected her. A babble of incomprehensible syllables followed. Finally Vor Nollig turned to the nun and said softly, "Pardon my breach of etiquette, but Vor Betla doesn't understand your language too well. She had never heard of a cat, and I was explaining that they are dumb animals kept as pets. We do not keep such animals on Pogathan.''

"I see," said Sister Mary Magdalene, trying to keep the chill out of her voice. She was not pleased by the slighting reference to the cat. "If everything is fine, I'll look after my other guests. If you need anything, just ask."

"Of course, Sister," said Vor Nollig, closing the door.

The nun repressed what would have been an irrational and sinful current of anger. She swept on down the hall to the next apartment and knocked. "Poor Felicity," she murmured soothingly to the cat resting on her other arm. "Don't let their insults upset you. After all, they aren't humans, you know."

The door opened.

"I beg pardon?" said the green-skinned Vor Gontakel.

"Oh," Sister Mary Magdalene said, feeling awkward. "Sorry. I was talking to Felicity."

"Ah," said the green Pogatha.

"We came to see if everything was comfortable in your room. Didn't we, Felicity?"

"Meerorow," Felicity said.

"Oh, yes," said Vor Gontakel. "All is quite as should be. Quite."

"Meerowou," Felicity said. "Mrourr."

Vor Gontakel said, "This means what?"

Sister Mary Magdalene smiled. "Felicity says she hopes you'll call us if anything is not to your liking."

Vor Gontakel smiled broadly, showing her golden teeth. "I am quite comfortable, thank you, Sister. And thank you, Felicity."

The door closed. Sister Mary Magdalene felt more cheerful. Vor Gontakel had at least been pleasant.

One more trip to make. The last, thank Heaven. The nun rapped on the final door.

Vor Vun slowly opened her door, peered out, stepped back in alarmed distaste. "A cat!" she exclaimed.

"I'm sorry if I frightened you," Sister Mary Magdalene said quickly.

"Frightened? No. I just do not like cats. When I was a prisoner aboard one of your spaceships, they had a cat." The alien woman held out a saffron-skinned arm. Three furrows of scar tissue stood out darkly. "I was scratched. Infection set in, and none of the Earthmen's medicine could be used. It is a good thing that there was an exchange of prisoners, or I might have died."

The alien paused, as if realizing that her speech was not precisely diplomatic. "I am sorry," she said, forcing a smile. "But—you understand?"

"Certainly," the nun said. For the third time in ten minutes she went through the necessary ritual of asking after her guest's comfort, and for the third time she was assured that all was well.

Sister Mary Magdalene returned to her office. "Come on, Felicity," she whispered soothingly. "Can't have you worrying our star boarders."

Father Destry was waiting for Sister Mary Magdalene when she came back from Mass the following morning. He was looking at her with a puzzled air.

"Where is everyone?"

Ignoring his question for the moment, Sister Mary Magdalene jabbed furiously at the air conditioner button. "Isn't this thing working?" she asked fretfully of no one in particular. "It seems as though I can still smell it." Then she realized that the priest had addressed her, and that he was still waiting with imperious patience for an answer.

"Father Pierce kindly invited us to use the monastery chapel this morning," she said, feeling a twinge of embarrassment at her own unintentional rudeness. "Our own is too close to the kitchen."

Father Destry's face showed his lack of comprehension. "You went over to the monastery? Kitchen?"

Sister Mary Magdalene sighed patiently. "Father Destry, I'm morally certain that it would have been impossible for anyone to have retained a properly reverent attitude at Mass if it was held in a chapel that smelled to high Heaven of long-dead fish!"

Her voice had risen in pitch during the last few words, and she cut off the crescendo with a sudden clamping together of her lips before her indignation distressed the priest. "The Pogatha rose early for breakfast. They wouldn't let Sister Elizabeth cook it. Vor Vun—that's the yellow one—did the honors, and each one ate in his—her—own room. That meant that those meals were carried from the kitchen to the rooms. You should have been here. We just barely made it through Lauds."

Father Destry was obviously trying to control a smile which inwardly pleased Sister Mary Magdalene. It was encouraging to know that even Father Destry could be amused by something.

"I imagine the air conditioners have taken care of it by now," he said carefully. "I didn't notice a thing when I came through the courtyard." He glanced at the big clock on the wall. "The first meeting between the official representatives of Pogathan and Earth begins in an hour. I want—"

There was a rap at the door.

"Yes?"

Sister Martha, one of the younger nuns, entered. There was a vaguely apprehensive look on her young face. "The Pogatha are here to see you, Sister."

She stood aside while the four aliens trooped in, led by the imposing Blue, Vor Nollig. Sister Mary Magdalene greeted them with as much heartiness as she could muster, considering the episode of breakfast.

Vor Nollig said, "If it is at all possible, we would like to stroll around the grounds, look at your buildings. Perhaps you could take us on a tour?"

Hostess or not, the last thing Sister Mary Magdalene wanted to do now was shepherd the four aliens around the Cathedral grounds. She glanced meaningfully at Father Destry, who scowled faintly, then brightened and nodded.

"It would be a pleasure," the priest said. "I'll be glad to show you the Cathedral grounds."

And bless you for it, the nun thought as the little group left. After they had gone, she rubbed a finger speculatively across the tip of her nose. Was she wrong or did there seem to be something peculiar in the actions of the aliens? They had seemed to be in a tremendous hurry to leave, and the expressions on their faces were strained. Or were they? It was hard to correlate any Pogatha expressions with their human equivalents. And, of course, Sister Mary Magdalene was no expert on extraterrestrial psychology.

Abruptly she ceased worrying about the behavior of the

Pogatha. With her finger still on her nose, she caught the aroma of the morning's coffee drifting from the kitchen, where it was being prepared. She smiled. Then she indulged in the first, deep, joyous laugh she had had in two weeks.

That evening, after the Pogatha had returned to their quarters, Sister Mary Magdalene's private meditations were interrupted by a phone call from Secretary Masterson, the heavyset U.N. man. His fleshy face had a tense, worried look on it.

"Sister, I know this might be overstepping my authority, but I have the fate of a war to deal with."

"Just what's the trouble, Mr. Masterson?"

"At the meeting today, the Pogatha seemed—I don't quite know how to put it—*offended,* I suppose. They were touchy and unreasonable, and they quarrelled among themselves during the conference—all in a strictly diplomatic way, of course. I'm afraid we got rather touchy ourselves."

"How sad," the nun said. "We all have such high hopes for the success of these negotiations."

"Was there some incident that might have irritated them, Sister? I don't mean to imply any carelessness, but was there anything that might have upset them?"

"The only thing I can think of is the smell of the morning coffee," said the nun. "They came to me asking to be taken on a tour of the Cathedral grounds, and they seemed in an awful hurry to get out of the building. When they were gone I smelled the coffee being prepared. It must have nauseated them as much as their foods bother us."

Masterson's face cleared a little. "That might be it. They *are* touchy people, and maybe they thought the coffee odor that they found so revolting had been generated for their benefit." He paused for a long moment before he said, "Well, that sort of thing is too much for you, and it's obviously too much for them. I'll speak to Bishop Courtland tonight. We'll have to make better arrangements. Meanwhile, do you think you could do something about supper tonight? Get them out of there somehow, and—"

"That might be a little difficult," said Sister Mary Magdalene. "I think it would be better if we ate out."

"Very well. And I'll talk to the bishop."

She waited a moment for the screen to clear after Secretary Masterson broke contact, then dialed the number of the Holy Cross Monastery on the far side of the Cathedral. The face of a monk appeared on the screen, the cowl of his white robe lying in graceful folds around his throat.

Sister Mary Magdalene said, "Father Pierce, you were gracious enough to ask us to your chapel this morning because of the alien aroma here. I wonder if you'd be good enough to ask us to dinner tonight? Our alien friends don't seem to like our odors any more than we like theirs, and so we can't cook here."

Father Pierce laughed cheerfully. "We'll have to use the public dining hall, of course. But I think we can manage it."

"It'll have to be in two shifts," the nun said. "We can't leave this place deserted, much as we'd like to while they're eating."

"Don't worry, Sister. We'll arrange something. But what about tomorrow and the next day?"

Sister Mary Magdalene smiled. "We'll worry about that if we have to, but I think the Pogatha are on their way out of here. Secretary Masterson is going to make different arrangements with the bishop."

"You don't think they'll be transferred to *us*?"

"Hardly, Father Pierce. They'll have to leave the Cathedral entirely."

It was a pleasant, if ungracious thought. But Sister Mary Magdalene had taken no vows to put herself and her nuns into great inconvenience for the sake of unpleasant alien creatures. She would be glad to see them go.

Morning came. Sister Mary Magdalene sat in Choir, listening to the words of the Divine Office and wondering why the Church had been chosen as a meeting place for the two so alien races. It had not been a successful meeting thus far; but, she pondered, was there some deeper reason for the coming-together than mere political negotiation?

The soft, sweet voices of the women, singing alternately from opposite sides of the chapel in the *Domine, Dominus noster,* were like the ringing of crystal chimes rather than the deeper, bell-like ringing that resounded from the throats of the monks on the opposite sides of the great cathedral.

And, like crystal, their voices seemed to shatter under the impact of the hoarse, ugly, bellowing scream that suddenly filled the air.

A moment later, the singing resumed, uncertainly but gamely, as monks and nuns compelled themselves to continue the service regardless. Sister Mary Magdalene felt the unaccustomed tingle of fear within her. What had happened? Trouble with the aliens? Or merely an excitable visitor taken aback by a surprise encounter with one of the Pogatha?

It might be almost anything. Tension grew within the nun. She had to know.

She rose from her seat and slipped away down the aisle. Behind her, the singing continued with renewed vigor. But that ungodly scream still echoed in her ears.

God in Heaven, thought Sister Mary Magdalene an hour later. *What are You doing to Your servants and hand-maidens now? Whoever heard of a convent full of cops?*

She hadn't realized that she had spoken the last sentence half aloud until she saw Father Destry's astonished and reproachful expression. She reddened at once.

"Please, Sister!" the priest murmured. "They're not 'cops'—they're World Bureau of Criminal Investigation officers!"

Sister Mary Magdalene nodded contritely and glanced through the open door of her office at the trio of big, bulky men who were conferring in low tones in the corridor. The label, she thought glumly, made no difference. WBCI or not, they were still *cops.*

The nun felt dazed. Too much had happened in the past hour. Sister Mary Magdalene felt as though everything were twisted and broken around her, as the body of Vor Nollig had been twisted and broken.

Vor Nollig, the Blue; Vor Nollig, the female Pogath; Vor Nollig, the Chief Diplomat of Pogathan—dead, with a common carving knife plunged into her abdomen and her alien blood all over the floor of the room in which she had slept the night before.

She still slept there. She would sleep eternally. The WBCI men had not yet removed the body.

Vor Betla, the other Blue, had found her, and it had been the outraged scream of Vor Betla that had broken the peace of

the convent. Sister Mary Magdalene wondered bleakly if that
peace would ever be whole again.

First the scream, then the violence of the raging fight as the
other two Pogatha had tried to subdue Vor Betla, who seemed
to be intent on destroying the convent with her bare hands.
And now, the quiet warmth of Sister Mary Magdalene's in-
violate little world had suddenly and jarringly been defiled by
the entrance of a dozen men, one right after another. But they
had come too late. The blood had already been shed.

"You look ill, Sister," said Father Destry, suddenly
solicitous. "Wouldn't you like to lie down for a while!"

Sister Mary Magdalene shook her head violently. "No! No,
I'll be all right. It's just the—the shock."

"The bishop gave me strict orders to make sure that none of
this disturbs you."

"I know what he said, and I appreciate it. But I'm afraid we
have already been disturbed." There was a touch of acid in her
voice.

Bishop Courtland, his fine old face looking haggard and
unhappy, had come and gone again. Sister Mary Magdalene
wished he had not gone, but there was no help for it; the
bishop had to deal with the stratoplane load of high officials
who had rocketed in as soon as the news had reached the
Capital.

One of the WBCI men removed his hat in a gesture of
respect and stepped into the nuns' office. She noticed out of
the corner of her eye that the other WBCI men, belatedly
remembering where they were, were taking their hats off, too.

"I'm Major Brock, Sister. Captain Lehmann told me that
you're the sister-in-charge here."

Sister Mary Magdalene nodded wordlessly. Captain Lehmann had been in charge of the group that had come rushing
in at Father Destry's call; they had been hidden outside the
cathedral grounds, ostensibly to protect the alien visitors.

"I know this is—unpleasant," Major Brock said. He was a
big man who was obviously finding it difficult to keep his
voice at the soft level he believed was appropriate in here.
"It's more than a matter of one life at stake, Sister. We have
to find out who did this."

Sister Mary Magdalene nodded, thinking, *The sooner you
find out, the sooner all of you will leave here.* "I'll do all I can
to help," she told him.

"We'd like to question the sisters," he said apologetically. "We'd like to know if any of them saw or heard anything unusual during the night."

The nun frowned. "What time was the alien killed, Major?"

"We don't know. If she were human, we'd be able to pinpoint it within a matter of seconds. But we don't know how fast the blood—" He stopped suddenly on the "d" of "blood," as though he had realized that such gory subjects might not be proper conversation here.

Sister Mary Magdalene was amused at the WBCI man's exaggerated tact. "How fast the blood coagulates," she completed, a bit surprised at her own calmness. "Nor, I suppose, how soon *rigor mortis* sets in, nor how long it takes the body to cool."

"That's about it. We'll just have to check with everybody to see if anyone saw anything that might help us."

"Would you tell me one thing?" Sister Mary Magdalene said, glancing hesitantly at the silent, glowering figure of Father Destry. "Can you tell me who the suspects are? And please don't say 'everybody'—I mean the immediate suspects."

"Frankly," said Major Brock, "we think it might be one of the aliens. But I'm afraid that might just be prejudice. There are other possibilities."

"You don't suspect one of us!"

"Not now. But I can't overlook the possibility. If any of the sisters has a brother or a father in the Space Service—"

"I concede the possibility," said Sister Mary Magdalene reluctantly. "And I suppose the same thing might hold true for anyone else."

"It might, but conditions here pretty well confine the suspects to the sisters and the aliens. After all, you've been pretty closely guarded, and you're pretty secure here." The WBCI man smiled. "Except from invasion by cops." He won Sister Mary Magdalene's undying love with that last sentence.

Father Destry swallowed hard to maintain his composure and said, "I suppose I'll have to remain if the sisters are to be questioned. The bishop—"

"I understand, Father. I'll try not to take too long."

Sister Mary Magdalene sighed and checked the schedule of Masses in the Cathedral of the Blessed Sacrament. There would be little chance of her hearing Mass in the chapel here, with all this going on.

The nightmarish morning dragged slowly along. Sister Mary Magdalene phoned the Mother Superior of the order in Wisconsin to assure her that everything was under control; it was true, if not wholly accurate. Then it was the nun's task to interview each of her Sisters, one by one, to learn her story of the night before.

They knew nothing. None of them was lying, Sister Mary Magdalene knew, and none of them was capable of murder.

Not until the Major came to Sister Angela did anything new come up. Sister Angela was asked if she had noticed anything unusual.

"Yes," she said flatly. "There was someone in the court-yard last night. I saw him from my window."

"Him?" Sister Mary Magdalene repeated in astonishment, sitting bolt upright in her chair. *"Him?"*

Sister Angela nodded nervously. "It—it looked like a monk."

"How do you know it was a monk?" asked the Major.

"Well, he was wearing a robe—with the cowl down. The moon was pretty bright. I could see him clearly."

"Did you recognize him?"

"It wasn't *that* bright, Major. But I'm sure it was—well, a man dressed in a monk's habit."

Major Brock frowned and chewed at the ends of his mustache. "We'll have to investigate this more fully."

Sister Mary Magdalene rose. A quick glance at the clock told her that it was her last chance to make it to Mass. For an instant, a niggling inward voice told her that missing Mass just this once would be excusable under the circumstances, but she fought it down.

"Would you excuse me?" she said to Brock. "I must attend Mass at this hour."

"Of course, Sister." Brock did not seem pleased at the prospect of having to carry on without her, but, as always, he maintained careful respect for the churchly activities going on about him.

Sister Mary Magdalene went out, headed for the cathedral. Outside, everything looked so normal that she could hardly believe anything had really happened. It was not until she reached the cathedral itself that depression again struck her.

The vestment radiations were off.

The vestments of the clergy were fluorescent; under the radiation from the projectors in the walls, the chasubles, tunics and dalmatics, the stoles, maniples and altar frontal, all glowed with color. The color depended on the wave-length of the radiation used. There was the somber violet of the penitential seasons of Lent and Advent, the restful green of Epiphany and the long weeks after Trinity, the joyous white of Christmas and Easter, and the blazing red of Pentecost. But without the radiations, the vestments were black—the somber black of the Requiem, the Mass of the Dead.

For a moment Sister Mary Magdalene's thoughts were as black as the hangings on the altar. And then she realized that, again, there was Reason behind whatever was going on here. There was no doubt in her own mind that the Pogatha were intelligent, reasoning beings, although the question had never been settled on a theological level by the Church. She would pray for the repose of the soul of Vor Nollig.

Forty-five minutes later, she was walking back toward the convent, her own soul strangely at rest. For just a short time, there toward the end, she had felt oddly apprehensive about having had Vor Nollig in mind while the celebrant intoned the *Agnus Dei:* "O Lamb of God that takest away the sins of the world, grant them rest eternal." But then the words of the Last Gospel had come to reassure her: "All things were made by Him, and without Him was not anything made." Surely it could not be wrong to pray for the happiness of one of God's creatures, no matter how strangely made.

She was to think that thought again within the next five minutes.

Sister Elizabeth, round and chubby and looking almost comically penguinlike, was standing at the gate, tears rolling down her plump cheeks.

"Why, Sister Elizabeth—what's the trouble?"

"Oh, Sister, Sister!" She burst into real sobs and buried her head miserably in Sister Mary Magdalene's shoulder. "She's dead—*murdered!*"

For a wild moment, Sister Mary Magdalene thought that Sister Elizabeth was referring to the dead Pogatha, Vor Nollig, but then she knew it was not so, and her numbed mind refused to speculate any further. She could only shake Sister Elizabeth and say, "Who? Who is dead? Who?"

"Her—her little head's all burned off!" sobbed the tearful nun. She was becoming hysterical now, shaking convulsively. Sister Mary Magdalene gripped Sister Elizabeth's shoulders firmly.

"Who?"

Sister Elizabeth looked up. When she spoke it was in a shocked whisper. "Felicity, Sister. Your cat! She's dead!"

Sister Mary Magdalene remained quite still, letting the first tide of grief wash over her. A moment later she was calm again. The cat had been her beloved companion for years, but Sister Mary Magdalene felt no grief now. Merely pity for the unfortunate one who could have done such a brutal deed, and sorrow over the loss of a dear friend. A moment later the anger began, and Sister Mary Magdalene prayed for the strength to unravel the mystery of the sudden outbreak of violence in these peaceful precincts.

When she returned to her office a few moments later, the three living aliens were standing grouped together near one wall of the room. Secretary Masterson and Secretary Bass were not too far away. Major Brock was seated in the guest chair, with Father Destry standing behind him. Brock was speaking.

". . . and that's about it. Someone—we don't know who— came in here last night. One of the Sisters saw him heading toward the back gate of the courtyard, and another has told us that the back gate was unlocked this morning—and it shouldn't have been, because she's positive she locked it the night before." Brock looked up at Sister Mary Magdalene and his expression changed as he saw the frozen mask of her face. The nun was filled with hot anger, burning and righteous, but under complete and icy control.

"What is it, Sister?"

"Would you come with me, Major Brock? I have something to show you. And Father Destry, if you would. I would prefer that the rest of you remain here." She spoke crisply. This was, after all, her domain.

She led the two men, priest and policeman, to the courtyard and around to the rear of the convent. Then they went out to the broad park beyond. Fifteen yards from the gate lay the charred, pitiful remains of the cat.

Major Brock knelt to look at it. "A dead cat," he said in a blank voice.

"Felicity," said Father Destry. "I'm sorry, Sister." The nun knew the sorrow was for her; Father Destry had never felt much warmth for the little animal.

Major Brock rose and said, softly, "I'm afraid I don't quite see what this has to do with—"

"Look at her head," said the nun in a hot-cold voice. "Burned! That's the work of a Brymer beamgun. Close range; not more than ten feet, possibly less."

Brock knelt again, picking up the body and studying it closely for a silent moment. When he looked up, the cat still in his hands, there was new respect in his eyes. "You're right, Sister. There's the typical hardening of the tissues around the burn. This wasn't done with a torch."

Father Destry blinked confusedly. "Do you think the killing of Sister Mary Magdalene's pet has something to do with the—uh—murder of Vor Nollig?"

"I don't know," Brock said slowly. "Sister? What do you think?"

"I think it does. But I'm not sure how. I think you'll find a connection."

"This brings something new into the picture, at least," said the Major. "Now we can look for a Brymer beamgun."

Vor Betla, the second Blue, who had never been able to speak English well, had given it up completely. She was snarling and snapping at Vor Vun, who was translating as best she could. It appeared that all three of the aliens seemed to feel that they might be the next to get a carving knife in their insides.

Vor Vun said, "We feel that you are not doing as well as you might, Major Brock. We don't blame the government of Earth directly for this insult, but obviously the precautions that were taken to protect us were insufficient."

The Major shook his head. "The entire grounds around the Cathedral were patrolled and guarded by every detection instrument known to Earth. No one could have gotten in."

Vor Gontakel put the palms of her green hands together, almost as if she were praying. "It makes a sense. You would not want us to get out, of course, so you would have much of safeguards around."

"We grant that," agreed Vor Vun. "But someone nonetheless killed Vor Nollig, and her loss is great."

Vor Betla snarled and yapped.

Vor Vun translated: "You must turn the killer over to us. If you do not, there can be no further talk of peace."

"How do we know it wasn't one of you three?" asked Secretary Masterson suddenly.

Vor Betla barked something. Vor Vun said, "We would have no reason for it."

Major Brock sighed. "I know. That's what's bothered me all along. Where's the motive?"

Sister Mary Magdalene, watching silently, eyed the three aliens. Which one of them would have killed Vor Nollig? Which one might have killed Felicity?

Vor Vun? She hated cats; had she also hated Vor Nollig? Or had it been Vor Gontakel, the despised Green? But why would she kill Felicity? Had Vor Betla done it so she could be head of the delegation? That made even less sense.

Motive. What was the motive?

Had someone else done it? One of the secretaries, perhaps? Was there a political motive behind the crime?

And then—she had to force herself to think of it—there was the possibility that one of the monks, or, worse yet, one of her own sisters had done it.

If an Earthman had done it, it was either a political motive or one of hatred; there could be nothing personal in it. Vor Nollig, if she had been killed by an Earthman, had been killed for some deep, unknown or unknowable political machination, probably by order of the government itself, or else she had been killed because some Earthman just hated the enemy to such an extent that—

Sister Mary Magdalene did not want to think of blind hatred such as that.

On the other hand, if one of the three remaining Pogatha had done it, the motive could be any one of several. It could be personal, or political, or it might even have a basis in racial prejudice.

The nun thought it over for several minutes without reaching any conclusions. Motive would have to be abandoned as a way of finding the killer. For once, motive could not enter into the solution at all.

Method, then. What was the method?

Major Brock was saying: "Even the best of modern aids to

crime detection can't reconstruct the past for us. But we do know part of the killer's actions. He—"

There was a rap on the door, and Captain Lehmann thrust his head inside. "Excuse me if I'm interrupting. See you a minute, Major?"

Brock frowned, rose, and went outside, closing the door behind him. Father Destry leaned over and whispered to the nun, "They may suspect me."

"Nonsense, Father!"

Father Destry pursed his lips suddenly and said nothing more. Major Brock put his head in the door. "Sister, would you come here a minute?"

She stepped into the hall to confront two very grim WBCI men. Captain Lehmann was holding a Brymer beamgun in one hand and a bundle of black cloth in the crook of his arm. A faint but decidedly foul stench was perceptible.

"This is the gun," Lehmann said, "that killed your cat. At least, as far as we know. An energy beam has no traceable ballistics characteristics. We found it wrapped in this—" He gestured toward the black bundle. "And shoved under one of the pews in the chapel."

With a sudden movement he flipped out the cloth so it was recognizable. Sister Mary Magdalene had no difficulties in recognizing it. It was the habit of a nun.

"The lab men have already gone over it," Major Brock said. "We can prove who the owner is by perspiration comparison, but there also happens to be an identification strip in it. The odor is the blood of Vor Nollig. It spurted out when she was stabbed through the heart."

Brock opened the habit so the ID tag became visible.

It said, *Sister Elizabeth, S.H.N.*

"We'll have to talk to her," said the Major.

"Of course," said Sister Mary Magdalene calmly. "I imagine you'll find it was stolen from her room. Tell me, why should Father Destry think you suspect him?"

The sudden, casual change of subject apparently puzzled Major Brock. He paused a moment before answering. "We don't, really. That is—" Again he paused. "He had a brother. A colonist on Pogathan. The Pogatha caught him. He died—not pleasantly, I'm afraid." He looked at the floor. "We have a similar bit of information on Sister Elizabeth. An uncle."

"You haven't mentioned my nephew yet," said Sister Mary Magdalene.

The Major looked surprised. "No. We hadn't."

"It's of no importance, anyway. Let's go check with Sister Elizabeth. I can tell you now that she knows nothing about it. She probably doesn't even know her spare habit is missing yet, because it was stolen from the laundry. The laundry room is right across from the aliens' quarters."

"Wait," Brock said. "You'd rather we didn't talk to her, don't you?"

"It would only upset her."

"How do you know she didn't do it?"

"For the same reason you don't think she did, Major. This thing is beginning to make sense. I'm beginning to understand the mind that did this awful thing."

He looked at her curiously. "You have a strange mind yourself, Sister. I didn't realize that nuns knew so much about crime."

"Major," she said evenly, "when I took my vows, I chose the name 'Mary Magdalene.' I didn't pick it out of the hat."

The Major nodded silently, and his gaze shifted to the closed door of the nun's office. "The thing is that the whole pattern *is* beginning to make sense. But I can't quite see it."

"It was a badly fumbled job, really," said Sister Mary Magdalene. "If an Earthman had done it, you'd have spotted him immediately."

Again the Major nodded. "I agree. That much of the picture is clear. It *was* one of those three. But unless we know which one, and know beyond any smidgen of doubt, we don't dare make any accusations."

The nun turned to Captain Lehmann. "Did your lab men find out where that gun was discharged?"

"Why, yes. We found faint burn marks on the floor near the door to Vor Nollig's room."

"In the corridor outside, about four or five feet away?"

"That's right."

"Now—and this is important—where were they in relation to the door? I mean, if a person were facing the door, looking at someone inside the room, would the burn marks be behind him or in front?"

"Well—let's see—the door opens in, so they'd have to stand at an angle—mmm. Behind."

"I thought so!" Sister Mary Magdalene exclaimed in triumph.

Major Brock frowned. "It almost makes sense, but I don't quite—"

"That's because I have a vital clue that you don't have, Major."

"Which is?"

She told him.

"We know what was done," said Major Brock levelly. "We know *how* it was done." He looked the three aliens over. "One of you will tell us *why* it was done."

"If you are going to accuse one of us," said Vor Gontakel, rubbing her green hands carefully, "I'm afraid we will have to resist arrest. Is it not called a 'frame'?"

"Is insult!" snapped Vor Betla. "Is stupid! Is lie!"

The Major leaned back in his chair and looked at the two Terran diplomats, Bass and Masterson. "What makes this so tough," he said, "is that we don't know the motive. If the plot was hatched by all three of them, we're going to have a hell of a time—excuse me, Sister—proving it, or at least a rough time doing anything about it."

Masterson considered. "Do you think you could prove it to the satisfaction of an Earth court?"

"Maybe." Brock paused. "I *think* so. I'm a cop, not a prosecuting attorney."

Masterson and Bass conferred a moment. "All right—go ahead," Masterson said finally. "If it's a personal motive, then the other two will be sensible enough to see that the killer has greatly endangered the peace negotiations, besides murdering their leader. And I don't think it's a political motive on the part of all three."

"Though if it is," Bass interjected, "nothing we say will matter anyhow."

"Okay," Brock said. "Here's what happened. Sometime early this morning, around two—if Sister Angela's testimony is accurate—the killer went into the laundry room and picked up one of the nun's habits. Then the killer went to the kitchen, got a carving knife, came back and knocked on the door of

Vor Nollig's room. Vor Nollig woke and came to the door. She opened the door a crack and saw what appeared to be a nun in the dim corridor. Not suspecting anything, Vor Nollig opened the door wider and stepped into full view. The killer stabbed her in the heart with the knife.''

"Earthman," said Vor Betla positively.

"No. Where's your heart, Vor Betla?"

The Pogath patted the base of her throat.

"Ours is here," Brock said. "An Earthman would have instinctively stabbed much lower, you see."

Sister Mary Magdalene repressed a smile. The Major was bluffing there. Plenty of human beings had been stabbed in the throat by other human beings.

Brock said, "But now comes the puzzling part. You do not like cats, Vor Vun. What would you do if one came near you? Are you afraid of them?"

Vor Vun sniffed. "Afraid? No. They are harmless. They can be frightened easily. I would not pick one up, or allow it too close, but I am not afraid."

"How about you, Vor Betla?"

"Do? Don't know. Know nothing of cats, but that they harmless dumb animals. Maybe kick if came too close."

"Vor Gontakel?"

"I too know nothing of cats. I only saw one once."

"One of you," said the Major judiciously, "is telling an untruth. Let's go on with the story."

Sister Mary Magdalene watched their faces, trying to read emotion in those alien visages as the Major spoke.

"The killer did a strange thing. She turned around and saw Felicity, the cat. Possibly it had meowed from behind her and attracted her attention. And what does the killer do? She draws a Brymer beamgun and kills the cat! Why?"

The Pogatha looked at each other and then back at the Major. Their faces, thought Sister Mary Magdalene, were utterly unreadable.

"Then the killer picked up the cat, walked outdoors through the rear gate and threw it into the meadow. It was the killer that Sister Angela saw last night, but the killer had pushed the cowl back, so she didn't recognize the fact that it was a nun's habit, not a monk's. When the killer had disposed of the cat, she removed the habit, wrapped the beamgun in it and went into the chapel and put it under one of the pews."

"Very plausible," said Vor Vun. "But not proof that one of *us* did it."

"Not so far. But let's keep plugging. Why did the killer wear the nun's habit?"

"Because was nun!" said Vor Betla. She pointed an accusing blue finger at Sister Mary Magdalene.

"No," Brock said. "Because she wanted Vor Nollig to let her get close enough to stab her. You see, we've eliminated you, Vor Betla. You shared the room; you would have been allowed in without question. But Vor Nollig would never have allowed a Green or a Yellow into her room, would she?"

"No," admitted the Blue, looking troubledly at Vor Vun and Vor Gontakel.

"Another point in your favor is the fact that the killer looked like a monk to Sister Angela. There are no dark-skinned monks at this cathedral, and Sister Angela would have commented on it if the skin had looked as dark as yours does. But colors are almost impossible to see in moonlight. A yellow or light green would have looked pretty much like human skin, and the features at a distance would be hard to recognize as belonging to a Pogath."

"You are playing on prejudices," said Vor Vun angrily. "This is an inexpensive trick!"

"A *cheap* trick," corrected Major Brock. "Except that it isn't. However, we must now prove that it was a Pogath. We've smelled each others' food, haven't we? Now, a burnt cat would smell no differently than, say, a broiled steak—except maybe a little more so. Why would the killer take the trouble to remove the cat from the building? Why not leave it where it was? If she expected to get away with one killing, she could have expected to get away with two. She took the cat out simply because she couldn't stand the overpowering odor! There was no other possible reason to expose herself that way to the possible spying eyes of Sister Angela or any other nun who happened to be looking out the window. It was clever of the killer to think of dropping the wimple back and disposing of the white part of the headdress so that she would appear to be a monk. I imagine it also took a lot of breathholding to stand to carry that burnt cat that far."

The Pogatha were definitely eyeing each other now, but the final wedge remained to be driven.

"Vor Gontakel!" the Major said sharply. "What would you say if I told you that another cat at the far end of the corridor saw you stab Vor Nollig and burn down Felicity?"

Vor Gontakel looked perfectly unruffled and imperturbed. No Earthman's bluff was going to get by *her!* "I would say the cat was lying," she said.

"The other two Pogatha got a confession out of her," said Major Brock that evening. "They'll take her back to Pogathan to stand trial."

Father Destry folded his hands and smiled. "Sister, you seem to have all the makings of a first-class detective. How did you figure out that it was Vor Gontakel? I mean, what started you on that train of thought?"

"Sister Elizabeth," the nun said. "She told me that Felicity had been murdered. And she *had* been—murdered, I mean, not just 'killed.' Vor Gontakel saw me talking to the cat, and Felicity meowed back. How was she to know that the cat wasn't intelligent? She knew nothing about Terrestrial life. The other two did. Felicity was murdered because Vor Gontakel thought she was a witness. It was the only possible motive for Felicity's murder."

"What about the motive for Vor Nollig's murder?" Father Destry said to the Major.

"Political. There's a group of Greens, it seems, that has the idea the war should go on. Most of the war is being fought by Blues, and if they're wiped out the so-called minority groups could take over. I doubt if it would work that way, but that's what this bunch thinks. Vor Gontakel simply wanted to kill a Blue and have it blamed on the Earthmen in order to stop the peace talks. But there's one thing I think we left untied here, Sister. Have you stopped to wonder why she used a knife on Vor Nollig instead of the beamgun she was carrying?"

Sister Mary Magdalene nodded. "She didn't want every sister in the place coming out to catch her before she had a chance to cover up. She knew that burnt Pogatha would smell as bad to us as burnt cat did to her. But she didn't have a chance to use a knife on Felicity; the cat would have run away."

Major Brock nodded in appreciation. "A very neat summation, Sister. I bow to your fine deductive abilities. And now, I imagine, we can get our staff off the cathedral premises and leave you people to your devotions."

"It's unfortunate we had to meet under such unhappy circumstances, Major," the nun said.

"But you were marvelously helpful, Sister."

The Major smiled at the nun, shook Father Destry's hand tentatively, as if uncertain that such a gesture was appropriate, and left. Sister Mary Magdalene sighed gently in relief.

Police and aliens and all were leaving. The cathedral was returning to its normal quietude. In the distance the big bell was tolling, and it was time for prayer. She was no longer a detective; she was simply sister Mary Magdalene of the Sisters of the Holy Nativity.

It would be good to have peace here again. But, she admitted wryly to herself, the excitement had been a not altogether unwelcome change from normal routine. The thought brought up old memories of a life long buried and sealed away with vows. Sister Mary Magdalene frowned gently, dispelling the thoughts, and quietly began to pray.

The Cat

Here's a rarity: the first—and, so far as we know, the only—short story set in the strange and evocative universe of Gene Wolfe's *The Book of the New Sun* tetralogy.

Come with us now to the far, far future, when the sun has grown old and red and dim, the moon has grown green with forests, and old Urth groans under the almost insupportable weight of her own unnumbered years.

The scene is the mysterious House Absolute, the immense and labyrinthine palace of the Autarch, home also to the sinister and enigmatic Father Inire, whose blazing magic circle of specula can circumfuse travelers and send them to the stars—or coalesce strange spectral beings from the ethereal waves. . . .

I am Odilo the Steward, the son of Odilo the Steward. I am he who is charged by our Autarch Severian the Great—whose desires are the dreams of his subjects—with the well-being of the Hypogeum Apotropaic. It is now the fifth year of his reign.

As all who know the ways of our House Absolute (and I may say here that I neither hope nor wish for other readers) are aware, our Hypogeum Apotropaic is that part devoted to the needs and comforts of Father Inire; and in the twenty years in which I have given satisfaction (as I hope) at my post, and in the years before them when I assisted my father, also Odilo the Steward, I have seen and heard many a strange thing. My father likewise.

This evening, when I had reached a respite in the unending tasks entailed by such a position as mine, I took myself, as my custom is, to the culina magna of our Hypogeum to obtain some slight refreshment. The cooks' labors too were ended, or nearly; and half or more, with a kitchen boy or three and a gaggle of scullery maids, sat about the dying fire, seeking, as such people will, to amuse one another by diverse boasts and recitals.

Having little better to do and being eager to rest, I bid the chief cook surrender his chair to me and heard them as I ate. It is now Hallowmas Eve (which is to say, the full of the Spading Moon) and their talk had turned to all manner of ghosts and bogeys. In the brief time required for me to chew my bread

and beef and sluice them down with hot spiced ale, I heard
such recountings of larva, lemures, and the like as would
terrify every child in the Commonwealth—and make every
man in it laugh most heartily.

So I myself laughed when I returned here to my study,
where I will scrutinize and doubtless approve the bills of fare
for Hallowmas; and yet I find I am bemused by these tales and
lost amid many wondering speculations. As every thinking
man acknowledges, mighty powers move through this dark
universe of Briah, though for the most part hidden from us by
its infinite night. Is it not every man's duty to record what
little he has glimpsed that may give light to it? And do not
such idle tales as I heard by the fire but serve to paint yet
blacker that gloom through which we grope? I am therefore
determined to set down here, for the enlightenment (as it may
be) of my successors and whoever else may read, the history,
whole and in entire in so far as I know it, of a series of inci-
dents that culminated (as I believe) this night ten years gone.
For the earlier events, I give the testimony of my father, Odilo
the Steward also, a contemporary of the Chatelaine Sancha.

She was (so my father said) an extraordinarily charming
child, with the face of a peri and eyes that were always laughing, darker than most exulted children but so tall that she
might have been supposed, at the age of seven or eight, to be a
young woman of sixteen.

That such a child should have attracted the attention of
Father Inire is scarcely to be wondered at. He has always been
fond of children (and particularly of girls), as the oldest
records of our Hypogeum show; and I sometimes think that he
has chosen to remain on Urth as a tutor to our race because he
finds even the wisest of us to be children in his sight. Permit
me to say at once that these children have often benefited from
his attention. It is true, perhaps, that they have sometimes suffered for it, but that has been seldom and I think by no means
by his wish.

It has ever been the custom of the exultants resident in our
House Absolute to keep their children closely confined to their
own apartments and to permit them to travel the ten thousand
corridors that wind such distances beneath the surface of the
land (even so far as the Old Citadel of Nessus, some say) only
under the watchful eyes of some trustworthy upper servant
And it has ever been the custom of those children to escape the

upper servants charged with their supervision whenever they can, to join in the games of the children of the staff, so much more numerous, and to wander at will through the numberless leagues of the ten thousand corridors, by which frolic many have been lost at one time or another, and some forever.

Whenever Father Inire encounters such a child not already known to him, he speaks to her, and if her face and her answers please him, he may pause in the conduct of great affairs to tell her some tale of the worlds beyond Dis. (No person grown has heard these tales, for the children do not recall them well enough to recount them afterward, though they are often quite charmed by them; and before they are grown themselves they have forgotten them, as indeed I have forgotten all but a few scraps of the tale Father Inire once told me.) If he cannot take the time for that, he often confers upon the child some many-hued toy of the kind that wise men and humble men such as I, and all women and children, call magical.

Should he encounter that child a second time, as often happens, he asks her what has become of the toy, or whether she wishes to hear some other story from his store. Should he find that the toy remains unbroken and that it is still in the possession of the child, he may give another, and should the child ask politely (for Father Inire values courtesy above all knowledge), he may tell another. But if, as only very rarely happens, the child has received a toy and exhibits it still whole, but asks on this occasion for a tale of the worlds beyond Dis instead of a second toy, then Father Inire takes that child as a particular friend and pupil for so long as she—or more rarely he—may live. (I boast no scholarship of words, as you that have read this account do already well know; but once I heard a man who was such a scholar say that this word *pupil* in its most ancient and purest state denominates the image of oneself one sees in another's eyes.)

Such a pupil Sancha became, one winter morning when she was of seven years or thereabout and my father much the same. All her replies must have pleased Father Inire; and he was doubtless returning to his apartments in our Hypogeum Apotropaic from some night-long deliberation with the Autarch. He took her with him; and so my father met them, as he often told me, in that white corridor we call the Luminary Way. Even then, when my father was only a child himself, he was struck by the sight of them walking and chatting together,

Father Inire bent nearly double, like a gnome in a nursery
book, with no more nose than an alouatte; Sancha already
towering over him, straight as a sapling, sable of hair and
bright of eye, with her cat in her arms.

Of what passed between them in Father Inire's apartments,
I can only relay what Sancha herself told a maid called Aude,
many years later. Father Inire showed the girl many wonderful
and magical appurtenances, and at last that marvelous circle
of specula by whose power a living being may be coalesced
from the ethereal waves, or, should such a being boldly enter
them, circumfused to the borders of Briah. Then Sancha,
doubtless thinking it but a toy, cast her cat into the circle. It
was a gray cat, so my father told me, with many stripes of a
darker gray.

Knowing Father Inire as I have been privileged to know him
these many years, I feel certain he must have promised poor
Sancha that he would do all that lay in his power to retrieve
her pet, and that he must have kept faithfully to that promise.
As for Sancha, Aude said she believed the cat the only creature
Sancha was ever to love, beyond herself; but that, I think, was
spite; and Aude was but a giddypate, who knew the Chatelaine
only when she was old.

As I have often observed, rumor in our House Absolute is a
self-willed wind. Ten thousand corridors there well may be
(though I, with so many more immediate concerns, have for-
borne to count them), and a million chambers or more; and in
truth no report reaches them all. And yet in a day or less, the
least gossip comes to a thousand ears. So it became known,
and quickly, that the girl Sancha was attended by some fey
thing. When she and some friend sat alone at play, a pochette
was knocked from a table and broken, or so it was said. On
another occasion, a young man who sat conversing with
Sancha (who must, I should think, have been somewhat older
then) observed the ruffled body of a sparrow lying on the
carpet at her feet, though she could scarcely have sat where she
did without stepping upon it, had it been present when they
began their talk.

Of the scandal concerning Sancha and a certain Lomer,
then seneschal to the Chatelaine Nympha, I shall say nothing—or at least very little, although the matter was only too
well known at the time. She was still but a child, being then
fourteen years of age, or as some alleged, fifteen. He was a

man of nearly thirty. They were discovered together in that state which is too easily imagined. Sancha's rank and age equally exempted her from formal punishment; her age and her rank equally ensured that the disrepute would cling to her for life. Lomer was sentenced to die; he appealed to the Autarch, and as the Chatelaine Nympha exerted herself on his behalf, his appeal was accepted. He was sent to the ante-chamber to await a hearing; but if his case was ever disposed of, I do not recall it. The Chatelaine Leocadia, who was said to have concocted the affair to injure Nympha, suffered nothing.

When Sancha came of age, she received a villa in the south by her father's will, so becoming the Chatelaine Sancha. The Autarch Appian permitted her to leave our House Absolute at once; and no one was surprised, to hear soon after that she had wed the heir of Fors—it was a country family not liable to know much of the gossip of the court, not apt to care greatly for what it heard, while the Chatelaine was a young woman of some fortune, excellent family, and extraordinary beauty. Insofar as we interested ourselves in her doings, she then vanished for the space of fifty years.

During the third year in which I performed the consequential charge which had once been my father's, she returned and requested a suite in this Hypogeum, which Father Inire granted in observance of their old friendship. At that time, I conversed with her at length, it being necessary to arrange a thousand details to her satisfaction.

Of the celebrated beauty that had been hers, only the eyes remained. Her back was as bent as Father Inire's, her teeth had been made for her by a provincial ivory-turner, and her nose had become the hooked beak of a carrion bird. For whatever reason, her person now carried a disagreeable odor; she must have been aware of it, for she had ordered fires of sandalwood to counter it.

Although she never mentioned her unfortunate adventure in our Hypogeum, she described to me, in much greater detail than I shall give here, her career at Fors. Suffice it to say that she had borne several children, that her husband was dead, and that her elder son now directed the family estate. The Chatelaine did not get along well with his wife and had many disagreeable anecdotes to relate of her, of which the worst was that she had once denounced the Chatelaine as a *gligua*, such

being the name the autochthons of the south employ for one
who has traffic with diakka, casts spells, and the like.

Till that time, no thought of the impalpable cat said to accompany this old woman had crossed my mind; but the odd
word suggested the odd story, and from that moment I kept
the most careful watch, though I neither saw nor heard the
least sign of the phantom. Several times I sought to lead our
talk to her former relations with Father Inire or to the subject
of felines per se—remarking, for example, that such an animal
might be a source of comfort to one now separated by so many
leagues from her family. The first evoked only general praises
of Father Inire's goodness and learning, and the latter talk of
birds, marmosets, and similar favorites.

As I was about to go, Aude (whom I had assigned to the
Chatelaine Sancha's service already, for the Chatelaine had
brought but little staff with her from Fors) entered to com-
plain that she had not been told the Chatelaine had a pet, and
that it would be necessary to arrange for its food and the
delivery of clean sand. The Chatelaine quite calmly denied she
possessed such an animal and demanded that the one Aude
reported be expelled from the suite.

As the years passed, the Chatelaine Sancha had little need of
birds or marmosets. The scandal was revived by doddering
women who recollected it from childhood, and she attracted
to herself a host of protégées, the daughters of armigers and
exultants, eager to exhibit their tolerance and bathe in a
notoriety that was without hazard. Rumors of a spectral cat
persisted—it being said to walk upon the keyboard of the
choralcelo—but there are many rumors in our Hypogeum,
and they were not the strangest.

It is one of my duties to pay my respects, as the prolocutor
of all Father Inire's servants, to those who endure their mortal
illness here. Thus I called upon the Chatelaine Sancha as she
lay dying, and thus I came to be in her bedchamber when,
after having spoken with me only a moment before, she cried
out with her final breath.

Having now carried my account to its conclusion, I scarcely
know how to end it, save by an unembellished recitation of the
facts.

At the dying Chatelaine's cry, all turned to look at her. And
all saw, as did I, that upon the snowy counterpane covering
her withered body there had appeared the dark pawprint o

some animal, and beside it a thing not unlike a doll. This was no longer than my hand, and yet it seemed in each detail a lovely child just become a woman. Nor was it of painted wood, or any other substance of which such toys are made; for when the physician pricked it with his lancet, a ruby drop shone forth.

By the strict instructions of Father Inire, this little figure was interred with the Chatelaine Sancha. Our laundresses having proved incapable of removing the stain left by the creature's paw, I ordered the counterpane sent to the Chatelaine Leocadia, who being of the most advanced age was even then but dim of sight.

She has since gone blind, and yet her maids report that she sees the cat, which stalks her in her dreams. It is not well for those of high station to involve the servants of their enemies in their quarrels.

Afternoon
at Schrafft's

By Gardner Dozois, Jack Dann,
and Michael Swanwick

The next story is about a large brindle cat who has the bad
luck to be the familiar of a very ungrateful wizard. Like
Rodney Dangerfield, familiars never get any respect. . . .

Wizards have had terrific PR over the last few thousand
years—they've managed to convince almost everybody that
they cast those magical spells that transmute lead into gold
and transform frogs into princes *all by themselves*.

But that's simply not true. Just ask the next dinosaur you
pass on the street. . . .

Jack Dann and Gardner Dozois are (in case you haven't
noticed yet) the editors of this book. You can find *our* bios on
the *About the Editors* page. Michael Swanwick is a Nebula
and World Fantasy Award finalist, as well as a finalist for the
John W. Campbell Award, and is one of the most respected
new talents to emerge in the 1980's. His stories have appeared
in *Universe, New Dimensions, Penthouse, Omni,* and *Tri-
quarterly*, among other places. He is currently at work on his
first novel, tentatively titled *The Drift*, for the upcoming "Ace
Specials" line.

The wizard sat alone at a table in Schrafft's, eating a tuna sandwich on rye. He finished off the last bite of his sandwich, sat back, and licked a spot of mayonnaise off his thumb. There was an ozone crackle in the air, and his familiar, a large brindle cat, materialized in the chair opposite him.

The cat coldly eyed the wizard's empty plate. "And where, may I ask, is my share?" he demanded.

The wizard coughed in embarrassment.

"You mean you didn't even leave me a crumb, is that it?"

The wizard shrugged and looked uncomfortable. "There's still a pickle left," he suggested.

The cat was not mollified.

"Or some chips. Have some potato chips."

"Feh," sneered the cat. "Potato chips I didn't want. What I *wanted* was a piece of your sandwich, Mister Inconsiderate."

"Listen, aggravation I don't need from you. Don't make such a big deal—it's only a *tunafish sandwich*. So who cares!"

"So who *cares*?" the cat spat. "So *I* care, that's who. Listen, it's not just the sandwich. It's everything! It's your *attitude*."

"Don't talk to *me* about *my* attitude—"

"Somebody should. You think you're *so* hot. Mister Big Deal! The Big-Time Wizard!" The cat sneered at him. "Hah! You need me more than I need you, believe me, Mister Oh-I'm-So-Wonderful!"

"Don't make me laugh," the wizard said.

"You couldn't get along without me, and you know it!"

"I'm laughing," the wizard said. "It's such a funny joke you're making, look at me, I'm laughing. Hah. Hah. Hah."

The cat fluffed itself up, enraged. "Without me, you couldn't even get through the day. What an ingrate! You refuse to admit just how much you really need me. Why, without me, you couldn't even"—the cat paused, casting about for an example, and his gaze fell on the check—"without me, you couldn't even pay the *check*."

"Oh yeah?"

"Yeah. Even something as simple as *that,* you couldn't do it by yourself. You couldn't handle it."

"*Sure* I could. Don't get too big for your britches. Stuff like this I was handling before *you* were even weaned, bubbie, let *alone* housebroken. So don't puff yourself up."

The cat sneered at him again. "Okay, so go ahead! Show me! Do it!"

"Do what?" said the wizard after a pause, a trace of uneasiness coming into his voice.

"Pay the check. Take care of it yourself."

"All right," the wizard said. "All right, then, I will!"

"So go ahead, already. I'm watching. This ought to be good." The cat smiled nastily and faded away, slowly disappearing line by line—the Cheshire cat was one of his heroes, and this was a favorite trick, although for originality's sake he left his nose behind instead of his grin. The nose hung inscrutably in midair, like a small black-rubber UFO. Occasionally it would give a sardonic twitch.

The wizard sighed and sat staring morosely down at the check. Then, knowing in advance that it would be useless, he pulled out his battered old change-purse and peered inside: nothing, except for some lint, the tiny polished skull of a bat, and a ticket stub from the 1876 Centennial Exposition. The wizard never carried money—ordinarily, he'd have just told the cat to conjure up whatever funds were necessary, an exercise so simple and trivial that it was beneath his dignity as a Mage even to consider bothering with it himself. That was what familiars were *for*, to have tasks like that delegated to them. Now, though . . .

"Well?" the cat's voice drawled. "So, I'm waiting. . . ."

"All right, all right, big shot," the wizard said. "I can handle this, don't worry yourself."

"I'm not worried—I'm *waiting*."

"All right, already." Mumbling to himself, the wizard began to work out the elements of the spell. It was a very *small* magic, after all. Still . . . He hesitated, drumming his fingers on the table. . . . Still, he hadn't had to do anything like this for himself for years, and his memory wasn't what it used to be. . . . Better ease his hand in slowly, try a still smaller magic first. Practice. Let's see now . . . He muttered a few words in a hissing sibilant tongue, sketched a close pattern in the air, and then rested his forefinger on the rim of his empty coffee cup. The cup filled with coffee, as though his finger was a spigot. He grunted in satisfaction, and then took a sip of his coffee. It was weak and yellow, and tasted faintly of turpentine. So far, so good, he thought. . . .

Across the table, the nose sniffed disdainfully.

The wizard ignored it. *Now* for the real thing. He loosened his tie and white starched collar and drew the pentagram of harmony, the *Sephiroth,* using salt from the shaker, which was also the secret symbol for the fifth element of the pentagram, the *akasha,* or ether. He made do with a glass of water, catsup, mustard, and toothpicks to represent the four elements and the worlds of Emanation, Creation, Formation, and Action. He felt cheap and vulgar using such substitutes, but what else could he do?

Now . . . he thought, that *is* the pentagram of harmony . . . isn't it? For an instant he was uncertain. Well, it's close enough. . . .

He tugged back his cuffs, leaving his wrists free to make the proper passes over the pentagram. Now . . . what was the spell to make money? It was either the first or the second Enochian Key . . . *that* much he did remember. It must be the second Key, and that went . . . *"Piamoel od Vaoan!"* No, no, that wasn't it. Was it *"Giras ta nazodapesad Roray I"*? That *must* be it.

The wizard said the words and softly clapped his hands together . . . and nothing seemed to happen.

For an instant there was no noise, not even a breath. It was as if he were hovering, disembodied, between the worlds of emanation.

There was a slow shift in his equilibrium, like a wheel revolving ponderously in darkness.

But magic didn't just disappear, he told himself querulously—it had to go *somewhere*.

As if from the other side of the world, the wizard heard the soft voice of his familiar, so faint and far away that he could barely make it out. What was it saying?

"Putz," the cat whispered, "you used the Pentagram of Chaos, the *Qliphoth*."

And suddenly, as if he really had been turned upside down for a while, the wizard felt everything right itself. He was sitting at a table in Schrafft's, and there was the usual din of people talking and shouting and pushing and complaining.

But something was odd, something was wrong. Even as he watched, the table splintered and flew to flinders before him, and his chair creaked and groaned and swayed like a high-masted ship in a strong wind, and then broke, dumping him heavily to the floor. The room shook, and the floor cracked and starred beneath him.

What was wrong? What ethers and spheres had he roiled and foiled with his misspoken magicking? Why did he feel so *strange*? Then he saw himself in the goldflecked smoked-glass mirrors that lined the room between rococo plaster pillars, and the reflection told him the terrible truth.

He had turned himself into some kind of giant lizard. A dinosaur. Actually, as dinosaurs go, he was rather small. He weighed about eight hundred pounds and was eleven feet long—a pachycephalosaurus, a horn-headed, pig-snouted her-bivore that was in its prime in the Upper Cretaceous. But for Schrafft's, at lunch time—big enough. He clicked his stubby tusks and tried to say "Gevalt!" as he shook his head ruefully. Before he could stop the motion, his head smashed into the wooden booth partition, causing it to shudder and crack.

Across from him, two eyes appeared, floating to either side of the hovering black nose. Slowly, solemnly, one eye winked. Then—slowly and very sinisterly—eyes and nose faded away and were gone.

That was a bad sign, the wizard thought. He huddled glumly against the wall. Maybe nobody would notice, he thought. His tail twitched nervously, splintering the booth behind him. The occupants of the booth leaped up, screaming, and fled the restaurant in terror. Out-of-towners, the wizard thought. Everyone else was eating and talking as usual, paying no attention, although the waiter *was* eyeing him somewhat sourly.

As he maneuvered clumsily away from the wall, pieces of wood crunching underfoot, the waiter came up to him and stood there making little *tsk*ing noises of disapproval. "Look, mister," the waiter said. "You're going to have to pay up and go. You're creating a disturbance. . . ." The wizard opened his mouth to utter a mild remonstrance, but what came out instead was a thunderous roaring belch, grindingly deep and loud enough to rattle your bones, the sort of noise that might be produced by having someone stand on the bass keys of a giant Wurlitzer. Even the wizard could smell the fermenting rotting-egg, bubbling-prehistoric-swamp stink of sulfur that his belch had released, and he winced in embarrassment. "I'm sorry," the wizard said, enunciating with difficulty through the huge, sloppy mouth. "It's the tunafish. I know I shouldn't eat it, it always gives me gas, but—" But the waiter no longer seemed to be listening—he had gone pale, and now he turned abruptly around without a word and walked away, ignoring as he passed the querulous demands for coffee refills from the people two tables away, marching in a straight line through the restaurant and right out into the street.

The wizard sighed, a gusty, twanging noise like a cello being squeezed flat in a winepress. Time—and *past* time—to work an obviation spell. So, then. Forgetting that he was a dinosaur, the wizard hurriedly tried to redraw the pentagram, but he couldn't pick up the salt, which was in a small pile around the broken glass shaker. And everything else he would need for the spell was buried under the debris of the table.

"Not doing so hot now, Mister Big Shot, are you?" a voice said, rather smugly.

"All right, all right, give me a minute, will you?" said the wizard, a difficult thing to say when your voice croaks like a gigantic frog's—it was hard to be a dinosaur and talk. But the wizard still had his pride. "You don't make soup in a second," he said. Then he began thinking feverishly. He didn't really *need* the elements and representations of the four worlds and the pentagram of cabalistic squares, not for an obviation spell, although, of course, things would be much more elegant *with* them. But. He *could* work the obviation spell by words alone—*if* he could remember the words. He needed something from the Eighteenth Path, that which connects *Binah* and *Geburah*, the House of Influence. Let's see, he thought. *"E pluribus unum."* No, no. . . . Could it be *"Micaoli beranusaji UK"*? No, that was a pharmacological spell. . . . But, yes, of *course*, this was it, and he began to chant *"Tstske, tstskeleh, tchotchike, tchotchkeleh, trayf, Qu-a-a-on!''*

That should do it.

But nothing happened. Again! The wizard tried to frown, but hadn't the face for it. "Nothing happened," he complained.

The cat's head materialized in midair. "That's what *you* think. As a matter of fact, all the quiches at Maxim's just turned into frogs. Great big ones," he added maliciously. "Great big green *slimy* ones."

The wizard dipped his great head humbly. "All right," he grumbled. "Enough is enough. I give up. I admit defeat. I was wrong. From now on, I promise, I'll save you a bite of every sandwich I ever order."

The cat appeared fully for a moment, swishing its tail thoughtfully back and forth. "You do know, don't you, that I prefer the part in the middle, without the crust . . .?"

"I'll never give you the crust, always from the middle—"

The waiter had come back into the restaurant, towing a policeman behind him, and was now pointing an indignant finger toward the wizard. The policeman began to slouch slowly toward them, looking bored and sullen and mean.

"I mean, it's not really the sandwich, you know," the cat said.

"I know, I know," the wizard mumbled.

"I get insecure too, like everyone else. I need to know that I'm wanted. It's the *thought* that counts, knowing that you're thinking about me, that you want me around—"

"All right, all right!" the wizard snapped irritably. Then he sighed again, and (with what would have been a gesture of final surrender if he'd had hands to spread) said, "So, okay, I want you around." He softened and said almost shyly, "I *do,* you know."

"I know," the cat said. They stared at each other with affection for a moment, and then the cat said, "For making money, it's the new moon blessing, *"Steyohn, v's-keyah-lahnough—"*

"Money I don't need anymore," the wizard said grumpily. "Money it's gone beyond. Straighten out all of *this"*—gesturing with his piglike snout at his—feh!—scaly green body.

"Not to worry. The *proper* obviation spell is that one you worked out during the Council of Trent, remember?"

The cat hissed out the words. Once again the wheel rotated slowly in darkness.

And then the wizard was sitting on the floor, in possession of his own spindly limbs again. Arthritically, he levered himself to his feet.

The cat watched him get up, saying smugly, "And as a bonus, I even put money in your purse, not bad, huh? I told—" And then the cat fell silent, staring off beyond the wizard's shoulder. The wizard looked around.

Everyone else in Schrafft's had turned into dinosaurs.

All around them were dinosaurs, dinosaurs in every possible variety, dinosaurs great and small, four-footed and two-footed, horned and scaled and armor-plated, striped and speckled and piebald, all busily eating lunch, hissing and grunting and belching and slurping, huge jaws chewing noisily, great fangs flashing and clashing, razor-sharp talons clicking on tile. The din was horrendous. The policeman had turned into some sort of giant spiky armadillo, and was contentedly munching up the baseboard. In one corner, two nattily pinstriped allosaurs were fighting over the check, tearing huge bloody pieces out of each other. It was impossible to recognize the waiter.

The cat stared at the wizard.

The wizard stared at the cat.

The cat shrugged.

After a moment, the wizard shrugged too.

They both sighed.

"Lunch tomorrow?" the wizard asked, and the cat said, "Suits me."

Behind them, one of the triceratops finished off its second egg cream and made a rattling noise with the straw.

The wizard left the money for the check near the cash register, and added a substantial tip.

They went out of the restaurant together, out into the watery city sunshine, and strolled away down the busy street through the fine mild air of spring.

Selected Bibliography

ANTHOLOGIES

The Book of Cats, ed. George Mac Beth and Martin Booth (Penguin, 1983)
Supernatural Cats, ed. Claire Necker (Doubleday, 1972)
Beware of the Cats, ed. Michel Parry (Gollancz, 1972)
Kitten Caboodle, ed. Barbara Silverberg (Holt, Rinehart & Winston)

SHORT STORIES

Joan Aiken, "Listening," *A Touch of Chill*
Poul and Karen Anderson, "Kitten," *Frights,* ed. McCauley
Stephen Vincent Benét, "The King of the Cats," *The Collected Works of*
Ambrose Bierce, "Cargo of Cat," *Complete Short Stories of*
Algernon Blackwood, "Ancient Sorceries," *Best Ghost Stories of*
Robert Bloch, "Catnip," *Pleasant Dreams and Nightmares*
Frederic Brown, "Aelurophobe," *Paradox Lost*
_____, "Cat Burglar," *Nightmares and Geezenstacks*
_____, "Satan one-and-a-half," *Shaggy Dog and Other Murders*
Tom Browne, "The Cat Was Black," *F&SF*, March 1953
Edward Bryant, "The Overly Familiar," *Mile High Futures,* November 1983

_____, "Bean Bag Cats" *Omni*, November 1983

Doris Pitkan Buck, "Please Close the Gate On Account of the Kitten," *F&SF*, April 1975

Truman Capote, "A Lamp in a Window," *Music for Chameleons*

Cleve Cartmill, "The Green Cat," *Supernatural Cats*

Roald Dahl, "Edward the Conqueror," *Kiss, Kiss*

Jack Dann, "Rags," *Fantastic*, April 1973

Miriam Allen De Ford, "The Cats of Rome," *Weird Tales*, Winter 1973

Walter de la Mare, "Broomsticks," *Supernatural Cats*

August Derleth, "Balu" *Supernatural Cats*

Tom Disch, "The Black Cat," *Shenandoah*, Summer 1976

Phyllis Gotleib, "Son of the Morning," *F&SF*, June 1972

Nicholas Stuart Gray, "The Thunder Cat," *Mainly in Moonlight*

Shirley Jackson, "Strangers in Town," *Saturday Evening Post Stories*, 1959

Rudyard Kipling, "The Cat Who Walked by Himself," *Just So Stories*

_____, "The Sending of Dana Da," *Indian Stories*

Tanith Lee, "Meow," *Shadows 4*, ed. Grant

Joseph Sheridan Le Fanu, "The White Cat of Drumgunniol," *Beware of the Cats*

Fritz Leiber, "Cat's Cradle," *The Book of Fritz Leiber*

_____, "The Cat Hotel," *F&SF*, October 1983

_____, "Cat Three," *F&SF*, October 1973

_____, "Kreativity for Kats," *Galaxy*, April 1961

_____, "The Lotus Eaters," *F&SF*, October 1972

_____, "Scylla's Daughter," *Fantastic*, May 1961

H. P. Lovecraft, "The Cats of Ulthar," *Beware of the Cats*

Ward Moore, "The Boy Who Spoke Cat," *Venus*, December 1973

Lewis Padgett, "Compliments of the Author," *Supernatural Cats*

Edgar Pangborn, "Darius," *Good Neighbors and Other Strangers*

Edgar Allan Poe, "The Black Cat," *Beware of the Cats*

Bill Pronzini, "Cat," *F&SF*, November 1978

Kit Reed, "Automatic Tiger" *F&SF*, March 1964

Joanna Russ, "The Zanzibar Cat," *The Zanzibar Cat and Other Stories*

Saki, "Tobermory," *The Book of Cats, Supernatural Cats*
Pamela Sargent, "The Mountain Gate," *The Mountain Gate*
Dorothy Sayers, "The Cyprian Cat," *Supernatural Cats*
James H. Schmitz, "Novice," *Analog,* June 1962
Cordwainer Smith, "The Ballad of Lost C'mell," *The Best of*
Theodore Sturgeon, "Fluffy," *Beware of the Cats*
_____, "Helix the Cat" *Astounding,* ed. Harrison
Mark Twain, "The Vampire Cat," *Beware of the Cats*
James White, "The Conspirators," *Supernatural Cats*
P. G. Wodehouse, "The Story of Webster," *Mulliner Nights*
Gene Wolfe, "Feather Tigers," *Edge,* ed. McAllister
Jane Yolen, "The Cat Bride," *Cricket Magazine*

ABOUT THE EDITORS

GARDNER DOZOIS was born and raised in Salem, Massachusetts, and now lives in Philadelphia. He is the author or editor of fifteen books, including the novel *Strangers* and the collection *The Visible Man;* he also edits the annual series *The Year's Best Science Fiction*. His short fiction has appeared in *Playboy, Penthouse, Omni*, and most of the leading SF magazines and anthologies, and he has many times been a finalist for the Hugo and Nebula awards. His critical work has appeared in *Writer's Digest, Starship, Thrust, Writing and Selling Science Fiction, The Writer's Handbook*, and *Science Fiction Writers*, and he is the author of the critical chapbook *The Fiction of James Tiptree, Jr.* His most recent book is *Unicorns!*, an anthology edited in collaboration with Jack Dann. He is currently at work on another novel, *Flash Point*.

JACK DANN is the author or editor of thirteen books, including the novels *Junction* and *Starhiker,* and the collection *Timetipping*. He is the editor of the anthology *Wandering Stars*, one of the most acclaimed anthologies of the 1970's, and several other well-known anthologies, including the recently published *More Wandering Stars*. His short fiction has appeared in *Playboy, Penthouse, Omni, Gallery*, and most of the leading SF magazines and anthologies. He has been a Nebula Award finalist five times, as well as a finalist for the World Fantasy Award and the British Science Fiction

Association Award. His critical work has appeared in *Starship, Nickelodeon, The Bulletin of the Science Fiction Writers of America, Empire, Future Life,* and *The Fiction Writer's Handbook,* and he is the author of the chapbook, *Christs and Other Poems.* His most recent books are *Unicorns!,* an anthology edited in collaboration with Gardner Dozois, and *The Man Who Melted,* a novel; he is at work on another new novel, *Counting Coup.* Dann lives with his family in Johnson City, New York.